The Collected Supernatural and Weird Fiction of Mrs. Henry Wood Volume 1

The Collected Supernatural and Weird Fiction of Mrs. Henry Wood Volume 1

Including One Novel "Featherston's Story," One Novella "A Mystery," One Novelette "Gina Montani," and Ten Short Stories of the Strange and Unusual

Mrs. Henry Wood

LEONAUR

The Collected
Supernatural and Weird
Fiction of
Mrs. Henry Wood
Volume 1
Including One Novel "Featherston's Story," One Novella "A Mystery," One Novelette
"Gina Montani," and Ten Short Stories of the Strange and Unusual
by Mrs. Henry Wood

FIRST EDITION

Leonaur is an imprint
of Oakpast Ltd

ISBN: 978-1-78282-052-9 (hardcover)
ISBN:978-1-78282-053-6 (softcover)

http://www.leonaur.com

Publisher's Notes

Contents

Featherston's Story

I have called this Featherston's story, because it was through him that I heard about it—and, indeed, saw a little of it towards the end.

1

Buttermead, the wide straggling district to which Feathers ton enjoyed the honour of being doctor-in-ordinary, was as rural as any that can be found in Worcestershire. Featherston's house stood at the end of the village. Whitney Hall lay close by; as did our school, Dr. Frost's. In the neighbourhood were scattered a few other substantial residences, some farmers' homesteads and labourers' cottages. Featherston was a slim man, with long thin legs and a face grey and careworn. His patients (like the soldier's steam arm) gave him no rest day or night.

There is no need to go into details here about Featherston's people. His sister, Mary Ann, lived in his house at one time, and for everyday ailments was almost as good a doctor as he. She was not at all like him: a merry, talkative, sociable little woman, with black hair and quick, kindly dark eyes.

Our resident French master in those days at Dr. Frost's was one Monsieur Jules Carimon: a small man with honest blue eyes in his clean-shaven face, and light brown hair cropped close to his head. He was an awful martinet at study, but a genial little gentleman out of it. To the surprise of Buttermead, he and Mary Featherston set up a courtship. It was carried on in sober fashion, as befitted a sober couple who had both left thirty years, and the rest, behind them; and after a summer or two of it they laid plans for their marriage and for living in France.

"I'm sure I don't know what on earth I shall do amongst the French, Johnny Ludlow," Mary said to me in her laughing way, when I and Bill Whitney were having tea at Featherston's one half-holiday, the week before the wedding. "Jules protests they are easier to get on with than the English; not so stiff and formal; but I don't pay attention to all he says, you know."

Monsieur Jules Carimon was going to settle down at his native place, Sainteville—a town on the opposite coast, which had a service of English steamers running to it two or three times a-week. He had obtained the post of first classical master at the college there, and meant to eke out his salary (never large in French colleges) by teaching French and mathematics to as many English pupils as he could obtain out of hours. Like other northern French seaport towns, Sainteville had its small colony of British residents.

"We shall get on; I am not afraid," answered Mary Featherston to a doubting remark made to her by old Mrs. Selby of the Court. "Neither I nor Jules have been accustomed to luxury, and we don't care for it. We would as soon make our dinner of bread-and-butter and radishes, as of chicken and apple-tart."

So the wedding took place, and they departed the same day for Sainteville. And of the first two or three years after that there's nothing good or bad to record.

Selby Court lay just outside Buttermead. Its mistress, an ancient lady now, was related to the Preen family, of whom I spoke in that story which told of the tragical death of Oliver. Lavinia Preen, sister to Oliver's father, Gervase Preen, but younger, lived with Mrs. Selby as a sort of adopted daughter; and when the death of the father, old Mr. Preen, left nearly all his large family with scarcely any cheese to their bread, Mrs. Selby told Ann Preen, the youngest of them all, that she might come to her also. So Lavinia and Ann Preen lived at the Court, and had no other home.

These two ladies were intimate with Mary Featherston, all three being much attached to one another. When Mary mar-

8

ried and left her country for France, the Miss Preens openly resented it, saying she ought to have had more consideration. Did some premonitory instinct prompt that unreasonable resentment? I cannot say. No one can say. But it is certain that had Mary Featherston not gone to live abroad, the ominous chain of events fated to engulf the sisters could not have touched them, and this account, which is a perfectly true one, would never have been written.

For a short time after the marriage they and Mary Carimon exchanged a letter now and then; not often, for foreign postage was expensive; and then it dropped altogether,

Mrs. Selby became an invalid, and died. She left each of the two sisters seventy pounds a-year for life; if the one died, the other was to enjoy the whole; when both were dead, it would lapse back to the Selby estate.

"Seventy pounds a-year!" remarked Ann Preen to her sister. "It does not seem very much, does it, Lavinia? Shall we be able to live upon it?"

They were seated in the wainscoted parlour at Selby Court, talking of the future. The funeral was over, and they must soon leave; for the house was waiting to be done up for the reception of its new master, Mr. Paul Selby, an old bachelor full of nervous fancies.

"We must live upon it, Nancy," said Lavinia in answer to her.

She was the stronger-minded of the two, and she looked it. A keen, practical woman, of rather more than middle height, with smooth brown hair, pleasant, dark hazel eyes, and a bright glow in her cheeks. Ann (or Nancy, as she was more often called) was smaller and lighter, with a pretty face, a shower of fair ringlets, and mild, light-blue eyes; altogether not unlike a pink-and-white wax doll.

"We should have been worse off, Nancy, had she not left us anything; and sometimes I have feared she might not," remarked Lavinia cheerfully. "It will be a hundred and forty pounds between us, dear; we can live upon that."

9

"Of course we can, if you think so, Lavinia," said the other, who deemed her elder sister wiser than anyone in the world, and revered her accordingly.

"But we should live cheaper abroad than here, I expect," continued Lavinia. "It's said money goes twice as far in France as in England. Suppose we were to go over, Nancy, and try? We could come back if we did not like it."

Nancy's eyes sparkled. "I think it would be delightful," she said. "Money go further in France—why, to be sure it does! Aunt Emily is able to live like a princess at Tours, by all accounts. Yes, yes, Lavinia, let us try France!"

★★★★★★

One fine spring morning the Miss Preens packed up their bag and baggage and started for the Continent. They went direct to Tours, intending to make that place their *pied-à-terre*, as the French phrase it; at any rate, for a time. It was not, perhaps, the wisest thing they could have done.

For Mrs. Magnus, formerly Emily Preen, and their late father's sister, did not welcome them warmly. She lived in style herself, one of the leading stars in the society of Tours; and she did not at all like that two middle-aged nieces, of straitened means, should take up their abode in the next street. So Mrs. Magnus met her nieces with the assurance that Tours would not do for them; it was too expensive a place; they would be swamped in it. Mrs. Magnus was drawing near to the close of her life then; had she known it, she might have been kinder, and let them remain; but she was not able to foresee the hour of that great event which must happen to us all any more than other people are. Oliver Preen was with her then, revelling in the sunny days which were flitting away on gossamer wings.

"Lavinia, do you think we can stay at Tours?"

The Miss Preens had descended at a fourth-rate hotel, picked out of the guide-book. When Ann asked this question, they were sitting after dinner in the *table d'hôte* room, their feet on the sanded floor. Sanded floors were quite usual at that time in many parts of France.

"Stay here to put up with Aunt Emily's pride and insolence!" quickly answered Miss Preen. "No. I will tell you what I have done, Ann. I wrote yesterday to Mary Carimon, asking her about Sainteville; whether she thinks it will suit us, and so on. As soon as her answer comes—she's certain to say yes—we will go, dear, and leave Mrs. Magnus to her grandeur. And, once we are safe away, I shall write her a letter," added Lavinia, in decisive tones; "a letter which she won't like."

Madame Carimon's answer came by return of post. It was as cordial as herself Sainteville would be the very place for them, she said, and she should count the hours until they were there.

The Miss Preens turned their backs upon Tours, shaking its dust off their shoes. Lavinia had a little nest of accumulated money, so was at ease in that respect. And when the evening of the following day the railway terminus at Sainteville was reached, the pleasant, smiling face of Mary Carimon was the first they saw outside the *barrière*. She must have been nearly forty now, but she did not look a day older than when she had left Buttermead. Miss Lavinia was a year or two older than Mary; Miss Ann a year or two younger.

"You must put up at the Hôtel des Princes," remarked Madame Carimon. "It is the only really good one in the town. They won't charge you too much; my husband has spoken to the landlady. And you must spend tomorrow with me."

The hotel omnibus was waiting for them and other passengers, the luggage was piled on the roof, and Madame Carimon accompanied them to the hotel. A handsome hotel, the sisters thought; quite another thing from the one at Tours. Mary Carimon introduced them to the landlady, Madame Podevin, saw them seated down to tea and a cold fowl, and then left for the night.

With Sainteville the Miss Preens were simply charmed. It was a fresh, clean town, with wide streets, and good houses and old families, and some bright shops. The harbour was large, and the pier extended out to the open sea.

"I *should* like to live here!" exclaimed Miss Lavinia, sitting down at Madame Carimon's, in a state of rapture. "I never saw such a nice town, or such a lovely market."

They had been about all the morning with Madame Carimon. It was market-day, Wednesday. The market was held on the Grande Place; and the delicious butter, the eggs, the fresh vegetables, the flowers and the poultry, took Miss Lavinia's heart by storm. Nancy was more taken with the picturesque market-women, in their white caps and long gold ear-rings. Other ladies were doing their marketing as well as Madame Carimon. She spoke to most of them, in French or in English, as the case might be. Under the able tuition of her husband, she talked French fluently now.

Madame Carimon's habitation—very nice, small and compact—was in the Rue Pomme Cuite. The streets have queer names in some of these old French towns. It was near the college, which was convenient for Monsieur Carimon. Here they lived, with their elderly servant, Pauline. The same routine went on daily in the steady little domicile from year's end to year's end.

"Jules goes to the college at eight o'clock every week-day, after a cup of coffee and a *petit pain*," said *madame* to her guests, "and he returns at five to dinner. He takes his *déjeûner* in the college at twelve, and I take mine alone at home. On Sundays he has no duty: we attend the French Protestant Church in a morning, dine at one o'clock, and go for a walk in the afternoon."

"You have no children, Mary?"

Mary Carimon's lively face turned sad as she answered: "There was one little one; she stayed with us six months, and then God took her. I wrote to you of it, you know, Lavinia. No, we have not any children. Best not, Jules says; and I agree with him. They might only leave us when we have learnt to love them; and that's a trial hard to bear. Best as it is."

"I'm sure I should never learn to speak French, though we lived here for a century," exclaimed Miss Lavinia. "Only to hear you jabbering to your servant, Mary, quite distracts one's ears."

"Yes, you would. You would soon pick up enough to be un-

12

derstood in the shops and at market."

At five o'clock, home came Monsieur Carimon. He welcomed the Miss Preens with honest, genuine pleasure, interspersed with a little French ceremony; making them about a dozen bows apiece before he met the hands held out to him.

They had quite a gala dinner. Soup to begin with—broth, the English ladies inwardly pronounced it—and then fish. A small cod, bought by Madame Carimon at the fish-market in the morning, with oyster sauce. Ten *sous* she had given for the cod, for she knew how to bargain now, and six *sous* for a dozen oysters, as large as a five-*franc* piece. This was followed by a delicious little *fricandeau* of veal, and that by a *tarte à la crême* from the pastrycook's. She told her guests unreservedly what all the dishes cost, to show them how reasonably people might live at Sainteville.

Over the coffee, after dinner, the question of their settling in the place was fully gone into, for the benefit of Monsieur Carimon's opinions, who gave them in good English.

"Depend upon it, Lavinia, you could not do better," remarked Mary Carimon. "If you cannot make your income do here, you cannot anywhere."

"We want to make it do well; not to betray our poverty, but to be able to maintain a fairly good appearance," said Lavinia. "You understand me, I am sure, *monsieur.*"

"But certainly, *mademoiselle*," he answered; "it is what we all like to do at Sainteville, I reckon."

"And *can* do, if we are provident," added *madame*. "French ways are not English ways. Our own income is small, Lavinia, yet we put by out of it."

"A fact that goes without saying," confirmed the pleasant little man. "If we did not put by, where would my wife be when I am no longer able to work?"

"Provisions being so cheap—— What did you say, Nancy?" asked Madame Carimon, interrupting herself.

"I was going to say that I could live upon oysters, and should like to," replied Nancy, shaking back her flaxen curls with a

13

laugh. "Half-a-dozen of those great big oysters would make me a lovely dinner any day—and the cost would be only three half-pence."

"And only fivepence the cost of that beautiful fish," put in her sister. "In Sainteville our income would amply suffice."

"It seems to me that it would, *mesdemoiselles*," observed Monsieur Carimon. "Three thousand five hundred *francs* yearly! We French should think it a sufficient sum. Doubtless much would depend upon the way in which you laid it out."

"What should we have to pay for lodgings, Mary?" inquired Lavinia. "Just a nice sitting-room and two small bedrooms; or a large room with two beds in it; and to be waited on "

"Oh, you won't find that at Sainteville," was the unexpected answer. "Nobody lets lodgings English fashion: it's not the custom over here. You can find a furnished apartment, but the people will not wait upon you. There is always a little kitchen let with the rooms, and you must have your own servant."

It was the first check the ladies had received. They sat thinking. "Dear me!" exclaimed Nancy. "No lodgings!"

"Would the apartments you speak of be very dear?" asked Lavinia.

"That depends upon the number of rooms and the situation," replied Madame Carimon. "I cannot call to mind just now any small apartment that is vacant. If you like, we will go tomorrow and look about."

It was so arranged. And little Monsieur Carimon attended the ladies back to the Hôtel des Princes at the sober hour of nine, and bowed them into the *porte coch*ère with two sweeps of his hat, wishing them the good-evening and the very goodnight.

2

Thursday morning. Nancy Preen awoke with a sick head-ache, and could not get up. But in the afternoon, when she was better, they went to Mary Carimon's, and all three set out to look for an apartment—not meeting with great success.

All they saw were too large, and priced accordingly. There was one, indeed, in the Rue Lamartine, which suited as to size, but the rooms were inconvenient and stuffy; and there was another small one on the Grande Place, dainty and desirable, but the rent was very high. Madame Carimon at once offered the landlord half-price, French custom: she dealt at his shop for her groceries. No, no, he answered; his apartment was the nicest in the town for its size, as *mesdames* saw, and it was in the best situation—and not a single *sou* would the worthy grocer abate.

They were growing tired, then; and five o'clock, the universal hour at Sainteville for dinner, was approaching.

"Come round to me after dinner, and we will talk it over," said Mary Carimon, when they parted. "I will give you a cup of tea."

They dined at the *table d'hôte*, which both of them thought charming, and then proceeded to the Rue Pomme Cuite. Monsieur Carimon was on the point of going out, to spend an hour at the Café Pillaud, but he put down his hat to wait awhile, out of respect to the ladies. They told him about not having found an apartment to suit them.

"Of course we have not searched all parts of the town, only the most likely ones," said Madame Carimon. "There are large apartments to be had, but no small ones. We can search again tomorrow."

"I suppose there's not a little house to be had cheap, if we cannot find an apartment?" cried Miss Nancy, who was in love with Sainteville, and had set her heart upon remaining there.

"*Tiens*," quickly spoke Monsieur Carimon in French to his wife, "there's the Petite Maison Rouge belonging to Madame Veuve Sauvage, in the Place Ronde. It is still to let: I saw the *affiche* in the shop window today. What do you think of it, Marie?"

Madame Carimon did not seem to know quite what to think. She looked at her husband, then at the eager faces of her two friends; but she did not speak.

About half-way down the Rue Tessin, a busy street leading to the port, was a wide opening, giving on to the Place Ronde. The Place Ronde agreed with its name, for it was somewhat in form of a horseshoe. Some fifteen or sixteen substantial houses were built round it, each having a shop for its basement; and trees, green and feathery, were scattered about, affording a slight though pleasant shelter from the hot sun in summer weather.

The middle house at the bottom of the Place Ronde, exactly facing the opening from the Rue Tessin, was a very conspicuous house indeed, inasmuch as it was painted red, whilst the other houses were white. All of them had green *persienne* shutters to the upper windows. The shop, a large one, belonging to this red house was that of the late Monsieur Jean Sauvage, "*Marchand de Vin en gros et en détail*," as the announcement over his door used to run in the later years of his life. But when Jean Sauvage commenced business, in that same shop, it was only as a retail vendor. Casting about in his mind one day for some means by which his shop might be distinguished from other wine-shops and attract customers, he hit upon the plan of painting the house red. No sooner thought of than done. A painter was called, who converted the white walls into a fiery vermilion, and stretched a board across the upper part, between the windows of the first and second floors, on which appeared in large letters "*A la Maison Rouge.*"

Whether this sort of advertisement drew the public, or whether it might have been the sterling respectability and devotion to business of Monsieur Sauvage, he got on most successfully. The *Marchand en détail* became also *Marchand en gros*, and in course of time he added liqueurs to his wines. No citizen of Sainteville was more highly esteemed than he, both as a man and a tradesman. Since his death the business had been carried on by his widow, aided by the two sons, Gustave and Emile. Latterly Madame Veuve Sauvage had given up all work to them; she was now in years, and had well earned her rest. They lived in the rooms over the shop, which were large and handsome. In former days, when the energies of herself and her husband were chiefly devoted to acquiring and saving money, they had let these upper rooms for a good sum yearly. Old Madame Sauvage might be seen any day now sitting at a front-window, looking out upon the world between her embroidered white curtains.

The door of this prosperous shop was between the two windows. The one window displayed a few bottles of wine, most of them in straw cases; in the other window were clear flacons of liqueurs: *chartreuse*, green and yellow; *curaçoa*, warm and ruby; *eau de vie de Danzick*, with its fluttering gold leaf; and many other sorts.

However, it is not with the goods of Madame Veuve Sauvage that we have to do, but with her premises. Standing in front of the shop, as if coveting a bottle of that choice wine for today's dinner, or an immediate glass of delicious liqueur, you may see on your right hand, but to the left of the shop, the private door of the house. On the other side the shop is also a door which opens to a narrow entry. The entry looks dark, even in the midday sun, for it is pretty long, extending down a portion of the side of the Maison Rouge, which is a deep house, and terminating in a paved yard surrounded by high buildings. At the end of the yard is a small dwelling, with two modern windows, one above the other. Near the under window is the entrance-door, painted oak colour, with a brass knob, a bell-wire with a curious handle, and a knocker. This little house the late Monsieur Sauvage had also caused to be converted into a red one, the same as the larger.

In earlier days, when Jean Sauvage and his wife were putting their shoulders to the wheel, they had lived in the little house with their children; the two sons and the daughter, Jeanne. Jeanne Sauvage married early and very well, an *avocat*. But since they had left it, the house in the yard seemed to have been, as the Widow Sauvage herself expressed it, unlucky. The first of the tenants had died there; the second had disappeared—decamped in fact, to avoid paying rent and other debts; the third had moved into a better house; and the fourth, an old widow lady, had also died, owing a year's rent to Madame Sauvage, and leaving no money to pay it.

It was of this small dwelling, lying under the shadow of the Maison Rouge, that Monsieur Carimon had thought. Turning to the Miss Preens, he gave them briefly a few particulars, and said he believed the house was to be had on very reasonable terms.

"What do you call it?" exclaimed Lavinia. "The little red house?"

"Yes, we call it so," said Monsieur Carimon. "Emile Sauvage was talking of it to me the other evening at the *café*, saying they would be glad to have it tenanted."

"I fear our good friends here would find it dull," remarked Madame Carimon to him. "It is in so gloomy a situation, you know, Jules."

"*Mon amie,* I do not myself see how that signifies," said he in reply, "If your house is comfortable inside, does it matter what it looks out upon?"

"Very true," assented Miss Lavinia, whose hopes had gone up again. "But this house may not be furnished, Mary."

"It is partly furnished," said Madame Carimon. "When the old lady who was last in it died, they had to take her furniture for the rent. It was not much, I have heard."

"We should not want much, only two of us," cried Miss Ann eagerly. "Do let us go to look at it tomorrow!"

On the following day, Friday, the Miss Preens went to the Place Ronde, piloted by Mary Carimon. They were struck with admiration at the Maison Rouge, all a fiery glow in the morning sun, and a novelty to English eyes. Whilst Madame Carimon went into the shop to explain and ask for the key, the sisters gazed in at the windows. Lying on the wine-bottles was a small black board on which was written in white letters, "*Petite Maison à louer.*"

Monsieur Gustave Sauvage, key in hand, saluted the ladies in English, which he spoke fairly well, and accompanied them to view the house. The sun was very bright that day, and the confined yard did not look so dull as at a less favourable time; and perhaps the brilliant red of the little house, at which Nancy laughed, imparted a cheerfulness to it. Monsieur Gustave opened the door with a latch-key, drew back, and waited for them to enter.

The first to do so, or to attempt to do so, was Miss Preen. But no sooner had she put one foot over the threshold than she drew back with a start, somewhat discomposing the others by the movement.

"What is it, Lavinia?" inquired Ann.

"Something seemed to startle me, and throw me backward!" exclaimed Lavinia Preen, regaining her breath. "Perhaps it was the gloom of the passage: it is very dark."

"*Pardon, mesdames,*" spoke Monsieur Gustave politely. "If the ladies will forgive my entering before them, I will open the *salon* door."

The passage was narrow. The broad shoulders of Monsieur Gustave almost touched the wall on either side as he walked along. Almost at the other end of it, on his left hand, was the *salon* door; he threw it open, and a little light shone forth. The passage terminated in a small square recess. At the back of this was fixed a shallow marble slab for holding things, above which was a cupboard let into the wall. On the right of the recess was the staircase; and opposite the staircase the kitchen-door, the kitchen being behind the *salon*.

The *salon* was nice when they were in it; the paint was fresh, the paper light and handsome. It was of good size, and its large window looked to the front. The kitchen opened upon a small backyard, furnished with a pump and a shed for wood or coal. On the floor above were two very good chambers, one behind the other. Opposite these, on the other side of the passage, was another room, not so large, but of fair size. It was apparently built out over some part of the next-door premises, and was lighted by a skylight. All the rooms were fresh and good, and the passage had a window at the end.

Altogether it was not an inconvenient abode for people who did not go in for show. The furniture was plain, clean and useful, but it would have to be added to. There were no grates, not even a cooking-stove in the kitchen. It was very much the Sainteville custom at that period for tenants to provide grates for themselves, plenty of which could be bought or hired for a small sum. An easy-chair or two would be needed; tea-cups and saucers and wine-glasses; and though there were washing-stands, these contained no jugs or basins; and there were no sheets or tablecloths or towels, no knives or forks, no brooms or brushes, and so on.

"There is only this one sitting-room, you perceive," remarked Madame Carimon, as they turned about, looking at the *salon* again, after coming downstairs.

"Yes, that's a pity, on account of dining," replied Miss Nancy.

"One of our tenants made a pretty *salon* of the room above this, and this the *salle à manger*," replied Monsieur Gustave. "*Mesdames* might like to do the same, possibly?"

He had pointedly addressed Miss Laviaia, near whom he stood. She did not answer. In fact—it was a very curious thing, but a fact—Miss Lavinia had not spoken a word since she entered. She had gone through the house taking in its features in complete silence, just as if that shock at the door had scared away her speech.

The rent asked by Monsieur Gustave, acting for his mother, was very moderate indeed—twenty pounds a-year, including the use of the furniture. There would be no taxes to pay, he said; absolutely none; the taxes of this little house, being upon their premises, were included in their own. But to ensure this low rental, the house must be taken for five years.

"Of course we will take it—won't we, Lavinia? "cried Miss Ann in a loud whisper. "Only twenty pounds a-year! Just think of it!"

"Sir," Miss Lavinia said to Monsieur Gustave, speaking at last, "the house would suit us in some respects, especially as regards rent. But we might find it too lonely: and I should hardly like to be bound for five years."

All that was of course for *mesdames'* consideration, he frankly responded. But he thought that if the ladies were established in it with their *ménage* about them, they would not find it lonely.

"We will give you an answer tomorrow or Monday," decided Miss Lavinia.

They went about the town all that day with Madame Carimon; but nothing in the shape of an apartment could be found to suit them. *Madame* invited them again to tea in the evening. And by that time they had decided to take the house. Nancy was wild about it. What with the change from the monotony of their country house to the bright and busy streets, the gay outdoor life, the delights of the *table d'hôte*, Ann Preen looked upon Sainteville as an earthly paradise.

"The house is certainly more suited to you than anything else we have seen," observed Madame Carimon. "I have nothing to say against the Petite Maison Rouge, except its dull situation."

"Did it strike you, Mary, apart from its situation, as being gloomy?" asked Lavinia.

"No. Once you are in the rooms they are cheerful enough."

"It did me. Gloomy, with a peculiar gloom, you understand, I'm sure the passage was dark as night. It must have been its darkness that startled me as we were going in."

"By the way, Lavinia, what was the matter with you then?" interrupted her sister.

"I don't know, Nancy; I said at the time I did not know. With my first step into the passage, some horror, seemed to meet me and drive me backward."

"Some horror!" repeated Nancy.

"I seemed to feel it so. I had still the glare of the streets and the fiery red walls in my eyes, which must have caused the house passage to look darker than it ought. That was all, I suppose—but it turned me sick with a sort of fear; sick and shivery."

"That *salon* may be made as pretty a room as any in Sainteville," remarked Madame Carimon. "Many of the English residents here have only one *salon* in their apartments. You see, we don't go in for ceremony; France is not like England."

On the morrow the little house under the wing of the Maison Rouge was secured by the Miss Preens. They took it in their joint names for five years. To complete the transaction they were ushered upstairs to the *salon* and presence of Madame Veuve Sauvage—a rather stately looking old lady, attired in a voluminous black silk robe and a mourning cap of fine muslin. *Madame*, who could not speak a syllable of English, conversed graciously with her future tenants through the interpretation of Mary Carimon, offering to be useful to them in any way she could. Lavinia and Ann Preen both signed the *bail*, or agreement, and Madame Veuve Sauvage likewise signed it; by virtue of which she became their landlady, and they her tenants of the little house for five years. Madame Carimon, and a shopman who came upstairs for the purpose, signed as witnesses.

Wine and the little cakes called *pistolets* were then introduced; and so the bargain was complete.

Oh if some kindly spirit from the all-seeing world above could only have whispered a hint to those ill-fated sisters of what they were doing!—had only whispered a warning in time to prevent it! Might not that horror, which fell upon Lavinia as she was about to pass over the door-sill, have served her as such? But who regards these warnings when they come to us? Who personally applies them? None.

Having purchased or hired the additional things required, the Miss Preens took possession of their house. Nancy had the front bed-chamber, which Lavinia thought rather the best, and so gave it up to her; Lavinia took the back one. The one opposite, with the skylight, remained unoccupied, as their servant did not sleep in the house. Not at all an uncommon custom at Sainteville.

An excellent servant had been found for them in the person of Flore Pamart, a widow, who was honest, cooked well, and could talk away in English; all recommendations that the ladies liked. Flore let herself in with a latch-key before breakfast, and left as soon after five o'clock in the evening as she could get the dinner things removed. Madame Flore Pamart had one little boy named Dion, who went to school by day, but was at home night and morning; for which reason his mother could only take a daily service.

Thus the Miss Preens became part of the small colony of English at Sainteville. They took sittings in the English Protestant Church, which was not much more than a room; and they subscribed to the casino on the port when it opened for the summer season, spending many an evening there, listening to the music, watching the dancing when there was any, and chattering with the acquaintances they met. They were well regarded, these new-comers, and they began to speak French after a fashion. Now and then they went out to a *soirée*; once in a way gave one in return. Very sober *soirées* indeed were those of Sainteville; consisting (as Sam Weller might inform us) of tea at seven o'clock with hot *galette*, conversation, cake at ten (*gâteau Suisse* or *gâteau au rhum*), and a glass of Picardin wine.

They were pleased with the house, once they had settled down in it, and never a shadow of regret crossed either of them for having taken the Petite Maison Rouge.

In this way about a twelvemonth wore on.

3

It was a fine morning at the beginning of April; the sun being particularly welcome, as Sainteville had latterly been favoured with a spell of ill-natured, bitter east winds. About eleven o'clock, Miss Preen and her sister turned out of their house to take a walk on the pier—which they liked to do most days, wind and weather permitting. In going down the Rue des Arbres, they were met by a fresh-looking little elderly gentleman, with rather long white hair, and wearing a white necktie. He stopped to salute the ladies, bowing ceremoniously low to each of them. It was *Monsieur le Docteur* Dupuis, a kindly man of skilful reputation, who had now mostly, though not altogether, given up practice to his son, Monsieur Henri Dupuis. Miss Lavinia had a little acquaintance with the doctor, and took occasion to ask him news of the public welfare; for there was raging in the town the malady called "*la grippe*," which, being interpreted, means influenza.

It was not much better at present. Monsieur Dupuis answered; but this genial sunshine he hoped would begin to drive it away; and, with another bow, he passed onward.

The pier was soon reached, and they enjoyed their walk upon it. The sunlight glinted on the rather turbulent waves of the sea in the distance, but there was not much breeze to be felt on land. When nearing the end of the pier their attention was attracted to a fishing-boat, which was tumbling about rather unaccountably in its efforts to make the harbour.

"It almost looks from here as though it had lost its rudder, Nancy," remarked Miss Lavinia.

They halted, and stood looking over the side at the object of interest; not particularly noticing that a gentleman stood near them, also looking at the same through an opera-glass. He was spare, of middle height and middle age; his hair was grey, his face pale and impassive; the light over-coat he wore was of fashionable English cut.

"Oh, Lavinia, look, look! It is coming right on to the end of the pier," cried Ann Preen.

"Hush, Nancy, don't excite yourself," said Miss Lavinia, in lowered tones. "It will take care not to do that."

The gentleman gave a wary glance at them. He saw two ladies dressed alike, in handsome black velvet mantles, and bonnets with violet feathers; by which he judged them to be sisters, though there was no resemblance in face. The elder had clear-cut features, a healthy colour, dark brown hair, worn plain, and a keen, sensible expression. The other was fair, with blue eyes and light ringlets.

"Pardon me," he said, turning to them, and his accent was that of a gentleman. "May I offer you the use of my glasses?"

"Oh, thank you!" exclaimed Nancy, in a light tone bordering on a giggle; and she accepted the glasses. She was evidently pleased with the offer and with the stranger.

Lavinia, on the contrary, was not. The moment she saw his full face she shrank from it—shrank from him. The feeling might have been as unaccountable as that which came over her when she had been first entering the Petite Maison Rouge; but it was there. However, she put it from her, and thanked him.

"I don't think I see so well with the glasses as without them; it seems all a mist," remarked Nancy, who was standing next the stranger.

"They are not properly focused for you. Allow me," said he, as he took the glasses from her to alter them. "Young eyes need a less powerful focus than elderly ones like mine."

He spoke in a laughing tone; Nancy, fond of compliments, giggled outright this time. She was approaching forty; he might have been ten years older. They continued standing there, watching the fishing-boat, and exchanging remarks at intervals. When it had made the harbour without accident, the Miss Preens wished him good-morning, and went back down the pier; he took off his hat to them, and walked the other way.

"What a *charming* man!" exclaimed Nancy, when they were at a safe distance.

"I don't like him," dissented Lavinia.

"Not like him! "echoed the other in surprise. "Why, Lavinia, his manners are delightful. I wonder who he is?"

When nearly home, in turning into the Place Ronde, they met an English lady of their acquaintance, the wife of Major Smith. She had been ordering a dozen of *vin* Picardin from the Maison Rouge. As they stood talking together, the gentleman of the pier passed up the Rue de Tessin. He lifted his hat, and they all, including Mrs. Smith, bowed.

"Do you know him?" quickly asked Nancy, in a whisper.

"Hardly that," answered Mrs. Smith. "When we were passing the Hôtel des Princes this morning, a gentleman turned out of the courtyard, and he and my husband spoke to one another. The major said to me afterwards that he had formerly been in the—I forget which—regiment. He called him Mr. Fennel."

Now, as ill-fortune had it, Miss Preen found herself very poorly after she got home. She began to sneeze and cough, and thought she must have taken cold through standing on the pier to watch the vagaries of the fishing-smack.

"I hope you are not going to have the influenza!" cried Nancy, her blue eyes wide with concern.

But the influenza it proved to be. Miss Preen seemed about to have it badly, and lay in bed the next day. Nancy proposed to send Flore for Monsieur Dupuis, but Lavinia said she knew how to treat herself as well as he could treat her.

The next day she was no better. Poor Nancy had to go out alone, or to stay indoors. She did not like doing the latter at all; it was too dull; her own inclination would have led her abroad all day long and every day.

"I saw Captain Fennel on the pier again," said she to her sister that afternoon, when she was making the tea at Lavinia's bedside, Flore having carried up the tray.

"I hope you did not talk to him, Ann," spoke the invalid, as well as she could articulate.

"I talked a little," said Nancy, turning hot, conscious that she had gossiped with him for three-quarters-of-an-hour. "He stopped to speak to me; I could not walk on rudely."

"Anyway, don't talk to him again, my dear. I do not like that man."

"What is there to dislike in him, Lavinia?"

"That I can't say. His countenance is not a good one; it is shifty and deceitful. He is a man you could never trust."

"I'm sure I've heard you say the same of other people."

"Because I can read faces," returned Lavinia.

"Oh—well—I consider Captain Fennel's is a *handsome* face," debated Nancy.

"Why do you call him 'Captain'?"

"He calls himself so," answered Nancy. "I suppose it was his rank in the army when he retired. They retain it afterwards by courtesy, don't they, Lavinia?"

"I am not sure. It depends upon whether they retire in rotation or sell out, I fancy. Mrs. Smith said the major called him Mr. Fennel, and he ought to know. There, I can't talk any more, Nancy, and the man is nothing to us, that we need discuss him."

La grippe had taken rather sharp hold of Lavinia Preen, and she was upstairs for ten days. On the first afternoon she went down to the salon. Captain Fennel called, very much to her surprise; and, also to her surprise, he and Nancy appeared to be pretty intimate.

In point of fact, they had met every day, generally upon the pier. Nancy had said nothing about it at home. She was neither sly nor deceitful in disposition; rather notably simple and unsophisticated; but, after Lavinia's reproof the first time she told about meeting him, she would not tell again.

Miss Preen behaved coolly to him; which he would not appear to see. She sat over the fire, wrapped in a shawl, for it was a cold afternoon. He stayed only a little time, and put his card down on the slab near the stairs when he left. Lavinia had it brought to her.

"Mr. Edwin Fennel."

"Then he is not Captain Fennel," she observed. "But, Nancy, what in the world could have induced the man to call here? And how is it you seem to be familiar with him?"

"I have met him out-of-doors, sometimes, while you were ill," said Nancy. "As to his calling here—he came, I suppose, out of politeness. There's no harm in it, Lavinia."

Miss Lavinia did not say there was. But she disliked the man too much to favour his acquaintanceship. Instinct warned her against him.

How little was she prepared for what was to follow! Before she was well out-of-doors again, before she had been anywhere except to church, Nancy gave her a shock. With no end of simperings and blushings, she confessed that she had been asked to marry Captain Fennel.

Had Miss Lavinia Preen been herself politely asked to marry a certain gentleman popularly supposed to reside underground, she would not have been much more indignantly startled. Perhaps "frightened" would be the better word for it.

"But—you *would* not, Nancy!" she gasped, when she found her voice.

"I don't know," simpered foolish Nancy. "I—I—think him very nice and gentlemanly, Lavinia."

Lavinia came out of her fright sufficiently to reason. She strove to show Nancy how utterly unwise such a step would be. They knew nothing of Captain Fennel or his antecedents; to become his wife might just be courting misery and destruction.

Nancy ceased to argue; and Lavinia hoped she had yielded.

Both sisters kept a diary. But for that fact, and also that the diaries were preserved, Featherston could not have arrived at the details of the story so perfectly. About this time, a trifle earlier or later, Ann Preen wrote as follows in hers:

April 16th.—I met Captain Fennel on the pier again this morning. I do think he goes there because he knows he may meet me. Lavinia is not out yet; she has not quite got rid of that Grip, as they stupidly call it here. I'm sure it has gripped *her*. We walked quite to the end of the pier, and then I sat down on the edge for a little while, and he stood talking to me. I do wish I could tell Lavinia of these meetings; but she was so cross the first day I met him, and told her of it, that I don't like to. Captain Fennel lent me his glasses as usual, and I looked at the London steamer, which was coming in. Somehow we fell to talking of the Smiths; he said they were poor, had not much more than the major's half-pay. 'Not like you rich people. Miss Nancy,' he said—he thinks that's my right name. 'Your income is different from theirs.' 'Oh,' I screamed out, 'why, it's only a hundred and forty pounds a-year!' 'Well,' he answered, smiling, 'that's a comfortable sum for a place like this; five *francs* will buy as much at Sainteville as half-a-sovereign will in England.' Which is pretty nearly true.

Skipping a few entries of little importance, we come to another:

May 1st, and such a lovely day!—It reminds me of one May-day at home, when the Jacks-in-the-green were dancing on the grass-plot before the Court windows at Buttermead, and Mrs. Selby sat watching them, as pleased as they were, saying she should like to dance, too, if she could only go first to the mill to be ground young again. Jane and Edith Peckham were spending the day with us. It was just such a day as this, warm and bright; light, fleecy clouds flitting across the blue sky. I wish Lavinia were out to enjoy it! but she is hardly strong enough for long walks yet, and only potters about, when she does get out, in the Rue des Arbres or the Grande Place, or perhaps over to see Mary Carimon.

I don't know what to do. I lay awake all last night, and sat moping yesterday, thinking what I *could* do. Edwin wants me to marry him; I told Lavinia, and she absolutely forbids it, saying I should rush upon misery. *He* says I should be happy as the day's long. I feel like a distracted lunatic, not knowing which of them is right, or which opinion I ought to yield to. I have obeyed Lavinia all my life; we have never had a difference before; her wishes have been mine, and mine have been hers. But I *can't* see why she need have taken up this prejudice against him, for I'm sure he's more like an angel than a man; and, as he whispers to me, Nancy Fennel would be a prettier name than Nancy Preen. I said to him today, 'My name is Ann, not really Nancy.' 'My dear,' he answered, ' I shall always call you Nancy; I love the simple name.'

I no longer talk about him to Lavinia, or let her suspect that we still meet on the pier. It would make her angry, and I can't bear that. I dare not hint to her what Edwin said today—-that he should take matters into his own hands. He means to go over to Dover, *via* Calais; stay at Dover a fortnight, as the marriage law requires, and then come back to fetch me; and after the marriage has taken place we shall return here to live.

Oh dear, what am I to do? It will be a *dreadful* thing to deceive Lavinia; and it will be equally dreadful to lose *him*. He declares that if I do not agree to this he shall set sail for India (where he used to be with his regiment), and never, never see me again. Good gracious! *never* to see me again!

The worst is, he wants to go off to Dover at once, giving one no time for consideration! Must I say Yes, or No? The uncertainty shakes me to pieces. He laughed today when

I said something of this, assuring me Lavinia's anger would pass away like a summer cloud when I was his wife; that sisters had no authority over one another, and that Lavinia's opposition arose from selfishness only, because she did not want to lose me. '*Risk it*, Nancy,' said he; 'she will receive you with open arms when I bring you back from Dover,' If I could only think so! Now and then I feel inclined to confide my dilemma to Mary Carimon, and ask her opinion, only that I fear she might tell Lavinia.

Mr. Edwin Fennel quitted Sainteville. When he was missed people thought he might have gone for good. But one Saturday morning some time onwards, when the month of May was drawing towards its close, Miss Lavinia, out with Nancy at market, came full upon Captain Fennel in the crowd on the Grande Place. He held out his hand.

"I thought you had left Sainteville, Mr. Fennel," she remarked, meeting his hand and the sinister look in his face unwillingly.

"Got back this morning," he said; "travelled by night. Shall be leaving again today or tomorrow. How are *you*, Miss Nancy?"

Lavinia pushed her way to the nearest poultry stall. "Will you come here, Ann?" she said. "I want to choose a fowl."

She began to bargain, half in French, half in English, with the poultry man, all to get rid of that other man, and she looked round, expecting Nancy had followed her. Nancy had not stirred from the spot near the butter-baskets: she and Captain Fennel had their heads together, he talking hard and fast.

They saw Lavinia looking at them; looking angry, too, "Remember," impressively whispered Captain Fennel to Nancy: and, lifting his hat to Lavinia, over the white caps of the market-women, he disappeared across the Place.

"I wonder what that man has come back for?" cried Miss Preen, as Nancy reached her—not that she had any suspicion. "And I wonder you should stay talking with him, Nancy!" Nancy did not answer.

Sending Flore—who had attended them with her market-basket—home with the fowl and eggs and vegetables, they called at the butcher's and the grocer's, and then went home themselves. Miss Preen then remembered that she had forgotten one or two things, and must go out again. Nancy remained at home. When Lavinia returned, which was not for an hour, for she had met various friends and stayed to gossip, her sister was in her room. Flore thought Mademoiselle Nancy was setting her drawers to rights: she had heard her opening and shutting them.

Time went on until the afternoon. Just before five o'clock, when Flore came in to lay the cloth for dinner, Lavinia, sitting at the window, saw her sister leave the house and cross the yard, a good-sized paper parcel in her hand.

"Why, that is Miss Nancy," she exclaimed, in much surprise. "Where can she be going to now?"

"Miss Nancy came down the stairs as I was coming in here," replied Flore. "She said to me that she had just time to run to Madame Carimon's before dinner."

"Hardly," dissented Miss Lavinia. "What can she be going for?"

As five o'clock struck, Flore (always punctual, from self-interest) came in to ask if she should serve the fish; but was told to wait until Miss Nancy returned. When half-past five was at hand, and Nancy had not appeared, Miss Preen ordered the fish in, remarking that Madame Carimon must be keeping her sister to dinner.

Afterwards Miss Preen set out for the *casino*, expecting she should meet them both there; for Lavinia and Nancy had intended to go. Madame Carimon was not a subscriber, but she sometimes paid her ten *sous* and went in. It would be quite a pretty sight tonight—a children's dance. Lavinia soon joined some friends there, but the others did not come.

At eight o'clock she was in the Rue Pomme Cuite, approaching Madame Carimon's. Pauline, in her short woollen petticoats, and shoeless feet thrust into wooden *sabots*, was splashing buckets of water before the door to scrub the pavement, and keeping up a screaming chatter with the other servants in the street, who were doing the same, Saturday-night fashion.

Madame Carimon was in the *salon*, sitting idle in the fading light; her sewing lay on the table. Lavinia's eyes went round the room, but she saw no one else in it.

"Mary, where is Nancy?" she asked, as Madame Carimon rose to greet her with outstretched hands.

"I'm sure I don't know," answered Madame Carimon lightly. "She has not been here. Did you think she had?"

"She dined here—did she not?"

"What, Nancy? Oh no! I and Jules dined alone. He is out now, giving a French lesson. I have not seen Nancy since—let me see—since Thursday, I think; the day before yesterday."

Lavinia Preen sat down, half-bewildered. She related the history of the evening.

"It is elsewhere that Nancy is gone," remarked Madame Carimon. "Flore must have misunderstood her."

Concluding that to be the case, and that Nancy might already be at home, Lavinia returned at once to the Petite Maison Rouge, Mary Carimon bearing her company in the sweet summer twilight. Lavinia opened the door with her latch-key. Flore had departed long before. There were three latch-keys to the house, Nancy possessing one of them.

They looked into every room, and called out "Nancy! Nancy!" But she was not there.

Nancy Preen had gone off with Captain Fennel by the six-o'clock train, *en route* for Dover, there to be converted into Mrs. Fennel.

And had Nancy foreseen the terrible events and final crime which this most disastrous step would bring about, she might have chosen, rather than take it, to run away to the Protestant cemetery outside the gates of Sainteville, there to lay herself down to die.

4

"Where *can* Nancy be?"

Miss Preen spoke these words to Mary Carimon in a sort of flurry. After letting themselves into the house, the Petite Maison Rouge, and calling up and down it in vain for Nancy, the ques-

32

tion as to where she could be naturally arose.

"She must be spending the evening with the friends she stayed to dine with," said Madame Carimon.

"I don't know where she would be likely to stay. Unless—yes—perhaps at Mrs. Hardy's."

"That must be it, Lavinia," pronounced Madame Carimon.

It was then getting towards nine o'clock. They set out again for Mrs. Hardy's to escort Nancy home. She lived in the Rue Lothaire; a long street, leading to the railway-station.

Mrs. Hardy was an elderly lady. When near her door they saw her grand-nephew, Charles Palliser, turn out of it. Charley was a good-hearted young fellow, the son of a rich merchant in London. He was staying at Sainteville for the purpose of acquiring the art of speaking French as a native.

"Looking for Miss Ann Preen!" cried he, as they explained in a word or two. "No, she is not at our house; has not been there. I saw her going off this evening by the six-o'clock train."

"Going off by the six-o'clock train!" echoed Miss Lavinia, staring at him. "Why, what do you mean, Mr, Charles? My sister has not gone off by any train."

"It was in this way," answered the young man, too polite to flatly contradict a lady. "Mrs. Hardy's cousin, Louise Soubitez, came to town this morning; she spent the day with us, and after dinner I went to see her off by the train. And there, at the station, was Miss Ann Preen."

"But not going away by train," returned Miss Lavinia.

"Why, yes, she was. I watched the train out of the station. She and Louise Soubitez sat in the same compartment."

A smile stole to Charles Palliser's face. In truth, he was amused at Miss Lavinia's consternation. It suddenly struck her that the young man was joking.

"Did you speak to Ann, Mr. Charles?"

"Oh yes; just a few words. There was not time for much conversation; Louise was late."

Miss Preen felt a little shaken.

"Was Ann alone?"

"No; she was with Captain Fennel."

And, with that, a suspicion of the truth, and the full horror of it, dawned upon Lavinia Preen. She grasped Madame Carimon's arm and turned white as death.

"It never can be," she whispered, her lips trembling; "it never can be! She cannot have—have—run away—with that man!"

Unconsciously perhaps to herself, her eyes were fixed on Charles. He thought the question was put to him, and answered it.

"Well—I—I'm afraid it looks like it, as she seems to have said nothing to you," he slowly said. "But I give you my word, Miss Preen, that until this moment that aspect of the matter never suggested itself to me. I supposed they were just going up the line together for some purpose or other; though, in fact, I hardly thought about it at all."

"And perhaps that is all the mystery!" interposed Madame Carimon briskly. "He may have taken Ann to Drecques for a little jaunt, and they will be back again by the last train. It must be almost due, Lavinia."

With one impulse they turned to the station, which was near at hand. Drecques, a village, was the first place the trains stopped at on the up-line. The passengers were already issuing from the gate. Standing aside until all had passed, and not seeing Nancy anywhere, Charley Palliser looked into the omnibuses. But she was not there.

"They may have intended to come back and missed the train. Miss Preen; it's very easy to miss a train," said he in his good nature.

"I think it must be so, Lavinia," spoke up Madame Carimon. "Any way, we will assume it until we hear to the contrary. And, Charley, we had better not talk of this tonight."

"*I* won't," answered Charley earnestly. "You may be sure of me."

Unless Captain Fennel and Miss Ann Preen chartered a balloon, there was little probability of their reaching Sainteville that evening, for this had been the last train. Lavinia Preen passed a night of discomfort, striving to *hope against hope*, as the saying runs. Not a very wise saying; it might run better, striving to hope against despair.

When Sunday did not bring back the truants, or any news of them, the three in the secret—Mary Carimon, Lavinia, and Charley Palliser—had little doubt that the disappearance meant an elopement. Monsieur Jules Carimon, not easily understanding such an escapade, so little in accordance with the customs and manners of his own country, said in his wife's ear he hoped it would turn out that there was a marriage in the case.

Miss Preen received a letter from Dover pretty early in the week, written by Ann. She had been married that day to Captain Fennel.

Altogether, the matter was the most bitter blow ever yet dealt to Lavinia Preen. No living being knew, or ever would know, how cruelly her heart was wrung by it. But, being a kindly woman of good sound sense, she saw that the best must be made of it, not the worst; and this she set herself out to do. She began by hoping that her own instinct, warning her against Captain Fennel, might be a mistaken one, and that he had a good home to offer his wife and would make her happy in it.

She knew no more about him—his family, his fortune, his former life, his antecedents—than she knew of the man in the moon. Major Smith perhaps did; he had been acquainted with him in the past. Nancy's letter, though written the previous day, had been delivered by the afternoon post. As soon as she could get dinner over, Lavinia went to Major Smith's. He lived at the top of the Rue Lambeau, a street turning out of the Grande Place. He and his wife, their own dinner just removed, were sitting together, the major indulging in a steaming glass of *schiedam* and water, flavoured with a slice of lemon. He was a very jolly little man, with rosy cheeks and a bald head. They welcomed Miss Lavinia warmly. She, not quite as composed as usual, opened her business without preamble; her sister Ann had married Captain Fennel, and she had come to ask Major Smith what he knew of him.

"Not very much," answered the major.

There was something behind his tone, and Lavinia burst into tears. Compassionating her distress, the major offered her a comforting glass, similar to his own. Lavinia declined it.

"You will tell me what you know," she said: and he proceeded to do so.

Edwin Fennel, the son of Colonel Fennel, was stationed in India with his regiment for several years. He got on well enough, but was not much liked by his brother officers: they thought him unscrupulous and deceitful. All at once, something very disagreeable occurred, which obliged Captain Fennel to quit Her Majesty's service. The affair was hushed up, out of consideration to his family and his father's long-term of service. "In fact, I believe he was allowed to retire, instead of being cashiered," added the major, "but I am not quite sure which it was."

"What was it that occurred—that Captain Fennel did, to necessitate his dismissal?" questioned Lavinia.

"I don't much like to mention it," said the major, shaking his head. "It might get about, you see. Miss Preen, which would make it awkward for him. I have no wish, or right either, to do the man a gratuitous injury."

"I promise you it shall not get about through me," returned Lavinia; "my sister's being his wife will be the best guarantee for that. You must please tell me. Major Smith."

"Well, Fennel was suspected—detected, in short—of cheating at cards."

Lavinia drew a deep breath. "Do you know," she said presently, in an undertone, "that when I first met the man I shrank from his face."

"Oh my! And it has such nice features!" put in Mrs. Smith, who was but a silly little woman.

"There was something in its shifty look which spoke to me as a warning," continued Lavinia. "It did, indeed. All my life I have been able to read faces, and my first instinct has rarely, if ever, deceived me. Each time I have seen this man since, that instinct against him has become stronger."

Major Smith took a sip at his *schiedam*. "I believe—between ourselves—he is just a *mauvais sujet*," said he. "He has a brother who is one, out and out; as I chance to know."

"What is Edwin Fennel's income, major?"

"I can't tell at all. I should not be surprised to hear that he has none."

"How does he live then?" asked Lavinia, her heart going at a gallop.

"Don't know that either," said the major. "His father is dead now and can't help him. A very respectable man, the old colonel, but always poor."

"He cannot live upon air; he must have some means," debated Lavinia.

"Lives upon his wits, perhaps; some men do. He wanted to borrow ten pounds from me a short time ago," added the major, taking another sip at his tumbler; "but I told him I had no money to lend—which was a fact. I have an idea that he got it out of Charley Palliser."

The more Lavinia Preen heard of this unhappy case, the worse it seemed to be. Declining to stay for tea, as Mrs. Smith wished, she betook her miserable steps home again, rather wishing that the sea would swallow up Captain Fennel.

The next day she saw Charles Palliser. Pouncing upon him as he was airing his long legs in the Grande Place, she put the question to him in so determined a way that Charley had no chance against her. He turned red.

"I don't know who can have set that about," said he. "But it's true. Miss Preen. Fennel pressed me to lend him ten pounds for a month; and I—well, I did it. I happened to have it in my pocket, you see, having just cashed a remittance from my father."

"Has he repaid you, Mr. Charles? "

"Oh, the month's not quite up yet," cried Charley. "Please don't talk of it. Miss Preen; he wouldn't like it, you know. How on earth it has slipped out I can't imagine."

"No, I shall not talk of it," said Lavinia, as she wished him good-day and walked onwards, wondering what sort of a home

Captain Fennel meant to provide for Ann.

Lavinia Preens cup of sorrow was not yet full. A morning or two after this she was seated at breakfast with the window open, when she saw the postman come striding across the yard with a letter. It was from the bride; a very short letter, and one that Miss Lavinia did not at once understand. She read it again.

My dear Lavinia,

All being well, we shall be home tomorrow; that is, on the day you receive this letter; reaching Sainteville by the last train in the evening. Please get something nice and substantial for tea, Edwin says, and please see that Flore has the bedroom in good order.

Your affectionate sister,

Ann Fennel.

The thing that Miss Lavinia did, when comprehension came to her, was to fly into a passion.

"Come home here—*he!*—is that what she means?" cried she. "Never. Have that man in my house? Never, never."

"But what has *mademoiselle* received?" exclaimed Flore, appearing just then with a boiled egg. "Is it bad news?"

"It is news that I will not put up with—will not tolerate," cried Miss Lavinia. And, in the moment's dismay, she told the woman what it was.

"*Tiens!*" commented Flore, taking a common-sense view of matters: "they must be coming just to show themselves to *mademoiselle* on their marriage. Likely enough they will not stay more than a night or two, while looking out for an apartment."

Lavinia did not believe it; but the very suggestion somewhat soothed her. To receive that man even for a night or two, as Flore put it, would be to her most repugnant, cruel pain, and she resolved not to do it. Breakfast over, she carried the letter and her trouble to the Rue Pomme Cuite.

"But I am afraid, Lavinia, you cannot refuse to receive them," spoke Madame Carimon, after considering the problem.

"Not refuse to receive them!" echoed Lavinia. "Why do you

say that?"

"Well," replied Mary Carimon uneasily, for she disliked to add to trouble, "you see the house is as much Ann's as yours. It was taken in your joint names. Ann has the right to return to it; and also, I suppose"—more dubiously—"to introduce her husband into it."

"Is that French law?"

"I think so. I'll ask Jules when he comes home to dinner. Would it not be English law also, Lavinia?"

Lavinia was feeling wretchedly uncomfortable. With all her plain common-sense, this phase of the matter had not struck her.

"Mary," said she—and there stopped, for she was seized with a violent shivering, which seemed difficult to be accounted for. "Mary, if that man has to take up his abode in the house, I can never remain in it, I would rather die."

"Look here, dear friend," whispered Mary: "life is full of trouble—as Job tells us in the Holy Scriptures—none of us are exempt from it. It attacks us all in turn. The only one thing we can do is to strive to make the best of it, under God; to ask Him to help us. I am afraid there is a severe cross before you, Lavinia; better *bear* it than fight against it."

"I will never bear *that*," retorted Lavinia, turning a deaf ear in her anger. "You ought not to wish me to do so."

"And I would not if I saw anything better for you."

Madame Veuve Sauvage, sitting as usual at her front-window that same morning, was surprised at receiving an early call from her tenant, Miss Preen. *Madame* handed her into her best crimson velvet *fauteuil*, and they began talking.

Not to much purpose, however; for neither very well understood what the other said. Lavinia tried to explain the object of her visit, but found her French was not equal to it. Madame called her maid, Mariette, and sent her into the shop below to ask Monsieur Gustave to be good enough to step up.

Lavinia had gone to beg of them to cancel the agreement for the little house, so far as her sister was concerned, and to place it in her name only.

Monsieur Gustave, when he had mastered the request, politely answered that such a thing was not practicable; Miss Ann's name could not be struck out of the lease without her consent, or, as he expressed it, breaking the *bail*. His mother and himself had every disposition to oblige Miss Preen in any way, as indeed she must know, but they had no power to act against the law.

So poor Miss Lavinia went into her home wringing her hands in despair. She was perfectly helpless.

5

The summer days went on. Mr. Edwin Fennel, with all the impudence in the world, had taken up his abode in the Petite Maison Rouge, without saying with your leave or by your leave.

"How could you *think* of bringing him here, Ann?" Lavinia demanded of her sister in the first days.

"I did not think of it; it was he thought of it," returned Mrs. Fennel in her simple way. "I feared you would not like it, Lavinia; but what could I do? He seemed to look upon it as a matter of course that he should come."

Yes, there he was; "a matter of course;" making one in the home. Lavinia could not show fight; he was Ann's husband, and the place was as much Ann's as hers. The more Lavinia saw of him the more she disliked him; which was perhaps unreasonable, since he made himself agreeable to her in social intercourse, though he took care to have things his own way. If Lavinia's will went one way in the house and his the other, she found herself smilingly set at naught. Ann was his willing slave; and when opinions differed she sided with her husband.

It was no light charge, having a third person in the house to live upon their small income, especially one who studied his appetite. For a very short time Lavinia, in her indignation at affairs generally, turned the housekeeping over to Mrs. Fennel. But she had to take to it again. Ann was naturally an incautious manager; she ordered in delicacies to please her husband's palate without regard to cost, and nothing could have come of that but debt and disaster.

That the gallant ex-Captain Fennel had married Ann Preen just to have a roof over his head, Lavinia felt as sure of as that the moon occasionally shone in the heavens. She did not suppose he had any other refuge in the wide world. And through something told her by Ann she judged that he had believed he was doing better for himself in marrying than he had done.

The day after the marriage Mr. and Mrs. Fennel were sitting on a bench at Dover, romantically gazing at the sea, honeymoon fashion, and talking of course of hearts and darts. Suddenly the bridegroom turned his thoughts to more practical things.

"Nancy, how do you receive your money—half-yearly or quarterly?" asked he.

"Oh, quarterly," said Nancy. "It is paid punctually to us by the acting-trustee, Colonel Selby."

"Ah, yes. Then you have thirty-five pounds every quarter?"

"Between us, we do," assented Nancy. "Lavinia has seventeen pounds ten, and I have the same; and the colonel makes us each give a receipt for our own share."

Captain Fennel turned his head and gazed at her with a hard stare.

"You told me your income was a hundred and forty pounds a-year."

"Yes, it is that exactly," said she quietly; "mine and Lavinia's together. We do not each have that, Edwin; I never meant to imply—"

Mrs. Fennel broke off, frightened. On the captain's face, cruel enough just then, there sat an expression which she might have thought diabolical had it been anyone else's face. Any way, it scared her.

"What is it?" she gasped.

Rising rapidly, Captain Fennel walked forward, caught up some pebbles, flung them from him and waited, apparently watching to see where they fell. Then he strolled back again.

"Were you angry with me?" faltered Nancy. "Had I done anything?"

41

"My dear, what should you have done? Angry?" repeated he, in a light tone, as if intensely amused. "You must not take up fancies, Mrs. Fennel."

"I suppose Mrs. Selby thought it would be sufficient income for us, both living together," remarked Nancy. "If either of us should die it all lapses to the other. We found it quite enough last year, I assure you, Edwin; Sainteville is so cheap a place."

"Oh, delightfully cheap!" agreed the captain.

It was this conversation that Nancy repeated to Lavinia; but she did not speak of the queer look which had frightened her. Lavinia saw that Mr. Edwin Fennel had taken up a wrong idea of their income. Of course the disappointment angered him.

An aspect of semi-courtesy was outwardly maintained in the intercourse of home life. Lavinia was a gentlewoman; she had not spoken unpleasant things to the captain's face, or hinted that he was a weight upon the housekeeping pocket; whilst he, as yet, was quite officiously civil to her. But there was no love lost between them; and Lavinia could not divest her mind of an undercurrent of conviction that he was, in some way or other, a man to be dreaded.

Thus Captain Fennel (as he was mostly called), being domiciled with the estimable ladies in the Petite Maison Rouge, grew to be considered one of the English colony of Sainteville, and was received as such. As nobody knew aught against him, nobody thought anything. Major Smith had not spoken of antecedents, neither had Miss Preen; the Carimons, who were in the secret, never spoke ill of any one: and as the captain could assume pleasing manners at will, he became fairly well liked by his country-people in a passing sort of way.

Lavinia Preen sat one day upon the low edge of the pier, her back to the sun and the sea. She had called in at the little shoe-shop on the port, just as you turn out of the Rue Tessin, and had left her parasol there. The sun was not then out in the grey sky, and she did not miss it. Now that the sun was shining, and the grey canopy above had become blue, she said to herself that she had been stupid. It was September weather, so the sun was not unbearable.

Lavinia Preen was thinner; the thraldom of the past three months had made her so. Now and then it would cross her mind to leave the Petite Maison Rouge to its married inmates; but for Nancy's sake she hesitated. Nancy had made the one love of her life, and Nancy had loved her in return. Now, the love was chiefly given to the new tie she had formed; Lavinia was second in every respect.

"They go their way now, and I have to go mine," sighed Lavinia, as she sat this morning on the pier. "Even my walks have to be solitary."

A cloud came sailing up and the sun went in again. Lavinia rose; she walked onwards till she came to the end of the pier, where she again sat down. The next moment, chancing to look the way she had come, she saw a lady and gentleman advancing arm-in-arm.

"Oh, *they* are on the pier, are they!" mentally spoke Lavinia. For it was Mr. and Mrs. Edwin Fennel.

Nancy sat down beside her. "It is a long walk!" cried she, drawing a quick breath or two. "Lavinia, what do you think we have just heard?"

"How can I tell?" returned the elder sister.

"You know those queer people, an old English aunt and three nieces, who took Madame Gibon's rooms in the Rue Ménar? They have all disappeared and have paid nobody," continued Nancy. "Charley Palliser told us just how; he was laughing like anything over it."

"I never thought they looked like people to be trusted," remarked Lavinia. "Dear me! here's the sun coming out again."

"Where is your parasol?"

Lavinia recounted her negligence in having left it at the shoe-mart. Captain Fennel had brought out a small silk umbrella; he turned from the end of the pier, where he stood looking out to sea, opened the umbrella, and offered it.

"It is not much larger than a good-sized parasol," remarked he. "Pray take it, Miss Lavinia."

Lavinia did so after a moment's imperceptible hesitation, and thanked him. She hated to be under the slightest obligation to him, but the sun was now full in her eyes, and might make her head ache.

The pleasant smell of a cigar caused them to look up. A youngish man, rather remarkably tall, with a shepherd's plaid across his broad shoulders, was striding up the pier. He sat down near Miss Preen, and she glanced round at him. Appearing to think that she looked at his cigar, he immediately threw it into the sea behind him.

"Oh, I am sorry you did that," said Lavinia, speaking impulsively. "I like the smell of a cigar."

"Oh, thank you; thank you very much," he answered. "I had nearly smoked it out."

Voice and manner were alike pleasant and easy, and Lavinia spoke again—some trivial remark about the fine expanse of sea; upon which they drifted into conversation. We are reserved enough with strangers at home, we Islanders, as the world knows, but most of us are less ungracious abroad.

"Sainteville seems a clean, healthy place," remarked the newcomer.

"Very," said Miss Lavinia. "Do you know it well?"

"I never saw it before today," he replied. "I have come here from Douai to meet a friend, having two or three days to spare."

"Douai is a fine town," remarked Captain Fennel, turning to speak, for he was still looking out over the sea, and had his opera-glasses in his hand. "I spent a week there not long ago."

"Douai!" exclaimed Nancy. "That's the place where the great Law Courts are, is it not? Don't you remember the man last year, Lavinia, who committed some dreadful crime, and was taken up to Douai to be tried at the Assizes there?"

"We have a great case coming on there as soon as the Courts meet," said the stranger, who seemed a talkative man; "and that's what I am at Douai for. A case of extensive swindling."

"You are a lawyer, I presume?" said Miss Preen.

44

The stranger nodded; "Being the only one of our London firm who can speak French readily, and we are four of us in it, I had to come over and watch this affair and wait for the trial. For the young fellow is an Englishman, I am sorry to say, and his people, worthy and well-to-do merchants, are nearly mad over it."

"But did he commit it in England?" cried Miss Preen.

"Oh no; in France, within the *arrondissement* of the Douai Courts. He is in prison there. I dare say you get some swindling in a petty way even at Sainteville," added the speaker.

"That we do," put in Nancy. "An English family of ladies ran away only yesterday, owing twenty pounds at least, it is said."

"Ah," said the stranger, with a smile, "I think the ladies are sometimes more clever at that game than the men. By the way," he went on briskly, "do you know a Mr. Dangerfield at Sainteville?"

"No," replied Lavinia.

"He is staying here, I believe, or has been."

"Not that I know of," said Lavinia. "I never heard his name."

"Changed it again, probably," carelessly observed the young man.

"Is Dangerfield not his true name, then?"

"Just as much as it is mine, madam. His real name is Fennel; but he has found it convenient to drop that on occasion."

Now it was a curious fact that Nancy did not hear the name which the stranger had given as the true one. Her attention was diverted by some men who were working at the mud in the harbour, for it was low water, and who were loudly disputing together. Nancy had moved to the side of the pier to look down at them.

"Is he a swindler, that Mr. Dangerfield?" asked she, half-turning her head to speak. But the stranger did not answer.

As to Lavinia, the avowal had struck her speechless. She glanced at Captain Fennel. He had his back to them, and stood immovable, apparently unconcerned, possibly not having heard. A thought struck her—and frightened her.

45

"Do you know that Mr. Dangerfield yourself?" she asked the stranger, in a tone of indifference.

"No, I do not," he said; "but there's a man coming over in yonder boat who does."

He pointed over his shoulder at the sea as he spoke. Lavinia glanced quickly in the same direction.

"In yonder boat?" she repeated vaguely.

"I mean the London boat, which is on its way here, and will get in this evening," he explained.

"Oh, of course," said Lavinia, as if her wits had been wool-gathering.

The young man took out his watch and looked at it. Then he rose, lifted his hat, and, with a general good-morning, walked quickly down the pier.

Nancy was still at the side of the pier, looking down at the men. Captain Fennel put up his glasses and sat down beside Lavinia, his impassive face still as usual.

"I wonder who that man is?" he cried, watching the footsteps of the retreating stranger,

"Did you hear what he said?" asked Lavinia, dropping her voice.

"Yes. Had Nancy not been here, I should have given him a taste of my mind; but she hates even the semblance of a quarrel. He had no right to say what he did."

"What could it have meant?" murmured Lavinia.

"It meant my brother, I expect," said Captain Fennel savagely, and, as Lavinia thought, with every appearance of truth. "But he. has never been at Sainteville, so far as I know; the fellow is mistaken in that."

"Does he pass under the name of Dangerfield?"

"Possibly. This is the first I've heard of it. He is an extravagant man, often in embarrassment from debt. There's nothing worse against him."

He did not say more; neither did Lavinia. They sat on in silence. The tall figure in the Scotch plaid disappeared from sight; the men in the harbour kept on disputing.

"How long are you going to stay here?" asked Nancy, turning towards her husband.

"I'm ready to go now," he answered. And giving his arm to Nancy, they walked down the pier together.

Never a word to Lavinia; never a question put by him or by Nancy, if only to say, "Are you not coming with us?" It was ever so now. Nancy, absorbed in her husband, neglected her sister.

Lavinia sighed. She sat on a little while longer, and then took her departure.

The shoe-shop on the port was opposite the place in the harbour where the London steamers were generally moored. The one now there was taking in cargo. As Lavinia was turning into the shop for her parasol, she heard a stentorian English voice call out to a man who was superintending the work in his shirt-sleeves: "At what hour does this boat leave tonight?"

"At eight o'clock, sir," was the answer. "Eight sharp; we want to get away with the first o' the tide."

From Miss Lavinia Preen's Diary.

September 22nd.—The town clocks have just struck eight, and I could almost fancy that I hear the faint sound of the boat steaming down the harbour in the dark night, carrying Nancy away with it, and carrying him. However, that is fancy and nothing else, for the sound could not penetrate to me here.

Perhaps it surprised me, perhaps it did not, when Nancy came to me this afternoon as I was sitting in my bedroom reading Scott's *Legend of Montrose*, which Mary Carimon had lent me from her little stock of English books, and said she and Captain Fennel were going to London that night by the boat. He had received a letter, he told her, calling him thither. He might tell Nancy that if he liked, but it would not do for me. He is going, I can only believe, in consequence of what that gentleman in the shepherd's plaid said on the pier today. Can it be that the "Mr. Dangerfield" spoken of applies to Edwin Fennel himself and not to his brother? Is he finding himself in some dangerous strait, and is running away from the individual coming over in the approaching boat, who personally knows Mr. Dangerfield? "Can you lend me a five-pound note, Lavinia?" Nancy went on, when she had told me the news; "lend it to myself, I mean. I will repay you when I receive my next quarter's income, which is due, you know, in a few days." I chanced to have a five-pound note by me in my own private store, and I gave it her, reminding her that unless she did let me have it again, it would be so much less in hand to meet expenses with, and that I had found difficulty enough in the past quarter.

"On the other hand," said Nancy, "if I and Edwin stay away a week or two, you will be spared our housekeeping; and when our money comes, Lavinia, you can open my letter and repay yourself if I am not here. I don't at all know where we are going to stay," she said, in answer to my question. "I was beginning to ask Edwin just now in the other room, but he was busy packing his portmanteau, and told me not to bother him."

And so, there it is: they are gone, and I am left here all alone.

I wonder whether any Mr, Dangerfield has been at Sainteville? I think we should have heard the name. Why, that is the door-bell! I must go and answer it.

It was Charley Palliser. He had come with a message from Major and Mrs. Smith. They are going to Drecques to-morrow morning by the eleven-o'clock train with a few friends and a basket of provisions, and had sent Charley to say they would be glad of my company. "Do come. Miss Preen," urged Charley as I hesitated; "you are all alone now, and I'm sure it must be dreadfully dull."

"How do you know I am alone?" I asked.

"Because," said Charley, "I have been watching the London boat out, and I saw Captain Fennel and your sister go by it. Major and Mrs. Smith were with me. It is a lovely night."

"Wait a moment," I said, as Charley was about to depart when I had accepted the invitation. "Do you know whether an Englishman named Dangerfield is living here?"

"Don't think there is; I have not met with him," said Charley "Why, Miss Preen?"

"Oh, only that I was asked today whether I knew any one of that name," I returned carelessly. "Goodnight, Mr. Charles. Thank you for coming."

They have invited me, finding I was left alone, and I think it very kind of them. But the Smiths are both kind-hearted people.

September 23rd.—Half-past nine o'clock, p.m. Have just returned from Drecques by the last train after spending a pleasant day. Quiet, of course, for there is not much to do at Drecques except stroll over the ruins of the old castle, or saunter about the quaint little ancient town, and go into the grand old church. It was so fine and warm that we had dinner on the grass, the people at the cottage bringing our plates and knives and forks. Later in the day we took tea indoors. In the afternoon, when all the rest were scattered about and the major sat smoking his cigar on the bench under the trees, I sat down by him to tell him what happened yesterday, and I begged him to give me his opinion. It was no betrayal of confidence, for Major Smith is better acquainted with the shady side of the Fennels than I am.

"I heard there was an English lawyer staying at the Hotel des Princes, and that he had come here from Douai," observed the major. "His name's Lockett. It must have been he who spoke to you on the pier."

"Yes, of course. Do you know, major, whether anyone has stayed at Sainteville passing as Mr. Dangerfield?"

"I don't think so," replied the major. "Unless he has kept himself remarkably quiet."

"Could it apply to Captain Fennel?"

"I never knew that he had gone under an assumed name. The accusation is one more likely to apply to his brother than to himself. James Fennel is unscrupulous, very incautious: notwithstanding that, I like him better than I like the other. There's something about Edwin Fennel that repels you; at least, it does me; but one can hardly help liking James, *mauvais sujet* though he is," added the speaker, pausing to flirt off the ashes of his cigar.

"The doubt pointing to Edwin Fennel in the affair is his suddenly decamping," continued Major Smith. "It was quite *impromptu*, you say, Miss Preen?"

"Quite so, I feel sure he had no thought of going away in the morning; and he did not receive any letter from England later, which was the excuse he gave Nancy for departing. Rely upon it that what he heard about the Mr. Dangerfield on the pier drove him away."

"Well, that looks suspicious, you see."

"Oh yes, I do see it," I answered, unable to conceal the pain I felt. "It was a bitter calamity. Major Smith, when Nancy married him."

"I'll make a few cautious inquiries in the town, and try to find out if there's anything against him in secret, or if any man named Dangerfield has been in the place and got into a mess. But, indeed, I don't altogether see that it could apply to him," concluded the major after a pause. "One can't well go under two names in the same town; and everyone knows him as Edwin Fennel.—Here they are, some of them, coming back!" And when the wanderers were close up, they found Major Smith arguing with me about the architecture of the castle.

Ten o'clock. Time for bed. I am in no haste to go, for I don't sleep as well as I used to.

A thought has lately sometimes crossed me that this miserable trouble worries me more than it ought to do. "Accept it as your cross, and *yield* to it, Lavinia," says Mary Carimon to me. But I *cannot* yield to it; that is, I cannot in the least diminish the anxiety which always clings to me, or forget the distress and dread that lie upon me like a shadow. I know that my life has been on the whole an easy life—that during all the years I spent at Selby Court I never had any trouble; I know that crosses do come to us all, earlier or later, and that I ought not to be surprised that "no new thing has happened to me," the world being full of such experiences. I suppose it is because I have been so exempt from care, that I feel this the more.

Half-past ten! just half-an-hour writing these last few lines and *thinking!* Time I put up. I wonder when I shall hear from Nancy?

6

A curious phase, taken in conjunction with what was to follow, now occurred in the history. Miss Preen began to experience a nervous dread at going into the Petite Maison Rouge at night.

She could go into the house ten times a-day when it was empty; she could stay in the house alone in the evening after Flore took her departure; she could be its only inmate all night long; and never at these times have the slightest sense of fear. But if she went out to spend the evening, she felt an unaccountable dread, amounting to horror, at entering it when she arrived home.

It came on suddenly. One evening when Lavinia had been at Mrs. Hardy's, Charley Palliser having run over to London, she returned home a little before ten o'clock. Opening the door with her latch-key, she was stepping into the passage when a sharp horror of entering it seized her. A dread, as it seemed to her, of going into the empty house, up the long, dark, narrow passage. It was the same sort of sensation that had struck her the first time she attempted to enter it under the escort of Monsieur Gustave Sauvage, and it came on now with as little reason as it had come on then. For Lavinia this night had not a thought in her mind of fear or loneliness, or anything else unpleasant. Mrs. Hardy had been relating a laughable adventure that Charley Palliser met with on board the boat when going over, the account of which he had written to her, and Lavinia was thinking brightly of it all the way home. She was smiling to herself as she unlatched the door and opened it. And then, without warning, arose the horrible fear.

How she conquered it sufficiently to enter the passage and reach the slab, where her candle and matches were always placed, she did not know. It had to be done, for Lavinia Preen could not remain in the dark yard all night, or patrol the streets; but her face had turned moist, and her hands trembled.

That was the beginning of it. Never since had she come home in the same way at night but the same terror assailed her; and I must beg the reader to understand that this is no invention. Devoid of reason and unaccountable though the terror was, Lavinia Preen experienced it.

She went out often—two or three times a-week, perhaps—either to dine or to spend the evening. Captain Fennel and Nancy were still away, and friends, remembering Miss Preen's solitary position, invited her.

October had passed, November was passing, and as yet no news came to Lavinia of the return of the travellers. At first they did not write to her at all, leaving her to infer that as the boat reached London safely they had done the same. After the lapse of a fortnight she received a short letter from Nancy telling her really nothing, and not giving any address. The next letter came towards the end of November, and was as follows:

My dear Lavinia,
I have not written to you, for, truly, there is nothing to write about, and almost every day I expect Edwin to tell me we are going home. Will you *kindly* lend me a ten-pound note? Please send it in a letter. We are staying at Camberwell, and I enclose you the address in strict confidence. Do not repeat it to any one—not even to Mary Carimon. It is a relation of Edwin's we are staying with, but he is not well off! I like his wife. Edwin desires his best regards.
     Your loving sister,   Nancy.

Miss Preen did not send the ten-pound note. She wrote to tell Nancy that she could not do it, and was uncomfortably pressed for money herself in consequence of Nancy's own action.

The five-pound note borrowed from Lavinia by Nancy on her departure had not been repaid; neither had Nancy's share of the previous quarter's money been remitted. On the usual day of payment at the end of September, Lavinia's quarterly income came to her at Sainteville, as was customary; not Nancy's. For Nancy there came neither money nor letter. The fact was, Nancy, escorted by her husband, had presented herself at Colonel Selby's bank—he was junior partner and manager of a small private bank in the City—the day before the dividends were due, and personally claimed the quarterly payment, which was paid to her.

But now, the summary docking of just half their income was a matter of embarrassment to Miss Preen, as may readily be imagined. The house expenses had to go on, with only half the money to meet them. Lavinia had a little nest-egg of her own, it has been said before, saved in earlier years; and this she drew upon, and so kept debt down. But it was very inconvenient, as well as vexatious. Lavinia told the whole truth now to Mary Carimon and her husband, with Nancy's recent application for a ten-pound note, and her refusal. Little Monsieur Carimon muttered a word between his closed lips which sounded like "Rat," and was no doubt applied to Edwin Fennel.

Pretty close upon this, Lavinia received a blowing-up letter from Colonel Selby. Having known Lavinia when she was in pinafores, the colonel, a peppery man, considered he had a right to take her to task at will. He was brother to Paul Selby, of Selby Court, and heir presumptive to it. The colonel had a wife and children, and much ado at times to keep them, for his income was not large at present, and growing-up sons are expensive.

Dear Lavinia,
What in the name of common sense could have induced you to imagine that I should pay the two quarterly incomes some weeks before they were due, and to send Ann

53

and that man Fennel here with your orders that I should do so? Pretty ideas of trusteeship you must have! If you are over head and ears in debt, as they tell me, and for that reason wish to forestall the time for payment, *I* can't help it. It is no reason with me. Your money will be forwarded to Sainteville, at the proper period, to *yourself.* Do not ask me again to pay it into Ann's hands, and to accept her receipt for it. I can do nothing of the kind. Ann's share will be sent at the same time. She tells me she is returning to you. She must give me her own receipt for it, and you must give me yours.

Your affectionate kinsman,

William Selby.

Just for a few minutes Lavinia Preen did not understand this letter. What could it mean? Why had Colonel Selby written it to her? Then the truth flashed into her mind.

Nancy (induced, of course, by Edwin Fennel) had gone with him to Colonel Selby, purporting to have been sent by Lavinia, to ask him to pay them the quarter's money not due until the end of December, and not only Nancy's share but Lavinia's as well.

"Why, it would have been nothing short of swindling!" cried Lavinia, as she gazed in dismay at the colonel's letter.

In the indignation of the moment, she took pen and ink and wrote an answer to William Selby. Partly enlightening him—not quite—but telling him that her money must never be paid to anyone but herself, and that the present matter had better be hushed up for Ann's sake, who was as a reed in the hands of the man she had married.

Colonel Selby exploded a little when he received this answer. Down he sat in his turn, and wrote a short, sharp note to Edwin Fennel, giving that estimable man a little of his mind, and warning him that he must not be surprised if the police were advised to look after him.

When Edward Fennel received this decisive note through an address he had given to Colonel Selby, but not the one at Camberwell, he called Miss Lavinia Preen all the laudatory names in the thieves' dictionary.

And on the feast of St. Andrew, which as everyone knows is the last day of November, the letters came to an end with the following one from Nancy:

All being well, my dear Lavinia, we propose to return home by next Sunday's boat, which ought to get in before three o'clock in the afternoon. On Wednesday, Edwin met Charley Palliser in the Strand, and had a chat with him, and heard all the Sainteville news; not that there seemed much to hear. Charley says he runs over to London pretty often now, his mother being ill. Of course you will not mind waiting dinner for us on Sunday.

Ever your loving sister,

Ann.

So at length they were coming! Either that threat of being looked after by the police had been too much for Captain Fennel, or the failure to obtain funds was cutting short his stay in London. Any way, they were coming. Lavinia laid the letter beside her breakfast-plate and fell into thought. She resolved to welcome them graciously, and to say nothing about bygones.

Flore was told the news, and warned that instead of dining at half-past one on the morrow, the usual Sunday hour, it would be delayed until three. Flore did not much like the prospect of her afternoon's holiday being shortened, but there was no help for it. Lavinia provided a couple of ducks for dinner, going into the market after breakfast to buy them; the dish was an especial favourite of the captain's. She invited Mary Carimon to partake of it, for Monsieur Carimon was going to spend Sunday at Lille with an old friend of his, who was now master of the college there.

On this evening, Saturday, Lavinia dined out herself. Some ladies named Bosanquet, three sisters, with whom she had become pretty intimate, called at the Petite Maison Rouge, and carried her off to their home in the Rue Lamar tine, where they had lived for years. After a very pleasant evening with them, Lavinia left at ten o'clock.

And when she reached her own door, and was putting the latch-key into the lock, the old fear came over her. Dropping her hands, she stood there trembling. She looked round at the silent, deserted yard, she looked up at the high encircling walls; she glanced at the frosty sky and the bright stars; and she stood there shivering.

But she must go in. Throwing the door back with an effort of will, she turned sick and faint: to enter that dark, lonely, empty house seemed beyond her strength and courage. What could this strange feeling portend?—why should it thus attack her? It was just as if some fatality were in the house waiting to destroy her, and a subtle power would keep her from entering it.

Her heart beating wildly, her breath laboured, Lavinia went in; she shut the door behind her and sped up the passage. Feeling for the match-box on the slab, put ready to her hand, she struck a match and lighted the candle. At that moment, when turning round, she saw, or thought she saw, Captain Fennel. He was standing just within the front-door, which she had now come in at, staring at her with a fixed gaze, and with the most malignant expression on his usually impassive face. Lavinia's terror partly gave place to astonishment. Was it he himself? How had he come in?

Turning to take the candle from the slab in her bewilderment, when she looked again he was gone. What had become of him? Lavinia called to him by name, but he did not answer. She took the candle into the salon, though feeling sure he could not have come up the passage; but he was not there. Had he slipped out again? Had she left the door open when thinking she closed it, and had he followed her in, and was now gone again? Lavinia carried her lighted candle to the door, and found it was fastened. She had not left it open.

Then, as she undressed in her room, trying all the while to solve the problem, an idea crept into her mind that the appearance might have been supernatural. Yet—supernatural visitants of the living do not appear to us, but of the dead. Was Edwin Fennel dead?

So disturbed was the brain of Lavinia Preen that she could not get to sleep; but tossed and turned about the bed almost until daybreak, At six o'clock she fell into an uneasy slumber, and into a most distressing dream.

It was a confused dream; nothing in it was clear. All she knew when she awoke, was that she had appeared to be in a state of inexplicable terror, of most intense apprehension throughout it, arising from some evil threatened her by Captain Fennel.

7

It was a fine, frosty day, and the first of December. The sun shone on the fair streets of Sainteville and on the small congregation turning out of the English Protestant Church after morning service.

Lavinia Preen went straight home. There she found that Madame Carimon, who was to spend the rest of the day with her—*monsieur* having gone to Lille—had not yet arrived, though the French Church Evangélique was always over before the English. After glancing at Flore in the kitchen, busy over the fine ducks, Lavinia set off for the Rue Pomme Cuite.

She met Mary Carimon turning out of it. "Let us go and sit under the wall in the sun," said Mary. "It is too early yet for the boat."

This was a high wall belonging to the strong north gates of the town, near Madame Carimon's. The sun shone full upon the benches beneath it, which it sheltered from the bleak winds; in front was a patch of green grass, on which the children ran about amidst the straight poplar trees. It was very pleasant sitting there, even on this December day—bright and cheerful; the wall behind them was quite warm, the sunshine rested upon all.

Sitting there, Lavinia Preen told Madame Carimon of the curious dread of entering her house at night, which had pursued her for the past two months that she had been alone in it, and which she had never spoken of to any one before. She went on to speak of the belief that she had seen Captain Fennel the previous night in the passage, and of the dream which had visited her when at length she fell asleep.

Madame Carimon turned her kindly, sensible face and her quiet, dark, surprised eyes upon Lavinia. "I cannot understand you," she said.

"You mean, I suppose, that you cannot understand the facts, Mary. Neither can I. Why this fear of going into the house should lie upon me is most strange. I never was nervous before."

"I don't know that that is so very strange," dissented Mary Carimon, after a pause. "It must seem lonely to let one's self into a dark, empty house in the middle of the night; and your house is in what may be called an isolated situation; I should not much like it myself. That's nothing. What I cannot understand, Lavinia, is the fancy that you saw Captain Fennel."

"He appeared to be standing there, and was quite visible to me. The expression on his face, which seemed to be looking straight into mine, was most malicious. I never saw such an expression upon it in reality."

Mary Carimon laughed a little, saying she had never been troubled with nervous fears herself; she was too practical for anything of the sort.

"And I have been practical hitherto," returned Lavinia. "When the first surprise of seeing him there, or fancying I saw him there, was over, I began to think, Mary, that he might be dead; that it was his apparition which had stood there looking at me.

Mary Carimon shook her head. "Had anything of that sort happened, Nancy would have telegraphed to you. Rely upon it, Lavinia, it was pure fancy. You have been disagreeably exercised in mind lately, you know, about that man; hearing he was coming home, your brain was somewhat thrown off its balance."

"It may be so. The dream followed on it; and I did not like the dream."

"We all have bad dreams now and then. You say you do not remember much of this one."

"I think I did not know much of it when dreaming it,"

quaintly spoke Lavinia. "I was in a sea of trouble, throughout which I seemed to be striving to escape some evil menaced me by Captain Fennel, and could not do so. Whichever way I turned, there he was at a distance, scowling at me with a threatening, evil countenance. Mary," she added in impassioned tones, "I am sure some ill awaits me from that man."

"I am sure, were I you, I would put these foolish notions from me," calmly spoke Madame Carimon. "If Nancy set up a vocation for seeing ghosts and dreaming dreams, one would not so much wonder at it. *You* have always been reasonable, Lavinia; be so now."

Miss Preen took out her watch and looked at it. "We may as well be walking towards the port, Mary," she remarked. "It is past two. The boat ought to be in sight."

Not only in sight was the steamer, but rapidly nearing the port. She had made a calm and quick passage. When at length she was in and about to swing round, and the two ladies were looking down at it, with a small crowd of other assembled spectators, the first passengers they saw on board were Nancy and Captain Fennel, who began to wave their hands in greeting and to nod their heads.

"Anyway, Lavinia, it could not have been his ghost last night," whispered Mary Carimon.

★★★★★★

Far from presenting an evil countenance to Lavinia, as the days passed on. Captain Fennel appeared to wish to please her, and was all suavity. So at present nothing disturbed the peace of the Petite Maison Rouge.

"What people were they that you stayed with in London, Nancy?" Lavinia inquired of her sister on the first favourable opportunity.

Nancy glanced round the *salon* before answering, as if to make sure they were alone; but Captain Fennel had gone out for a stroll,

"We were at James Fennel's, Lavinia."

"What—the brother's! And has he a wife?"

"Yes; a wife, but no children. Mrs. James Fennel has money of her own, which she receives weekly."

"Receives weekly!" echoed Lavinia.

"She owns some little houses which are let out in weekly tenements; an agent collects the rents, and brings her the money every Tuesday morning. She dresses in the shabbiest things sometimes, and does her own housework, and altogether is not what I should call quite a lady, but she is very good-hearted, She did her best to make us comfortable, and never grumbled at our staying so long. I expect Edwin paid her something. James only came home by fits and starts. I think he was in some embarrassment—debt, you know. He used to dash into the house like a whirlwind when he did come, and steal out of it when he left, peering about on all sides."

"Have they a nice house?" asked Lavinia.

"Oh, good gracious, no! It's not a house at all, only small lodgings. And Mrs. James changed them twice over whilst we were there. When we first went they were at a place called Ball's Pond."

"Why did you remain all that time?"

Mrs. Edwin Fennel shook her head helplessly; she could not answer the question. "I should have liked to come back before," she said; "it was very wearisome, knowing nobody and having nothing to do. Did you find it dull here, Lavinia, all by yourself?"

"'Dull' is not the right word for it," answered Lavinia, catching her breath with a sigh. "I felt more lonely, Ann, than I shall ever care to feel again. Especially when I had to come home at night from some *soirée*, or from spending the evening quietly with Mary Carimon or any other friend." And she went on to tell of the feeling of terror which had so tried her.

"I never heard of such a thing!" exclaimed Ann, "How silly you must be, Lavinia! What could there have been in the house to frighten you?"

"I don't know; I wish I did know," sighed Lavinia, just as she had said more than once before,

Nancy, who was attired in a bright ruby cashmere robe, with a gold chain and locket, some blue ribbons adorning her light ringlets, for she had made a point of dressing more youthfully than ever since her marriage, leaned back in her chair, as she sat staring at her sister and thinking.

"Lavinia," she said huskily, "you remember the feeling you had the day we were about to look at the house with Mary Carimon, and which you thought was through the darkness of the passage striking you unpleasantly? Well, my opinion is that it must have given you a scare."

"Why, of course it did."

"Ah, but I mean a scare which lasts," said Ann; "one of those scares which affect the mind and take very long to get rid of You recollect poor Mrs, Hunt, at Buttermead? She was frightened at a violent thunderstorm, though she never had been before; and for years afterwards, whenever it thundered, she became so alarmingly ill and agitated that Mr. Featherston had to be run for. He called it a scare. I think the fear you felt that past day must have left that sort of scare upon you. How else can you account for what you tell me?"

Truth to say, the same idea had more than once struck Lavinia. She knew how devoid of reason some of these "scares" are, and yet how terribly they disturb the mind on which they fasten.

"But I had quite forgotten that fear, Ann," she urged in reply. "We had lived in the house eighteen months when you went away, and I had never recalled it."

"All the same, I think you received the scare; it had only lain dormant," persisted Ann.

"Well, well; you are back again now, and it is over," said Lavinia. "Let us forget it. Do not speak of it again at all to any one, Nancy love."

8

Winter that year had quite set in when Sainteville found itself honoured with rather a remarkable visitor; one Signor Talcke, who descended, one morning at the beginning of December, at the Hôtel des Princes. Though he called himself "*Signor*," it seemed uncertain to what country he owed his birth. He spoke five or six languages as a native, including Hindustani. Signor Talcke was a professor of occult sciences; he was a great astronomer; astrology he had at his fingers' ends. He was a powerful mesmerist; he would foretell the events of your life by your hands, or your fortune by the cards.

For a fee of twenty-five *francs*, he would attend an evening party, and exhibit some of his powers. Amidst others who engaged him were the Miss Bosanquets, in the Rue Lamartine. A relative of theirs, Sir George Bosanquet, K.C.B., had come over with his wife to spend Christmas with them. Sir George laughed at what he heard of Signor Talcke's powers of reading the future, and said he should much like to witness a specimen of it. So Miss Bosanquet and her sisters hastily arranged an evening entertainment, engaged the mystical man, and invited their friends and acquaintances, those of the Petite Maison Rouge included.

It took place on the Friday after Christmas-Day. Something that occurred during the evening was rather remarkable. Miss Preen's diary gives a full account of it, and that shall be transcribed here. And I, Johnny Ludlow, take this opportunity of assuring the reader that what she wrote was in faithful accordance with the facts of the case.

From Miss Preen's Diary.

Saturday morning.—I feel very tired; fit for nothing. Nancy has undertaken to do the marketing, and is gone out for that purpose with her husband. It is to be hoped she will be moderate, and not attempt to buy up half the market. I lay awake all night, after the evening at Miss Bosanquet's, thinking how foolish Ann was to have had her "future cast," as that Italian (if he is Italian) called it, and how worse than foolish I was to let what he said worry me. "As if there could be anything in it!" laughed Ann, as we were coming home; fortunately she is not as I am in temperament—nervously anxious. "It is only nonsense," said

Miss Anna Bosanquet to me when the *signor's* predictions were at an end; "he will tell someone else just the same next time." But *I* did not think so. Of course, one is at a loss how to trust this kind of man. Take him for all in all, I rather like him; and he appears to believe implicitly in what he says: or, rather, in what he tell us the cards say.

They are charming women, these three sisters—Grace, Rose, and Anna Bosanquet; good, considerate, high-bred ladies, I wonder how it is they have lived to middle life without any one of them marrying? And I often wonder how they came to take up their residence at Sainteville, for they are very well off, and have great connections. I remember, though, Anna once said to me that the dry, pure air of the place suited her sister Rose, who has bad health, better than any other they had tried.

When seven o'clock struck, the hour named, Nancy and I appeared together in the sitting-room, ready to start, for we observe punctuality at Sainteville. I wore my black satin, handsome yet, trimmed with the rich white lace that Mrs. Selby gave me. Nancy looked very nice and young in her lilac silk. She wore a white rose in her hair, and her gold chain and locket round her neck. Captain Fennel surprised us by saying he was not going—his neuralgia had come on. I fancied it was an excuse—that he did not wish to meet Sir George Bosanquet. He had complained of the same thing on Christmas-Day, so it might be true. Ann and I set off together, leaving him nursing his cheek at the table.

It was a large gathering for Sainteville—forty guests, I should think; but the rooms are large. Professor Talcke exhibited some wonderful feats in—what shall I call it?—necromancy?—as good a word, perhaps, as any other. He mesmerized some people, and put one of them into a state of clairvoyance, and her revelations took my breath away. Signer Talcke assured us that what she said would be found minutely true. I think he has the strangest eyes

I ever saw: grey eyes, with a sort of light in their depths. His features are fair and delicate, his voice is gentle as a woman's, his manner retiring; Sir George seemed much taken with him.

Later, when the evening was passing, he asked if any one present would like to have their future cast, for he had cards which would do it. Three of his listeners pressed forward at once; two of them with gay laughter, the other pale and awestruck. The *signor* went into the recess in the small room, and sat down behind the little table there, and as many as could crowd round to look on, did so. I don't know what passed; there was no room for me; or whether the "Futures" he disclosed were good or bad. I had sat on the sofa at a distance, talking with Anna Bosanquet and Madame Carimon.

Suddenly, as we were for a moment silent, Ann's voice was heard, eager and laughing:

"Will you tell my fortune, Signor Talcke? I should like to have mine revealed."

"With pleasure, *madame*," he answered. We got up and drew near. I felt vexed that Ann should put herself forward in any such matter, and whispered to her; but she only shook her curls, laughed at me, and persisted. Signor Talcke put the cards in her hands, telling her to shuffle them.

"It is all fun, Lavinia," she whispered to me. "Did you hear him tell Miss Peet she was going to have money left her?"

After Ann had shuffled the cards, he made her cut them into three divisions, and he then turned them up on the table himself, faces upwards, and laid them out in three rows. They were not like the cards we play with; quite different from those; nearly all were picture-cards, and the plain ones bore cabalistic characters. We stood looking on with two or three other people; the rest had dispersed, and had gone into the next room to listen to the singing.

At first Signor Talcke never spoke a word. He looked at

the cards, and looked at Nancy; looked, and looked again. "They are not propitious," he said in low tones, and picked them up, and asked Nancy to shuffle and cut them again. Then he laid them as before, and we stood waiting in silence.

Chancing at that moment to look at Signor Talcke, his face startled me. He was frowning at the cards in so painful a manner as to quite alter its expression. But he did not speak. He still only gazed at the cards with bent eyes, and glanced up at Ann occasionally. Then, with an impatient sweep of the hand, he pushed the cards together.

"I must trouble you to shuffle and cut them once more, *madame*," he said. "Shuffle them well."

"Are they still unpropitious?" sked a jesting voice at my elbow. Turning, I saw Charley Palliser's smiling face. He must have been standing there, and heard Signor Talcke's previous remark.

"Yes, sir, they are," replied the *signor*, with marked emphasis. "I never saw the cards so unpropitious in my life."

Nancy took up the cards, shuffled them well, and cut them three times. Signor Talcke laid them out as before, bent his head, and looked attentively at them. He did not speak, but there was no mistaking the vexed, pained, and puzzled look on his face.

I do not think he knew Nancy, even by name. I do not think he knew me, or had the least notion that we were related. Neither of us had ever met him before. He put his hand to his brow, still gazing at the cards.

"But when are you going to begin my fortune, sir?" broke in Nancy.

"I would rather not tell it at all, *madame*," he answered.

"*Cannot* you tell it?—have your powers of forecasting inconveniently run away?" said she incautiously, her tone mocking in her disappointment.

"I could tell it, all too surely; but you might not like to hear it," returned he.

"Our magician has lost his divining-rod just when he needed it," observed a gentleman with a grey beard, a stranger to me, who was standing opposite, speaking in a tone of ill-natured satire; and a laugh went round,

"It is not that," said the *signor*, keeping his temper perfectly. "I could tell what the cards say, all too certainly; but it would not give satisfaction."

"Oh yes, it would," returned Nancy. "I should like to hear it, every bit of it. Please do begin."

"The cards are dark, very dark indeed," he said; "I don't remember ever to have seen them like it. Each time they have been turned the darkness has increased. *Nothing* can show worse than they do now."

"Never mind that," gaily returned Ann. "You undertook to tell my fortune, sir; and you ought not to make excuses in the middle of it. Let the cards be as dark as night, we must hear what they say."

He drew in his thin lips for a moment, and then spoke, his tone quiet, calm, unemotional.

"Some great evil threatens you," he began; "you seem to be living in the midst of it. It is not only you that it threatens; there is another also—"

"Oh, my goodness!" interrupted Nancy, in her childish way. "I hope it does not threaten Edwin. What *is* the evil?—sickness?"

"Worse than that. It—is—" Signor Talcke's attention was so absorbed by the aspect of the cards that, as it struck me, he appeared hardly to heed what he was saying. He had a long, thin black pencil in his long, thin fingers, and kept pointing to different cards as if in accordance with his thoughts, but not touching them. "There is some peculiar form of terror here," he went on. "I cannot make it out; it is very unusual. It does not come close to you; not yet, at any rate; and it seems to surround you. It seems to be in the house. May I ask"—quickly lifting his eyes to Ann—"whether you are given to superstitious fears?"

"Do you mean ghosts?" cried Ann, and Charley Palliser burst out laughing. "Not at all, sir; I don't believe in ghosts. I'm sure there are none in our house."

Remembering my own terror in regard to the house, and the nervous fancy of having seen Captain Fennel in it when he was miles away, a curious impression came over me that he must surely be reading my fortune as well as Nancy's. But I was not prepared for her next words. Truly she has no more reticence than a child.

"My sister has a feeling that the house is lonely. She shivers when she has to go into it after nightfall."

Signor Talcke let his hands fall on the table, and lifted his face. Apparently, he was digesting this revelation. I do not think he knew the "sister" was present. For my part, disliking publicity, I slipped behind Anna Bosanquet, and stood by Charley Palliser.

"Shivers?" repeated the Italian.

"Shivers and trembles, and turns sick at having to go in," affirmed Nancy. "So she told me when I arrived home from England."

"If a feeling of that sort assailed me, I should never go into the house again," said the *signor*.

"But how could you help it, if it were your home?" she argued.

"All the same. I should regard that feeling as a warning against the house, and never enter it. Then you are not yourself troubled with superstitious fears?" he broke off, returning to the business in hand, and looking at the cards. "Well—at present—it does not seem to touch you, this curious terror which is assuredly in the house—"

"I beg your pardon," interrupted Ann. "Why do you say 'at present'? Is it to touch me later?"

"I cannot say. Each time that the cards have been spread it has shown itself nearer to you. It is not yet very near. Apart from that terror—or perhaps remotely connected with it—I see evil threatening you—great evil."

"Is it in the house?"

"Yes; hovering about it. It is not only yourself it seems to threaten. There is someone else. And it is nearer to that person than it is to you."

"But who is that person?—man or woman?"

"It is a woman. See this ugly card," continued he, pointing with his pencil; "it will not be got rid of, shuffle as you will; it has come nearer to that woman each time."

The card he pointed to was more curious-looking than any other in the pack. It was not unlike the nine of spades, but crowded with devices. The gentleman opposite, whom I did not know, leaned forward and touched the card with the tip of his forefinger.

"*Le cercueil, n'est-ce-pas?*" said he.

"My" whispered an English lad's voice behind me. "*Cercueil?* that means coffin."

"How did you know?" asked Signer Talcke of the grey-bearded man.

"I was at the *Sous-Préfect's soirée* on Sunday evening when you were exhibiting. I heard you tell him in French that that was the ugliest card in the pack: indicating death."

"Well, it is not this lady the card is pursuing," said the *signor*, smiling at Ann to reassure her. "Not yet awhile, at least. And we must all be pursued by it in our turn, whenever that shall come," he added, bending over the cards again. "Pardon me, *madame*—may I ask whether there has not been some unpleasantness in the house concerning money?"

Nancy's face turned red. "Not—exactly," she answered with hesitation. "We are like a great many more people—not as rich as we should wish to be."

"It does not appear to lie precisely in the want of money: but certainly money is in some way connected with the evil," he was beginning to say, his eyes fixed dreamily on the cards, when Ann interrupted him.

"That is too strong a word—evil. Why do you use it?"

"I use it because the evil is there. No lighter word would be appropriate. There is some evil element pervading your house, very grave and formidable; it is most threatening; likely to go on to—to—darkness. I mean that it looks as if there would be some great break-up," he corrected swiftly, as if to soften the other word.

"That the house would be broken up?" questioned Ann. He stole a glance at her. "Something of that sort," he said carelessly.

"Do you mean that the evil comes from an enemy?" she went on.

"Assuredly."

"But we have no enemy. I'm sure we have not one in all the world."

He slightly shook his head. "You may not suspect it yet, though I should have said"—waving the pencil thoughtfully over some of the cards—"that he was already suspected—doubted."

Nancy took up the personal pronoun briskly. "He!—then the evil enemy must be a man? I assure you we do not know any man likely to be our enemy or to wish us harm. No, nor woman either. Perhaps your cards don't tell true tonight, Signor Talcke?"

"Perhaps not, *madame*; we will let it be so if you will," he quietly said, and shuffled all the cards together.

That ended the *séance*. As if determined not to tell any more fortunes, the *signor* hurriedly put up the cards and disappeared from the recess. Nancy did not appear to be in the least impressed.

"What a curious 'future' it was!" she exclaimed lightly to Mary Carimon. "I might as well not have had it cast. He told me nothing."

They walked away together. I went back to the sofa and Anna Bosanquet followed me.

"Mrs. Fennel calls it 'curious,'" I said to her. "I call it more than that—strange; ominous. I wish I had not heard it."

"Dear Miss Preen, it is only nonsense," she answered. "He will tell someone else the same next time." But she only so spoke to console me.

A wild wish flashed into my mind—that I should ask the man to tell *my* future. But had I not heard enough? Mine was blended with this of Ann's. I was the other woman whom the dark fate was more relentlessly pursuing. There could be no doubt of that. There could be as little doubt that it was I who already suspected the author of the "evil." What can the "dark fate" be that we are threatened with? Debt? Will his debts spring upon us and break up our home, and turn us out of it? Or will it be something worse? That card which followed me meant a coffin, they said. Ah me! Perhaps I am foolish to dwell upon such ideas. Certainly they are more fitting for the world's dark ages than for this enlightened nineteenth century of it.

Charley Palliser gallantly offered to see us home. I said no; as if we were not old enough to go by ourselves; but he would come with us. As we went along Ann began talking of the party, criticizing the dresses, and so on. Charley seemed to be unusually silent.

"Was not mine a grand fortune?" she presently said with a laugh, as we crossed the Place Ronde.

"Stunning," said he.

"As if there could be anything in it, you know! Does the man think we believe him, I wonder?"

"Oh, these conjurers like to fancy they impose on us," remarked Charley, shaking hands as we halted before the house of Madame Sauvage.

And I have had a wretched night, for somehow the thing has frightened me. I never was superstitious; never; and I'm sure I never believed in conjurers, as Charles had it. If I should come across Signor Talcke again while he stays here, I would ask him——Here comes Nancy! and Flore behind her with the marketings. I'll put up my diary.

"I've bought such a lovely capon," began Nancy, as Lavinia

went into the kitchen. "Show it to *madame*, Flore."

It was one that even Lavinia could praise; they both understood poultry. "It really is a beauty," said Lavinia. "And did you remember the *salsifis*? And, Ann, where have you left your husband?"

"Oh, we met old Mr. Griffin, and Edwin has gone up to Drecques with him. My opinion is, Lavinia, that that poor old Giiffin dare not go about far by himself since his attack. He had to see his landlord at Drecques today, and he asked Edwin to accompany him. They went by the eleven-o'clock train."

Lavinia felt it a relief. Even that little absence, part of a day, she felt thankful for, so much had she grown to dislike the presence in the house of Edwin Fennel.

"Did you tell your husband about your 'fortune,' Nancy?"

"No; I was too sleepy last night to talk, and I was late in getting up this morning. I'm not sure that I shall tell him," added Mrs. Fennel thoughtfully; "he might be angry with me for having had it done."

"That is more than likely," replied Lavinia.

Late in the afternoon, as they were sitting together in the *salon*, they saw the postman come marching up the yard. He brought two letters—one for Miss Preen, the other for her sister.

"It is the remittance from William Selby," said Lavinia as she opened hers. "He has sent it a day or two earlier than usual; it is not really due until Monday or Tuesday."

Seventeen pounds ten shillings each. Nancy, in a hasty sort of manner, put her cheque into the hands of Lavinia, almost as if she feared it would burn her own fingers. "You had better take it from me whilst you can," she said in low tones.

"Yes; for I must have it, Ann," was the answer. "We are in debt—as you may readily conceive—with only half the usual amount to spend last quarter."

"It was not my fault; I was very sorry," said Ann humbly; and she rose hastily to go to the kitchen, saying she was thirsty, and wanted a glass of water. But Lavinia thought she went to avoid being questioned.

Lavinia carried the two cheques to her room and locked them up. After their five-o'clock dinner, each sister wrote a note to Colonel Selby, enclosing her receipt. Flore took them out to post when she left. The evening passed on. Lavinia worked; Nancy nodded over the fire: she was very sleepy, and went to bed early.

It was past eleven o'clock when Captain Fennel came in, a little the worse for something or other. After returning from Drecques by the last train, he had gone home with Mr. Griffin to supper. He told Lavinia, in words running into one another, that the jolting train had made him giddy. Of course she believed as much of that as she liked, but did not contradict it. He went to the cupboard in the recess, unlocked it to get out the cognac, and then sat down with his pipe by the embers of the dying fire. Lavinia, unasked, brought in a decanter of water, put it on the table with a glass, and wished him goodnight.

All next day Captain Fennel lay in bed with a racking headache. His wife carried up a choice bit of the capon when they were dining after morning service, but he could not so much as look at it. Being a fairly cautious man as a rule, he had to pay for—for the jolting of the train.

He was better on Monday morning, but not well, still shaky, and did not come down to breakfast. It was bitterly cold—a sort of black frost; but Lavinia, wrapping herself up warmly, went out as soon as breakfast was over.

Her first errand was to the bank, where she paid in the cheques and received French money for them. Then she visited sundry shops; the butcher's, the grocer's, and others, settling the accounts due. Last of all, she made a call upon Madame Veuve Sauvage, and paid the rent for the past quarter. All this left her with exactly nineteen pounds, which was all the money she had to go on with for every purpose until the end of March—three whole months.

Lunch was ready when she returned. Taking off her things upstairs and locking up her cash, she went down to it. Flore had made some delicious *soupe maigre*. Only those who have tried it know how good it is on a sharp winter's day. Captain Fennel seemed to relish it much, though his appetite had not quite come back to him, and he turned from the dish of scrambled eggs which supplemented the soup. In the evening they went, by appointment, to dine at Madame Carimon's, the other guests being Monsieur Henri Dupuis with his recently married wife, and Charles Palliser.

After dinner, over the coffee, Monsieur Henri Dupuis suddenly spoke of the *soirée* at Miss Bosanquet's the previous Friday, regretting that he and his wife had been unable to attend it. He was engaged the whole evening with a patient dangerously ill, and his wife did not like to appear at it without him. Nancy—Nancy!—then began to tell about the "fortune" which had been forecast for her by Signor Talcke, thinking possibly that her husband could not reproach her for it before company. She was very gay over it; a proof that it had left no bad impression on her mind.

"What's that, Nancy?" cried Captain Fennel, who had listened as if he disbelieved his ears. "The fellow told you we had something evil in our house?"

"Yes, he did," assented Nancy. "An evil influence, he said, which was destined to bring forth something dark and dreadful."

"I am sorry you did not tell this before," returned the captain stiffly. "I should have requested you not again to allude to such folly. It was downright insolence."

"I—you—you were out on Saturday, you know, Edwin, and in bed with your headache all Sunday; and today I forgot it," said Nancy in less brave tones.

"Suppose we have a game at wholesome card-playing," interposed Mary Carimon, bringing forth a new pack. "Open them, will you, Jules? Do you remember, *mon ami*, having your fortune told once by a gipsy woman when we were in Sir John Whitney's coppice with the two Peckham girls? She told you you would fall into a rich inheritance and marry a Frenchwoman."

73

"Neither of which agreeable promises is yet fulfilled," said little Monsieur Carimon with his happy smile. Monsieur Carimon had heard the account of Nancy's "forecast" from his wife; he was not himself present, but taking a hand at whist in the card-room.

They sat down to a round game—spin. Monsieur Henri Dupuis and his pretty young wife had never played it before, but they soon learned it and liked it much. Both of them spoke English well; she with the prettiest accent imaginable. Thus the evening passed, and no more allusion was made to the fortune-telling at Miss Bosanquet's.

That was Monday. On Tuesday, Miss Preen was dispensing the coffee at breakfast in the Petite Maison Rouge to her sister and Mr. Fennel, when Flore came bustling in with a letter in her hand.

"*Tenez, madame*," she said, putting it beside Mrs. Fennel. "I laid it down in the kitchen when the *facteur* brought it, whilst I was preparing the *déjeûner*, and forgot it afterwards."

Before Nancy could touch the letter, her husband caught it up. He gazed at the address, at the postmark, and turned it about to look at the seal. The letters of gentlefolk were generally fastened with a seal in those days: this had one in transparent bronze wax.

Mr. Fennel put the letter down with a remark peevishly uttered. "It is not from London; it is from Buttermead."

"And from your old friend, Jane Peckham, Nancy," struck in Lavinia. "I recognize her handwriting."

"I *am* glad," exclaimed Nancy. "I have not heard from them for ages. Why now—is it not odd?—that Madame Carimon should mention the Peckhams last night, and I receive a letter from them this morning?"

"I supposed it might be from London, with your remittance," said Mr. Fennel to his wife. "It is due, is it not?"

"Oh, that came on Saturday, Edwin," she said, as she opened her letter.

"Came on Saturday!" echoed Captain Fennel ungraciously, as

74

if disputing the assertion.

"By the afternoon post; you were at Drecques, you know."

"The *money* came? *Your* money?"

"Yes," said Nancy, who had stepped to the window to read her letter, for it was a dark day, and stood there with her back to the room.

"And where is it?" demanded he.

"I gave it to Lavinia. I always give it to her."

Captain Fennel glared at his wife for a moment, then smoothed his face to its ordinary placidity, and turned to Lavinia.

"Will you be good enough to hand over to me my wife's money. Miss Preen?"

"No," she answered quietly.

"I must trouble you to do so, when breakfast shall be finished."

"I cannot," pursued Lavinia. "I have paid it away."

"That I do not believe. I claim it from you in right of my wife; and I shall enforce the claim."

"The money is Nancy's, not yours," said Lavinia. "In consequence of your having stopped her share last quarter in London, I was plunged here into debt and great inconvenience. Yesterday morning I went out to settle the debts—and it has taken the whole of her money to do it. That is the state of things, Captain Fennel."

"I am in debt here myself," retorted he, but not angrily. "I owe money to my tailor and bootmaker; I owe an account at the chemist's; I want money in my pockets—and I must indeed have it."

"Not from me," returned Lavinia,

Edwin Fennel broke into a little access of temper. He dashed his serviette on the table, strode to the window, and roughly caught his wife by the arm. She cried out.

"How dared you hand your money to anyone but me?" he asked in a low voice of passion.

"But how are we to live if I don't give it to Lavinia for the housekeeping? "returned Nancy, bursting into tears. "It takes all we have; her share and mine; every farthing of it."

"Let my sister alone, Mr. Fennel," spoke up Lavinia with authority. "She is responsible for the debts we contract in this house, just as much as I am, and she must contribute her part to pay them. You ought to be aware that the expenses are now increased by nearly a third; I assure you I hardly like to face the difficulties I see before me."

"Do you suppose I can stop in the place without some loose cash to keep me going?" he asked calmly. "Is that reasonable, Miss Lavinia?"

"And do you suppose I can keep you and Ann here without her money to help me to do it?" she rejoined. "Perhaps the better plan will be for me to take up my abode elsewhere, and leave the house to you and Ann to do as you please in it."

Captain Fennel dropped his argument, returned to the table, and went on with his breakfast. The last words had startled him. Without Lavinia, which meant without her money, they could not live in the house at all.

Matters were partly patched up in the course of the day. Nancy came upstairs to Lavinia, begging and praying, as if she were praying for her life, for a little ready money for her husband—just a hundred *francs*. Trembling and sobbing, she confessed that she dared not return to him without it; she should be too frightened at his anger.

And Lavinia gave it to her.

9

Matters went on to the spring. There were no outward differences in the Petite Maison Rouge, but it was full of an undercurrent of discomfort. At least for Lavinia. Captain Fennel was simply to her an incubus; and now and again petty accounts of his would be brought to the door by tradespeople who wanted them settled. As to keeping up the legitimate payments, she could not do it.

March was drawing to an end, when a surprise came to them. Lavinia received a letter from Paris, written by Colonel Selby. He had been there for two days on business, he said, and purposed returning via Sainteville, to take a passing glimpse at herself and her sister. He hoped to be down that afternoon by the three-o'clock train, and he asked them to meet him at the Hôtel des Princes afterwards, and to stay and dine with him. He proposed crossing to London by the night boat.

Lavinia read the letter aloud. Nancy went into ecstasies, for a wonder; she had been curiously subdued in manner lately. Edwin Fennel made no remark, but his pale face wore a look of thought.

During the morning he betook himself to the Rue Lothaire to call upon Mr. Griffin; and he persuaded that easy-natured old gentleman to take advantage of the sunny day and make an excursion *en voiture* to the nearest town, a place called Pontipette. Of course the captain went also, as his companion.

Colonel Selby arrived at three. Lavinia and Nancy met him at the station, and went with him in the omnibus to the hotel. They then showed him about Sainteville, to which he was a stranger, took him to see their *domicile*, the little red house (which he did not seem to admire), and thence to Madame Carimon's. In the Buttermead days, the colonel and Mary Featherston had been great friends. He invited her and her husband to join them at the *table d'hôte* dinner at five o'clock.

Lavinia and Nancy went home again to change their dresses for it. Nancy put on a pretty light green silk, which had been recently modernized. Mrs. Selby had kept up an extensive wardrobe, and had left it between the two sisters.

"You should wear your gold chain and locket," remarked Lavinia, who always took pride in her sister's appearance. "It will look very nice upon that dress."

She alluded to a short, thick chain of gold, the gold locket attached to it being set round with pearls, Nancy's best ornament; nay, the only one she had of any value; it was the one she had worn at Miss Bosanquet's celebrated party. Nancy made no answer. She was turning red and white.

"What's the matter?" cried Lavinia,

The matter was, that Mr. Edwin Fennel had obtained possession of the chain and locket more than a month ago. Silly Nancy confessed with trembling lips that she feared he had pledged it.

Or sold it, thought Lavinia. She felt terribly vexed and indignant. "I suppose, Ann, it will end in his grasping everything," she said, "and starving us out of house and home: *myself*, at any rate."

"He expects money from his brother James, and then he will get it back for me," twittered Nancy.

Monsieur Jules Carimon was not able to come to the *table d'hôte*; his duties that night would detain him at the college until seven o'clock. It happened so on occasion. Colonel Selby sat at one end of their party, Lavinia at the other; Mary Carimon and Nancy between them, A gentleman was on the other side of Lavinia whom she did not particularly notice; and, upon his asking the waiter for something, his voice seemed to strike upon her memory. Turning, she saw that it was the tall Englishman they had seen on the pier some months before in the shepherd's plaid, the lawyer named Lockett. He recognized her face at the same moment, and they entered into conversation.

"Are you making any stay at Sainteville?" she inquired.

"For a few days. I must be back in London on Monday morning."

Colonel Selby's attention was attracted to the speakers. "What, is it you, Lockett?" he exclaimed.

Mr. Lockett bent forward to look beyond Lavinia and Madame Carimon. "Why, colonel, are you here?" he cried. So it was evident that they knew one another.

But you can't talk very much across people at a *table d'hôte*; and Lavinia and Mr. Lockett were, so to say, left together again. She put a question to him, dropping her voice to a whisper.

"Did you ever find that person you were looking for?"

"The person I was looking for?" repeated the lawyer, not remembering. "What person was that?"

"The one you spoke of on the pier that day—a Mr. Dangerfield."

"Oh, ay; but I was not looking for him myself. No; I believe he is not dropped upon yet. He is keeping quiet, I expect."

"Is he still being looked for?"

"Little doubt of that. My friend here, on my left, could tell you more about him than I can, if you want to know."

"No, thank you," said Lavinia hastily, in a sort of fear. And she then observed that next to Mr. Lockett another Englishman was sitting, who looked very much like a lawyer also.

After dinner Colonel Selby took his guests, the three ladies, into the little *salon*, which opened to Madame Podevin's *bureau*; for it was she who, French fashion, kept the *bureau* and all its accounts, not her husband. Whilst the coffee which the colonel ordered was preparing, he took from his pocket-book two cheques, and gave one each to Lavinia and Mrs. Fennel. It was their quarterly income, due about a week hence.

"I thought I might as well give it you now, as I am here, and save the trouble of sending," he remarked. "You can write me a receipt for it; here's pen, ink and paper."

Each wrote her receipt, and gave it him. Nancy held the cheque in her hand, looking at her sister in a vacillating manner. "I suppose I ought to give it you, Lavinia," she said. "Must I do so?"

"What do you think about it yourself?" coldly rejoined Lavinia.

"He was so very angry with me the last time," sighed Nancy, still withholding the cheque. "He said I ought to keep possession of my own, and he ordered me to do so in future."

"That he may have the pleasure of spending it," said Mary Carimon in a sharp tone, though she laughed at the same time. "Lavinia has to pay for the bread-and-cheese that you and he eat, Nancy; how can she do that unless she receives your money?"

"Yes, I know; it is very difficult," said poor Nancy, "Take the cheque, Lavinia; I shall tell him that you and Mary Carimon both said I must give it up."

"Oh, tell him I said so, and welcome," spoke Madame Carimon. "I will tell him so myself, if you like."

As Colonel Selby returned to the room—he had been seeing to his luggage—the coffee was brought in, and close upon it came Monsieur Carimon.

The boat for London was leaving early that night—eight o'clock; they all went down to it to see William Selby off. It was a calm night, warm for the time of year, the moon beautifully bright. After the boat's departure, Lavinia and Ann went home, and found Captain Fennel there. He had just got in, he said, and wanted some supper.

Whilst he was taking it, his wife told him of Mr. Lockett's having sat by them at the *table d'hôte*, and that he and Colonel Selby were acquainted with one another. Captain Fennel drew a grim face at the information, and asked whether the lawyer had also "cleared out" for London.

"I don't think so; I did not see him go on board," said Nancy. "Lavinia knows; she was talking with Mr. Lockett all dinner-time."

Captain Fennel turned his impassive face to Lavinia, as if demanding an answer to his question.

"Mr. Lockett intends to remain here until Sunday, I fancy; he said he had to be in London on Monday morning. He has some friend with him here. I inquired whether they had found the Mr. Dangerfield he spoke of last autumn," added Lavinia slowly and distinctly. "'Not yet,' he answered, 'but he is still being looked for.'"

Whether Lavinia said this with a little spice of malice, or whether she really meant to warn him, she best knew. Captain Fennel finished his supper in silence.

"I presume the colonel did not hand you over your quarter's money?" he next said to his wife in a mocking sort of way. "It is not due for a week yet; he is not one to pay beforehand."

Upon which Nancy began to tremble and looked imploringly at her sister, who was putting the plates together upon the tray. After Flore went home they had to wait upon themselves.

"Colonel Selby did hand us the money," said Lavinia. "I hold both cheques for it."

Well, there ensued a mild disturbance; what schoolboys might call a genteel row. Mr. Edwin Fennel insisted upon his wife's cheque being given to him. Lavinia decisively refused. She went into a bit of a temper, and told him some home truths. He said he had a right to hold his wife's money, and should appeal to the law on the morrow to enforce it. He might do that, Lavinia retorted; no French law would make her give it up. Nancy began to cry.

Probably he knew his threats were futile. Instead of appealing to the law on the morrow, he went off by an early train, carrying Nancy with him. Lavinia's private opinion was that he thought it safer to take her, though it did increase the expense, than to leave her; she might get talking with Mr. Lockett. Ann's eyes were red, as if she had spent the night in crying.

"Has he beaten you?" Lavinia inquired, snatching the opportunity of a private moment.

"Oh, Lavinia, don't, don't! I shall *never* dare to let you have the cheque again," she wailed.

"Where is it that you are going?"

"He has not told me," Nancy whispered back again. "To Calais, I think, or else up to Lille. We are to be away all the week."

"Until Mr. Lockett and his friend are gone," thought Lavinia. "Nancy, how can he find money for it?"

"He has some *napoleons* in his pocket—borrowed yesterday, I think, from old Griffin."

Lavinia understood. Old Griffin, as Nancy styled him, had been careless of his money since his very slight attack of paralysis; he would freely lend to anyone who asked him. She had not the slightest doubt that Captain Fennel had borrowed of him— and not for the first time.

It was on Wednesday morning that they went away, and for the rest of the week Lavinia was at peace. She changed the cheques at the bank as before, and paid the outstanding debts. But it left her so little to go on with, that she really knew not how she should get through the months until midsummer.

On Friday two of the Miss Bosanquets called. Hearing she was alone, they came to ask her to dine with them in the evening.

Lavinia did so. But upon returning home at night, the old horror of going into the house came on again. Lavinia was in despair; she had hoped it had passed away for good.

On Saturday morning at market she met Madame Carimon, who invited her for the following day, Sunday. Lavinia hesitated. Glad enough indeed she was at the prospect of being taken out of her solitary home for a happy day at Mary Carimon's; but she shrank from again risking the dreadful feeling which would be sure to attack her when going into the house at night.

"You must come, Lavinia," cheerily urged Madame Carimon. "I have invited the English teacher at Madame Deauville's school; she has no friends here, poor thing."

"Well, I will come, Mary; thank you," said Lavinia slowly.

"To be sure you will. Why do you hesitate at all? "

Lavinia could not say why in the midst of the jostling market-place; perhaps would not had they been alone. "For one thing, they may be coming home before tomorrow," observed Lavinia, alluding to Mr. and Mrs. Fennel.

"Let them come. You are not obliged to stay at home with them," laughed Mary.

From the Diary of Miss Preen.

Monday morning.—Well, it is over. The horror of last night is over, and I have not died of it. That will be considered a strong expression, should any eye save my own see this diary: but I truly believe the horror would kill me if I were subjected many more times to it.

I went to Mary Carimon's after our service was over in the morning, and we had a pleasant day there. The more I see of Monsieur Jules the more I esteem and respect him. He is so genuine, so good at heart, so simple in manner. Miss Perry is very agreeable; not so young as I had thought—thirty last birthday, she says. Her English is good and refined, and that is not always the ease with the English teachers who come over to France—the French ladies who engage them cannot judge of our accent.

Miss Perry and I left together a little before ten. She wished me goodnight in the Rue Tessin, Madame Deauville's house lying one way, mine another. The horror began to come over me as I crossed the Place Ronde, which had never happened before. Stay; not the horror itself, but the dread of it. An impulse actually crossed me to ring at Madame Sauvage's, and ask Mariette to accompany me up the entry, and stand at my open door whilst I went in to light the candle. But I could see no light in the house, not even in *madame's salon*, and supposed she and Mariette might be gone to bed. They are early people on Sundays, and the two young men have their latch-keys.

I will try to overcome it this time, I bravely said to myself, and not allow the fear to keep me halting outside the door as it has done before. So I took out my latch-key, put it straight into the door, opened it, went in, and closed it again. Before I had well reached the top of the passage and felt for the matchbox on the slab, I was in a paroxysm of horror. Something, like an icy wind coming up the passage, seemed to flutter the candle as I lighted it. Can I have left the door open? I thought, and turned to look. There stood Edwin Fennel. He stood just inside the door, which appeared to be shut, and he was looking straight at me with a threatening, malignant expression on his pale face. "Oh! have you come home tonight?" I exclaimed aloud. For I really thought it was so.

The candle continued to flicker quickly as if it meant to go out, causing me to glance at it. When I looked up again Mr. Fennel was gone. *It was not himself who had been there; it was only an illusion.*

Exactly as he had seemed to appear to me the night before he and Nancy returned from London in December, so he had appeared again, his back to the door, and the evil menace on his countenance. Did the appearance come to me as a warning? or was the thing nothing but a delusion of my own optic nerves?

I dragged my shaking limbs upstairs, on the verge of screaming at each step with the fear of what might be behind me, and undressed and went to bed. For nearly the whole night I could not sleep, and when I did get to sleep in the morning I was tormented by a distressing dream. All, all as it had been that other night from three to four months ago.

A confused dream, no method in it. Several people were about—Nancy for one; I saw her fair curls. We all seemed to be in grievous discomfort and distress; whilst I, in worse fear than this world can know, was ever striving to hide myself from Edwin Fennel, to escape some dreadful fate which he held in store for me. And I knew I should not escape it.

10

Like many another active housewife, Madame Carimon was always busy on Monday mornings. On the one about to be referred to, she had finished her household duties by eleven o'clock, and then sat down in her little *salle-à-manger*, which she also made her workroom, to mend some of Monsieur Carimon's cotton socks. By her side, on the small work-table, lay a silver brooch which Miss Perry had inadvertently left behind her the previous evening. Mary Carimon was considering at what hour she could most conveniently go out to leave it at Madame Deauville's when she heard Pauline answer a ring at the door-bell, and Miss Preen came in.

"Oh, Lavinia, I am glad to see you. You are an early visitor. Are you not well?" continued Madame Carimon, noticing the pale, sad face. "Is anything the matter?"

"I am in great trouble, Mary; I cannot rest; and I have come to talk to you about it," said Lavinia, taking the sable boa from her neck and untying her bonnet-strings. "If things were to continue as they are now, I should die of it."

Drawing a chair near to Mary Carimon, Lavinia entered upon her narrative. She spoke first of general matters. The home discomfort, the trouble with Captain Fennel regarding Nancy's money, and the difficulty she had to keep up the indispensable payments to the tradespeople, expressing her firm belief that in future he would inevitably seize upon Nancy's portion when it came and confiscate it. Next, she went on to tell the story of the past night—Sunday: how the old terrible horror had come upon her of entering the house, of a fancied appearance of Edwin Fennel in the passage, and of the dream that followed. All this latter part was but a repetition of what she had told Madame Carimon three or four months ago. Hearing it for the second time, it impressed Mary Carimon's imagination. But she did not speak at once.

"I never in my life saw anything plainer or that looked more life-like than Captain Fennel, as he stood and gazed at me from the end of the passage with the evil look on his countenance," resumed Lavinia. "And I hardly know why I tell you about it again, Mary, except that I have no one else to speak to. You rather laughed at me the first time, if you remember; perhaps you will laugh again now."

"No, no," dissented Mary Carimon. "I did not put faith in it before, believing you were deceived by the uncertain light in the passage, and were, perhaps, thinking of him, and that the dream afterwards was merely the result of your fright; nothing else. But now that you have had a second experience of it, I don't doubt that you do see this spectre, and that the dream follows as a sequence to it. And I think," she added, slowly and emphatically, "that it has come to warn you of some threatened harm."

"I seem to see that it has," murmured Lavinia. "Why else should it come at all? I wish I could picture it to you half vividly enough: the reality of it and the horror. Mary, I am growing seriously afraid."

"Were I you, I should get away from the house," said Madame Carimon. "Leave them to themselves."

"It is what I mean to do, Mary. I cannot remain in it, apart from this undefined fear—which of course *may* be only superstitious fancy," hastily acknowledged Lavinia. "If things continue in the present state—and there is no prospect of their changing—"

"I should leave at once—as soon as they arrive home," rather sharply interrupted Mary Carimon, who seemed to like the aspect of what she had heard less and less.

"As soon as I can make arrangements. They come home tonight; I received a letter from Nancy this morning. They have been only at Pontipette all the time."

"Only at Pontipette!"

"Nancy says so. It did as well as any other place. Captain Fennel's motive was to hide away from the lawyers we met at the *table d'hôte.*"

"Have they left Sainteville, I wonder, those lawyers?"

"Yes," said Lavinia. "On Friday I met Mr, Lockett when I was going to the Rue Lamartine, and he told me he was leaving for Calais with his friend on Saturday morning. It is rather remarkable," she added, after a pause, "that the first time I saw that appearance in the passage and dreamed the dream, should have been the eve of Mr. Fennel's return here, and that it is the same again now."

"You must leave the house, Lavinia," reiterated Madame Carimon.

"Let me see," considered Lavinia. "April comes in this week. Next week will be Passion Week, preceding Easter. I will stay with them over Easter, and then leave."

Monsieur Jules Carimon's sock, in process of renovation, had been allowed to fall upon the mender's lap. She slowly took it up again, speaking thoughtfully.

"I should leave at once; before Easter. But you will see how he behaves, Lavinia. If not well; if he gives you any cause of annoyance, come away there and then. We will take you in, mind, if you have not found a place to go to."

Lavinia thanked her, and rearranged her bonnet preparatory to returning home. She went out with a heavy heart. Only one poor twelvemonth to have brought about all this change!

At the door of the Petite Maison Rouge, when she reached it, stood Flore, parleying with a slim youth, who held an open paper in his outstretched hand. Flore was refusing to touch the paper, which was both printed and written on, and looked official.

"I tell him that *Monsieur le Capitaine* is not at home; he can bring it when he is," explained Flore to her mistress in English.

Lavinia turned to the young man. "Captain Fennel has been away from Sainteville for a few days; he probably will be here tomorow," she said. "Do you wish to leave this paper for him?"

"Yes," said the messenger, evidently understanding English but speaking in French, as he contrived to slip the paper into Miss Preen's unconscious hand. "You will have the politeness to give it to him, *madame*."

And, with that, he went off down the entry, whistling.

"Do you know what the paper is, Flore?" asked Lavinia.

"I think so," said Flore. "I've seen these papers before today. It's just a sort of order from the law court on Captain Fennel, to pay up some debt that he owes; and, if he does not pay, the court will issue a *procès* against him. That's what it is, *madame*."

Lavinia carried the paper into the *salon*, and sat studying it. As far as she could make it out, Mr. Edwin Fennel was called upon to pay to some creditor the sum of one hundred and eighty-three *francs*, without delay.

"Over seven pounds! And if he does not pay, the law expenses, to enforce it, will increase the debt perhaps by one-half," sighed Lavinia. "There may be, and no doubt *are*, other things at the back of this. Will he turn us out of house and home? "

Propping the paper against the wall over the mantelpiece, she left it there, that it might meet the captain's eye on his return.

Not until quite late that evening did Madame Carimon get her husband to herself, for he brought in one of the young under-masters at the college to dine with them. But as soon as they were sitting cosily alone, he smoking his pipe before bedtime, she told him all she had heard from Lavinia Preen.

"I don't like it, Jules; I don't indeed," she said. "It has made a strangely disagreeable impression on me. What is your opinion?"

Placid Monsieur Jules did not seem to have much opinion one way or the other. Upon the superstitious portion of the tale he, being a practical Frenchman, totally declined to have any at all. He was very sorry for the uncomfortable position Miss Preen found herself in, and he certainly was not surprised she should wish to quit the Petite Maison Rouge if affairs could not be made more agreeable there. As to the Capitaine Fennel, he felt free to confess there was something about him which he did not like: and he was sure no man of honour ought to have run away clandestinely, as he did, with Miss Nancy.

"You see, Jules, what the man aims at is to get hold of Nancy's income and apply it to his own uses—and for Lavinia to keep them upon hers."

"I see," said Jules.

"And Lavinia *cannot* do it; she has not half enough. It troubles me very much," flashed Madame Carimon. "She says she shall stay with them until Easter is over. *I* should not; I should leave them to it tomorrow."

"Yes, my dear, that's all very well," nodded Monsieur Jules; "but we cannot always do precisely what we would. Miss Preen is responsible for the rent of that house, and if Fennel and his wife do not pay it, she would have to. She must have a thorough understanding upon that point before she leaves it."

By the nine-o'clock train that night they came home, Lavinia, pleading a bad headache and feeling altogether out of sorts, got Flore to remain for once, and went herself to bed. She dreaded the very sight of Captain Fennel,

In the morning she saw that the paper had disappeared from the mantelpiece. He was quite jaunty at breakfast, talking to her and Nancy about Pontipette; and things passed pleasantly. About eleven o'clock he began brushing his hat to go out.

"I'm going to have a look at Griffin, and see how he's getting on," he remarked. "Perhaps the old man would enjoy a drive this fine day; if so, you may not see me back till dinner-time."

But just as Captain Fennel turned out of the Place Ronde to the Rue Tessin, he came upon Charles Palliser, strolling along.

"Fine day, Mr. Charles," he remarked graciously.

"Capital," assented Charles, "and I'm glad of it; the old gentleman will have a good passage. I've just seen him off by the eleven train."

"Seems to me you spend your time in seeing people off by trains. Which old gentleman is it now?—him from below? "

Charley laughed. "It's Griffin this time," said he. "Being feeble, I thought I might be of use in starting him, and went up."

"Griffin!" exclaimed Captain Fennel. "Why, where's he gone to?"

"To Calais. *En route* for Dover and—"

"What's he gone for? When's he coming back?" interrupted the captain, speaking like a man in great amazement.

"He is not coming back at all; he has gone for good," said Charley. "His daughter came to fetch him."

"Why on earth should she do that?"

"It seems that her husband, a clergyman at Kensington, fell across Major Smith last week in London, and put some pretty close questions to him about the old man, for they had been made uneasy by his letters of late. The major—"

"What business had the major in London?" questioned Captain Fennel impatiently.

"You can ask him," said Charles equably, "I didn't. He is back again. Well, Major Smith, being questioned, made no bones about it at all; said Griffin and Griffin's money both wanted looking after. Upon that, the daughter came straight off, arriving here on Sunday morning; she settled things yesterday, and has carried her father away today. He was as pleased as Punch, poor childish old fellow, at the prospect of a voyage in the boat."

Whether this information put a check upon any little plan Captain Fennel may have been entertaining, Charles Palliser could not positively know; but he thought he had never seen so evil an eye as the one glaring upon him. Only for a moment; just a flash; and then the face was smoothed again. Charley had his ideas—and all his wits about him; and old Griffin had babbled publicly.

Captain Fennel strolled by his side towards the port, talking of Pontipette and other matters of indifference. When in sight of the harbour, he halted.

"I must wish you good-day now, Palliser; I have letters to write," said he; and walked briskly back again.

Lavinia and Nancy were sitting together in the *salon* when he reached home. Nancy was looking scared.

"Edwin," she said, leaving her chair to meet him—"Edwin, what do you think Lavinia has been saying? That she is going to leave us."

"Oh, indeed," he carelessly answered.

"But it is true, Edwin; she means it."

"Yes, I mean it," interposed Lavinia very quietly. "You and Nancy will be better without me; perhaps happier."

He looked at her for a full minute in silence, then laughed a little. "Like Darby and Joan," he remarked, as he put his writing-case on the table and sat down to it.

Mrs. Fennel returned to her chair by Lavinia, who was sitting close to the window mending a lace collar which had been torn in the ironing. As usual Nancy was doing nothing.

"You *couldn't* leave me, Lavinia, you know," she said in coaxing tones.

"I know that I never thought to do so, Ann, but circumstances alter cases," answered the elder sister. Both of them had dropped their voices to a low key, not to disturb the letter-writer. But he could hear if he chose to listen. "I began putting my things together yesterday, and shall finish doing it at leisure. I will stay over Easter with you; but go then I shall."

"You must be cruel to think of such a thing, Lavinia."

"Not cruel," corrected Lavinia. "I am sorry, Ann, but the step is forced upon me. The anxieties in regard to money matters are wearing me out; they would wear me out altogether if I did not end them. And there are other things which urge upon me the expediency of departure from this house."

"What things?"

"I cannot speak of them. Never mind what they are, Ann.

They concern myself; not you."

Ann Fennel sat twirling one of her fair silken ringlets between her thumb and finger; a habit of hers when thinking:.

"Where shall you live, Lavinia, if you do leave? Take another apartment at Sainteville?"

"I think not. It is a puzzling question. Possibly I may go back to Buttermead, and get some family to take me in as a boarder," dreamily answered Lavinia. "Seventy pounds a-year will not keep me luxuriously."

Captain Fennel lifted his face. "If it will not keep one, how is it to keep two?" he demanded, in rather defiant tones.

"I don't know anything about that," said Lavinia civilly. "I have not two to keep; only one."

Nancy chanced to catch a glimpse of his face just then, and its look frightened her. Lavinia had her back to him, and did not see it. Nancy began to cry quietly.

"Oh, Lavinia, you will think better of this; you will not leave us!" she implored. "We could not do at all without you and your half of the money."

Lavinia had finished her collar, and rose to take it upstairs. "Don't be distressed, Nancy," she paused to say; "it is a thing that *must be*. I am very sorry; but it is not my fault. As you——"

"You can stay in the house if you choose!" flashed Nancy, growing feebly angry.

"No, I cannot. I *cannot*," repeated Lavinia. "I begin to foresee that I might—might die of it."

11

Sainteville felt surprised and sorry to hear that Miss Preen was going to leave it to its own devices, for the town had grown to like her. Lavinia did not herself talk about going, but the news somehow got wind. People wondered why she went. Matters, as connected with the financial department of the Petite Maison Rouge, were known but imperfectly—to most people not known at all; so that reason was not thought of. It was quite understood that Ann Preen's stolen marriage, capped by the bringing home of her husband to the Petite Maison Rouge, had been a sharp blow to Miss Preen: perhaps, said Sainteville now, she had tried living with them and found it did not answer. Or perhaps she was only going away for a change, and would return after a while.

Passion week passed, and Easter week came in, and Lavinia made her arrangements for the succeeding one. On the Tuesday in that next week, all being well, she would quit Sainteville. Her preparations were made; her larger box was already packed and corded. Nancy, of shallow temperament and elastic spirits, seemed quite to have recovered from the sting of the proposed parting; she helped Lavinia to put up her laces and other little fine things, prattling all the time. Captain Fennel maintained his suavity. Beyond the words he had spoken—as to how she expected the income to keep two if it would not keep one—he had said nothing. It might be that he hardly yet believed Lavinia would positively go.

But she was going. At first only to Boulogne-sur-Mer. Monsieur Jules Carimon had a cousin, Madame Degravier, who kept a superior boarding-house there, much patronized by the English; he had written to her to introduce Miss Preen, and to intimate that it would oblige him if the terms were made *très facile*. *Madame* had written back to Lavinia most satisfactorily, and, so far, that was arranged.

Once at Boulogne in peace and quietness, Lavinia would have leisure to decide upon her future plans. She hoped to pay a visit to Buttermead in the summer-time, for she had begun to yearn for a sight of the old place and its people. After that—well, she should see. If things went on pleasantly at Sainteville—that is, if Captain Fennel and Nancy were still in the Petite Maison Rouge, and he was enabled to find means to continue in it— then, perhaps, she might return to the town. Not to make one of the household—never again that; but she might find a little *pied-à-terre* in some other home.

Meanwhile, Lavinia heard no more of the *procès*, and she wondered how the captain was meeting it. During the Easter week she made her farewell calls. That week she was not very much at home; one or other of her old acquaintances wanted her. Major and Mrs. Smith had her to spend a day with them; the Miss Bosanquets invited her also; and so on.

One call, involving also private business, she made upon old Madame Sauvage, Mary Carimon accompanying her. Monsieur Gustave was called up to the *salon* to assist at the conference. Lavinia partly explained her position to them in strict confidence, and the motive, as touching pecuniary affairs, which was taking her away: she said nothing of that other and greater motive, her superstitious fear.

"I have come to speak of the rent," she said to Monsieur Gustave, and Mary Carimon repeated the words in French to old Madame Sauvage. "You must in future look to Captain Fennel for it; you must make him pay it if possible. At the same time, I admit my own responsibility," added Lavinia, "and if it be found totally impracticable to get it from Captain Fennel or my sister, I shall pay it to you. This must, of course, be kept strictly between ourselves, Monsieur Gustave; you and *madame* understand that. If Captain Fennel gained any intimation of it, he would take care not to pay it."

Monsieur Gustave and *madame* his mother assured her that they fully understood, and that she might rely upon their honour. They were grieved to lose so excellent a tenant and neighbour as Miss Preen, and wished circumstances had been more kindly. One thing she might rest assured of—that they should feel at least as mortified at having to apply to her for the rent as she herself would be, and they would not leave a stone unturned to extract it from the hands of Captain Fennel.

"It has altogether been a most bitter trial to me," sighed Lavinia, as she stood up to say farewell to *madame*.

The old lady understood, and the tears came into her compassionate eyes as she held Lavinia's hands between her own. "Ay, for certain," she replied in French. "She and her sons had said so privately to one another ever since the abrupt coming home of the strange captain to the petite *maison à côté*."

On Sunday, Lavinia, accompanied by Nancy and Captain

Fennel, attended morning service for the last time. She spoke to several acquaintances coming out, wishing them goodbye, and was hastening to overtake her sister, when she heard rapid steps behind her, and a voice speaking. Turning, she saw Charley Palliser.

"Miss Preen," cried he, "my aunt wants you to come home and dine with us. See, she is waiting for you. You could not come any one day last week, you know."

"I was not able to come to you last week, Mr, Charles; I had so much to do, and so many engagements," said Lavinia, as she walked back to Mrs. Hardy, who stood smiling.

"But you will come today, dear Miss Preen," said old Mrs. Hardy, who had caught the words. "We have a lovely *fricandeau* of veal, and—"

"Why, that is just our own dinner," interrupted Lavinia gaily. "I should like to come to you, Mrs. Hardy, but I cannot. It is my last Sunday at home, and I could not well go out and leave them."

They saw the force of the objection. Mrs. Hardy asked whether she should be at church in the evening. Lavinia replied that she intended to be, and they agreed to bid each other farewell then.

"You don't know what you've lost. Miss Preen," said Charley comically. "There's a huge cream tart—lovely."

Captain Fennel was quite lively at the dinner-table. He related a rather laughable story which had been told him by Major Smith, with whom he had walked for ten minutes after church, and was otherwise gracious.

After dinner, while Flore was taking away the things, he left the room, and came back with three glasses of liqueur, on a small waiter, handing one to Lavinia, another to his wife, and keeping the third himself. It was the yellow *chartreuse*; Captain Fennel kept a bottle of it and of one or two other choice liqueurs in the little cupboard at the end of the passage, and treated them to a glass sometimes.

"How delightful!" cried Nancy, who liked *chartreuse* and anything else that was good.

They sat and sipped it, talking pleasantly together. The captain soon finished his, and said he should take a stroll on the pier. It was a bright day with a brisk wind, which seemed to be getting higher.

"The London boat ought to be in about four o'clock," he remarked. "It's catching it sweetly, I know; passengers will look like ghosts. *Au revoir*, don't get quarrelling." And thus, nodding to the two ladies, he went out gaily.

Not much danger of their quarrelling. They turned their chairs to the fire, and plunged into conversation, which chanced to turn upon Buttermead. In calling up one reminiscence of the old place after another, now Lavinia, now Nancy, the time passed on. Lavinia wore her silver-grey silk dress that day, with some yellowish-looking lace falling at the throat and wrists.

Flore came in to bring the tea-tray; she always put it on the table in readiness on a Sunday afternoon. The water, she said, would be on the boil in the kitchen by the time they wanted it. And then she went away as usual for the rest of the day.

Not long afterwards, Lavinia, who was speaking, suddenly stopped in the middle of a sentence. She started up in her chair, fell back again, and clasped her hands below her chest with a great cry.

"Oh, Nancy!— Nancy!"

Nancy dashed across the hearthrug. "What is it?" she exclaimed. "What is it, Lavinia?"

Lavinia apparently could not say what it was. She seemed to be in the greatest agony; her face had turned livd. Nancy was next door to an imbecile in any emergency, and fairly wrung her hands in her distress.

"Oh, what can be the matter with me?" gasped Lavinia, "Nancy, I think I am dying."

The next moment she had glided from the chair to the floor, and lay there shrieking and writhing. Bursting away, Nancy ran round to the next house, all closed today, rang wildly at the private door, and when it was opened by Mariette, rushed upstairs to *madame's salon.*

Madame Veuve Sauvage, comprehending that something was amiss, without understanding Nancy's frantic words, put a shawl on her shoulders to hasten to the other house, ordering Mariette to follow her. Her sons were out.

There lay Lavinia, in the greatest agony. Madame Sauvage sent Mariette off for Monsieur Dupuis, and told her to fly. "Better bring Monsieur Henri Dupuis, Mariette," she called after her: "he will get quicker over the ground than his old father."

But Monsieur Henri Dupuis, as it turned out, was absent. He had left that morning for Calais with his wife, to spend two days with her friends who lived there, purposing to be back early on Tuesday morning. Old Monsieur Dupuis came very quickly. He thought Mademoiselle Preen must have inward inflammation, he said to Madame Sauvage, and inquired what she had eaten for dinner. Nancy told him as well as she could between her sobs and her broken speech.

A *fricandeau* of veal, potatoes, a cauliflower *au gratin*, and a *frangipane* tart from the pastrycook's. No fruit or any other dessert. They took a little Bordeaux wine with dinner, and a liqueur glass of *chartreuse* afterwards.

All very wholesome, pronounced Monsieur Dupuis, with satisfaction; not at all likely to disagree with *mademoiselle.* Possibly she had caught a chill.

Mariette had run for Flore, who came in great consternation. Between them all they got Lavinia upstairs, undressed her and laid her in bed, applying hot flannels to the pain—and Monsieur Dupuis administered in a wine-glass of water every quarter-of-an-hour some drops from a glass phial which he had brought in his pocket.

It was close upon half-past five when Captain Fennel came in. He expressed much surprise and concern, saying, like the doctor, that she must have eaten something which had disagreed with her. The doctor avowed that he could not otherwise account for the seizure; he did not altogether think it was produced by a chill; and he spoke again of the dinner. Captain

Fennel observed that as to the dinner they had all three partaken of it, one the same as another; he did not see why it should affect his sister-in-law and not himself or his wife. This reasoning was evident, admitted Monsieur Dupuis; but Miss Preen had touched nothing since her breakfast, except at dinner. In point of fact, he felt very much at a loss, he did not scruple to add; but the more acute symptoms were showing a slight improvement, he was thankful to perceive, and he trusted to bring her round.

As he did. In a few hours the pain had so far abated, or yielded to remedies, that poor Lavinia, worn out, dropped into a comfortable sleep. Monsieur Dupuis was round again early in the morning, and found her recovered, though still feeling tired and very weak. He advised her to lie in bed until the afternoon; not to get up then unless she felt inclined; and he charged her to take chiefly milk food all the day—no solids whatever.

Lavinia slept again all the morning, and awoke very much refreshed. In the afternoon she felt quite equal to getting up, and did so, dressing herself in the grey silk she had worn the previous day, because it was nearest at hand. She then penned a line to Madame Degravier, saying she was unable to travel to Boulogne on the morrow, as had been fixed, but hoped to be there on Wednesday, or, at the latest, Thursday.

Captain Fennel, who generally took possession of the easiest chair in the salon, and the warmest place, resigned it to Lavinia the instant she appeared downstairs. He shook her by the hand, said how glad he was that she had recovered from her indisposition, and installed her in the chair with a cushion at her back and a rug over her knees. All she had to dread now, he thought, was cold; she must guard against that. Lavinia replied that she could not in the least imagine what had been the matter with her; she had never had a similar attack before, and had never been in such dreadful pain.

Presently Mary Carimon came in, having heard of the affair from Mariette, whom she had met in the fish-market during the morning. All danger was over, Mariette said, and *mademoiselle* was then sleeping quietly: so Madame Carimon, not to disturb

her, put off calling until the afternoon. Captain Fennel sat talking with her a few minutes, and then went out. For some cause
or other he never seemed to be quite at ease in the presence of
Madame Carimon.

"I know what it must have been," cried Mary Carimon,
coming to one of her rapid conclusions after listening to the
description of the illness. "Misled by the sunny spring days last
week, you went and left off some of your warm underclothing,
Lavinia, and so caught cold."

"Good gracious!" exclaimed Nancy, who had curled herself
up on the sofa like a ball, not having yet recovered from her
fatigue and fright. "Leave off one's warm things the beginning
of April! I never heard of such imprudence! How came you to
do it, Lavinia?"

"I did not do it," said Lavinia quietly. "I have not left off"
anything. Should I be so silly as to do that with a journey before
me?"

"Then what caused the attack?" debated Madame Carimon.
"Something you had eaten?"

Lavinia shook her head helplessly. "It could hardly have been
that, Mary. I took nothing whatever that Nancy and Captain
Fennel did not take. I wish I did know—that I might guard, if
possible, against a similar attack in future. The pain seized me all
in a moment. I thought I was dying."

"It sounds odd," said Madame Carimon. "Monsieur Dupuis
does not know either, it seems. That's why I thought you might
have been leaving off your things, and did not like to tell him."

"I conclude that it must have been one of those mysterious
attacks of sudden illness to which we are all liable, but for which
no one can account," sighed Lavinia. "I hope I shall never have
it again. This experience has been enough for a lifetime."

Mary Carimon warmly echoed the hope as she rose to take
her departure. She advised Lavinia to go to bed early, and promised to come again in the morning.

While Captain Fennel and Nancy dined, Flore made her
mistress some tea, and brought in with it some thin bread-and-

butter. Lavinia felt all the better for the refreshment, laughingly remarking that by the morning she was sure she should be as hungry as a hunter. She sat chatting, and sometimes dozing between whiles, until about a quarter to nine o'clock, when she said she would go to bed.

Nancy went to the kitchen to make her a cup of arrowroot. Lavinia then wished Captain Fennel goodnight, and went upstairs. Flore had left as usual, after washing up the dinner-things.

"Lavinia, shall I—— Oh, she has gone on," broke off Nancy, who had come in with the breakfast-cup of arrowroot in her hand. "Edwin, do you think I may venture to put a little brandy into this?"

Captain Fennel sat reading with his face to the fire and the lamp at his elbow. He turned round.

"Brandy?" said he. "I'm sure I don't know. If that pain meant inflammation, brandy might do harm. Ask Lavinia; she had better decide for herself. No, no; leave the arrowroot on the table here," he hastily cried, as Nancy was going out of the room with the cup. "Tell Lavinia to come down, and we'll discuss the matter with her. Of course a little brandy would do her an immense deal of good, if she might take it with safety."

Nancy did as she was told. Leaving the cup and saucer on the table, she went up to her sister. In a minute or two she was back again.

"Lavinia won't come down again, Edwin; she is already half-undressed. She thinks she had better be on the safe side, and not have the brandy."

"All right," replied the captain, who was sitting as before, intent on his book. Nancy took the cup upstairs.

She helped her sister into bed, and then gave her the arrowroot, inquiring whether she had made it well.

"Quite well, only it was rather sweet," answered Lavinia.

"Sweet!" echoed Nancy, in reply. "Why, I hardly put any sugar at all into it; I remembered that you don't like it."

Lavinia finished the cupful. Nancy tucked her up, and gave

her a goodnight kiss. "Pleasant dreams, Lavinia dear," she called back, as she was shutting the door.

"Thank you, Nancy; but I hope I shall sleep tonight without dreaming," answered Lavinia.

As Nancy went downstairs she turned into the kitchen for her own arrowroot, which she had left all that time in the saucepan. Being fond of it, she had made enough for herself as well as for Lavinia.

12

It was between half-past ten and eleven, and Captain and Mrs. Fennel were in their bedroom preparing to retire to rest. She stood before the glass doing her hair, having thrown a thin print cotton cape upon her shoulders as usual, to protect her dress; he had taken off his coat.

"What was that?" cried she, in startled tones.

Some sound had penetrated to their room. The captain put his coat on a chair and bent his ear. "I did not hear anything, Nancy," he answered.

"There it is again!" exclaimed Nancy. "Oh, it is Lavinia! I do believe it is Lavinia!"

Flinging the comb from her hand, Nancy dashed out at the room-door, which was near the head of the stairs; Lavinia's door being nearly at the end of the passage. Unmistakable sounds, now a shriek, now a wail, came from Lavinia's chamber. Nancy flew into it, her fair hair falling on her shoulders.

"What is it, Lavinia? Oh, Edwin, Edwin, come here!" called Mrs. Fennel, beside herself with terror. Lavinia was rolling about the bed, as she had the previous day rolled on the *salon* floor; her face was distorted with pain, her moans and cries agonizing.

Captain Fennel stayed to put on his coat, came to Lavinia's door, and put his head inside it. "Is it the pain again?" he asked.

"Yes, it is the pain again," gasped Lavinia, in answer. "I am dying, I am surely dying!"

That put the finishing-touch to timorous Nancy.

"Edwin, run, run for Monsieur Dupuis!" she implored. "Oh, what shall we do? What shall we do?"

100

Captain Fennel descended the stairs. When Nancy thought he must have been gone out at least a minute or two, he appeared again with a wine-glass of hot brandy-and-water, which he had stayed to mix.

"Try and get her to take this," he said. "It can't do harm; it may do good. And if you could put hot flannels to her, Nancy, it might be well; they eased the pain yesterday. I'll bring Dupuis here as soon as I can."

Lavinia could not take the brandy-and-water, and it was left upon the grey marble top of the chest of drawers. Her paroxysms increased; Nancy had never seen or imagined such pain, for this attack was worse than the other, and she almost lost her wits with terror. Could she see Lavinia die before her eyes?—no helping hand near to strive to save her? Just as Nancy had done before, she did again now.

Flying down the stairs and out of the house, across the yard and through the dark entry, she seized the bell-handle of Madame Veuve Sauvage's door and pulled it frantically. The household had all retired for the night.

Presently a window above opened, and Monsieur Gustave—Nancy knew his voice—looked out.

"Who's there?" he asked in French. "What's the matter?"

"Oh, Monsieur Gustave, come in for the love of Heaven!" responded poor Nancy, looking up, "She has another attack, worse than the first; she's dying, and there's no one in the house but me."

"Directly, *madame*; I am with you on the instant," he kindly answered. "I but wait to put on my effects."

He was at the Petite Maison Rouge almost as soon as she; his brother Emile followed him in, and Mariette, whom they had called, came shortly. Miss Preen lay in dreadful paroxysms; it did appear to them that she must die. Nancy and Mariette busied themselves in the kitchen, heating flannels.

The doctor did not seem to come very quickly. Captain Fennel at length made his appearance and said Monsieur Dupuis would be there in a minute or two.

"I am content to hear that," remarked Monsieur Gustave in reply. "I was just about to despatch my brother for the first doctor he could find."

"Never had such trouble in ringing up a doctor before," returned Captain Fennel. "I suppose the old man sleeps too soundly to be easily aroused; many elderly people do."

"I fear she is dying," whispered Monsieur Gustave.

"No, no, surely not!" cried Captain Fennel, recoiling a step at the words. "What can it possibly be? What causes the attacks?"

Whilst Monsieur Gustave was shaking his head at this difficult question. Monsieur Dupuis arrived. Monsieur Emile, anxious to make himself useful, was requested by Mariette to go to Flore's *domicile* and ring her up. Flore seemed to have been sleeping with her clothes on, for they came back together.

Monsieur Dupuis could do nothing for his patient. He strove to administer drops of medicinal remedies; he caused her to be nearly smothered in scalding-hot flannels—all in vain. He despatched Monsieur Emile Sauvage to bring in another doctor, Monsieur Podevin, who lived near. All in vain. Lavinia died. Just at one o'clock in the morning, before the cocks had begun to crow, Lavinia Preen died.

The shock to those in the house was great. It seemed to stun them, one and all. The brothers Sauvage, leaving a few words of heartfelt sympathy with Captain Fennel, withdrew silently to their own home. Mariette stayed. The two doctors, shut up in the salon, talked with one another, endeavouring to account for the death.

"Inflammation, no doubt," observed Monsieur Dupuis; "but even so, the death has been too speedy."

"More like poison," rejoined the younger man, Monsieur Podevin. He was brother to the proprietor of the Hôtel des Princes, and was much respected by his fellow-citizens as a safe and skilful practitioner.

"The thought of poison naturally occurred to me on Sunday, when I was first called to her," returned Monsieur Dupuis, "but it could not be borne out. You see, she had partaken of nothing, either in food or drink, but what the other inmates had taken; absolutely nothing. This was assured me by them all, herself included."

"She seems to have taken nothing today, either, that could in any way harm her," said Monsieur Podevin.

"Nothing. She took a cup of tea at five o'clock, which the servant, Flore, prepared and also partook of herself—a cup out of the same teapot. Later, when the poor lady went to bed, her sister made her a basin of arrowroot, and made herself one at the same time."

"Well, it appears strange."

"It could not have been a chill. The symptoms—"

"A chill?—bah!" interrupted Monsieur Podevin. "We shall know more after the post-mortem," he added, taking up his hat. "Of course there must be one."

Wishing his brother practitioner goodnight, he left. Monsieur Dupuis went looking about for Captain Fennel, and found him in the kitchen, standing by the hot stove, and drinking a glass of hot brandy-and-water. The rest were upstairs.

"This event has shaken my nerves, doctor," apologized the captain, in reference to the glass. "I never was so upset. Shall I mix you one?"

Monsieur Dupuis shook his head. He never took anything so strong. The most calming thing, in his opinion, was a glass of *eau sucrée*, with a teaspoonful of orange-flower water in it.

"Sir," he went on, "I have been conversing with my esteemed *confrère*. We cannot, either of us, decide what *mademoiselle* has died of, being unable to see any adequate cause for it; and we wish to hold a post-mortem examination. I presume you will not object to it?"

"Certainly not; I think there should be one," briskly spoke Captain Fennel after a moment's pause, "For our satisfaction, if for nothing else, doctor."

"Very well. Will nine o'clock in the morning suit you, as to time? It should be made early."

"I—expect it will," answered the captain, reflecting, "Do you hold it here?"

"Undoubtedly. In her own room."

"Then wait just one minute, will you, doctor, whilst I speak to my wife. Nine o'clock seems a little early, but I dare say it will suit."

Monsieur Dupuis went back into the *salon*. He had waited there a short interval, when Mrs. Fennel burst in, wild with excitement. Her hair still hung down her back, her eyes were swollen with weeping, her face was one of piteous distress. She advanced to Monsieur Dupuis, and held up her trembling hands.

The old doctor understood English fairly well when it was quietly spoken; but he did not in the least understand it in a storm. Sobbing, trembling, Mrs. Fennel was beseeching him not to hold a post-mortem on her poor dead sister, for the love of mercy.

Surprised and distressed, he placed her on the sofa, soothed her into calmness, and then bade her tell him quietly what her petition was. She repeated it—begging, praying, imploring him not to disturb her sister now she was at rest; but to let her be put into her grave in peace. Well, well, said the compassionate old man; if it would pain the relatives so greatly to have it done, he and Monsieur Podevin would, of course, abandon the idea. It would be a satisfaction to them both to be able to decide upon the cause of death, but they did not wish to proceed in it against the feelings of the family.

Sainteville woke up in the morning to a shock. Half the townspeople still believed that Miss Preen was leaving that day, Tuesday, for Boulogne; and to hear that she would not go on that journey, that she would never go on any earthly journey again, that she was *dead*, shook them to the centre.

What had been the matter with her?—what had killed her so quickly in the midst of life and health? Groups asked this; one group meeting another. "Inflammation," was the answer—for that report had somehow started itself. She caught a chill on the Sunday, probably when leaving the church after morning service; it induced speedy and instant inflammation, and she had died of it.

With softened steps and mournful faces, hosts of people made their way to the Place Ronde. Only to take a glimpse at the outside of the Maison Rouge brought satisfaction to excited feelings. Monsieur Gustave Sauvage had caused his white shop window-blinds to be drawn half-way down, out of respect to the dead; all the windows above had the green *persiennes* closed before them. The calamity had so greatly affected old Madame Sauvage that she lay in bed.

When her sons returned indoors after the death had taken place, their mother called them to her room. Nancy's violent ringing had disturbed her, and she had lain since then in anxiety, waiting for news.

"Better not tell the mother tonight," whispered Emile to his brother outside her door.

But the mother's ears were quick; she was sitting up in bed, and the door was ajar. "Yes, you will tell me, my sons," she said. "I am fearing the worst."

"Well, mother, it is all over," avowed Gustave. "The attack was more violent than the one last night, and the poor lady is gone."

"May the good God have taken her to His rest!" fervently aspirated *madame*. But she lay down in the bed in her distress and covered her face with the white-frilled pillow and sobbed a little. Gustave and Emile related a few particulars.

"And what was really the malady? What is it that she has died of?" questioned the mother, wiping her eyes.

"That is not settled; nobody seems to know," replied Gustave.

Madame Veuve Sauvage lay still, thinking. "I—hope—that—man—has—not—done—her—any—injury!" she slowly said.

"I hope not either; there is no appearance of it," said Monsieur Gustave. "Any way, mother, she had two skilful doctors with her, honest men and upright. Better not admit such thoughts."

"True, true," murmured *madame*, appeased. "I fear the poor dear lady must have taken a chill, which struck inwardly. That handsome *demoiselle*, the cousin of *Monsieur le Procureur*, died of the same thing, you may remember. Goodnight, my sons; you leave me very unhappy."

About eight o'clock in the morning, Monsieur Jules Carimon heard of it. In going through the large iron entrance-gates of the college to his day's work, he found himself accosted by one of two or three young *gamins* of pupils, who were also entering. It was Dion Pamart. The well-informed reader is of course aware that the French educational colleges are attended by all classes, high and low, indiscriminately.

"*Monsieur*, have you heard?" said the lad, with timid deprecation. "*Mademoiselle* is dead."

Monsieur Jules Carimon turned his eyes on the speaker. At first he did not recognize him: his own work lay with the advanced desks.

"Ah, *c'est Pamart, n'est-ce-pas?*" said he, "What did you say, my boy? Someone is dead?"

Dion Pamart repeated his information. The master, inwardly shocked, took refuge in disbelief.

"I think you must be mistaken, Pamart," said he.

"Oh no, I'm not, sir. *Mademoiselle* was taken frightfully ill again last night, and they fetched my mother. They had two doctors to her and all; but they couldn't do anything for her, and she died. Grandmother gave me my breakfast just now; she said my mother was crying too much to come home. The other lady, the captain's wife, has been in hysterics all night."

"Go on to your desks," commanded Monsieur Carimon to the small fry now gathered round him.

He turned back home himself. When he entered *the salle-à-manger*, Pauline was carrying away the last of the breakfast-things. Her mistress stood putting a little water on a musk plant in the window.

"Is it you, Jules?" she exclaimed. "Have you forgotten something?"

Monsieur Jules shut the door. "I have not forgotten anything," he answered. "But I have heard of a sad calamity, and I have come back to prepare you, Marie, before you hear it from others."

He spoke solemnly; he was looking solemn. His wife put down the jug of water on the table. "A calamity?" she repeated.

"Yes. You will grieve to hear it. Your friend. Miss Preen, was—was taken ill last night with the same sort of attack, but more violent; and she—"

"Oh, Jules, don't tell me, don't tell me!" cried Mary Carimon, lifting her hands to ward off the words with a too sure prevision of what they were going to be.

"But, my dear, you must be told sooner or later," remonstrated he; "you cannot go through even this morning without hearing it from one person or another. Flore's boy was my informant. In spite of all that could be done by those about her, poor lady—in spite of the two doctors who were called to her aid—she died."

Madame Carimon was a great deal too much stunned for tears. She sank back in a chair with a face of stone, feeling that the room was turning upside down about her.

An hour later, when she had somewhat gathered her scattered senses together, she set off for the Petite Maison Rouge. Her way lay past the house of Monsieur Podevin; old Monsieur Dupuis was turning out of it as she went by. Madame Carimon stopped.

"Yes," the doctor said, when a few words had passed, "it is a most desolating affair. But, as *madame* knows, when Death has laid his grasp upon a patient, medical craft loses its power to resist him."

"Too true," murmured Mary Carimon. "And what is it that she has died of?"

Monsieur Dupuis shook his head to indicate that he did not know.

"I could have wished for an examination, to ascertain the true cause of the seizure," continued the doctor, "and I come now from expressing my regrets to my *confrère*, Monsieur Podevin. He agrees with me in deciding that we cannot press it in opposition to the family. Captain Fennel was quite willing it should take place, but his wife, poor distressed woman, altogether objects to it."

Mary Carimon went on to the house of death. She saw Lavinia, looking so peaceful in her stillness. A happy smile sat on her countenance. On her white attire lay some sweet fresh primroses, which Flore had placed there. Lavinia loved primroses. She used to say that when she looked at them they brought to her mind the woods and dales of Buttermead, always carpeted with the pale, fair blossoms in the spring of the year. Mrs. Fennel lay in a heavy sleep, exhausted by her night of distress, Flore informed Madame Carimon; and the captain, anxious about her, was sitting in her room, to guard against her being disturbed.

On the next day, Wednesday, in obedience to the laws of France relating to the dead, Lavinia Preen was buried. All the English gentlemen in the town, and some Frenchmen, including Monsieur Carimon and the sons of Madame Veuve Sauvage, assembled in the Place Ronde, and fell in behind the coffin when it was brought forth. They walked after it to the portion of the cemetery consecrated to Protestants, and there witnessed the interment. The tears trickled down Charley Palliser's face as he took his last look into the grave, and he was honest enough not to mind who saw them.

13

In their new mourning, at the English Church, the Sunday after the interment of Lavinia Preen, appeared Captain and Mrs. Fennel. The congregation looked at them more than at the parson. Poor Nancy's eyes were so blinded with tears that she could not see the letters in her Prayer-book. Only one little week ago when she had sat there, Lavinia was on the bench at her side, alive and well; and now—It was with difficulty Nancy kept herself from breaking down.

Two or three acquaintances caught her hand on leaving the church, whispering a few words of sympathy in her ear. Not one but felt truly sorry for her. The captain's hat, which had a wide band round it, was perpetually raised in acknowledgment of silent greetings, as he piloted his wife back to their house, the Petite Maison Rouge.

A very different dinner-table, this which the two sat down to, from last Sunday's, in the matter of cheerfulness. Nancy was about half-way through the wing of the fowl her husband had helped her to, when a choking sob caught her throat. She dropped her knife and fork.

"Oh, Edwin, I cannot! I cannot eat for my unhappy thoughts! This time last Sunday Lavinia was seated at the table with us. Now—" Nancy's speech collapsed altogether.

"Come, come," said Captain Fennel. "I hope you are not going to be hysterical again, Nancy. It is frightfully sad; I know that; but this prolonged grief will do no good. Go on with your dinner; it is a very nice chicken."

Nancy gave a great sob, and spoke impulsively, "I don't believe you regret her one bit, Edwin!"

Edwin Fennel in turn laid down his knife and fork and stared at his wife. A curious expression sat on his face.

"Not regret her," he repeated with emphasis. "Why, Nancy, I regret her every hour of the day. But I do not make a parade of my regrets. Why should I?—to what end? Come, come, my dear; you will be all the better for eating your dinner."

He went on with his own as he spoke. Nancy took up her knife and fork with a hopeless sigh.

Dinner over, Captain Fennel went to his cupboard and brought in some of the *chartreuse*. Two glasses, this time, instead of three. He might regret Lavinia, as he said, every hour of the day; possibly he did so; but it did not seem to affect his appetite, or his relish for good things.

Most events have their dark and their light sides. It could hardly escape the mind of Edwin Fennel that by the death of Lavinia the whole income became Nancy's. To him that must have been a satisfactory consolation.

In the afternoon he went with Nancy for a walk on the pier. She did not want to go; said she had no spirits for it; it was miserable at home; miserable out; miserable everywhere. Captain

Fennel took her off, as he might have taken a child, telling her she should come and see the fishing-boats. After tea they went to church—an unusual thing for Captain Fennel. Lavinia and Nancy formerly went to evening service; he, never.

That night something curious occurred. Nancy went up to bed leaving the captain to follow, after finishing his glass of grog. He generally took one the last thing. Nancy had taken off her gown, and was standing before the glass about to undo her hair, when she heard him leave the parlour. Her bedroom door, almost close to the head of the stairs, was not closed, and her ears were on the alert. Since Lavinia died, Nancy had felt timid in the house when alone, and she was listening for her husband to come up. She heard him lock up the spirit bottle in the little cupboard below, and begin to ascend the stairs, and she opened her door wider, that the light might guide him, for the staircase was in darkness.

Captain Fennel had nearly gained the top, when something— he never knew what—induced him to look round sharply, as though he fancied someone was close behind him. In fact, he did fancy it. In a moment, he gave a shout, dashed onwards into the bedroom, shut the door with a bang, and bolted it. Nancy, in great astonishment, turned to look at him. He seemed to have shrunk within himself in a fit of trembling, his face was ghastly, and the perspiration stood upon his brow.

"Edwin!" she exclaimed in a scared whisper, "what is the matter?"

Captain Fennel did not answer at first. He was getting up his breath.

"Has Flore not gone?" he then said.

"*Flore!*" exclaimed Nancy in surprise. "Why, Edwin, you know Flore goes away on Sundays in the middle of the afternoon! She left before we went on the pier. Why do you ask?"

"I—I thought—some person—followed me upstairs," he replied, in uneasy pauses.

"Oh, my goodness." cried timid Nancy. "Perhaps a thief has got into the house!"

She went to the door, and was about to draw it an inch open, intending to peep out gingerly and listen, when her husband pulled her back with a motion of terror, and put his back against it. This meant, she thought, that he *knew* a thief was there. Perhaps two of them!

"Is there more than one?" she whispered. "Lavinia's silver—my silver, now—is in the basket on the console in the *salon*."

He did not answer. He appeared to be listening. Nancy listened also. The house seemed still as death.

"Perhaps I was mistaken," said Captain Fennel; beginning to recover himself after a bit. "I dare say I was."

"Well, I think you must have been, Edwin; I can't hear anything. We had better open the door."

She undid the bolt as she spoke, and he moved away from it. Nancy cautiously took a step outside, and kept still. Not a sound met her ear. Then she brought forth the candle and looked down the staircase. Not a sign of anything or anyone met her eye.

"Edwin, there's nothing, there's nobody; come and see. You must have fancied it."

"No doubt," answered Captain Fennel. But he did not go to see, for all that.

Nancy went back to the room. "Won't you just look downstairs?" she said. "I—I don't much mind going with you."

"Not any necessity," replied he, and began to undress—and slipped the bolt again.

"Why do you bolt the door tonight?" asked Nancy.

"To keep the thief out," said he, in grim tones, which Nancy took for jesting. But she could not at all understand him.

His restlessness kept her awake. "It *must* have been all fancy," she more than once heard him mutter to himself.

When he rose in the morning, his restlessness seemed still to hang upon him. Remarking to Nancy, who was only half-awake, that his nerves were out of order, and he should be all the better for a sea-bath, he dressed and left the room. Nancy got down at the usual hour, half-past eight; and was told by Flore that *monsieur* had left word *madame* was not to wait breakfast for

111

him: he was gone to have a dip in the sea, and should probably take a long country walk after it.

Flore was making the coffee at the kitchen stove; her mistress stood by, as if wanting to watch the process. These last few days, since Lavinia had been carried from the house, Nancy had felt easier in Flore's company than when alone with her own.

"That's to steady his nerves; they are out of order," replied Nancy, who had as much idea of reticence as a child. "*Monsieur* had a great fright last night, Flore."

"Truly!" said Flore, much occupied just then with her coffee-pot.

"He was coming up to bed between ten and eleven; I had gone on. When nearly at the top of the stairs he thought he heard someone behind him. It startled him frightfully. Not being prepared for it, supposing that the house was empty, you see, Flore, of course it would startle him."

"Naturally, *madame*."

"He cried out, and dashed into the bedroom and bolted the door. I never saw any one in such a state of terror, Flore; he was trembling all over; his face was whiter than your apron."

"*Vraiment!*" returned Flore, turning to look at her mistress in a little surprise. "But, *madame*, what had terrified him? What was it that he had seen?"

"Why, he could have seen nothing," corrected Mrs. Fennel. "There was nothing to see."

"*Madame* has reason; there could have been nothing, the house being empty. But then, what could have frightened him?" repeated Flore.

"Why, he must have fancied it, I suppose. Anyway, he fancied someone was there. The first question he asked me was, whether you were in the house."

"*Moi! Monsieur* might have known I should not be in the house at that hour, *madame*. And why should he show terror if he thought it was me?"

Mrs. Fennel shrugged her shoulders. "It was a moment's scare; just that, I conclude; and it upset his nerves. A sea-bath will put him all right again."

Flore carried the coffee into the *salon*, and her mistress sat down to breakfast.

Now it chanced that this same week a guest came to stay with Madame Carimon. Stella Featherston, from Buttermead, was about to make a sojourn in Paris, and she took Sainteville on her route that she might stay a few days with her cousin, Mary Carimon, whom she had not seen for several years.

Lavinia and Ann Preen had once been very intimate with Miss Featherston, who reached Madame Carimon's on the Thursday. On the Friday morning Mrs. Fennel called to see her—and, in Nancy's *impromptu* way, she invited her and Mary Carimon to take tea at seven o'clock that same evening at the Petite Maison Rouge.

Nancy went home delighted. It was a little *divertissement* to her present saddened life. Captain Fennel knitted his brow when he heard of the arrangement, but made no objection in words. His wife shrank at the frown.

"Don't you like my having invited Miss Featherston to tea, Edwin?"

"Oh! I've no objection to it," he carelessly replied. "I am not in love with either Carimon or his wife, and don't care how little I see of them."

"He cannot come, having a private class on tonight. And I could not invite Miss Featherston without Mary Carimon," pleaded Nancy.

"Just so. I am not objecting."

With this somewhat ungracious assent, Nancy had to content herself. She ordered a *gâteau Suisse*, the nicest sort of *gâteau* to be had at Sainteville; and told Flore that she must for once remain for the evening.

The guests appeared punctually at seven o'clock. Such a thing as being invited for one hour, and strolling in an hour or two after it, was a mark of English breeding never yet heard of in the simple-mannered French town. Miss Featherston, a smart, lively young woman, wore a cherry-coloured silk; Mary Carimon was in black; she had gone into slight mourning for Lavinia. Good little Monsieur Jules had put a small band on his hat.

Captain Fennel was not at home to tea, and the ladies had it all their own way in the matter of talking. What with items of news from the old home, Buttermead, and Stella's telling about her own plans, the conversation never flagged a moment.

"Yes, that's what I am going to Paris for," said Stella, explaining her plans. "I don't seem likely to marry, for nobody comes to ask me, and I mean to go out in the world and make a little money. It is a sin and a shame that a healthy girl, the eldest of three sisters, should be living upon her poor mother in idleness. Not much of a girl, you may say, for I was three-and-thirty last week! but we all like to pay ourselves compliments when age is in question."

Nancy laughed. Almost the first time she had laughed since Lavinia's death.

"So you are going to Paris to learn French, Stella!"

"I am going to Paris to learn French, Nancy," assented Miss Featherston. "I know it pretty well, but when I come to speak it I am all at sea; and you can't get out as a governess now unless you speak it fluently. At each of the two situations I applied for in Worcestershire, it was the one fatal objection: 'We should have liked you, Miss Featherston, but we can only engage a lady who will speak French with the children.' So I made my mind up to *speak* French; and I wrote to good Monsieur Jules Carimon, and he has found me a place to go to in Paris, where not a soul in the household speaks English. He says, and I say, that in six months I shall chatter away like a native," she concluded, laughing.

14

About nine o'clock Captain Fennel came home. He was gracious to the visitors, Stella Featherston thought his manners were pleasing. Shortly afterwards Charley Palliser called. He apologized for the lateness of the hour, but his errand was a good-natured one. His aunt, Mrs. Hardy, had received a box of delicious candied fruits from Marseilles; she had sent him with a few to Mrs. Fennel, if that lady would kindly accept them. The truth was, everyone in Sainteville felt sorry just now for poor Nancy Fennel.

Nancy looked as delighted as a child. She called to Flore to bring plates, turned out the fruits and handed them round. Flore also brought in the *gateau Suisse* and glasses, and a bottle of Picardin wine, that the company might regale themselves. Charley Palliser suddenly spoke; he had just thought of something.

"Would it be too much trouble to give me back that book which I lent you a week or two ago—about the plans of the fortifications?" he asked, turning to Captain Fennel. "I want it sometimes for reference in my studies."

"Not at all; I ought to have returned it to you before this—but the trouble here has driven other things out of my head," replied Captain Fennel. "Let me see—where did I put it? Nancy, do you remember where that book is?—the heavy one, you know, with red edges and a mottled cover."

"That book? Why, it is on the drawers in our bedroom," replied Nancy.

"To be sure; I'll get it," said Captain Fennel.

His wife called after him to bring down the dominoes also; someone might like a game. The captain did not intend to take the trouble of going himself; he meant to send Flore. But Flore was not in the kitchen, and he took it for granted she was upstairs. In fact, Flore was in the yard at the pump; but he never thought of the yard or the pump. Lighting a candle, he strode upstairs.

He was coming down again, the open box of dominoes and Charley Palliser's book in one hand, the candlestick in the other, when the same sort of thing seemed to occur which had occurred on Sunday night. Hearing, as he thought, someone close behind him, almost treading, as it were, upon his heels, and thinking it was Flore, he turned his head round, intending to tell her to keep her distance.

Then, with a frightful yell, down dashed Captain Fennel the few remaining stairs, the book, the candlestick, and the box of dominoes all falling in the passage from his nerveless hands. The dominoes were hard and strong, and made a great crash. But it was the yell which had frightened the company in the *salon*.

They flocked out in doubt and wonder. The candle had gone out; and Charley Palliser was bringing forth the lamp to light up the darkness, when he was nearly knocked down by Captain Fennel, Flore, returning from the pump with her own candle, much damaged by the air of the yard, held it up to survey the scene.

Captain Fennel swept past Charley into the *salon*, and threw himself into a chair behind the door, after trying to dash it to; but they were trooping in behind him. His breath was short, his terrified face looked livid as one meet for the grave.

"Why, what has happened to you, sir?" asked Charles, intensely surprised.

"Oh! he must have seen the thief again!" shrieked Nancy.

"Shut the door; bolt it!" called out the stricken man.

They did as they were bid. This order, as it struck them all, could only have reference to keeping out some nefarious intruder, such as a thief Flore had followed them in, after picking up the debris. She put the book and the dominoes on the table, and stood staring over her mistress's shoulder.

"Has the thief got in again, Edwin?" repeated Mrs. Fennel, who was beginning to tremble. "Did you see him?—or hear him?"

"My foot slipped; it sent me headforemost down the stairs," spoke the captain at last, conscious, perhaps, that something must be said to satisfy the inquisitive faces around him. "I heard Flore behind me, and—"

"Not me, sir," put in Flore in her best English. "I was not upstairs at all; I was out at the pump. There is nobody upstairs, sir; there can't be." But Captain Fennel only glared at her in answer.

"What did you cry out at?" asked Charles Palliser, speaking soothingly, for he saw that the man was pitiably unstrung. "Have you had a thief in the house? Did you think you saw one?"

"I saw no thief; there has been no thief in the house that I

116

know of; I tell you I slipped—and it startled me," retorted the captain, his tones becoming savage.

"Then—why did you have the door bolted, captain?" struck in Miss Stella Featherston, who was extremely practical and matter-of-fact, and who could not understand the scene at all.

This time the captain glared at *her*. Only for a moment; a sickly smile then stole over his countenance.

"Somebody here talked about a thief: I said bolt him out," answered he.

With this general explanation they had to be contented; but to none of them did it sound natural or straightforward.

Order was restored. The ladies took a glass of wine each and some of the *gâteau*, which Flore handed round. Charles Palliser said goodnight and departed with his book. Captain Fennel went out at the same time. He turned into the *café* on the Place Ronde, and drank three small glasses of cognac in succession.

"Nancy, what did you mean by talking about a thief?" began Madame Carimon, the whole thing much exercising her mind.

Upon which, Mrs. Fennel treated them all, including Flore, to an elaborate account of her husband's fright on the Sunday night.

"It was on the stairs; just as it was again now," she said. "He thought he heard someone following behind him as he came up to bed. He fancied it was Flore; but Flore had left hours before. I never saw any one show such terror in all my life. He said it was Flore behind him tonight, and you saw how terrified he was."

"But if he took it to be Flore, why should he be frightened?" returned Mary Carimon.

"Pardon, *mesdames*, but it is the same argument I made bold to use to *madame*," interposed Flore from the background, where she stood. "There is not anything in me to give people fright."

"I—think—it must have been," said Mrs. Fennel, speaking slowly, "that he grew alarmed when he found it was not Flore he saw. Both times."

"Then who was it that he did see—to startle him like that?" asked Mary Carimon.

"Why, he must have thought it was a thief," replied Nancy. "There's nothing else for it."

At this juncture the argument was brought to a close by the entrance of Monsieur Jules Carimon, who had come to escort his wife and Stella Featherston home.

These curious attacks of terror were repeated; not often, but at a few days' interval; so that at length Captain Fennel took care not to go about the house alone in the dark. He went up to bed when his wife did; he would not go to the door, if a ring came after Flore's departure, without a light in his hand. By-and-by he improvised a lamp, which he kept on the slab.

What was it that he was scared at? An impression arose in the minds of the two or three people who were privy to this, that he saw, or fancied he saw, in the house the spectre of one who had just been carried out of it, Lavinia Preen. Nancy had no such suspicion as yet; she only thought her husband could not be well. She was much occupied about that time, having at length nerved herself to the task of looking over her poor sister's effects.

One afternoon, when sitting in Lavinia's room (Flore—who stayed with her for company—had run down to the kitchen to see that the dinner did not burn), Nancy came upon a small, thin green case. Between its leaves she found three one-hundred-*franc* notes—twelve pounds in English value. She rightly judged that it was all that remained of her sister's nest-egg, and that she had intended to take it with her to Boulogne.

"Poor Lavinia!" she aspirated, the tears dropping from her eyes. "Every farthing remaining of the quarter's money she left with me for housekeeping."

But now a thought came to Nancy. Placing the case on the floor near her, intending to show it to her husband—she was sitting on a stool before one of Lavinia's boxes—it suddenly occurred to her that it might be as well to say nothing to him about it. He would be sure to appropriate the money to his own private uses: and Nancy knew that she should need some for hers. There would be her mourning to pay for; and—

The room-door was wide open, and at this point in her reflections Nancy heard the captain enter the house with his latch-key, and march straight upstairs. In hasty confusion, she thrust the little case into the nearest hiding-place, which happened to be the front of her black dress bodice.

"Nancy, I have to go to England," cried the captain. "How hot you look! Can't you manage to do that without stooping?"

"To go to England!" repeated Nancy, lifting her flushed face.

"Here's a letter from my brother; the postman gave it me as I was crossing the Place Ronde. It's only a line or two," he added, tossing it to her. "I must take this evening's boat."

Nancy read the letter. Only a line or two, as he said, just telling the captain to go over with all speed upon a pressing matter of business, and that he could return before the week was ended.

"Oh, but, Edwin, you can't go," began Nancy, in alarm. "I cannot stay here by myself."

"Not go! Why, I must go," he said very decisively. "How do I know what it is that I am wanted for? Perhaps that property which we are always expecting to fall in."

"But I should be so lonely. I could not stay here alone."

"Nonsense!" he sharply answered. "I shall not be away above one clear day; two days at the furthest. This is Thursday, and I shall return by Sunday's boat. You will only be alone tomorrow and Saturday."

He turned away, thus putting an end to the discussion, and entered their own room. As Nancy looked after him in despair, it suddenly struck her how very thin and ill he had become; his face worn and grey.

"He wants a change," she said to herself; "our trouble here has upset him as much as it did me. I'll say no more; I must not be selfish. Poor Lavinia used to warn me against selfishness."

So Captain Fennel went off without further opposition, his wife enjoining him to be sure to return on Sunday. The steamer was starting that night at eight o'clock; it was a fine evening, and Nancy walked down to the port with her husband and saw him on board. Nancy met an acquaintance down there; no other than Charley Palliser. They strolled a little in the wake of the departing steamer; Charley then saw her as far as the Place Ronde, and there wished her goodnight.

And now an extraordinary thing happened. As Mrs. Fennel opened the door with her latch-key, Flore having left, and was about to enter the dark passage, the same curious and unaccountable terror seized her which had been wont to attack Lavinia. Leaving the door wide open, she dashed up the passage, felt for the matchbox, and struck a light. Then, candle in hand, she returned to shut the door; but her whole frame trembled with fear.

"Why, it's just what poor Lavinia felt!" she gasped. "What on earth can it be? Why should it come to me? I will take care not to go out tomorrow night or Saturday."

And she held to her decision. Mrs. Hardy sent Charley Palliser to invite her for either day, or both days; Mary Carimon sent Pauline with a note to the same effect; but Nancy returned a refusal in both cases, with her best thanks.

The boat came in on Sunday night, but it did not bring Captain Fennel. On the Sunday morning the post had brought Nancy a few lines from him, saying he found the business on which he had been called to London was of great importance, and he was obliged to remain another day or two.

Nancy was frightfully put out: not only vexed, but angry. Edwin had no business to leave her alone like that so soon after Lavinia's death. She bemoaned her hard fate to several friends on coming out of church, and Mrs. Smith carried her off to dinner. The major was not out that morning—a twinge of gout in the right foot had kept him indoors.

This involved Nancy's going home alone in the evening, for the major could not walk with her. She did not like it. The same horror came over her before opening the door. She entered somehow, and dashed into the kitchen, hoping the stove was alight: a very silly hope, for Flore had been gone since the afternoon.

Nancy lighted the candle in the kitchen, and then fancied she saw someone looking at her from the open kitchen-door. It looked like Lavinia. It certainly was Lavinia. Nancy stood spellbound; then she gave a cry of desperate horror and dropped the candlestick.

How she picked it up she never knew; the light had not gone out. Nothing was to be seen then. The apparition, if it had been one, had vanished. She got up to bed somehow, and lay shivering under the bedclothes until morning.

Quite early, when Nancy was at breakfast, Madame Carimon came in. She had already been to the fish-market, and came on to invite Nancy to her house for the day, having heard that Mr. Fennel was still absent. With a scared face and trembling lips, Nancy told her about the previous night—the strange horror of entering which had begun to attack her, the figure of Lavinia at the kitchen-door.

Madame Carimon, listening gravely, took, or appeared to take, a sensible view of it. "You have caught up this fear of entering the house, Nancy, through remembering that it attacked poor Lavinia," she said. "Impressionable minds—and yours is one of them—take fright just as children catch measles. As to thinking you saw Lavinia—"

"She had on the gown she wore the Sunday she was taken ill: her silver-grey silk, you know," interrupted Nancy. "She looked at me with a mournful, appealing gaze, just as if she wanted something."

"Ay, you were just in the mood to fancy something of the kind," lightly spoke Madame Carimon. "The fright of coming in had done that for you. I dare say you had been talking of Lavinia at Major Smith's."

"Well, so we had," confessed Nancy.

"Just so; she was already on your mind, and therefore that and the fright you were in caused you to fancy you saw her. Nancy, my dear, you cannot imagine the foolish illusions our fancies play us,"

Easily persuaded, Mrs. Fennel agreed that it might have been

121

so. She strove to forget the matter, and. went out there and then with Mary Carimon.

But this state of things was to continue. Captain Fennel did not return, and Nancy grew frightened to death at being alone in the house after dark. Flore was unable to stay longer than the time originally agreed for, her old mother being dangerously ill. As dusk approached, Nancy began to hate her destiny. Apart from nervousness, she was sociably inclined, and yearned, for company. Now and again the inclination to accept an invitation was too strong to be resisted, or she went out after dinner, uninvited, to this friend or that. But the pleasure was counterbalanced by having to go in again at night; the horror clung to her.

If a servant attended her home, or any gentleman from the house where she had been, she made them go indoors with her whilst she lighted her candle; once she got Monsieur Gustave's errand-boy to do so. But it was almost as bad with the lighted candle—the first feeling of being in the lonely house after they had gone. She wrote letter after letter, imploring her husband to return. Captain Fennel's replies were rich in promises: he would be back the very instant business permitted; probably "tomorrow, or the next day." But he did not come.

One Sunday, when he had been gone about three weeks, and Nancy had been spending the day in the Rue Pomme Cuite, Mary Carimon walked home with her in the evening. Monsieur Jules had gone to see his cousin off by the nine-o'clock train—Mademoiselle Priscille Carimon, who had come in to spend the day with them. She lived at Drecques.

"You will come in with me, Mary?" said Ann Fennel, as they gained the door.

"To be sure I will," replied Madame Carimon, laughing lightly, for none knew about the fears better than she.

Nancy took her hand as they went up the passage. She lighted the candle at the slab, and they went into the *salon*, Madame Carimon sat down for a few minutes, by way of reassuring her. Nancy took off her bonnet and mantle. On the table was a small

tray with the tea-things upon it. Flore had left it there in readiness, not quite certain whether her mistress would come in to
tea or not.

"I had such a curious dream last night," began Nancy; "those
tea-things put me in mind of it. Lavinia—"

"For goodness' sake don't begin upon dreams tonight!" interposed Madame Carimon. "You know they always frighten
you."

"Oh, but this was a pleasant dream, Mary. I thought that I and
Lavinia were seated at a little table, with two teacups between
us full of tea. The cups were very pretty; pale amber with gilt
scrolls, and the china so thin as to be transparent. I can see them
now. And Lavinia said something which made me smile; but I
don't remember what it was. Ah, Mary! if she were only back
again with us!"

"She is better off, you know," said Mary Carimon in tender
tones.

"All the same, it was a cruel fate that took her; I shall never
think otherwise. I wish I knew what it was she died of! Flore
told me one day that Monsieur Podevin quite laughed at the
idea of its being a chill."

"Well, Nancy, it was you who stopped it, you know."

"Stopped what?" asked Nancy.

"The investigation the doctors would have made after death.
Both of them were much put out at your forbidding it: for their
own satisfaction they wished to ascertain particulars. I may tell
you now that I thought you were wrong to interfere."

"It was Captain Fennel," said Nancy calmly.

"Captain Fennel!" echoed Mary Carimon. "Monsieur Dupuis told me that Captain Fennel wished for it as much as he
and Monsieur Podevin."

Captain Fennel's wife shook her head. "They asked him
about it before they left, after she died. He came to me, and I
said, Oh, let them do what they would; it could not hurt her
now she was dead. I was in such terrible distress, Mary, that I
hardly knew or cared what I said. Then Edwin drew so dreadful

123

a picture of what post-mortems are, and how barbarously her poor neck and arms would be cut and slashed, that I grew sick and frightened."

"And so you stopped it—by reason of the picture he drew?"

"Yes. I came running down here to Monsieur Dupuis—Monsieur Podevin had gone—for Edwin said it must be my decision, not his, and his name had better not be mentioned; and I begged and prayed Monsieur Dupuis not to hold it. I think I startled him, good old man. I was almost out of my mind; quite wild with agitation; and he promised me it should be as I wished. That's how it all was, Mary."

Mary Carimon's face wore a curious look. Then she rallied, speaking even lightly.

"Well, well; it could not have brought her back to life; and I repeat that we must remember she is better off And now, Nancy, I want you to show me the pretty purse that Miss Perry has knitted for you, if you have it at hand."

Nancy rose, opened her workbox, which stood on the side-table, and brought forth the purse. Of course Madame Carimon's motive had been to change her thoughts. After admiring the purse, and talking of other pleasant matters, Mary took her departure.

And the moment the outer door had closed upon her that feeling of terror seized upon Nancy. Catching up her mantle with one hand and the candle with the other, she made for the staircase, leaving her bonnet and gloves in the salon. The staircase struck cold to her, and she could hear the wind whistling, for it was a windy night. As to the candle, it seemed to burn with a pale flame and not to give half its usual light.

In her nervous agitation, just as she gained the uppermost stair, she dropped her mantle. Raising her head from stooping to pick it up, she suddenly saw some figure before her at the end of the passage. It stood beyond the door of her own room, close to that which had been her sister's.

It was Lavinia. She appeared to be habited in the silver-grey silk already spoken of. Her gaze was fixed upon Nancy, with the same imploring aspect of appeal, as if she wanted something; her pale face was inexpressibly mournful. With a terrible cry, Nancy tore into her own room, the mantle trailing after her. She shut the door and bolted it, and buried her face in the counterpane in wild agony.

And in that moment a revelation came to Ann Fennel. It was this apparition which had been wont to haunt her husband in the house and terrify him beyond control. Not a thief; not Flore—but Lavinia!

15

On the Monday morning Flore found her mistress in so sick and suffering and strange a state, that she sent for Madame Carimon. In vain Mary Carimon, after hearing Nancy's tale, strove to convince her that what she saw was fancy, the effect of diseased nerves. Nancy was more obstinate than a mule.

"What I saw was Lavinia," she shivered. "Lavinia's apparition. No good to tell me it was not; I have seen it now twice. It was as clear and evident to me, both times, as ever she herself was in life. That's what Edwin used to see; I know it now; and he became unable to bear the house. I seem to read it all as in a book, Mary. He got his brother to send for him, and he is staying away because he dreads to come back again. But you know I cannot stay here alone now."

Madame Carimon wrote off at once to Captain Fennel, Nancy supplying the address. She told him that his wife was ill; in a nervous state; fancying she saw Lavinia in the house. Such a report, she added, should if possible be kept from spreading to the town, and therefore she must advise him to return without delay.

The letter brought back Captain Fennel, Flore having meanwhile remained entirely at the Petite Maison Rouge. Perhaps the captain did not in secret like that little remark of its being well to keep it from the public; he may have considered it suggestive, coming from Mary Carimon. He believed she read him pretty correctly, and he hated her accordingly. Anyway, he deemed it well to be on the spot. Left to herself, there was no telling what ridiculous things Nancy might be saying or fancying.

Edwin Fennel did not return alone. His brother's wife was with him. Mrs. James, they called her, James being the brother's Christian name. Mrs. James was not a lady in herself or in manner; but she was lively and very good-natured, and these qualities were what the Petite Maison Rouge wanted in it just now; and perhaps that was Captain Fennel's motive in bringing her. Nancy was delighted. She almost forgot her fears and fancies. Flore was agreeable also, for she was now at liberty to return to ordinary arrangements. Thus there was a lull in the storm. They walked out with Mrs. James on the pier, and took her to see the different points of interest in the town; they even gave a little *soirée* for her, and in return were invited to other houses.

One day, when the two ladies were gossiping together, Nancy, in the openness of her heart, related to Mrs. James the particulars of Lavinia's unexpected and rather mysterious death, and of her appearing in the house again after it. Captain Fennel disturbed them in the midst of the story. His wife was taking his name in vain at the moment of his entrance, saying how scared *he* had been at the apparition.

"Hold your peace, you foolish woman!" he thundered, looking as if he meant to strike her. "Don't trouble Mrs. James's head with such miserable rubbish as that."

Mrs. James did not appear to mind it. She burst into a hearty laugh. She never had seen a ghost, she said, and was sure she never should; there were no such things. But she should like to hear all about poor Miss Preen's death.

"There was nothing else to hear," the captain growled. "She caught a chill on the Sunday, coming out of the hot church after morning service. It struck inwardly, bringing on inflammation, which the medical men could not subdue."

"But you know, Edwin, the church never is hot, and you know the doctors decided it was not a chill. Monsieur Podevin especially denied it," dissented Nancy, who possessed about as much insight as a goose, and a little less tact.

"Then what did she die of?" questioned Mrs. James. "Was she

poisoned?"

"Oh, how can you suggest so dreadful a thing!" shrieked Nancy. "Poisoned! Who would be so wicked as to poison Lavinia? Everyone loved her."

Which again amused the listening lady. "You have a quick imagination, Mrs. Edwin," she laughed. "I was thinking of mushrooms."

"And I of tinned meats and copper saucepans," supplemented Captain Fennel. "However, there could be no suspicion even of that sort in Lavinia's case, since she had touched nothing but what we all partook of. She died of inflammation, Mrs. James."

"Little doubt of it," acquiesced Mrs. James. "A friend of mine went, not twelve months ago, to a funeral at Brompton Cemetery; the ground was damp, and she caught a chill. In four days she was dead."

"Women have no business at funerals," growled Edwin Fennel. "Why should they parade their grief abroad? You see nothing of the kind in France."

"In truth I think you are not far wrong," said Mrs. James. "It is a fashion which has sprung up of late. A few years ago it was as much unknown with us as it is with the French."

"*They* will be catching it up next, I suppose," retorted the captain, as if the thing were a personal grievance to him.

"Little doubt of it," laughed Mrs. James.

After staying at Sainteville for a month, Mrs. James Fennel took her departure for London. Captain Fennel proposed to escort her over; but his wife went into so wild a state at the mere mention of it, that he had to give it up.

"I dare not stay in the house by myself, Edwin," she shuddered. "I should go to the Vice-Consul and to other influential people here, and tell them of my misery—that I am afraid of seeing Lavinia."

And Captain Fennel believed she would be capable of doing it. So he remained with her.

That the spectre of the dead-and-gone Lavinia did at times appear to them, or else their fancies conjured up the vision, was all too certain. Three times during the visit of Mrs. James the captain had been betrayed into one of his fits of terror: no need to ask what had caused it. After her departure the same thing took place. Nancy had not again seen anything, but she knew he had.

"We shall not be able to stay in the house, Edwin," his wife said to him one evening when they were sitting in the *salon* at dusk after Flore's departure; nothing having led up to the remark.

"I fancy we should be as well out of it," replied he.

"Oh, Edwin, let us go! If we can! There will be all the rent to pay up first."

"All the what?" said he.

"The rent," repeated Nancy; "up to the end of the term we took it for. About three years longer, I think, Edwin. That would be sixty pounds."

"And where do you suppose the sixty pounds would come from?"

"I don't know. There's the impediment, you see," remarked Nancy blankly. "We cannot leave without paying up."

"Unless we made a moonlight flitting of it, my dear."

"That I never will," she rejoined, with a firmness he could not mistake. "You are only jesting, Edwin."

"It would be no jesting matter to pay up that claim, and others; for there are others. Our better plan, Nancy, will be to go off by the London boat some night, and not let anyone know where we are until I can come back to pay. You may see it is the only thing to be done, and you must bring your mind to it."

"Never by me," said Nancy, strong in her innate rectitude. "As to hiding ourselves anywhere, that can never be; I should not conceal my address from Mary Carimon—I *could* not conceal it from Colonel Selby."

Captain Fennel ground his teeth. "Suppose I say that this shall be, that we will go, and order you to obey me? What then?"

"No, Edwin, I could not. I should go in to Monsieur Gustave Sauvage, and say to him, 'We were thinking of running away, but

I cannot do it; please put me in prison until I can pay the debt.'
And then—"

"Are you an idiot?" asked Captain Fennel, staring at her.

"And then, when I was in prison," went on Nancy, "I should write to tell William Selby; and perhaps he would come over and release me. Please don't talk in this kind of way again, Edwin. I should keep my word."

Mr. Edwin Fennel could not have felt more astounded had his wife then and there turned into a dromedary before his eyes. She had hitherto been tractable as a child. But he had never tried her in a thing that touched her honour, and he saw that the card which he had intended to play was lost.

Captain Fennel played another. He went away himself.

Making the best he could of the house and its haunted state (though day by day saw him looking more and more like a walking skeleton) throughout the greater part of June, for the summer had come in, he despatched his wife to Pontipette one market day—Saturday—to remain there until the following Wednesday. Old Mrs. Hardy had gone to the homely but comfortable hotel at Pontipette for a change, and she wrote to invite Nancy to stay a short time with her. Charles Palliser was in England. Captain Fennel proceeded to London by that same Saturday night's boat, armed with a letter from his wife to Colonel Selby, requesting the colonel to pay over to her husband her quarterly instalment instead of sending it to herself. Captain Fennel had bidden her do this; and Nancy, of strict probity in regard to other people's money, could not resist signing over her own,

"But you will be sure to bring it all back, won't you, Edwin? and to be here by Wednesday, the day I return?" she said to him.

"Why, of course I shall, my dear,"

"It will be a double portion now—thirty-five pounds."

"And a good thing, too; we shall want it," he returned.

"Indeed, yes; there's such a heap of things owing for," concluded Nancy.

Thus the captain went over to England in great glee, carrying with him the order for the money. But he was reckoning without his host.

Upon presenting himself at the bank in the City on Monday morning, he found Colonel Selby absent; not expected to return before the end of that week, or the beginning of the next. This was a check for Captain Fennel. He quite glared at the gentleman who thus informed him—Mr, West, who sat in the colonel's room, and was his *locum tenens* for the time being.

"Business is transacted all the same, I conclude?" said he snappishly.

"Why, certainly," replied Mr. West, marvelling at the absurdity of the question. "What can I do for you?"

Captain Fennel produced his wife's letter, requesting that her quarter's money should be paid over to him, and handed in her receipt for the same. Mr. West read them both, the letter twice, and then looked direct through his silver-rimmed spectacles at the applicant.

"I cannot do this," said he; "it is a private matter of Colonel Selby's."

"It is not more private than any other payment you may have to make," retorted Captain Fennel.

"Pardon me, it is. This really does not concern the bank at all. I cannot pay it without Colonel Selby's authority: he has neither given it nor mentioned it to me. Another thing: the payment, as I gather from the wording of Mrs. Ann Fennel's letter, is not yet due. Upon that score, apart from any other, I should decline to pay it."

"It will be due in two or three days. Colonel Selby would not object to forestall the time by that short period."

"That would, of course, be for the colonel's own consideration."

"I particularly wish to receive the money this morning."

Mr. West shook his head in answer. "If you will leave Mrs. Fennel's letter and receipt in my charge, sir, I will place them before the colonel as soon as he returns. That is all I can do. Or perhaps you would prefer to retain the latter," he added, handing back the receipt over the desk.

"Business men are the very devil to stick at straws," muttered Captain Fennel under his breath. He saw it was no use trying to move the one before him, and went out, saying he would call in a day or two.

Now it happened that Colonel Selby, who was only staying at Brighton for a rest (for he had been very unwell of late), took a run up to town that same Monday morning to see his medical attendant. His visit paid, he went on to the bank, surprising Mr. West there about one o'clock. After some conference upon business matters, Mr. West spoke of Captain Fennel's visit, and handed over the letter he had left.

Colonel Selby drew in his lips as he read it. He did not like Mr. Edwin Fennel; and he would most assuredly not pay Ann Fennel's money to him. He returned the letter to Mr. West.

"Should the man come here again, West, tell him, as you did this morning, that he can see me on my return—which will probably be on this day week," said the colonel. "No need to say I have been up here today."

And on the following day, Tuesday, Colonel Selby, being then at Brighton, drew out a cheque for the quarter almost due and sent it by post to Nancy at Sainteville.

Thus checkmated in regard to the money, Captain Fennel did not return home at the time he promised, even if he had had any intention of doing so. When Nancy returned to Sainteville on the Wednesday from Pontipette, he was not there. The first thing she saw waiting for her on the table was Colonel Selby's letter containing the cheque for five-and-thirty pounds.

"How glad I am it has come to me so soon!" cried Nancy; "I can pay the bills now. I suppose William Selby thinks it would not be legal to pay it to Edwin."

The week went on. Each time a boat came in, Nancy was promenading the port, expecting to see her husband land from it. On the Sunday morning Nancy received a letter from him, in which he told her he was waiting to see Colonel Selby, to get the money paid to him. Nancy wrote back hastily, saying it had been received by herself, and that she had paid it nearly all away in settling the bills. She begged him to come back by the next boat. Flore was staying in the house altogether, but at an inconvenience.

On the Monday evening Mrs. Fennel had another desperate fright. She went to take tea with an elderly lady and her daughter, Mrs. and Miss Lambert, bidding Flore to come for her at half-past nine o'clock. Half-past nine came, but no Flore; ten o'clock came, and then Mrs. Fennel set off alone, supposing Flore had misunderstood her and would be found waiting for her at home. The moonlit streets were crowded with promenaders returning from their summer evening-walk upon the pier.

Nancy rang the bell; but it was not answered. She had her latch-key in her pocket, but preferred to be admitted, and she rang again. No one came. "Flore must have dropped asleep in the kitchen," she petulantly thought, and drew out her key.

"Flore!" she called out, pushing the door back. "Flore, where are you?"

Flore apparently was nowhere, very much to the dismay of Mrs. Fennel. She would have to go in alone, all down the dark passage, and wake her up. Leaving the door wide open, she advanced in the dark with cautious steps, the old terror full upon her.

The kitchen was dark also, so far as fire or candlelight went, but a glimmer of moonlight shone in at the window. "Are you not here, Flore?" shivered Nancy. But there was no response.

Groping for the matchbox on the mantelshelf over the stove, and not at once finding it, Nancy suddenly took up an impression that someone was standing in the misty rays of the moon. Gazing attentively, it seemed to assume the shadowy form of Lavinia. And with a shuddering cry Nancy Fennel fell down upon the brick floor of the kitchen.

16

It was a lovely summer's day, and Madame Carimon's neat little slip of a kitchen was bright and hot with the morning sun. Madame, herself, stood before the paste-board, making a green-apricot tart. Of pies and tarts *à la mode Anglaise*, Monsieur Jules was more fond than a schoolboy; and of all tarts known to the civilized world, none can equal that of a green apricot.

Madame had put down the rolling-pin, and stood for the moment idle, looking at Flore Pamart, and listening to something that Flore was saying. Flore, whisking out of the Petite Maison Rouge a few minutes before, ostensibly to do her morning's marketings, had whisked straight off to the Rue Pomme Cuite, and was now seated at the corner of the pastry-table, telling a story to Madame Carimon.

"It was *madame's* own fault," she broke off in her tale to remark. "*Madame will* give me her orders in French, and half the time I can't understand them. She had an engagement to take tea at Madame Smith's in the Rue Lambeau, was what I thought she said to me, and that I must present myself there at half-past nine to walk home with her. Well, *madame*, I went accordingly, and found nobody at home there but the *bonne*, Thomasine. Her master was dining out at the *Sous-préfet's,* and her mistress had gone out with some more ladies to walk on the pier, as it was so fine an evening. Naturally I thought my mistress was one of the ladies, and sat there waiting for her and chatting with Thomasine. Madame Smith came in at ten o'clock, and then she said that my lady had not been there and that she had not expected her."

"She must have gone to tea elsewhere," observed Madame Carimon.

"Clearly, *madame*; as I afterwards found. It was to Madame Lambert's, in the Rue Lothaire, that I ought to have gone. I could only go home, as *madame* sees; and when I arrived there I found the house-door wide open. Just as I entered, a frightful cry came from the kitchen, and there I found her dropped down on the floor, half senseless with terror. *Madame*, she avowed to me that she had seen Mademoiselle Lavinia standing near her in the moonlight."

Madame Carimon took up her rolling-pin slowly before she spoke. "I know she has a fancy that she appears in the house."

"Madame Carimon, I think she is in the house," said Flore solemnly. And for a minute or two Madame Carimon rolled her paste in silence.

"Monsieur Fennel used to see her—I am sure he did—and now his wife sees her," went on the woman. "I think that is the secret of his running away so much: he can't bear the house and what is haunting it.

"It is altogether a dreadful thing; I lie awake thinking of it," bewailed Mary Carimon.

"But it cannot be let go on like this," said Flore; "and that's what has brought me running here this morning—to ask you, *madame*, whether anything can be done. If she is left alone to see these sights, she'll die of it. When she got up this morning she was shivering like a leaf in the wind. Has *madame* noticed that she is wasting away? For the matter of that, so was Monsieur Fennel."

Madame Carimon, beginning to line her shallow dish with paste, nodded in assent. "He ought to be here with her," she remarked.

"Catch him," returned Flore, in a heat. "Pardon, *madame*, but I must avow I trust not that gentleman. He is no good. He will never come back to stay at the house so long as there is in it— what is there. He dare not; and I would like to ask him why not. A man with the conscience at ease could not be that sort of coward. Honest men do not fly away, all scared, when they fancy they see a revenant."

Deeming it might be unwise to pursue the topic from this point, Madame Carimon said she would go and see Mrs. Fennel in the course of the day, and Flore clattered off, her wooden shoes echoing on the narrow pavement of the Rue Pomme Cuite.

But, as Madame Carimon was crossing the Place Ronde in the afternoon to pay her visit, she met Mrs. Fennel, Of course, Flore's communication was not to be mentioned.

"Ah," said Madame Carimon readily, "is it you? I was coming to ask if you would like to take a walk on the pier with me. It is a lovely afternoon, and not too hot."

"Oh, I'll go," said Nancy. "I came out because it is so miserable at home. When Flore went off to the fish-market after breakfast, I felt more lonely than you would believe. Mary," dropping her voice, "I saw Lavinia last night."

"Now I won't listen to that," retorted Mary Carimon, as if she were reprimanding a child. "Once give in to our nerves and fancies, there's no end to the tricks they play us. I wish, Ann, your house were in a more lively situation, where you might sit at the window and watch the passers-by."

"But it isn't," said Nancy sensibly. "It looks upon nothing but the walls."

Walking on, they sat down upon a bench that stood back from the port, facing the harbour. Nearly opposite lay the English boat, busily loading for London. The sight made Nancy sigh.

"I wish it would bring Edwin the next time it comes in," she said in low tones.

"When do you expect him?"

"I don't know *when*," said poor Nancy with emphasis. "Mary, I am beginning to think he stays away because he is afraid of seeing Lavinia."

"Men are not afraid of those foolish things, Ann."

"He is. Recollect those fits of terror he had. He used to hear her following him up and downstairs; used to see her on the landings."

Madame Carimon found no ready answer. She had witnessed one of those fits of terror herself.

"Last night," went on Mrs. Fennel, after a pause, "when Flore had left me and I could only shiver in my bed, and not expect to sleep, I became calm enough to ask myself *why* Lavinia should come back again, and what it is she wants. Can you think why, Mary?"

"Not I," said Madame Carimon lightly. "I shall only believe she does come when she shows herself to me."

"And I happened on the thought that, possibly, she may be wanting us to inquire into the true cause of her death. It might have been ascertained at the time, but for my stopping the action of the doctors, you know."

"Ann, my dear, you should exercise a little common sense. I would ask you what end ascertaining it now would answer, to her, dead, or to you, living?"

"It might be seen that she could have been cured, had we only known what the malady was."

"But you did not know; the doctors did not know. It could only have been discovered, even at your showing, after her death, not in time to save her."

"I wish Monsieur Dupuis had come more quickly on the Monday night!" sighed Nancy. "I am always wishing it. You can picture what it was, Mary—Lavinia lying in that dreadful agony and no doctor coming near her. Edwin was gone so long—so long! He could not wake up Monsieur Dupuis. I think now that the bell was out of order."

"Why do you think that now? Captain Fennel must have known whether the bell answered to his summons, or not."

"Well," returned Nancy, "this morning when Flore returned with the fish, she said I looked very ill. She had just seen Monsieur Dupuis in the Place Ronde, and she ran out again and brought him in—"

"Did you mention to him this fancy of seeing Lavinia?" hastily interrupted Madame Carimon.

"No, no; I don't talk of that to people. Only to you and Flore; and—yes—I did tell Mrs. Smith. I let Monsieur Dupuis think I was ill with grieving after Lavinia, and we talked a little about her. I said how I wished he could have been here sooner on the Monday night, and that my husband had rung several times before he could arouse him. Monsieur Dupuis said that was a mistake; he had got up and come as soon as he was called; he was not asleep at the time, and the bell had rung only once."

"What an extraordinary thing!" exclaimed Mary Carimon. "I know your husband said he rang many times."

"That's why I now think the bell must have been out of order; but I did not say so to Monsieur Dupuis," returned Nancy.

"He is a kind old man, and it would grieve him: for of course we know doctors *ought* to keep their door-bells in order."

Madame Carimon rose in silence, but full of thought, and they continued their walk. It was low water in the harbour, but the sun was sparkling and playing on the waves out at sea. On the pier they found Rose and Anna Bosanquet; and in chatting with them Nancy's mood became more cheerful.

That same evening, on that same pier, Mary Carimon spoke a few confidential words to her husband. They sat at the end of it, and the beauty of the night, so warm and still, induced them to linger. The bright moon sailed grandly in the heavens and glittered upon the water that now filled the harbour, for the tide was in. Most of the promenaders had turned down the pier again, after watching out the steamer. What a fine passage she would make, and was making, cutting there so smoothly through the crystal sea!

Mary Carimon began in a low voice, though no one was near to listen and the waves could not hear her. She spoke pretty fully of a haunting doubt that lay upon her mind, as to whether Lavinia had died a natural death.

"If we make the best of it," she concluded, "her dying in that strangely sudden way was unusual; you know that, Jules; quite unaccountable. It never *has* been accounted for."

Monsieur Jules, gazing on the gentle waves as they rose and fell in the moonlight at the mouth of the harbour, answered nothing.

"He had so much to wish her away for, that man: all the money would become Nancy's. And I'm sure there was secret enmity between them—on both sides. Don't you see, Jules, how suspicious it all looks?"

The moonbeams, illumining Monsieur Jules Carimon's face, showed it to be very impassive, betraying no indication that he as much as heard what his wife was talking about.

"I have not forgotten, I can never forget, Jules, the very singular Fate-reading, or whatever you may please to call it, spoken by the Astrologer Talcke last winter at Miss Bosanquet's *soirée*.

You were not in the room, you know, but I related it to you when we arrived home. He certainly foretold Lavinia's death, as I, recalling the words, look upon it now. He said there was some element of evil in their house, threatening and terrible; he repeated it more than once. *In their house,* Jules, and that it would end in darkness; which, as everyone understood, meant death: not for Mrs. Fennel; he took care to tell her that; but for another. He said the cards were more fateful than he had ever seen them. That evil in the house was Fennel."

Still Monsieur Jules offered no comment.

"And what could be the meaning of those dreams Lavinia had about him, in which he always seemed to be preparing to inflict upon her some fearful ill, and she knew she never could and never would escape from it?" ran on Mary Carimon, her eager, suppressed tones bearing a gruesome sound in the stillness of the night. "And what is the explanation of the fits of terror which have shaken Fennel since the death, fancying he sees Lavinia? Flore said to me this morning that she is sure Lavinia is in the house."

Glancing at her husband to see that he was at least listening, but receiving no confirmation of it by word or motion, Mary Carimon continued:

"Those dreams came to warn her, Jules. To warn her to get out of the house while she could. And she made arrangements to go, and in another day or two would have been away in safety. But he was too quick for her."

Monsieur Jules Carimon turned now to face his wife. "*Mon amie, tais toi,*" said he with authority. "Such a topic is not convenable," he added, still in French, though she had spoken in English. "It is dangerous."

"But, Jules, I believe it *to have been so.*"

"All the same, and whether or no, it is not your affair, Marie. Neither must you make it so. Believe me, my wife, the only way to live peaceably ourselves in the world is to let our neighbours' sins alone."

17

Captain Edwin Fennel was certainly in no hurry to return to Sainteville, for he did not come. Nancy, ailing, weak, wretchedly uncomfortable, wrote letter after letter to him, generally sending them over by some friend or other who might be crossing, to be put in a London letter-box, and so evade the foreign postage. Once or twice she had written to Mrs. James, telling of her lonely life and that she wanted Edwin either to take her out of the dark and desolate house, or else to come back to it himself Captain Fennel would answer now and again, promising to come—she would be quite sure to see him on one of the first boats if she looked out for their arrival. Nancy did look, but she had not yet seen him. She was growing visibly thinner and weaker. Sainteville said how ill Mrs. Fennel was looking.

One evening at the end of July, when the London steamer was due about ten o'clock, Nancy went to watch it in, as usual, Flore attending her. The port was gay, crowded with promenaders. There had been a concert at the Rooms, and the company was coming home from it. Mrs. Fennel had not made one: latterly she had felt no spirit for amusement. Several friends met her; she did not tell them she had come down to meet her husband, if haply he should be on the expected boat; she had grown tired and half ashamed of saying that; she let them think she was only out for a walk that fine evening. There was a yellow glow still in the sky where the sun had set; the north-west was clear and bright with its opal light.

The time went on; the port became deserted, excepting a few passing stragglers. Ten o'clock had struck, eleven would soon strike, Flore and her mistress, tired of pacing about, sat down on one of the benches facing the harbour. One of two young men, passing swiftly homewards from the pier, found himself called to.

"Charley! Charley Palliser!"

Charles turned, and recognized Mrs. Fennel. Stepping across to her, he shook hands.

"What do you think can have become of the boat?" she asked. "It ought to have been in nearly an hour ago."

"Oh, it will be here shortly," he replied. "The boat often makes a slow passage when there's no wind. What little wind we have had today has been dead against it."

"As I've just said to *madame*," put in Flore, always ready to take up the conversation. "Mr. Charles knows there's no fear it has gone down, though it may be a bit late."

"Why, certainly not," laughed Charley. "Are you waiting here for it, Mrs. Fennel?"

"Ye—s," she answered, but with hesitation.

"And as it's not even in sight yet, *madame* had much better go home and not wait, for the air is getting chilly," again spoke Flore,

"We can't see whether it's in sight or not," said her mistress. "It is dark out at sea."

"Shall I wait here with you, Mrs. Fennel?" asked Charley in his good nature.

"Oh no, no; no, thank you," she answered quickly. "If it does not come in soon, we shall go home."

He wished them goodnight, and went onwards.

"She is hoping the boat may bring that mysterious brute, Fennel," remarked Charles to his companion.

"Brute, you call him?"

"He is no better than one, to leave his sick wife alone so long," responded Charles in hearty tones. "She has picked up an idea, I hear, that the house is haunted, and shakes in her shoes in it from morning till night."

The two watchers sat on, Flore grumbling. Not for herself, but for her mistress. A sea-fog was rising, and Flore thought *madame* might take cold. Mrs. Fennel wrapped her light fleecy shawl closer about her chest, and protested she was quite hot. The shawl was well enough for a warm summer's night, but not for a cold sea-fog. About half-past eleven there suddenly loomed into view through the mist the lights of the steamer, about to enter the harbour.

"There she is!" exultingly cried Nancy, who had been shiver-ing inwardly for some time past, and doing her best not to shiver outwardly for fear of Flore. "And now, Flore, you go home as quickly as you can and make a fire in the *salon* to warm us. I'm sure he will need one—at sea in this cold fog."

"If he is come," mentally returned Flore in her derisive heart. She had no faith in the return of Monsieur Fennel by any boat, a day or a night one. But she needed no second prompting to hasten away; was too glad to do it.

Poor Nancy waited on. The steamer came very slowly up the port, or she fancied so; one must be cautious in a fog; and it seemed to her a long time swinging round and settling itself into its place. Then the passengers came on shore one by one, Nancy standing close to look at them. There were only about twenty in all, and Captain Fennel was not one of them. With misty eyes and a rising in her throat and spiritless footsteps, Nancy arrived at her home, the Petite Maison Rouge. Flore had the fire burning in the *salon*; but Nancy was too thoroughly chilled for any salon fire to warm her.

The cold she caught that night stuck to her chest. For some days afterwards she was very ill indeed. Monsieur Dupuis attended her, and brought his son once or twice, Monsieur Henri. Nancy got up again, and was, so to say, herself once more; but she did not get up her strength.

She would lie on the sofa in the *salon* those August days, which were very hot ones, too languid to get off it. Friends would call in to see her; Major and Mrs. Smith, the Miss Bosanquets, the Lamberts, and so on. Madame Carimon was often there. They would ask her why she did not "make an effort" and sit up and occupy herself with a book or a bit of work, or go out a little; and Nancy's answer was nearly always the same—she would do all that when the weather was somewhat cooler. Charley Palliser was quite a constant visitor. An English damsel, who was casting a covetous eye to Charles, though she might have spared herself the pains, took a fit of jealousy and said one might think sick Nancy Fennel was his sweetheart, going there so often. Charley rarely went empty-handed either. Now it would be half-a-dozen nectarines in their red-ripe loveliness, now some choice peaches, then a bunch of hot-house grapes, "purple and gushing," and again an amusing novel just out in England.

★★★★★★

"Mary, she is surely dying!"

The sad exclamation came from Stella Featherston. She and Madame Carimon, going in to take tea at the Petite Maison Rouge, had been sent by its mistress to her chamber above to take off their bonnets. The words had broken from Stella the moment they were alone.

"Sometimes I fear it myself," replied Madame Carimon. "She certainly grows weaker instead of stronger."

"Does any doctor attend her?"

"Monsieur Dupuis; a man of long experience, kind and clever, I was talking to him the other day, and he as good as said his skill and care seemed to avail nothing: were wasted on her."

"Is it consumption?"

"I think not. She caught a dreadful cold about a month ago through being out in a night fog, thinly clad; and there's no doubt it left mischief behind; but it seems to me that she is wasting away with inward fever."

"I should get George to run over to see her, if I were you, Mary," remarked Stella. "French doctors are very clever, I believe, especially as surgeons; "but for an uncertain case like this they don't come up to the English. And George knows her constitution."

They went down to the *salon*, Mary Carimon laughing a little at the remark. Stella Featherston had not been long enough in France to part with her native prejudices. The family with whom she lived in Paris had journeyed to Sainteville for a month for what they called "*les eaux*," and Stella accompanied them. They were in lodgings on the port.

Mrs. Fennel seemed more like her old self that evening than she had been for some time past. The unexpected presence of her companion of early days changed the tone of her mind and raised her spirits. Stella exerted all her mirth, talked of their doings in the past, told of Buttermead's doings in the present. Nan-

142

cy was quite gay.

"Do you ever sing now, Stella?" she suddenly asked.

"Why, no," laughed Stella, "unless I am quite alone. Who would care to hear old ditties sung without music?"

"I should. Oh, Stella, sing me a few!" urged the invalid, her tone quite imploring. "It would bring the dear old days back to me."

Stella Featherston had a most melodious voice, but she did not play. It was not unusual in those days for girls to sing without any accompaniment, as Stella had for the most part done.

"Have you forgotten your Scotch songs, Stella?" asked Mary Carimon.

"Not I; I like them best of all," replied Miss Featherston. And without more ado she broke into "*Ye banks and braes.*"

It was followed by "*The Banks of Allan Water,*" and others. Flore stole to the parlour-door, and thought she had never heard so sweet a singer. Last of all, Stella began a quaint song that was more of a chant than anything else, low and subdued:

Woe's me, for my heart is breakin',
I think en my brither sma',
And on my sister greetin',
When I cam' from home awa'.
And O, how my mither sobbit,
As she took from me her hand,
When I left the door of our old house
To come to this stranger land.

There's nae place like our ain home,
O, I would that I were there!
There's nae home like our ain home
To be met wi' onywhere.
And O, that I were back again
To our farm and fields sae green,
And heard the tongues of our ain folk,
And was what I hae been!

A feeling of despair ran through the whole words; and the

tears were running down Ann Fennel's hectic cheeks as the melody died away in a plaintive silence.

"It is what I shall never see again, Stella," she murmured—"the green fields of *our* home; or hear the tongues of all the dear ones there. In my dreams, sometimes, I am at Selby Court, light-hearted and happy, as I was before I left it for this ' stranger land.' Woe's *me*, also, Stella!"

And now I come into the story—I, Johnny Ludlow. For what I have told of it hitherto has not been from any personal knowledge of mine, but from diaries, and from what Mary Carimon related to me, and from Featherston. It may be regarded as singular that I should have been, so to say, present at its ending, but that I *was* there is as true as anything I ever wrote. The story itself is true in all its chief facts; I have already said that; and it is true that I saw the close of it.

18

To say that George Featherston, Doctor-in-ordinary at Buttermead, felt as if he were standing on his head instead of his heels, would not in the least express his mental condition as he stood in his surgery that September afternoon and read a letter, just delivered, from his sister, Madame Carimon.

"Wants me to go to Sainteville to see Ann Preen; thinks she will die if I refuse, for the French doctors can do nothing for her!" commented Featherston, staring at the letter in intense perplexity, and then looking off it to stare at me.

I wonder whether anything in this world happens by chance? In the days and years that have gone by since, I sometimes ask myself whether *that* did: that I should be at that particular moment in Featherston's surgery. Squire Todhetley was staying with Sir John Whitney for partridge shooting. He had taken me with him, Tod being in Gloucestershire; and on this Friday afternoon I had run in to say "How-d'ye-do" to Featherston.

"*Sainteville!*" repeated he, quite unable to collect his senses. "Why, I must cross the water to get *there!*"

I laughed. "Did you think Sainteville would cross to you, sir?"

"Bless me! just listen to this," he went on, reading parts of the letter aloud for my benefit. "'It is a dreadful story, George; I dare not enter into details here. But I may tell you this much: that she is dying of fright as much as of fever—or whatever it may be that ails her physically. I am sure it is not consumption, though some of the people here think it is. It is fright and superstition. She lives in the belief that the house is haunted: that Lavinia's ghost walks in it.'"

"Now what on earth can Mary mean by that?" demanded the doctor, looking off to ask me. "Ann Preen's wits must have left her. And Mary's too, to repeat so nonsensical a thing."

Turning to the next page of the letter, Featherston read on.

"'To see her dying by inches before my eyes, and not make any attempt to. save her, is what I cannot reconcile myself to, George. I should have it on my conscience afterwards. I think there is this one chance for her: that you, who have attended her before and must know her constitution, would see her now. You might be able to suggest some remedy or mode of treatment which would restore her. It might even be that the sight of a home face, of her old home doctor, would do for her what the strange doctors here cannot do. No one knows better than you how marvellously in illness the mind influences the body.'"

"True enough," broke off Featherston. "But it seems to me there must be something mysterious about the sickness," He read on again.

"'Stella, who is here, was the first to suggest your seeing her, but it was already exercising my thoughts. Do come, George! the sooner the better. I and Jules will be delighted to have you with us.'"

Featherston slowly folded up the letter. "What do you think of all this, Johnny Ludlow? Curious, is it not?"

"Very. Especially that hint about the house being haunted by the dead-and-gone Miss Preen."

"I have never heard clearly what it was Lavinia Preen died of," observed Featherston, leaving, doctor-like, the supernatural for the practical. "Except that she was seized with some sort of illness one day and died the next."

"But that's no reason why her ghost should walk. Is it?"

"Nancy's imagination," spoke Featherston slightingly. "She was always foolish and fanciful."

"Shall you go to Sainteville, Mr. Featherston?"

He gave his head a slow, dubious shake, but did not speak.

"Don't I wish such a chance were offered to me!"

Featherston sat down on a high stool, which stood before the physic shelves, to revolve the momentous question. And by the time he took over it, he seemed to find it a difficult task.

"One hardly likes to refuse the request, put as Mary writes it," remarked he presently. "Yet I don't see how I can go all the way over there; or how I could leave my patients here. What a temper some of them would be in!"

"They wouldn't die of it. It would be a rare holiday for you. Set you up in health for a year to come."

"I've not had a holiday since that time at Pumpwater," he rejoined dreamily; "when I went over for a day or two to see poor John Whitney. You remember it, Johnny; you were there."

"Ay, I remember it."

"Not that this is a question of a holiday for me or no holiday, and I wonder you should put it so, Johnny Ludlow; it turns upon Ann Preen. Ann Fennel, that's to say. If I thought I *could* do her any good, and those French doctors can't, why, I suppose I ought to make an effort to go."

"To be sure. Make one also to take me with you!"

"I dare say!" laughed Featherston. "What would the Squire say to that?"

"Bluster a bit, and then see it was the very thing for me, and ask what the cost would be. Mr. Featherston, I shall be ready to start when you are. Please let me go!"

Of course I said this half in jest. But it turned out to be earnest. Whether Featherston feared he might get lost if he crossed the sea alone, I can't say; but he said I might put the question to the Squire if I liked, and he would see him later and second it.

Featherston did another thing. He carried Mary Carimon's

letter that evening to Selby Court. Colonel Selby was staying with his brother for a week's shooting. Mr. Selby, a nervous valetudinarian, would not have gone out with a gun if bribed to it, but he invited his friends to do so. They had just finished dinner when Featherston arrived; the two brothers, and a short, dark, younger man with a rather keen but good-natured face and kindly dark eyes. He was introduced as Mr. David Preen, and turned out to be a cousin, more or less removed, of all the Preens and all the Selbys you have ever heard of, dead or living.

Featherston imparted his news to them, and showed his sister's letter. It was pronounced to be a very curious letter, and was read over more than once. Colonel Selby next told them what he knew and what he thought of Edwin Fennel: how he had persistently schemed to get the quarterly money of the two ladies into his own covetous hands, and what a shady sort of individual he was believed to be. Mr. Selby, nervous at the best of times, let alone the worst, became painfully impressed: he seemed to fear poor Nancy was altogether in a hornet's nest, and gave an impulsive opinion that some one of the family ought to go over with Featherston to look into things.

"Lavinia can't have been murdered, can she?" cried he, his thoughts altogether confused; "murdered by that man for her share of the money? Why else should her ghost come back?"

"Don't make us laugh, Paul," said the colonel to his brother. "Ghosts are all moonshine. There are no such things."

"I can tell you that there *are*, William," returned the elder. "Though mercifully the power to see them is accorded to very few mortals on earth. Can you go with Mr. Featherston to look into this strange business, William?"

"No," replied the colonel, "I could not possibly spare the time. Neither should I care to do it. Any inquiry of that kind would be quite out of my line."

"I will go," quietly spoke David Preen.

"Do so, David," said Mr. Selby eagerly. "It shall cost you nothing, you know." By which little speech, Featherston gathered that Mr. David Preen was not more overdone with riches than were many of the other Preens.

"Look into it well, David. See the doctor who attended Lavinia; see all and every one able to throw any light upon her death," urged Mr. Selby. "As to Ann, she was lamentably, foolishly blameable to marry as she did, but she must not be left at the villain's mercy now things have come to this pass."

To which Mr. David Preen nodded an emphatic assent.

The Squire gave in at last. Not to my pleading—he accused me of having lost my head only to think of it—but to Featherston. And when the following week was wearing away, the exigencies of Featherston's patients not releasing him sooner, we started for Sainteville; he, I, and David Preen. Getting in at ten at night after a boisterous passage, Featherston took up his quarters at Monsieur Garimon's, we ours at the Hôtel des Princes.

She looked very ill. Ill and changed. I had seen Ann Preen at Buttermead when she lived there, but the Ann Preen (or Fennel) I saw now was not much like her. The once bright face was drawn and fallen in, and very nearly as long and grey as Featherston's. Apart from that, a timid, shrinking look sat upon it, as though she feared some terror lay very near to her.

The sick have to be studied, especially when suffering from whims and fancies. So they invented a little fable to Mrs. Fennel—that Featherston and David Preen were taking an excursion together for their recreation, and the doctor had extended it as far as Sainteville to see his sister Mary; never allowing her to think that it was to see *her.* I was with them, but I went for nobody—and in truth that's all I was in the matter.

It was the forenoon of the day after we arrived. David Preen had gone in first, her kinsman and distant cousin, to the Petite Maison Rouge, paving the way, as it were, for Featherston. We went in presently. Mrs. Fennel sat in a large armchair by the salon fire, wrapped in a grey shawl; she was always cold now, she told us; David Preen sat on the sofa opposite, talking pleasantly of home news. Featherston joined him on the sofa, and I sat down near the table.

Oh, she was glad to see us! Glad to see us all. Ours were

home faces, you see. She held my hands in hers, and the tears ran down her face, betraying her state of weakness.

"You have not been very well of late, Mary tells me," Featherston said to her in a break of the conversation. "What has been the matter?"

"I—it came on from a bad cold I caught," she answered with some hesitation. "And there was all the trouble about Lavinia's death. I could not get over the grief."

"Well, I must say you don't look very robust," returned Featherston, in a half-joking tone. "I think I had better take you in hand whilst I am here, and set you up."

"I do not think you can set me up; I do not suppose anyone can," she replied, shaking back her curls, which fell on each side of her face in ringlets, as of old.

Featherston smiled cheerily. "I'll try," said he. "Some of my patients say the same when I am first called in to them; but they change their tone after I have brought back their roses. So will you; never fear. I'll come in this afternoon and have a professional chat with you."

That settled, they went on with Buttermead again; David Preen giving scraps and revelations of the Preen and Selby families; Featherston telling choice items of the rural public in general. Mrs. Fennel's spirits went up to animation.

"Shall you be able to do anything for her, sir?" I asked the doctor as we came away and went through the entry to the Place Ronde.

"I cannot tell," he answered gravely. "She has a look on her face that I do not like to see there."

Betrayed into confidence, I suppose, by the presence of the old friend of her girlhood, Ann Fennel related everything to Mr. Featherston that afternoon, as they sat on the sofa side by side, her hand occasionally held soothingly in his own. He assured her plainly that what she was chiefly suffering from was a disorder of the nerves, and that she must state to him explicitly the circumstances which brought it on before he could decide how to treat her for it.

149

Nancy obeyed him. She yearned to get well, though a latent impression lay within her that she should not do so. She told him the particulars of Lavinia's unexpected death just when on the point of leaving Sainteville; and she went on to declare, glancing over her shoulders with frightened eyes, that she (Lavinia) had several times since then appeared in the house.

"What did Lavinia die of?" inquired the doctor at this juncture.

"We could not tell," answered Mrs. Fennel. "It puzzled us. At first Monsieur Dupuis thought it must be inflammation brought on by a chill; but Monsieur Podevin quite put that opinion aside, saying it was nothing of the sort. He is a younger and more energetic practitioner than Monsieur Dupuis."

"Was it never suggested that she might, in one way or another, have taken something which poisoned her?"

"Why, yes, it was; I believe Monsieur Dupuis did think so—I am sure Monsieur Podevin did. But it was impossible it could have been the case, you see, because Lavinia touched nothing either of the days that we did not also partake of."

"There ought to have been an examination after death. You objected to that, I fancy," continued Featherston, who had talked a little with Madame Carimon.

"True—I did; and I have been sorry for it since," sighed Ann Fennel. "It was through what my husband said to me that I objected. Edwin thought it would be distasteful to me. He did not like the idea of it either. Being dead, he held that she should be left in reverence."

Featherston coughed. She was evidently innocent as any lamb of suspicion against *him*.

"And now," went on Mr. Featherston, "just tell me what you mean by saying you see your sister about the house."

"We do see her," said Nancy.

"Nonsense! You don't. It is all fancy. When the nerves are unstrung, as yours are, they play us all sorts of tricks. Why, I knew a man once who took up a notion that he walked upon his head, and he came to me to be cured!"

"But it is seeing Lavinia's apparition, and the constant fear of seeing it which lies upon me, that has brought on this nervousness," pleaded Nancy. "It is to my husband, when he is here, that she chiefly appears; nothing but that is keeping him away. I have seen her only three or four times."

She spoke quietly and simply, evidently grounded in the belief. Mr. Featherston wondered how he was to deal with this: and perhaps he was not himself so much of a sceptic in the supernatural as he thought fit to pretend. Nancy continued:

"It was to my husband she appeared first. Exactly a week after her death. No; a week after the evening she was first taken ill. He was coming upstairs to bed—I had gone on—when he suddenly fancied that someone was following him, though only he and I were in the house. Turning quickly round, he saw Lavinia. That was the first time; and I assure you I thought he would have died of it. Never before had I witnessed such mortal terror in man."

"Did he tell you he had seen her?"

"No; never. I could not imagine what brought on these curious attacks of fright, for he had others. He put it upon his health. It was only when I saw Lavinia myself after he went to England that I knew. I knew then what it must have been."

Mr. Featherston was silent.

"She always appears in the same dress," continued Nancy; "a silver-grey silk that she wore at church that Sunday. It was the last gown she ever put on: we took it off her when she was first seized with the pain. And in her face there is always a sad, beseeching aspect, as if she wanted something and were imploring us to get it for her. *Indeed* we see her, Mr. Featherston."

"Ah, well," he said, perceiving it was not from this quarter that light could be thrown on the suspicious darkness of the past, "let us talk of yourself. You are to obey my orders in all respects, Mistress Nancy. We will soon have you flourishing again."

Brave words. Perhaps the doctor half believed in them himself. But he and they received a check all too soon.

That same evening, after David Preen had left—for he went

in to spend an hour at the little red house to gossip about the folks at home—Nancy was taken with a fit of shivering. Flore hastily mixed her a glass of hot wine-and-water, and then went upstairs to light a fire in the bedroom, thinking her mistress would be the better for it. Nancy, who could hear Flore moving about overhead, suddenly remembered something that she wanted brought down. Rising from her chair, she went to the door of the *salon*, intending to call out. A sort of side light, dim and indistinct, fell upon her as she stood in the recess at the foot of the stairs from the lamp in the salon and from the stove in the kitchen, for both doors were open.

"Flore," she was beginning, "will you bring down my—"

And there Ann Fennel's words ended. With a wild cry, which reached the ears of Flore and nearly startled her into fits, Mrs. Fennel collapsed. The servant came dashing downstairs, expecting to hear that the ghost had appeared again.

It was not that. Her mistress was looking wild and puzzled; and when she recovered herself sufficiently to speak, declared that she had been startled by some animal. Either a cat or a rabbit, she could not tell which, the glimpse she caught of it was so brief and slight; it had run against her legs as she was calling out,

Flore did not know what to make of this. She looked about, but neither cat nor rabbit was to be seen; and she told her mistress it could have been nothing but fancy. Mrs. Fennel thought she knew better.

"Why, I felt it and saw it," she said. "It came right against me and ran over my feet. It seemed to be making for the passage, as if it wanted to get out by the front-door."

★★★★★★

We were gathered together in the *salon* of the Petite Maison Rouge the following morning, partly by accident. Ann Fennel, exceedingly weak and nervous, lay in bed. Featherston and Monsieur Dupuis were both upstairs. She put down her illness to the fright, which she talked of to them freely. They did not assure her it was only "nerves"—to what purpose? I waited in the *salon* with David Preen, and just as the doctors came down Madame Carimon came in.

David Preen seized upon the opportunity. Fearing that one so favourable might not again occur, unless formally planned, he opened the ball. Drawing his chair to the table, next to that of Madame Carimon, the two doctors sitting opposite, David Preen avowed, with straightforward candour, that he, with some other relatives, held a sort of doubt as to whether it might not have been something Miss Lavinia Preen took which caused her death; and he begged Monsieur Dupuis to say if any such doubt had crossed his own mind at the time.

The fair-faced little *médecin* shook his head at this appeal, as much as to say he thought that the subject was a puzzling one. Naturally the doubt had crossed him, and very strongly, he answered; but the difficulty in assuming that view of the matter lay in her having partaken solely of the food which the rest of the household had partaken of; that and nothing else. His *confrère*, Monsieur Podevin, held a very conclusive opinion—that she had died of poison.

David Preen drew towards him a writing-case which lay on the table, took a sheet of paper from it, and a pencil from his pocket. "Let us go over the facts quietly," said he; "it may be we shall arrive at some decision."

So they went over the facts, the chief speakers being. Madame Carimon and Flore, who was called in. David Preen dotted down from time to time something which I suppose particularly impressed him.

Miss Preen was in perfectly good health up to that Sunday— the first after Easter. On the following Tuesday she was about to quit Sainteville for Boulogne, her home at the Petite Maison Rouge having become intolerable to her through the residence in it of Captain Fennel.

"Pardon me if I state here something which is not positively in the line of facts; rather, perhaps, in that of imagination," said Madame Carimon, looking up. "Lavinia had gradually acquired a most painful dread of Captain Fennel. She had dreams which she could only believe came to warn her against him, in which he appeared to be threatening her with some evil that she could not escape from. Once or twice—and this I cannot in any way account for—she saw him in the house when he was not in it, not even at Sainteville—"

"What! saw his apparition?" cried Featherston. "When the man was living! Come, come, Mary, that is going too far!"

"*Quelle drole d'idée!*" exclaimed the little doctor.

"He appeared to her twice, she told me," continued Mary Carimon. "She had been spending the evening out each time; had come into the house, this house, closing the street-door behind her. When she lighted a candle at the slab, she saw him standing just inside the door, gazing at her with the same dreadful aspect that she saw afterwards in her dreams. You may laugh, George; Monsieur Dupuis, I think you are already laughing; but I fully believe that she saw what she said she did, and dreamt what she did dream."

"But it could not have been the man's apparition when he was not dead; and it could not have been the man himself when he was not at Sainteville," contended Featherston.

"And I believe that it all meant one of those mysterious warnings which are vouchsafed us from our spiritual guardians in the unseen world," added Madame Carimon, independently pursuing her argument. "And that it came to Lavinia to warn her to escape from this evil house."

"And she did not do it," remarked David Preen. "She was not quick enough. Well, let us go on."

"As Lavinia came out of church, Charles Palliser ran after her to ask her to go home to dine with him and his aunt," resumed Madame Carimon. "If she had only accepted it! The dinner here was a very simple one, and they all partook of it, including Flore—"

"And it was Flore who cooked and served it?" interrupted David Preen, looking at her.

"*Mais oui, monsieur.* The tart excepted; that was *frangipane*, and did come from the pastrycook," added Flore, plunging into

English. "Then I had my own dinner, and I had of every dish; and I drank of the wine. Miss Lavinia would give me a glass of wine on the Sunday, and she poured it out for me herself that day from the bottle of Bordeaux on their own table. Nothing was the matter with any of all that. The one thing I did not have of was the liqueur."

"What liqueur was that?"

"It was *chartreuse*, I believe," said Flore. "While I was busy removing the dinner articles from the *salon, monsieur* was busy at his cupboard outside there, where he kept his bottles. He came into the kitchen just as I had sat down to eat, and asked me for three liqueur glasses, which I gave to him on a plate. I heard him pour the liqueur into them, and he carried them to the ladies."

Mr. David Preen wrote something down here.

"After that the captain went out to walk, saying he would see the English boat enter; and when I had finished washing up I carried the tea-tray to the *salon*-table and went home. Miss Lavinia was quite well then; she sat in her *belle* robe of grey silk talking with her sister. Then, when I was giving my boy Dion his *collation*, a *tartine* and a cooked apple, I was fetched back here, and found the poor lady fighting with pain for her life."

"Did you wash those liqueur glasses?" asked Mr. Featherston,

"But yes, sir. I had taken them away when I carried in the tea-things, and washed them at once, and put them on the shelf in their places."

"You see," observed Monsieur Dupuis, "the ill-fated lady appears to have taken nothing that the others did not take also. I applied my remedies when I was called to her, and the following day she had, as I believed, recovered from the attack; nothing but the exhaustion left by the agony was remaining. But that night she was again seized, and I was again fetched to her. The attack was even more violent than the first one. I made a request for another doctor, and Monsieur Podevin was brought. He at once set aside my suggestion of inflammation from a chill, and said it looked to him more like a case of poison."

"She had had nothing but slops all day, *messieurs*, which I made and carried to her," put in Flore; "and when I left, at night, she was, as *Monsieur le Medecin* put it, 'all well to look at.'"

"Flore did not make the arrowroot which she took later," said Mary Carimon, taking up the narrative. "When Lavinia went up to bed, towards nine o'clock, Mrs. Fennel made her a cup of arrowroot in the kitchen—"

"And a cup for herself at the same time, as I was informed, *madame*," spoke the little doctor.

"Oh yes, I know that. Monsieur Dupuis. Mrs. Fennel brought her sister's arrowroot, when it was ready, into this room, asking her husband whether she might venture to put a little brandy into it. He sent her to ask the question of Lavinia, bidding her leave the arrowroot on the table here. She came down for it, saying Lavinia declined the brandy, carried it up to her and saw her take it. Mrs, Fennel wished her goodnight and came down for her own portion, which she had left in the kitchen. Before eleven o'clock, when they were going to bed, cries were heard in Lavinia's room; she was seized with the second attack, and—and died in it."

"This second attack was so violent, so unmanageable," said Monsieur Dupuis, as Mary Carimon's voice faltered into silence, "that I feel convinced I could not have saved her had I been present when it came on. I hear that Captain Fennel says he rang several times at my door before he could arouse me. Such was not the case. I am a very light sleeper, waking, from habit, at the slightest sound. But in this case I had not had time to fall asleep when I fancied I heard the bell sound very faintly. I thought I must be mistaken, as the bell is a loud bell, and rings easily; and people who ring me up at night generally ring pretty sharply. I lay listening, and sometime afterwards, not immediately, it did ring. I opened my window, saw Captain Fennel outside, and was dressed and with him in two minutes."

"That sounds as if he did not want you to go to her too quickly, *monsieur*," observed Mr. Featherston, which went, as the French have it, without saying. "And I have heard of another suspicious fact: that he put his wife up to stop the medical examination after death."

"It amounts to this," spoke David Preen, "according to our judgement, if anything wrong was administered to her, it was given in the glass of liqueur on the Sunday afternoon, and in the cup of arrowroot on the Monday evening. They were the only things affording an opportunity of being tampered with; and in each case the pain came on about two hours afterwards."

Grave suspicion, as I am sure they all felt it to be. But not enough, as Featherston remarked, to accuse a man of murder. There was no proof to be brought forward, especially now that months had elapsed.

"What became of the cup which had contained the arrowroot?" inquired David Preen, looking at Flore. "Was it left in the bedroom?"

"That cup, sir, I found in a bowl of water in the kitchen, and also the other one which had been used. The two were together in the wooden bowl. I supposed Madame Fennel had put them there; but she said she had not."

"Ah!" exclaimed David Preen, drawing a deep breath.

He had come over to look into this suspicious matter; but, as it seemed, nothing could be done. To stir in it, and fail, would be worse than letting it alone.

"Look you," said David Preen, as he put up his note-book. "If it be true that Lavinia cannot rest now she's dead, but shows herself here in the house, I regard it as a pretty sure proof that she was sent out of the world unjustly. But——"

"Then you hold the belief that spirits revisit the earth, *monsieur*," interrupted Monsieur Dupuis, "and that revenants are to be seen?"

"I do, sir," replied David. "We Preens see them. But I cannot stir in this matter, I was about to say, and the man must be left to his conscience."

And so the conference broke up.

The thing which lay chiefly on hand now was to try to bring health back to Ann Fennel. It was thought well to take her out of the house for a short time, as she had such fancies about it; so Featherston gave up his room at Madame Carimon's, and Ann was invited to move into it, whilst he joined us at the hotel. I thought her very ill, as we all did. But after her removal there, she recovered her spirits wonderfully, and went out for short walks and laughed and chatted: and when Featherston and David Preen took the boat back to return home, she went to the port to see them steam off.

"Will it be all right with her?" was the last question Mary Carimon whispered to her brother.

"I'm afraid *not*," he answered. "A little time will show one way or the other. Depends somewhat, perhaps, upon how that husband of hers allows things to go on. I have done what I can, Mary; I could not do more."

Does the reader notice that I did not include myself in those who steamed off? For I did not go. Good, genial little Jules Carimon, who was pleased to say he had always liked me much at school, invited me to make a stay at his house, if I did not mind putting up with a small bedroom in the *mansarde*. I did not mind it at all; it was large enough for me. Nancy was delighted. We had quite a gay time of it; and I made the acquaintance of Major and Mrs. Smith, the Misses Bosanquet and Charley Palliser, who was shortly to quit Sainteville. Charley's impression of Mrs. Fennel was that she would quit it before he did, but in a different manner.

One fine afternoon, when we were coming off the pier, Nancy was walking between me and Mary Carimon, for she needed the support of two arms if she went far—yes, she was as weak as that—someone called out that the London boat was coming in. Turning round, we saw her gliding smoothly up the harbour. No one in these Anglo-French towns willingly misses *that* sight, and we drew up on the quay to watch the passengers land. There were only eight or ten of them.

Suddenly Nancy gave a great cry, which bore a sound both of fear and of gladness—"Oh, there's Edwin!"—and the next moment began to shake her pocket-handkerchief frantically.

A thin, grey, weasel of a man, whose face I did not like, came stalking up the ladder. Yes, it was the ex-captain, Edwin Fennel.

"He has not come for her sake; he has come to grab the quarter's money," spoke Mary, quite savagely, in my ear. No doubt. It would be due the end of September, which was at hand.

The captain was elaborately polite; quite effusive in his greeting to us. Nancy left us and took his arm. At the turning where we had to branch off to the Rue Pomme Cuite, she halted to say goodbye.

"But you are coming back to us, are you not?" cried Madame Carimon to her.

"Oh, I could not let Edwin go home alone," said she, "Nobody's there but Flore, you know."

So she went back there and then to the Petite Maison Rouge, and never came out of it again. I think he was kind to her, that man. He had sometimes a scared look upon his face, and I guessed he had been seeing sights. The man would have given his head to be off again; to remain in that haunted house must have been to him a most intolerable penance; but he had some regard (policy dictating it) for public opinion, and could not well run away from his wife in her failing health.

It was curious how quickly Nancy declined. From the very afternoon she entered the house it seemed to begin. He had grabbed the money, as Mary Carimon called it, and brought her nice and nourishing things; but nothing availed. And a fine way he must have been in, to see that; for with his wife's death the money would go away from him for evermore.

Monsieur Dupuis, sometimes Monsieur Henry Dupuis, saw her daily; and Captain Fennel hastily called in another doctor who had the reputation of being the best in the town, next to Monsieur Podevin; one Monsieur Lamirand. Mary Carimon spent half her time there; I went in most days. It could not be said that she had any special complaint, but she was too weak to live.

In less than three weeks it was all over. The end, when it came, was quite sudden. For a day or two she had seemed so much better that we told her she had taken a turn at last. On the Thursday evening, quite late—it was between eight and nine o'clock—Madame Carimon asked me to run there with some jelly which she had made, and which was only then ready. When I arrived, Flore said she was sure her mistress would like me to go up to her room; she was alone, *monsieur* having stepped out.

Nancy, wrapped in a warm dressing-gown, sat by the fire in an easy-chair and a great shawl. Her fair curls were all put back under a small lace cap, which was tied at the chin with grey ribbon; her pretty blue eyes were bright. I told her what I had come for, and took the chair in front of her.

"You look so well this evening, Nancy," I said heartily—for I had learnt to call her so at Madame Carimon's, as they did. "We shall have you getting well now all one way."

"It is the spurt of the candle before going out," she quietly answered. "I have not the least pain left anywhere—but it is only that."

"You should not say or think so."

"But I know it; I cannot mistake my own feelings. Fancy any one, reduced as I am, getting well again!"

I am a bad one to keep up "make-believes." Truth to say, I felt as sure of it as she did.

"And it will not be very long first. Johnny," she went on, in a half-whisper, "I saw Lavinia today." I looked at her, but made no reply. "I have never seen her since I came back here. Edwin has, though; I am sure of it. This afternoon at dusk I woke up out of a doze, for getting up to sit here quite exhausts me, and I was moving forward to touch the hand-bell on the table there, to let Flore know I was ready for my tea, when I saw Lavinia. She was standing over there, just in the firelight. I thought she seemed to be holding out her hand to me, as if inviting me to go to her, and on her face there was the sweetest smile of welcome; sweeter than could be seen on any face in life. All the sad, mournful, beseeching look had left it. She stood there for about a minute, and then vanished."

"Were you very much frightened?"

"I had not a thought of fear, Johnny. It was the contrary. She looked radiantly happy; and it somehow imparted happiness to me. I think—I think," added Nancy impressively, though with some hesitation, "that she came to let me know I am going to her. I believe I have seen her for the last time. The house has, also, I fancy; she and I will shortly go out of it together."

What could I answer to that?

"And so it is over at last," she murmured, more to herself than to me. "Very nearly over. The distress and the doubt, the terror and the pain. *I* brought it all on; you know that, Johnny Ludlow. I feel sure now that she has pardoned me. I humbly hope that God has."

She caught up her breath with a long-drawn sigh.

"And you will give my dear love to all the old friends in England, Johnny, beginning with Mr. Featherston; he has been very kind to me; you will see them again, but I shall not. Not in this life. But we shall be together in the Life which has no ending."

★★★★★★

At twelve o'clock that night Nancy Fennel died. At least, it was as near twelve as could be told. Just after that hour Flore went into the room, preparatory to sitting up with her, and found her dead—just expired, apparently—with a sweet smile on her face, and one hand stretched out as if in greeting. Perhaps Lavinia had come to greet her.

We followed her to the grave on Saturday. Captain Fennel walked next the coffin—and I wondered how he liked it. I was close behind him with Monsieur Carimon. Charley Palliser came next with little *Monsieur le Docteur* Dupuis and Monsieur Gustave Sauvage. And we left Nancy in the cemetery, side by side with her sister.

Captain Edwin Fennel disappeared. On the Sunday, when we English were looking for him in church, he did not come—his grief not allowing him, said some of the ladies. But an English clerk in the broker's office, hearing this, told another tale. Fennel had gone off by the boat which left the port for London the previous night at midnight.

And he did not come back again. He had left sundry debts behind him, including that owing to Madame Veuve Sauvage. Monsieur Carimon, later, undertook the payment of these at the request of Colonel Selby. It was understood that Captain Edwin Fennel had emigrated to South America. If he had any conscience at all, it was to be hoped he carried it with him. He did not carry the money. The poor little income which he had schemed for, and perhaps worse, went back to the Selby's.

And that is the story. It is a curious history, and painful in more ways than one. But I repeat that it is true.

A Curious Experience

What I am about to tell of took place during the last year of John Whitney's life, now many years ago. We could never account for it, or understand it: but it occurred (at least, so far as our experience of it went) just as I relate it.

It was not the custom for schools to give a long holiday at Easter then: one week at most. Dr. Frost allowed us from the Thursday in Passion week, to the following Thursday; and many of the boys spent it at school.

Easter was late that year, and the weather lovely. On the Wednesday in Easter week, the squire and Mrs. Todhetley drove over to spend the day at Whitney Hall, Tod and I being with them. Sir John and Lady Whitney were beginning to be anxious about John's health—their eldest son. He had been ailing since the previous Christmas, and he seemed to get thinner and weaker. It was so perceptible when he got home from school this Easter, that Sir John put himself into a flurry (he was just like the squire in that and in many another way), and sent an express to Worcester for Henry Garden, asking him to bring Dr. Hastings with him.

They came. John wanted care, they said, and they could not discover any specific disease at present. As to his returning to school, they both thought that question might be left with the boy himself. John told them he should prefer to go back, and laughed a little at this fuss being made over him: he should soon be all right, he said; people were apt to lose strength more or less in the spring. He was sixteen then, a slender, upright boy, with a delicate, thoughtful face, dreamy, grey-blue eyes and brown hair, and he was ever gentle, sweet-tempered, and considerate. Sir John related to the squire what the doctors had said, avowing that he could not "make much out of it."

In the afternoon, when we were out of doors on the lawn in the hot sunshine, listening to the birds singing and the cuckoo calling, Featherston came in, the local doctor, who saw John nearly every day. He was a tall, grey, hard-worked man, with a face of care. After talking a few moments with John and his mother, he turned to the rest of us on the grass. The squire and Sir John were sitting on a garden bench, some wine and lemonade on a little table between them. Featherston shook hands.

"Will you take some?" asked Sir John.

"I don't mind a glass of lemonade with a dash of sherry in it," answered Featherston, lifting his hat to rub his brow. "I have been walking beyond Goose Brook and back, and upon my word it is as hot as midsummer."

"Ay, 'tis," assented Sir John. "Help yourself, doctor." He filled a tumbler with what he wanted, brought it over to the opposite bench, and sat down by Mrs. Todhetley. John and his mother were at the other end of it; I sat on the arm. The rest of them, with Helen and Anna, had gone strolling away; to the North Pole, for all we knew.

"John still says he shall go back to school," began Lady Whitney, to Featherston.

"Ay; tomorrow's the day, isn't it, John? Black Thursday, some of you boys call it."

"I like school," said John.

"Almost a pity, though," continued Featherston, looking up and about him. "To be out at will all day in this soft air, under the blue skies and the healing sunbeams, might be of more benefit to you, Master John, than being cooped up in a close schoolroom."

"You hear, John!" cried Lady Whitney. "I wish you would persuade him to take a longer rest at home, Mr. Featherston!"

Mr. Featherston stooped for his tumbler, which he had lodged on the smooth grass, and took another drink at it before replying. "If you and John would follow my advice. Lady Whitney, I'd give it"

"Yes?" cried she, all eagerness.

"Take John somewhere for a fortnight, and let him go back to school at the end," said the surgeon. "That would do him good."

"Why of course it would," called out Sir John, who had been listening. "And I say it shall be done. John, my boy, you and your mother shall go to the seaside—to Aberystwith."

"Well, I don't think I should quite say that. Sir John," said Featherston again. "The seaside would be all very well in this warm weather; but it may not last, it may change to cold and frost. I should suggest one of the inland watering places, as they are called: where there's a Spa, and a Pump Room, and a Parade, and lots of gay company. It would be lively for him, and a thorough change."

"What a nice idea! "cried Lady Whitney, who was the most unsophisticated woman in the world. "Such as Pumpwater."

"Such as Pumpwater: the very place," agreed Featherston. "Well, were I you, my lady, I would try it for a couple of weeks. Let John take a companion with him; one of his schoolfellows. Here's Johnny Ludlow: he might do."

"I'd rather have Johnny Ludlow than anybody," said John.

Remarking that his time was up, for a patient waited for him, and that he must leave us to settle the question, Featherston took his departure. But it appeared to be settled already.

"Johnny can go," spoke up the squire. "The loss of a fortnight's lessons is not much, compared with doing a little service to a friend. Charming spots are those inland watering-places, and Pumpwater is about the best of them all."

"We must get lodgings," said Lady Whitney presently, when they had done expatiating upon the gauds and glories of Pumpwater. "To stay at an hotel would be so noisy; and expensive besides."

"I know of some," cried Mrs. Todhetley, in sudden thought.

"If you could get into Miss Gay's rooms, you would be well off. Do you remember them?"—turning to the squire. "We stayed at her house on our way from "

"Why, bless me, to be sure I do," he interrupted. "Somebody had given us Miss Gay's address, and we drove straight to it to see if she had rooms at liberty; she had, and took us in at once. We were so comfortable there that we stayed at Pumpwater three days instead of two."

It was hastily decided that Mrs. Todhetley should write to Miss Gay, and she went indoors to do so. All being well, Lady Whitney meant to start on Saturday.

Miss Gay's answer came punctually, reaching Whitney Hall on Friday morning. It was addressed to Mrs. Todhetley, but Lady Whitney, as had been arranged, opened it. Miss Gay wrote that she should be much pleased to receive Lady Whitney. Her house, as it chanced, was then quite empty; a family, who had been with her six weeks, had just left: so Lady Whitney might take her choice of the rooms, which she would keep vacant until Saturday. In conclusion, she begged Mrs. Todhetley to notice that her address was changed. The old house was too small to accommodate the many kind friends who patronised her, and she had moved into a larger house, superior to the other and in the best position.

Thus all things seemed to move smoothly for our expedition; and we departed by train on the Saturday morning for Pumpwater.

★★★★★★

It was a handsome house, standing in the high road, between the parade and the principal street, and rather different from the houses on each side it, inasmuch as that it was detached and had a narrow slip of gravelled ground in front. In fact, it looked too large and handsome for a lodging-house; and Lady Whitney, regarding it from the fly which had brought us from the station, wondered whether the driver had made a mistake. It was built of red-brick, with ornamental white stone facings; the door, set in a pillared portico, stood in the middle, and three rooms, each with a bay window, lay one above another on both sides.

But in a moment we saw it was all right. A slight, fair woman, in a slate silk gown, came running out and announced herself as Miss Gay. She had a mild, pleasant voice, and a mild, pleasant face, with light falling curls, the fashion then for everybody, and she wore a lace cap, trimmed with pink. I took to her and to her face at once.

"I am glad to be here," said Lady Whitney, cordially, in answer to Miss Gay's welcome. "Is there anyone who can help with the luggage? We have not brought either man or maid-servant."

"Oh dear yes, my lady. Please let me show you indoors, and then leave all to me. Susannah!—Oh, here you are, Susannah! Where's Charity?—my cousin and chief help-mate, my lady."

A tall, dark person, about Miss Gay's own age, which might be forty, wearing brown ribbon in her hair and a purple bow at her throat, dropped a curtsey to Lady Whitney. This was Susannah. She looked strong-minded and capable. Charity, who came running up the kitchen stairs, was a smiling young woman-servant, with a coarse apron tied round her, and red arms bared to the elbow.

There were four sitting-rooms on the ground floor: two in front, with their large bay windows; two at the back, looking out upon some bright, semi-public gardens.

"A delightful house!" exclaimed Lady Whitney to Miss Gay, after she had looked about a little. "I will take one of these front rooms for our sitting-room," she added, entering, haphazard, the one on the right of the entrance-hall, and putting down her bag and parasol. "This one, I think. Miss Gay."

"Very good, my lady. And will you now be pleased to walk upstairs and fix upon the bedrooms."

Lady Whitney seemed to fancy the front of the house. "This room shall be my son's; and I should like to have the opposite one for myself," she said, rather hesitatingly, knowing they must be the two best chambers of all. "Can I, Miss Gay?"

Miss Gay seemed quite willing. We were in the room over our sitting-room on the right of the house looking to the front.

The objection, if it could be called one, came from Susannah.

"You can have the other room, certainly, my lady; but I think the young gentleman would find this one noisy, with all the carriages and carts that pass by, night and morning. The back rooms are much more quiet."

"But I like noise," put in John; "it seems like company to me. If I could do as I would, I'd never sleep in the country."

"One of the back rooms is very lively, sir; it has a view of the turning to the Pump Room," persisted Susannah, a kind of suppressed eagerness in her tone; and it struck me that she did not want John to have this front chamber. "I think you would like it best."

"No," said John, turning round from the window, out of which he had been looking, "I will have this. I shall like to watch the shops down that turning opposite, and the people who go into them."

No more was said. John took this chamber, which was over our sitting-room. Lady Whitney had the other front chamber, and I had a very good one at the back of John's. And thus we settled down.

Pumpwater is a nice place, as you would know if I gave its proper name, bright and gay, and our house was in the best of situations. The principal street, with its handsome shops, lay to our right; the Parade, leading to the Spa and Pump Room, to our left, and company and carriages were continually passing by. We visited some of the shops and took a look at the Pump Room.

In the evening, when tea was over, Miss Gay came in to speak of the breakfast. Lady Whitney asked her to sit down for a little chat. She wanted to ask about the churches.

"What a very nice house this is!" again observed Lady Whitney presently: for the more she saw of it, the better she found it. "You must pay a high rent for it. Miss Gay."

"Not so high as your ladyship might think," was the answer; "not high at all for what it is. I paid sixty pounds for the little house I used to be in, and I pay only seventy for this."

"Only seventy!" echoed Lady Whitney, in surprise. "How is it you get it so cheaply?"

A waggonette, full of people, was passing just then; Miss Gay seemed to want to watch it by before she answered. We were sitting in the dusk with the blinds up.

"For one thing, it had been standing empty for some time, and I suppose Mr. Bone, the agent, was glad to have my offer," replied Miss Gay, who seemed to be as fond of talking as anybody else is, once set on. "It had belonged to a good old family, my lady, but they got embarrassed and put it up for sale some six or seven years ago. A Mr. Calson bought it. He had come to Pumpwater about that time from foreign lands; and he and his wife settled down in the house. A puny, weakly little woman she was, who seemed to get weaklier instead of stronger, and in a year or two she died. After her death her husband got ill; he went away for change of air, and died in London; and the house was left to a little nephew living over in Australia."

"And has the house been vacant ever since?" asked John.

"No, sir. At first it was let furnished, then unfurnished. But it had been vacant some little time when I applied to Mr. Bone. I conclude he thought it better to let it at a low rent than for it to stand empty."

"It must cost you incessant care and trouble, Miss Gay, to conduct a house like this—when you are full," remarked Lady Whitney.

"It does," she answered. "One's work seems never done—and I cannot, at that, give satisfaction to all. Ah, my lady, what a difference there is in people!—you would never think it. Some are so kind and considerate to me, so anxious not to give trouble unduly, and so satisfied with all I do that it is a pleasure to serve them: while others make gratuitous work and trouble from morning till night, and treat me as if I were just a dog under their feet. Of course when we are full I have another servant in, two sometimes."

"Even that must leave a great deal for yourself to do and see to."

"The back is always fitted to the burden," sighed Miss Gay. "My father was a farmer in this county, as his ancestors had been before him, farming his three hundred acres of land, and looked upon as a man of substance. My mother made the butter, saw to the poultry, and superintended generally her household: and we children helped her. Farmers' daughters then did not spend their days in playing the piano and doing fancy work, or expect to be waited upon like ladies born."

"They do now, though," said Lady Whitney.

"So I was ready to turn my hand to anything when hard times came—not that I had thought I should have to do it," continued Miss Gay. "But my father's means dwindled down. Prosperity gave way to adversity. Crops failed; the stock died off; two of my brothers fell into trouble and it cost a mint of money to extricate them. Altogether, when father died, but little of his savings remained to us. Mother took a house in the town here, to let lodgings, and I came with her. She is dead, my lady, and I am left."

The silent tears were running down poor Miss Gay's cheeks.

"It is a life of struggle, I am sure," spoke Lady Whitney, gently. "And not deserved. Miss Gay."

"But there's another life to come," spoke John, in a half whisper, turning to Miss Gay from his favourite ground, the large bay-window. "None of us will be overworked *there*."

Miss Gay stealthily wiped her cheeks. "I do not repine," she said, humbly. "I have been enabled to rub on and keep my head above water, and to provide little comforts for mother in her need; and I gratefully thank God for it."

★★★★★★

The bells of the churches, ringing out at eight o'clock, called us up in the morning. Lady Whitney was downstairs first, I next. Susannah, who waited upon us, had brought up the breakfast. John followed me in.

"I hope you have slept well, my boy," said Lady Whitney, kissing him. "I have."

"So have I," I put in.

"Then you and the mother make up for me, Johnny," he said; "for I have not slept at all."

"Oh John!" exclaimed his mother.

"Not a wink all night long," added John. "I can't think what was the matter with me."

Susannah, then stooping to get the sugarbasin out of the sideboard, rose, turned sharply round and fixed her eyes on John. So curious an expression was on her face that I could but notice it.

"Do you not think it was the noise, sir?" she said to him. "I knew that room would be too noisy for you."

"Why the room was as quiet as could be," he answered. "A few carriages rolled by last night—and I liked to hear them; but that was all over before midnight; and I have heard none this morning."

"Well, sir, I'm sure you would be more comfortable in a back room," contended Susannah.

"It was a strange bed," said John. "I shall sleep all the sounder tonight."

Breakfast was half over when John found he had left his watch upstairs, on the chest of drawers. I went to fetch it.

The chamber door was open, and I stepped to the drawers, which stood just inside. Miss Gay and Susannah were making the bed and talking, too busy to see or hear me. A lot of things lay on the white cloth, and at first I could not see the watch.

"He declares he has not slept at all; *not at all*," Susannah was saying with emphasis. "If you had only seconded me yesterday, Harriet, they need not have had this room. But you never made a word of objection; you gave in at once."

"Well, I saw no cause to make it," said Miss Gay, mildly. "If I were to give in to your fancies, Susannah, I might as well shut up the room. Visitors must get used to it."

The watch had been partly hidden under one of John's neckties. I caught it up and decamped.

We went to church after breakfast. The first hymn sung was that nice one beginning, "Brief life."

Brief life is here our portion;
Brief sorrow, short-lived care;
The life that knows no ending,
The tearless life is there.

As the verses went on, John touched my elbow: "Miss Gay," he whispered; his eyelashes moist with the melody of the music. I have often thought since that we might have seen by these very moods of John—his thoughts bent upon Heaven more than upon earth—that his life was swiftly passing.

There's not much to tell of that Sunday. We dined in the middle of the day; John fell asleep after dinner; and in the evening we attended church again. And I think everybody was ready for bed when bedtime came. I know I was.

Therefore it was all the more surprising when, the next morning, John said he had again not slept.

"What, not at all!" exclaimed his mother.

"No, not at all. As I went to bed, so I got up—sleepless."

"I never heard of such a thing!" cried Lady Whitney. "Perhaps, John, you were too tired to sleep?"

"Something of that," he answered. "I felt both tired and sleepy when I got into bed; particularly so. But I got no sleep: not a wink. I could not lie still, either; I was frightfully restless all night; just as I was the night before. I suppose it can't be the bed?"

"Is the bed not comfortable?" asked his mother.

"It seems as comfortable a bed as can be when I first lie down in, and then I get restless and uneasy."

"It must be the restlessness of extreme fatigue," said Lady Whitney. "I fear the journey was rather too much for you, my dear."

"Oh I shall be all right as soon as I can sleep, mamma."

We had a surprise that morning. John and I were standing before a tart shop, our eyes glued to the window, when a voice behind us called out, "Don't they look nice, boys!" Turning round, there stood Henry Carden of Worcester, arm-in-arm with a little white-haired gentleman. Lady Whitney, in at the fishmonger's next door, came out while he was shaking hands with us.

"Dear me!—is it you" she cried to Mr. Carden.

"Ay," said he in his pleasant manner, "here am I at Pumpwater I come all this way to spend a couple of days with my old friend: Dr. Tambourine," added the surgeon, introducing him to Lady Whitney. Anyway, that was the name she understood him to say. John thought he said Tamarind, and I Carrafin. The street was noisy.

The doctor seemed to be chatty and courteous, a gentleman of the old school. He said his wife should do herself the honour of calling upon Lady Whitney if agreeable; Lady Whitney replied that it would be. He and Mr. Carden, who would be starting for Worcester by train that afternoon, walked with us up the Parade to the Pump Room, How a chance meeting like this in a strange place makes one feel at home in it!

The name turned out to be Parafin. Mrs. Parafin called early in the afternoon, on her way to some entertainment at the Pump Room: a chatty, pleasant woman, younger than her husband. He had retired from practice, and they lived in a white villa outside the town.

And what with looking at the shops, and parading up and down the public walks, and the entertainment at the Pump Room, to which we went with Mrs. Parafin, and all the rest of it, we felt uncommonly sleepy when night came, and were beginning to regard Pumpwater as a sort of Eden.

★★★★★★

"Johnny, have you slept?"

I was brushing my hair at the glass, under the morning sun, when John Whitney, half-dressed, and pale and languid, opened my door and thus accosted me.

"Yes; like a top. Why? Is anything the matter, John?"

"See here," said he, sinking into the easy-chair by the fireplace, "it is an odd thing, but I have again not slept. I *can't* sleep."

I put my back against the dressing-table and stood looking down at him, brush in hand. Not slept again! It *was* an odd thing.

"But what can be the cause, John?"

"I am beginning to think it must be the room."

"How can it be the room?"

"I don't know. There's nothing the matter with the room that I can see; it seems well-ventilated; the chimney's not stopped-up. Yet this is the third night that I cannot get to sleep in it."

"But *why* can you not get to sleep," I persisted

"I say I don't know why. Each night I have been as sleepy as possible; last night I could hardly undress I was so sleepy; but no sooner am I in bed than sleep goes right away from me. Not only that: I get terribly restless."

Weighing the problem this way and that, an idea struck me.

"John, do you think it is nervousness?"

"How can it be? I never was nervous in my life."

"I mean this: Not sleeping the first night, you may have got nervous about it the second and third."

He shook his head. "I have been nothing of the kind, Johnny. But look here: I hardly see what I am to do. I cannot go on like this without sleep; yet, if I tell the mother again, she'll say the air of the place does not suit me and run away from it—"

"Suppose we change rooms tonight, John?" I interrupted. "I can't think but you would sleep here. If you do not, why it must be the air of Pumpwater, and the sooner you are out of it the better."

"You'd not mind changing rooms for one night?" he said, wistfully.

"Mind! Why I shall be the gainer. Yours is the best room of the two."

At that it was settled; nothing to be said to anybody about the bargain. We did not want to be kidnapped out of Pumpwater— and Lady Whitney had promised us a night at the theatre.

Two or three more acquaintances were made, or found out, that day. Old Lady Scott heard of us, and came to call on Lady Whitney; they used to be intimate. She introduced some people at the Pump Room. Altogether, it seemed that we should not lack society.

Night came; and John and I went upstairs together. He undressed in his own room, and I in mine; and then we made the exchange. I saw him into my bed and wished him a goodnight.

"Goodnight, Johnny," he answered. "I hope you will sleep."

"Little doubt of that, John. I always sleep when I have nothing to trouble me. A very goodnight to *you*."

I had nothing to trouble me, and I was as sleepy as could be; and yet, I did not and could not sleep. I lay quiet as usual after getting into bed, yielding to the expected sleep, and I shut my eyes and never thought but it was coming.

Instead of that, came restlessness. A strange restlessness quite foreign to me, persistent and unaccountable. I tossed and turned from side to side, and I had not had a wink of sleep at morning light, nor any symptom of it. Was I getting nervous? Had I let the feeling creep over me that I had suggested to John? No; not that I was aware of. What could it be?

Unrefreshed and weary, I got up at the usual hour, and stole silently into the other room. John was in a deep sleep, his calm face lying still upon the pillow. Though I made no noise, my presence awoke him.

"Oh Johnny!" he exclaimed, "I have had *such* a night."

"Bad?"

"No; *good*. I went to sleep at once and never woke till now. It has done me a world of good. And you?"

"I? Oh well, I don't think I slept quite as well as I did here; it was a strange bed," I answered, carelessly.

The next night the same plan was carried out, he taking my bed; I his. And again John slept through it, while I *did not sleep at all*. I said nothing about it: John Whitney's comfort was of more importance than mine.

The third night came. This night we had been to the theatre, and had laughed ourselves hoarse, and been altogether delighted. No sooner was I in bed, and feeling dead asleep, than the door slowly opened and in came Lady Whitney, a candle in one hand, a wine-glass in the other.

"John, my dear," she began, "your tonic was forgotten this evening. I think you had better take it now. Featherston said, you know—Good gracious!" she broke off. "Why, it is Johnny!"

I could hardly speak for laughing, her face presented such a picture of astonishment. Sitting up in bed, I told her all; there was no help for it: that we had exchanged beds, John not having been able to sleep in this one.

"And do you sleep well in it?" she asked.

"No, not yet. But I feel very sleepy tonight, dear Lady Whitney."

"Well, you are a good lad, Johnny, to do this for him; and to say nothing about it," she concluded, as she went away with the candle and the tonic.

Dead asleep though I was, I could not get to sleep. It would be simply useless to try to describe my sensations. Each succeeding night they had been more marked. A strange, discomforting restlessness pervaded me; a feeling of uneasiness, I could not tell why or wherefore. I saw nothing uncanny, I heard nothing; nevertheless, I felt just as though some uncanny presence was in the room, imparting a sense of semi-terror. Once or twice, when I nearly dozed off from sheer weariness, I started up in real terror, wide awake again, my hair and face damp with a nameless fright.

I told this at breakfast, in answer to Lady Whitney's questions: John confessed that precisely the same sensations had attacked him the three nights he lay in the bed. Lady Whitney declared she never heard the like; and she kept looking at us alternately, as if doubting what could be the matter with us, or whether we had taken scarlet fever.

On this morning, Friday, a letter came from Sir John, saying that Featherston was coming to Pumpwater. Anxious on the score of his son, he was sending Featherston to see him, and take back a report, "I think he would stay a couple of days if you made it convenient to entertain him, and it would be a little holiday for the poor hardworked man," wrote Sir John, who was just as kind-hearted as his wife.

"To be sure I will," said Lady Whitney. "He shall have that room; I dare say he won't say he cannot sleep in it: it will be more comfortable for him than getting a bed at an hotel. Susannah shall put a small bed into the back room for Johnny. And when Featherston is gone, I will take the room myself. I am not like you two silly boys—afraid of lying awake."

Mr. Featherston arrived late that evening, with his grey face of care and his thin frame. He said he could hardly recall the time when he had had as much as two days' holiday, and thanked Lady Whitney for receiving him. That night John and I occupied the back room, having conducted Featherston in state to the front, with two candles; and both of us slept excellently well.

At breakfast Featherston began talking about the air. He had always believed Pumpwater to have a rather soporific air, but supposed he must be mistaken. Anyway, it had kept him awake; and it was not a little that did that for him.

"Did you not sleep well?" asked Lady Whitney.

"I did not sleep at all; did not get a wink of it all night long. Never mind, my lady," he added with a good-natured laugh, "I shall sleep all the sounder tonight."

But he did not. The next morning (Sunday) he looked grave and tired, and eat his breakfast almost in silence. When we had finished, he said he should like, with Lady Whitney's permission, to speak to the landlady. Miss Gay came in at once: in a light fresh print gown and black silk apron.

"Ma'am," began Featherston, politely, "something is wrong with that bedroom overhead. What is it?"

"Something wrong, sir?" repeated Miss Gay, her meek face flushing, "Wrong in what way, sir? "

"I don't know," answered Featherston; "I thought perhaps you could tell me: anyway, it ought to be seen to. It is something that scares away sleep. I give you my word, ma'am, I never had two such restless nights in succession in all my life. Two such *strange* nights. It was not only that sleep would not come near me; that's nothing uncommon you may say; but I lay in a state of uneasy, indescribable restlessness. I have examined the room

177

again this morning, and I can see no cause to induce it, yet a cause there must undoubtedly be. The paper is not made of arsenic, I suppose?"

"The paper is pale pink, sir," observed Miss Gay. "I fancy it is the green papers that have arsenic in them."

"Ay; well. I think there must be poison behind the paper; in the paste, say," went on Featherston. "Or perhaps another paper underneath has arsenic in it?"

Miss Gay shook her head, as she stood with her hand on the back of a chair. Lady Whitney had invited her to sit, but she declined.

"When I came into the house six months ago, that room was repapered, and I saw that the walls were thoroughly scraped. If you think there's anything—anything in the room that prevents people sleeping, and—and could point out what it is, I'm sure, sir, I should be glad to remedy it," said Miss Gay, with uncomfortable hesitation.

But this was just what Featherston, for all he was a doctor, could not point out. That something was amiss with the room, he felt convinced, but he had not discovered what it was, or how it could be remedied.

"After lying in torment half the night, I got up and lighted my candle," said he. "I examined the room and opened the window to let the cool breeze blow in. I could find nothing likely to keep me awake, no stuffed-up chimney, no accumulation of dust; and I shut the window and got into bed again. I was pretty cool by that time and reckoned I should sleep. Not a bit of it, ma'am. I lay more restless than ever, with the same unaccountable feeling of discomfort and depression upon me. Just as I had felt the night before."

"I am very sorry, sir," sighed Miss Gay, taking her hand from the chair to depart. "If the room is close, or anything of that—"

"But it is not close, ma'am. I don't know what it is. And I'm sure I hope you will be able to find out, and get it remedied," concluded Featherston as she withdrew.

We then told him of our experience: John's and mine. It

amazed him. "What an extraordinary thing!" he exclaimed. "One would think the room was haunted."

"Do you believe in haunted rooms, sir?" asked John.

"Well, I suppose such things are," he answered. "Folks say so. If haunted houses exist, why not haunted rooms?"

"It must lie in the Pumpwater air," said Lady Whitney, who was too practical to give in to haunted regions; "and I am very sorry you should have had your two nights' rest spoilt by it, Mr. Featherston. I will take the room myself: nothing keeps me awake."

"Did you ever see a ghost, sir?" asked John.

"No, never. But I know those who have seen them; and I cannot disbelieve what they say. One such story in particular is often in my mind; it was a very strange one."

"Won't you tell it us, Mr. Featherston?."

The doctor only laughed in answer. But after we came out of church, when he was sitting with me and John on the Parade, he told it. And I only wish I had space to relate it here.

He left Pumpwater in the afternoon, and Lady Whitney had the room prepared for her use at once, John moving into hers. So that I had mine to myself again, and the little bed was taken out of it.

The next day was Monday. When Lady Whitney came down in the morning the first thing she told us was, that she had not slept. All the curious symptoms of restless disturbance, of inward agitation, which we had experienced, had visited her.

"I will not give in, my dears," she said, bravely. "It may be, you know, that what I had heard against the room took all sleep out of me, though I was not conscious of it; so I shall keep to it. I must say it is a most comfortable bed."

She "kept" to the room until the Wednesday; three nights in all; getting no sleep. Then she gave in. Occasionally during the third night, when she was dropping asleep from exhaustion, she was startled up from it in sudden terror: terror of she knew not what. Just as it had been with me and with John. On the Wednesday morning she told Susannah that they must give her the back room opposite mine, and we would abandon that front room altogether.

"It is just as though there were a ghost in the room," she said to Susannah.

"Perhaps there is, my lady," was Susannah's cool reply.

★★★★★★

On the Friday evening Dr. and Mrs. Parafin came in to tea. Our visit would end on the morrow. The old doctor held John before him in the lamplight, and decided that he looked better—that the stay had done him good.

"I am sure it has," assented Lady Whitney. "Just at first I feared he was going backward: but that must have been owing to the sleepless nights."

"Sleepless nights!" echoed the doctor, in a curious tone.

"For the first three nights of our stay here, he never slept; *never slept at all.* After that—"

"Which room did he occupy?" interrupted the doctor, breathlessly. "Not the one over this?"

"Yes, it was. Why? Do you know anything against it?" questioned Lady Whitney, for she saw Dr. and Mrs. Parafin exchange glances.

"Only this; that I have heard of other people who were unable to sleep in that room," he answered.

"But what can be amiss with the room. Dr. Parafin?"

"Ah," said he, "there you go beyond me. It is, I believe, a fact, a singular fact, that there is something or other in the room which prevents people sleeping. Friends of ours who lived in the house before Miss Gay took it, ended by shutting the room up."

"Is it haunted, sir?" I asked. "Mr. Featherston thought it might be."

He looked at me and smiled, shaking his head. Mrs. Parafin nodded hers, as much as to say *It is.*

"Nobody has been able to get any sleep in that room since the Calsons lived here," said Mrs. Parafin, dropping her voice.

"How very strange!" cried Lady Whitney. "One might think murder had been done in it."

Mrs. Parafin coughed significantly. "The wife died in it," she said. "Some people thought her husband had—had—had at least hastened her death—"

"Hush, Matty!" interposed the doctor, warningly. "It was all rumour; all talk. Nothing was proved—or attempted to be."

"Perhaps there existed no proof," returned Mrs. Parafin. "And if there had—who was there to take it up? She was in her grave, poor woman, and he was left flourishing, master of himself and everybody about him. Anyway, Thomas, be that as it may, you cannot deny that the room has been like a haunted room since."

Dr. Parafin laughed lightly, objecting to be serious; men are more cautious than women. "I cannot deny that people find themselves unable to sleep in the room; I never heard that it was 'haunted' in any other way," he added, to Lady Whitney. "But there—let us change the subject; we can neither alter the fact nor understand it."

After they left us. Lady Whitney said she should like to ask Miss Gay what her experience of the room had been. But Miss Gay had stepped out to a neighbour's, and Susannah stayed to talk in her place. She could tell us more about it, she said, than Miss Gay.

"I warned my cousin she would do well not to take this house," began Susannah, accepting the chair to which Lady Whitney pointed. "But it is a beautiful house for letting, as you see, my lady, and that and the low rent tempted her. Besides, she did not believe the rumour about the room; she does not believe it fully yet, though it is beginning to worry her: she thinks the inability to sleep must lie in the people themselves."

"It has been an uncanny room since old Calson's wife died in it, has it not, Susannah?" said John, as if in jest. "I suppose he did not murder her?"

"*I think he did*," whispered Susannah.

The answer sounded so ghostly that it struck us all into silence.

Susannah resumed. "Nobody *knew*: but one or two suspected.

The wife was a poor, timid, gentle creature, worshipping the very ground her husband trod on, yet always in awe of him. She lay in the room, sick, for many many months before she died. Old Sarah—"

"What was her sickness?" interrupted Lady Whitney.

"My lady, that is more than I can tell you; more, I fancy, than anybody could have told. Old Sarah would often say to me that she did not believe there was any great sickness, only he made it out there was, and persuaded his wife so. He could just wind her round his little finger. The person who attended on her was one Astrea, quite a heathenish name I used to think, and a heathenish woman too: she was copper-coloured, and came with them from abroad. Sarah was in the kitchen, and there was only a man besides.

"I lived housekeeper at that time with an old lady on the Parade, and I looked in here from time to time to ask after the mistress. Once I was invited by Mr. Calson upstairs to see her: she lay in the room over this; the one that nobody can now sleep in. She looked so pitiful!—her poor, pale, patient face down deep in the pillow. Was she better, I asked; and what was it that ailed her. She thought it was not much beside weakness, she answered, and that she felt a constant nausea; and she was waiting for the warm weather: her dear husband assured her she would be better when that came."

"Was he kind to her, Susannah?"

"He seemed to be, Master Johnny, very kind and attentive indeed. He would sit by the hour together in her room, and give her her medicine, and feed her when she grew too weak to feed herself, and sit up at night with her. A doctor came to see her occasionally; it was said he could not find much the matter with her but debility, and that she seemed to be wasting away. Well, she died, my lady; died quietly in that room; and Calson ordered a grand funeral"

"So did Jonas Chuzzlewit," breathed John.

"Whispers got afloat when she was under ground—not before—that there had been something wrong about her death;

that she had not come by it fairly, or by the illness either," continued Susannah. "But they were not spoken openly; under the rose, as may be said; and they died away. Mr. Calson continued to live in the house as before; but he became soon ill. Real sickness, his was, my lady, whatever his wife's might have been.

"His illness was chiefly on the nerves; he grew frightfully thin; and the setting-in of some grave inward complaint was suspected: so if he did act in any ill manner to his wife it seemed he would not reap long benefit from it. All the medical men in Pumpwater were called to him in succession; but they could not cure him. He kept growing thinner and thinner till he was like a walking shadow. At last he shut up his house and went to London for advice; and there he died, fourteen months after the death of his wife."

"How long was the house kept shut up?" asked Lady Whitney, as Susannah paused.

"About two years, my lady. All his property was willed away to the little son of his brother, who lived over in Australia. Tardy instructions came from thence to Mr. Jermy the lawyer to let the house furnished, and Mr. Jermy put it into the hands of Bone the house-agent. A family took it, but they did not stay: then another family took it, and they did not stay. Each party went to Bone and told him that something was the matter with one of the rooms and nobody could sleep in it. After that, the furniture was sold off, and some people took the house by the year. They did not remain in it six months.

"Some other people took it then, and they stayed the year, but it was known that they shut up that room. Then the house stayed empty. My cousin, wanting a better house than the one she was in, cast many a longing eye towards it; finding it did not let, she went to Bone and asked him what the rent would be. Seventy pounds to her, he said; and she took it. Of course she had heard about the room, but she did not believe it; she thought, as Mr. Feathetston said the other morning, that something must be wrong with the paper, and she had the walls scraped and cleaned and a fresh paper put on."

"And since then—have your lodgers found aught amiss with the room?" questioned Lady Whitney.

"I am bound to say they have, my lady. It has been the same story with them all—not able to get to sleep in it. One gentleman, an old post-captain, after trying it a few nights, went right away from Pumpwater, swearing at the air. But the most singular experience we have had was that of two little girls. They were kept in that room for two nights, and each night they cried and screamed all night long, calling out that they were frightened. Their mother could not account for it; they were not at all timid children, she said, and such a thing had never happened with them before. Altogether, taking one thing with another, I fear, my lady, that something *is* wrong with the room. Miss Gay sees it now: but she is not superstitious, and she asks *what* it can be."

Well, that was Susannah's tale: and we carried it away with us on the morrow.

Sir John Whitney found his son looking all the better for his visit to Pumpwater. Temporarily he was so. Temporarily only; not materially: for John died before the year was out.

★★★★★★

Have I heard anything of the room since, you would like to ask. Yes, a little. Some eighteen months later, I was halting at Pumpwater for a few hours with the squire, and ran to the house to see Miss Gay. But the house was empty. A black board stood in front with big white letters on it *to be let.* Miss Gay had moved into another house facing the Parade.

"It was of no use my trying to stay in it," she said to me, shaking her head. "I moved into the room myself, Master Johnny, after you and my Lady Whitney left, and I am free to confess that I could not sleep. I had Susannah in, and she could not sleep; and, in short, we had to go out of it again. So I shut the room up, sir, until the year had expired, and then I gave up the house. It has not been let since, and people say it is falling into decay."

"Was anything ever seen in the room, Miss Gay?"

"Nothing," she answered, "or heard either; nothing whatever. The room is as nice a room as could be wished for in all respects,

184

light, large, cheerful, and airy; and yet nobody can get to sleep in it. I shall never understand it, sir."

I'm sure I never shall. It remains one of those curious experiences that cannot be solved in this world. But it is none the less true.

A Mesmerist of the Years Gone By

1

One afternoon in the spring of 1854, two distinguished-looking men might have been seen in Paris, strolling along the Boulevard des Italiens. Handsome, tall, and straight of limb they were, with sufficient resemblance in the general air and contour of feature to prove that kindred blood united them—that of brotherhood. The elder was of dark hue and of resolute, but sombre, cast of countenance; while the fair features, with their ever-ready smile, the wavy auburn hair, and bright complexion of the younger, seemed to say that he was cast in a less stern mould.

They were descendants of the old nobility, the *ancienne noblesse* of the Faubourg St. Germain, a race which seemed to be gradually disappearing from the surface of revolutionised France. Their father was a St. Sévron, but he had been dead some years, and they had been reared in all the pride, the exclusive ideas, and the poverty of their mother, who was of the family of the De Montcarsons. Gaston, the younger, was serving in the French army, as yet but a lieutenant, but André pursued no occupation.

They had met by chance on the *boulevards*, and Gaston put his arm through his brother's, and turned to pursue with him the same way. The utmost affection had always subsisted between them. The difference in their ages, ten years, caused Gaston to regard his elder brother with the love and reverence due to a father; whilst André was fervently attached to him, who in infancy had nestled his curly head upon his breast, as its resting-place,

186

and looked up to him through his childish tears, and told him all his little troubles.

"Where were you bound to?" asked the elder brother.

"I was looking for Cartier. He promised to meet me, and he has missed his appointment. And you?"

"I don't know. Anywhere, Gaston! I am nearly sick of this inert life."

"By Jove! I'm nearly sick of having too much to do," laughed the more active younger brother. "What with morning drills and mid-day exercises, afternoon visits and gossip, and evening amusements, I seldom find the day long enough."

"You were born to see things *couleur-de-rose!*" grumbled the melancholy elder brother.

"What's the use of looking at them *couleur-de-noir?*" retorted Gaston. "It is a pity you are not in the army, André: there will be occupation enough, if this war goes on."

"*I* in the army!" haughtily returned André. "You are mocking me. No, no. I must be my own master. If the Legitimists, indeed, were on the throne—— But it is profitless to enter upon these topics with you."

"That it is," replied Gaston, good-humouredly. "I am content to enjoy things as I find them, without tormenting myself after what's past. There goes Cartier! Where's he off to, in that quarter?"

Unlinking his arm from his brother's, Gaston de St. Sévron set off, full speed, to catch his friend Cartier. André pursued his way till he came to the Rue de Rivoli, where he ascended to a handsome *appartement* in one of its handsome houses. As he was shown into the drawing-room, a lady rose to receive him, a quiet calm English lady of middle age, Mrs. Elliot,

She had come to Paris a year previously, with her niece, bringing, amongst other letters of introduction, one for old Madame de St. Sévron. The families had become intimate, for they mutually liked each other. Mrs. Elliot admired the fine old dame of the ancient *régime*, so resigned, yet still so simply grand in her fallen fortunes, and the two young Frenchmen began by liking

Miss Alice Dare, and ended by loving her. She was so different, this English maiden, from all the young French ladies of their experience. Never losing the self-possession of her manners, her speech was frank, and her intercourse with them free and open as that of a sister. It surprised them with its novelty, while it charmed them with its pleasing trustingness; and when, at the end of three months' sojourn, the ladies quitted Paris, it may be questioned which of the two young men missed them most. "You will be sure to return?" they had said to her, and she had laughingly replied, "Perhaps yes: perhaps no."

She did return. One frosty day, some months afterwards, in the January of 1854, if the old *appartement* of the St. Sévrons, which, dirty and confined as it was, was situated in the aristocratic *quartier de St. Germain*, could have looked down into the street, which it could not, being so high, it would have seen Miss Dare's carriage at the great door, and Miss Dare, followed by her aunt, stepping out of it, to gladden the eyes of poor Madame de St. Sévron. To gladden another person's also, who was sitting there; but let that pass for the present. Mrs. Elliot had no other home than the one she enjoyed as the protectress of Miss Dare: for Miss Dare was an orphan and an heiress, and moreover being of age, she was mistress of herself and her fine fortune. She could not boast of beauty, this young English lady, but there was a peculiar charm of manner about her which rendered her eminently attractive.

To return. When André de St. Sévron made his call this day, he found Mrs. Elliot alone, and sat with her, almost in silence, restlessly watching the door—watching for one who did not enter. Presently he asked whether *mademoiselle* was out.

"Alice is not out," replied Mrs. Elliot. "I fancy she is writing letters. Judith," she added, rising to speak to a young woman who sat sewing in the ante-room, "see where Miss Alice is. Tell her Mr. de St. Sévron is here."

"My mistress is writing, ma'am," said the girl, presently returning. "She says she knew Mr. St. de Sévron was here, for she heard his voice, but she hopes he will excuse her, for she fears to be too late for the post."

A warmer shade, it could scarcely be called colour, rose in the dark cheek of André de St. Sévron. Ere it faded, to leave the face more sallow than before, the door opened and his brother entered.

He was at no loss for conversation. He chatted with Mrs. Elliot, he joked his brother on his idleness, he told a piquant anecdote of the day, he hummed over for them a song in the last new drama. And he did not break it off, the humming, when Miss Dare came in, but carried the tune through to the end.

"Will you pardon my rudeness?" he said, with his sunny smile, as he went up and held out his hand. "I had just caught the air, and Mrs. Elliot was anxious to hear it."

"You went, then, on Sunday night?" she exclaimed.

"To be sure," he replied. "I told you I should go. Don't frown, Miss Alice. You, in England, are taught to think these Sunday pleasures sins: it is part of our religion to enjoy them."

"Very good," returned Miss Dare, quietly. "But why do you say I frowned?"

"Because I feared you might. You must go and see this new drama, Miss Alice."

"Shall I get you places for tonight?" interposed André, eagerly. "It is creating a perfect furore."

"Then I think I shall wait till the furore's over," returned Miss Dare. "I don't like these crowded nights."

"Have you finished your letters, Alice?" said Mrs. Elliot.

"No. I got tired. They will do tomorrow."

"She would not come when she heard my voice: did she come at *his?*" asked André, of himself. And he continued to look at her, as she sat there smiling at the apt phrases of his gay and gallant brother. He rose to leave.

"Are you coming, Gaston?" he enquired.

"Not I; not for this hour," protested Gaston. "I am relating a story to Miss Alice, and you have interrupted it."

"What story?"

"Something Cartier told me today about the new court and

our charming *impératrice*. I would advise you not to enquire particulars: they will not suit your Legitimist reverence."

André left the house, and made his way home to the Faubourg St. Germain. Toiling up the five flights of stairs, he opened the outer door of the apartment, with his pass-key. A very narrow ante-chamber, encumbered with trunks and firewood, passed, he found himself in the small and dingy sitting-room. The cloth was laid for dinner, and his mother sat in an attitude of waiting, her hands and her black mittens crossed before her. She was remarkably like her eldest son, especially in the expression of the face and eye, half stern, half melancholy.

"It is a quarter-past five, my son, and Nannette is waiting to serve the soup," she said. "Have you seen your brother?"

"I left him in the Rue Rivoli," replied André. "Let us begin. I am sorry I kept you waiting, mother."

Nannette, an ancient *dame*, who had lived in *Madame's* family unheard-of years, and remembered some of its former grandeur, but who had long fallen to be the solitary maid-of-all-work, put the potage on the table, and they sat down to it. An hour afterwards, the repast concluded, Gaston was heard. He ascended the stairs in a great bustle, leaping up three at a time, and burst into the room.

"I hope you did not wait dinner for me!"

"No. But where have you been, my child!" It was the mother's familiar mode of expression: André was "my son," Gaston, "my child."

"I stayed on at Mrs. Elliot's, mother, unconscious of the time, and when I left, was astonished to find it was half-past five. Just then Cartier came up, and made me go to dine with him, knowing I should be late here."

"Where are you flying to now, child?" demanded Madame de St. Sévron, as Gaston opened the opposite door.

"To dress. I am going to the theatre: the Porte St. Martin. And it is late. I don't know who's not waiting for me."

He entered and closed the door, as he spoke. It was the joint dressing-room of himself and André. Their beds were in two enclosed recesses in the same chamber—shut-up cupboards, an English bedroom would call them. Madame de St. Sévron slept in a recess partitioned off from the ante-room, and where old Nannette slept never could be divined; unless it was on the pile of wood, outside, or on the *poële* in the kitchen.

Not long was Gaston dressing: he was never long over anything: and out he went, as dashing a young officer as Paris could show. André remained by the side of the fire, moodily looking into it. His mother sat, on the other side, lost in dreams of the nation's and her own departed greatness. As the clock struck eight, André rose and stretched himself.

"Going out, my son?"

"I shall take a stroll as far as the Porte St. Martin. They play a sterling afterpiece there tonight. Goodnight, dear mother. You may be in bed before I return."

André de St. Sévron reached the Porte St. Martin, but he found some difficulty in getting into the pit of the theatre. An attractive piece was on, and the audience were closely packed. He did manage, somehow, to wedge his way in, and obtain a side-view of the stage.

He obtained a view of something else. Ranging his eyes round the house, they were arrested by a box, amidst whose brilliant crowd was the distinguished form of his brother, laughing and talking to Miss Dare. *She* was not talking; she was only listening; the more dangerous pastime, in such a case, of the two; and André knew it.

André de St. Sévron looked no more at the stage. He bent his dark brows, and, covered by the crush and crowd around, watched keenly that box, in one of whose inmates all the hopes of his future life were concentred. Once he started up, and would have made for it, but he remembered his careless costume, and remained where he was. Before the close of the performance, he left the house, and walked rapidly home. His mother had retired, and André sat down before the nearly burnt-out fire. Mechanically, with the air of one whose mind knows not what his hands are doing, he pushed the pieces of wood together, that they

191

might blaze up, and fell into a train of thought.

"Is it real or imaginary, this nightmare which oppresses me? For some time, ever since she returned to Paris, its shadows have hovered over me. They are growing darker: more dark than ever have they been today. If I thought he loved her, I think I could give her up—psha! a soldier boy, of five-and-twenty, love? Not he. His heart is in his profession; in his amusements; in his companions, light and void of care as is the wind. Why, to tie that lad down to matrimony, even with her, would be like chaining him to the grave! And if she, if it be true"—André winced visibly—"if indeed her fancy is temporarily caught by him, the kinder course to him, to both, would be to remove him from the danger. I must look to it. Why did I suffer myself to become enthralled by this English girl? I, who have hitherto made a stone of my feelings as regards women? But—if one must marry sometime—as well Alice as another. We should be equally matched. Thirty-five years to her two-and-twenty: all well: the husband should have more experience than the wife. She has a large fortune, and I have an ancient name. What can either side desire more? "

Not many mornings after this, Paris awoke with the news that certain regiments were ordered to Marseilles, on their way to commence the war, now declared against Russia, the regiment in which Gaston de St. Sévron served not being one. "God be thanked!" murmured Madame de St. Sévron, though she said it not in the hearing of her sons. She owned a brave heart, this lady, one which did not disgrace her high lineage; and if needs must have been that her son had gone forth to meet his country's enemies, she would have struggled for a calm voice in which to bid God speed him. But there was something behind.

From the very first faint rumour of an impending war, certain mouldy prophecies, rummaged out from it is impossible to say what hidden archives of Paris, had been secretly circulated amongst parties inimical to the war and to the new Imperial power. They had found their way to the hands of Madame de St. Sévron. Not much could she make out of them: those who were able to read them in their original Latin, professed to make more. They were written in the reigns of Charles IX. and Henri IV. They were carried down to, and indeed beyond, the present time, pointing clearly to a war to be begun in the year 1854 against Russia, and which would bring desolation in its train; famine, pestilence, and wholesale slaughter, till the earth should be partially disseminated. "Oh not for that," murmured Madame de St. Sévron, "did I bear my son. Engaged with an open, honourable enemy, he must take his chance and trust in Heaven; but famine—pestilence—indiscriminate butchery—my God, I thank Thee that he is spared the risk!" She did not tell her sons she had seen these old, yellow sheets of parchment: she knew that André would have haughtily sneered over them, and Gaston made merry.

In the afternoon of this day, so full of gossip and excitement for Paris, Gaston went to call in the Rue Rivoli. Alice Dare rose and stood by the centre table as he entered, glancing at him with a searching gaze. "Is it true?" were her first words, scarcely replying to his greeting.

"Is what true, Miss Alice?"

"That the war has begun? That you soldiers are ordered off?"

"True that we are ordered off. But the war has not actually begun. And it never may begin. Some of our wiseacres think it never will."

"Are _you_ ordered out?" she continued, in a low voice.

"No: our regiment has not received the honour. We remain here."

She drew a long breath, as if relieved, took her hand from the table on which it had leaned, and sat down on her favourite sofa by the window. Her spirits seemed to rise high.

"Now don't impose upon us with the nonsense that you are disappointed!" she exclaimed, interrupting something he was saying to Mrs. Elliot. "You soldiers like to uphold your martial character, and so pretend to great bravery. Had you been ordered out. Monsieur Gaston, you might have gone with a downcast heart; or perhaps have invented some plausible excuse for staying at home, not caring to get into the way of cannon-balls."

"Alice! Alice!" remonstrated Mrs. Elliot. "She is fond of joking. Monsieur Gaston."

The young man's cheek and brow flushed a glowing red, showing that he felt her words. Not individually: for never did a braver or more courageous heart beat than that of Gaston de St. Sévron. And there was something in the conscious, averted eye of Alice, as she turned it from his gaze, which told him that she *knew* the reproach of cowardice never could come near him.

2

What could it be that André de St. Sévron was so busy over? For some days he was not seen in his old haunts; he did not call in the Rue Rivoli; he was only at home night and morning. He was mingling, instead, with military officers, a thing he rarely condescended to do; he was in and out of the *bureau* of financiers; he was haunting the cabinet of the ministers-at-war. The secret of the whole was, that he was endeavouring to accomplish the exchange of his brother from one regiment to another.

And he effected it. One afternoon it was settled.

André was at rest now. He had scarcely taken food for some days; but he now turned into a cheap restaurant, and dined for twenty-five *sous*, he, this proud descendant of the once-sumptuous *régime*. The lamps were lighted in the streets when he reached home, and he ascended the high staircase by feel, not by sight. His mother was reclining in her *fauteuil*, in the warm corner.

"You don't seem well, mother!" he exclaimed, affectionately, for both boys deeply loved and reverenced their mother. "Is it the old pain at your chest?"

"I am free tonight from bodily ailments, my son," replied Madame de St. Sévron, "but my spirits are unusually depressed. Some calamity seems to be hanging over me. My old friend, the Comtesse de Morny, was here this afternoon, and she was going on in a melancholy strain about this miserable war which is looming in the future. It set me thinking about Gaston. His regiment is left *tranquil* as yet; but how long may it remain so?"

194

"Mother," began André in a hesitating voice, as he drew his chair close to hers, and took her hand, "it would be fortunate for Gaston to go out to the war. Do you know what I have been occupied with these last few days?"

"How should I know, my son?"

"I have been effecting for Gaston what his own luck did not effect for him. I have procured his exchange into one of these departing regiments."

The old lady turned her face slowly towards the speaker, and her lips parted as if with extreme astonishment or perplexity; not so much yet with terror, for her senses had not fully taken in the purport of the words.

"You can't imagine the trouble I had," continued André, "the officers, one and all, are so eager to get out, and be doing. Marshal St. Arnaud managed it at last. He knows what a fine fellow Gaston is."

Oh, the sharp, shrill cry of anguish that issued from the lips of Madame de St. Sévron! She clenched André's arm with a pressure of which he had deemed her aged and thin fingers incapable, and a torrent of reproaches burst from her.

"*You* have done this! *you* have acted the part of Judas by your own brother! You would drive him out to swell the dead on those far-off plains!—where the corpses are to lie in heaps, stricken down by war and pestilence!"

"Oh, mother! don't talk like that. War! pestilence! What pestilence? And as to war, our brave soldiers can hold their lines against the Russians. Whence got you such ideas?"

"They are not my ideas," interrupted Madame de St. Sévron, fiercely; "they are the revelations of one who lived and died ages ago. Every political event that has since come to pass in France is written down in these dread prophecies, especially those of later times: the Revolution; the murder of the king; *our* downfall; the rising of the Eagle, its triumph, its bloody sway, and then its fall; the Orleans dynasty; the Republic, swayed over by a second Eagle; the second Empire, and this fearful war which is to destroy the flower of the Western armies, and bring pestilence, famine, woe, madness in its train!"

"Dear mother," interposed the astonished André, "you must be lapsing into your dotage. Prophecies!" he continued, in a tone of haughty scorn. "Because some fools—though more knaves than fools—are circulating these wicked absurdities to answer their own ends, you must attach importance to them—*you!* Mother, be yourself again: remember you are a De Montcarson."

"I will be myself again when you are again a brother," she retorted. "What are we to do without Gaston? how exist, wanting him? Is he not the sunshine of our miserable household—is it not he, with his sweet temper and joyous spirit, that brings what ray of light comes into it? Has he not been something for us both to love—an end to live for—a continuous happiness to look forward to day by day as we awake? André! if you indeed drive my child out to death, may God forgive you, for I never will!"

At this moment the door of the inner room opened, and Gaston came out. He had been making ready for a party at Mrs. Elliot's.

"Gaston," exclaimed André, drawing up his tall form fearlessly, "our mother seems to have some mist before her eyes, causing her to see things in false colours. I have been exerting all the energy and influence I possess to advance your interest, and have succeeded in effecting an exchange for you into one of the regiments ordered to the East. It—"

"*Parbleu!* but I think you might have consulted me first!" "ejaculated the amazed young soldier. "I may have interests that bind me, if possible, to Paris."

"Tush, my brother! guard against frittering away time until you become a useless dreamer, as I have done. I have had, in this step, but your true welfare at heart; I swear it to you, by the honour of our name! Go forth and prosper. Use your sword bravely, and come back to us a captain—a colonel—a general: no rank is inaccessible to him who shows himself a lion on the battlefield."

"The battlefield gives stepping-stones, and it blows off heads," returned the careless Gaston. "If I go out, I must bear my chance of one, as of the other; and I should flinch from neither."

Again that cry of anguish from Madame de St. Sévron, but this time it was low and wailing, as she threw her feeble hands round her boy. "Oh, Gaston, my latest born!" she murmured, "if you die out there, you take my life with you!"

André looked on, and saw, and heard. He might have hesitated, might have endeavoured to undo his work, but that he truly believed the interest of Gaston lay in his being in active service.

It was late in the evening when Gaston de St. Sévron entered the reception-rooms of Mrs. Elliot. A gay party was assembled. In the course of the night he contrived to find himself alone with Miss Dare. Some people were at cards, and others had gathered round the piano, where a lady was shrieking through some Italian songs.

"Why have you brought me into this room?" demanded Alice. "There's no one in it, you see."

"That is why I did bring you," replied Gaston. "I may not be able to call upon you again, so I would say a word of *adieu* to you now: and I hate saying it in a crowd."

"Just tell me what you mean!" she exclaimed. "I don't like riddles. Take leave till when? till tomorrow?"

"Tomorrow, no!" he replied. "Probably forever. I am going out to the East. Ere eight-and-forty hours, we shall be on our road."

Her face, even her lips, turned of a ghastly whiteness. Gaston saw it.

"Why did you deceive me?" was her first question. "The other day, you said your regiment remained in Paris."

"The regiment remains. But I have exchanged into one going out. You did me the honour to suggest that, were I ordered off, I might be capable of inventing some disgraceful ruse to evade it," he added, determined to hazard a little joke. "Do you not think the insinuation was enough to make a fellow apply for permission to seek the risk?"

"Oh, Gaston! "she exclaimed, wildly, her livid features one keen expression of dismay, "do not torture me! You knew that all I said was but in jest."

"How could I know it? On my honour, I did not know whether you were in jest or earnest."

"You are but jesting with me now! "she uttered, laying her trembling hands upon his arm in her excitement.

"Alice, my love, why this emotion?" he whispered, more tenderly than he had ever permitted himself to speak to her. "Sit down and be calm."

"You are not going!" she exclaimed, in agitation, rising her head and checking the tears, as the colour flashed into her cheeks. "And I am foolish and nervous tonight But you are not going?"

"My dear Alice, I am assuredly going. But when I said I made the exchange in consequence of your observations to me, that was not true. I never applied—I never wished to apply, or to leave Paris: and till eight o'clock this night, I knew no more of the matter than you knew. It is André who has done it. He believes that my interests lie in being in active service, and he has exerted himself to effect an exchange. I am now in the —— regiment."

The first shock had passed, and she was still and quiet. "When do you leave?" she asked.

"The day after tomorrow."

"And when return?"

"Alice! as well enquire when the next comet will be discovered, or any other event which may or may not happen. If I do return, you are the first friend I shall seek a welcome from. And now I must leave you."

She stood up by his side, her eyes cast down, and her cheeks crimson. He took her hand in his, and pressed it to his heart. He did more. He threw his arm round her waist, and kissed, five or six times, those glowing cheeks, and she resisted not. But when he had finally left the room, she flew upstairs to her chamber, and, bolting herself within, indulged in an hysterical burst of tears.

3

The following summer was one of suspense and anxiety to many people; to France, as well as to our own country. Sickness was not spared to the French capital, any more than to ours; and varied reports from the East, where the allied armies were gathered, kept up a continual excitement. Now they were at Malta, now at Gallipoli, now some of them at Constantinople, and now in the desert plains surrounding Varna. Rumours came to Paris of minor engagements with the enemy, more than rumours of fearfully devastating sickness: but a brave heart sat in every Parisian breast. "The British Lion and the French Eagle," they shouted, "can never be subdued!"

Several letters arrived from Gaston de St. Sévron: to his mother, to André, to former companions: letters as gay as himself. It was evident he contrived to lead a merry life amidst all the discomforts that attended the army; but Gaston carried happiness with him in his own sunny heart. André de St. Sévron had made no progress in his wooing—if it was wooing he meant. A few days after the departure of Gaston, Miss Dare had left, with her aunt, for Switzerland. "I am tired of Paris," was her reply to Mrs. Elliot's comment upon the suddenness of her resolution.

Now at that period, as is well remembered yet, a certain class of people had begun to exercise a wonderful influence in Paris—the mesmerists. Some persons called them charlatans; others bowed to their power, and were terrified at it. One of them was especially noted for her revelations, a woman; but for obvious reasons her name is not given here. It was a recognised fact that many a heavy transaction was done on the Bourse, the secret incentive to which was neither more nor less than a *séance* with one or other of the mesmerists regarding news from the seat of war. It was a curious thing, difficult to understand—that they should be able to reveal events passing in the far-off East. And when, days afterwards, authentic tidings would come to prove their truth, people knew not what to think.

Their fame grew. Individuals of all classes, high and low, scoffers once, scrupled not to consult the mesmerists in secret—few of them cared to own it. One gentleman, a well-known financier in Parisian circles, was banteringly accused, in evening society, of having gone that morning to visit one. He indignantly denied it, and was believed. Nevertheless, he had been. They assumed to possess the power of revealing everything; from the general doings of the army, to the thoughts and movements of those forming it.

One day, towards the latter end of September, André de St. Sévron was dragging himself and his legs along the Tuileries gardens, in his usual listless mood, when he suddenly encountered Miss Dare and her maid. He brightened up to energy.

"This is indeed an unexpected pleasure!" he exclaimed. "When did you arrive?"

"Last night," she replied; "and we have seen no one yet. What news is there?"

"The troops have landed in the Crimea," said André, thinking the word "news" could only refer to the all-engrossing topic. "Where is Mrs. Elliot?"

"She was busy with her packing-cases when I came out. I expect her to join me presently. Do you mind sitting down, for I am tired with yesterday's journey? Judith," she continued, turning to the girl, "you can go and execute the commission my aunt gave you. You will find me here." And the servant departed on her errand, and. André sat down on the bench by Miss Dare's side.

"Have you heard recently from your brother?" she enquired, turning her face away.

"No, we have not," answered André. "His letters used to come pretty regularly at first, but latterly we have received none. I may confess to you that I am getting anxious. Not that there's fear on Gaston's account, for if anything unfortunately happened to him, his, brother-officers would write, but my poor mother torments herself out of her life. She is now a mere skeleton."

"I attach no importance to the non-receipt of letters from this allied expedition of ours," observed Miss Dare. "My aunt has a son out there, a young ensign, and though we know he writes regularly, more of his letters are lost, or delayed, than come to hand."

"There has been a disagreeable rumour flying about Paris these last few hours," proceeded André, unconsciously dropping his voice, "but I cannot find that it proceeds from any source save the prolific brains of the mesmerists. I was at the Telegraph-office this morning, and nothing of it had been heard there."

"Mesmerists!" exclaimed Miss Dare. "Are they busying themselves about the war?"

"They are: and, what's worse, they keep Paris in a hotter fever than it would otherwise be. Some events, it cannot be denied, they have described exactly; aye, nearly in the very hour in which they occurred."

"But what is this present rumour you allude to?"

"I don't put any faith in it," said André, imperiously. Yet his uneasy, nervous movement, as he spoke, proved he *did*. "It is, that the troops have landed in Crimea—but that was known—that some days afterwards, upon encountering the Russians, a desperate battle ensued, and that thousands of the allies, men and officers, are down."

Miss Dare compressed her lips. "But, you say, even the telegraph has no news of this?" she observed, in a cheerful voice, after some minutes' thought.

"No, no; it all comes from these infernal mesmerists—I beg your pardon for the word. But, you see, as they have been right before, they may be again. I have been in a state of worry since the morning, lest the report should reach my mother."

"Have you been yourself to consult the mesmerists?" enquired Miss Dare.

"Thank you. There are enough idiots who go, without my making one."

"Then, were I you, I should go and hear what they do say," she rejoined, firmly, "and exercise my own judgment as to whether there was anything in it. It seems to me that such imposture, if it be imposture, must be readily detected."

André de St. Sévron sat silent. He did not choose to confess to her that it was the very plan he had been debating in his own mind.

"Do ladies go?" proceeded Miss Dare.

"Some have gone. I suppose you are aware that we have women speculators on the Bourse as well as men. And it is chiefly for these speculations that the *clairvoyantes* are consulted."

"Do you know," she said, in a low, timid voice, "I should much like to go."

"Go where?" ejaculated André

"To hear, or see—which do you call it?—one of these mesmerists. It has never fallen to my chance to be present at any of their exhibitions, though I have often wished it. Why not now, as well as at another time? Will you take me, André?"

"You English *demoiselles* are remarkably independent!" was André's observation,

"Yes," she said, "it is our privilege. But we retain our dignity and self-possession, André, and no harm can come near us. Will you go?"

"If you are in earnest in wishing it. When shall it be? Some hour that will suit Mrs. Elliot."

"I will not have Mrs. Elliot, or tell her of it," interrupted Miss Dare. "I ask you to accompany me, because it might not be right for a young lady to appear there alone. Take me to the first of them all; the woman with the wonderful reputation. I will be ready this evening."

"At what hour?"

"Seven."

It was before a house in the neighbourhood of the Rue St. Denis, that a hired *citadine* stopped that night, soon after the hour named by Miss Dare. She stepped out of it, attended by André de St. Sévron. Her own manservant sat on the box with the driver. This may be looked upon as a curious adventure for her, or any other English lady, to engage in, but she was troubled and anxious, and thought not of forms and ceremonies; and she went through with it.

It was the house of the renowned mesmerist, for André had

obeyed her wishes. They were shown into the waiting room, a sort of badly-furnished and worse-lighted *salle-à-manger*, and were told they would soon be called for, but the *clairvoyante* was just then engaged.

Alice Dare grew impatient at the delay, and began to pace the room. Perhaps she did not feel quite satisfied with what she had undertaken. "If we are kept here much longer," she observed to her companion, "I shall return."

André opened the door, with a view of looking for the person who had shown them in. He could see no one. On the right was the staircase they had ascended; on the left, a long corridor, which was lighted by a bit of candle, stuck in a tin sconce nailed to the wall. Suddenly, as he stood, a door at the extreme end of the passage opened and closed, and a gentleman was walking down the passage towards him. It was a friend of St. Sévron's, a man of sixty years.

"What! you here, St. Sévron!" was the exclamation. "Have you, the cynical, come to pray advice of the oracle?"

"I may retort by the same question," replied St. Sévron, drawing-to the door behind him, that Alice might not be seen. "What has the oracle done for you?"

"Little for me, by all that's sombre!" replied the old man. "If what she says is true, the funds will go down awfully."

"What does she say?"

"You'll hear enough, if you go in, without my telling you. One thing I trust she may be wrong in—that St. Arnaud's dead."

"Bah!"

"She affirms it. Not killed in the battle. Died of natural disease after it—after another attack of cholera![1] I say! a compact?"

"Well?" returned St. Sévron.

"That neither of us has seen the other here."

"Be it so."

As the gentleman passed down the staircase, St. Sévron and Miss Dare were summoned to the reception-room. A woman,

---

1. It is certain that the death and its cause, of Marshal de St. Arnaud was positively affirmed in secret, in Paris, some days before the telegraph brought news of the fact.

attired in black silk, with a white bandage over her eyes, leant back asleep—at least was in the attitude of sleep—in an easy-chair. A man, short of stature, with round, cunning eyes, likewise dressed in black, and well dressed, sat at a table.

"You must put your questions to *Madame* through me," he observed to the visitors. "What is it you wish to know?"

"Of the welfare of one who is serving in the Crimea," rejoined André. "An officer."

"Have you aught belonging to him about you?" enquired the man.

"I have a piece of his hair and a letter," was St. Sévron's reply. For, be it observed, the last time Gaston wrote to his mother from Varna, he enclosed to her a lock of his hair, according to a request she had made. This letter and hair André had borrowed, for that evening, knowing something of the requisitions of the mesmerists. The man returned the letter to André as useless, but he took the hair, *and placed it on the top of the woman's head.*

The woman became restless, stirred, and sighed heavily. It was some minutes before she spoke.

"What do you see?" enquired the man of her. "How is he employed now, from whom that hair was severed?"

"I see a plain whose heights are rugged and uneven," she murmured. "I see it strewn with corpses. They are burying them; but they are often called off. There are many wounded, hundreds upon hundreds. I see a wide expanse of water, and ships—"

"Is he, who owns that hair amongst the wounded? Ask her," interrupted André, eagerly, whilst Alice clung to his arm, partly in suspense, partly in terror. And the man put the question.

"I cannot find him," she went on to murmur, speaking at intervals, and with difficulty. "Ah! I see now. His luxuriant hair is fair and bright, but it is all bloody, and his face is white, and his jaw fallen. He is with the dead."

"Dead!" breathed André, who, much as he despised himself for it, could not shake off the feeling of horror that was creeping over him.

"Dead. One—two—three—four wounds, all in front. He

died bravely. Stay! stay! they have come to him—they are taking him—now they search his pockets—there's a knife, and letters, and—and things I can't see—they get in the light. Where to now? There they go! Ah! they are bearing him to the great pit, where so many are being thrown."

Nothing more could he get out of the woman—and the reader will probably think this was quite enough. She went rambling on to other sights she saw, or made believe to see, on the battlefield. André de St. Sévron conducted his companion from the room. She never spoke a word; nor he. But in the coach he recovered his spirits. His common sense and judgment returned to him with the fading away of the mesmeric scene, and he no longer condescended to admit apprehension for the fate of his brother. "It was all absurd; nothing but a clap-trap; a disgraceful mode of swindling the credulous out of money!" he indignantly exclaimed, but he was interrupted by the sound of a sob, and turning to Miss Dare, he found she was weeping silently. He went over to the side of the coach where she sat, and took her hand, and essayed to soothe her. But she shrank from him.

"Nay, do not push me away, Alice," he whispered, affectionately; "suffer me to comfort you. I have long hoped that I might be your comforter through life. I should have told you this in the spring, but for your sudden departure from Paris. I have only waited your return to speak."

"You my soother in life!" she passionately exclaimed, through her convulsive sobs—"you, who plotted and worked in slyness and in secret till you succeeded in driving your brave brother out to the death he has met!"

"Hush, hush, Alice," remonstrated André; "my brother has met with no death. How can you suffer the ridiculous farce we have come from to scare away your reason? Alice, you are the only woman I ever cared for: you must promise to be my dear wife."

"Listen!" spoke Miss Dare, arresting her sobs by a resolute effort. "I will tell you a history. I might shrink from repeating it at most times, but this night I am in no mood to stand on ceremony. I am the promised wife of one in my own land. When I engaged myself, I thought I liked him; and so I did. But I came to Paris; I saw your brother; I became intimate with him; and then I found I had mistaken liking for love. André de St. Sévron, I loved your brother; *I loved him*; had you not forced him from me, I know that in time I should have been his wife, for I would have given up that other engagement at his bidding. Are you answered?"

"These fancies will wear away in time," observed André, gloomily. "Let me hope —"

"Hope nothing," interrupted Alice, with fearless impetuosity. "When these fancies, as you call them, shall have worn away, I shall marry him who is waiting for me; and perhaps not make him the less good wife, because I, for a few months, passionately loved one who is in his grave."

"I would endeavour to render you happy, Alice," he persisted, clinging even against hope.

"Your endeavours have not been so directed hitherto," she retorted. "You have contrived to tear from me what romance I had in life; you have been the means of slaying your brother. Look there, André de St. Sévron!" she suddenly exclaimed, pulling him towards the coach window, "do you see these men who are passing home from their day's work—some in blouses, some in rags?—there is not one amongst them that I would not marry in preference to you!"

He left Alice Dare at her residence; and, dismissing the *citadine*, walked, with the moody step of grief and despair, to the Faubourg St. Germain. Her reproaches had told home. If it should indeed prove that Gaston had fallen, why, *he* had driven him out to perish. And what would be his own future? To live on alone—to hear that *she* had married one of her own nation, one to whom she had been engaged for years! He looked across the fireplace at his poor old mother, now so near her end, but there was no comfort for him there. Comfort! Even her life he had contributed to shorten. André de St. Sévron was apt to say he was born under a miserable star, but never had he felt the conviction so keenly as on that night.

Some days afterwards, on Sunday, the 1st of October, came the official tidings of the Battle of the Alma. And when the lists of killed and wounded appeared, the name of Gaston de St. Sévron was amongst the slain.

A Mysterious Visitor

On Monday morning, the 11th of May, 1857—the year, as the reader may remember, that England was destined to be shaken to its centre with the disastrous news of the rising in India—there sat in one of the quiet rooms of Enton Parsonage a young and pretty woman, playing with her baby. It was Mrs. Ordie. The incumbent of Enton was Dr. Ling, an honorary canon of the county cathedral. Mrs. Ling was from India: her family connections, uncles, brothers, and cousins, had been, or were, in the civil or military service of Bengal. Consequently, as the daughters of Dr. Ling had grown towards womanhood, they were severally shipped off, with high matrimonial views, according to a fashion that extensively prevails.

Miss Ling, Louisa, had gone out first, and had secured Captain Ordie. Constance went next, and espoused Lieutenant Main, to the indignation of all her relatives, both at home and out, for she was a handsome girl, and had been set down for nothing less than a major. The third daughter, Sarah Ann, very young and pretty she was, went out the following year, with a stern injunction not to do as Constance had done.

Before Sarah Ann could get there, Mrs. Ordie's health failed, and she was ordered immediately to her native climate. Upon landing, she proceeded to Enton. The voyage had been of much service to her, and her health was improved. And there we see her sitting, on the morning of the 11th of May, nearly twelve months after her arrival, playing with her infant, who was nine months old. In August she and the child were going back to India.

Mrs. Ordie was much attached to this child, very anxious and fidgety over it: her first child had died in India. She fancied, this morning, that it was not well, and had been sending in haste for Mrs. Beecher, who lived close by, just beyond the garden. The honorary canon and the rest of the family had gone to spend a week in the county town.

Mrs. Beecher came in without her bonnet. She had been governess to Louisa and Constance, had married the curate, and remained the deeply-attached friend and adviser of the Ling family. In any emergency Mrs. Beecher was appealed to.

"I am sure baby's ill" was Mrs. Ordie's salutation. "I have been doing all I can to excite her notice, but she will keep her head down. See how hot her cheeks are."

"I think she is sleepy," said Mrs. Beecher. "And perhaps a very little feverish."

"*Do* you think her feverish? What shall I do? Good mercy, if she should die as my other baby did!"

"Louisa," remonstrated Mrs. Beecher, "do not excite yourself causelessly. I thought you had left that habit off."

"Oh, but you don't know what it is to lose a child; you never had one," returned Mrs. Ordie, giving way to her excitement. " If she does, I can tell you I shall die with her."

"Hush," interrupted Mrs. Beecher. "I believe there is little, if anything, the matter with the child, excepting her teeth, which renders children somewhat feverish. But if she were dangerously ill, you have no right to say what you have just said."

"Oh yes, I have a right, for it is truth. I would rather lose everything I possess in the world, than my baby. What a long while Mr. Percival is!" she added, walking to the window and looking out.

"You surely have not sent for Mr. Percival?"

"I surely have. And if he does not soon make his appearance, I shall send again."

Mrs. Oldie had always been of most excitable temperament. As a girl, her imagination was so vivid, so prone to the marvellous, that story books and fairy tales were kept from her. She would get them unknown to her parents, and wake up in the night, shrieking with terror at what she had read. Hers was indeed a peculiarly active brain. It is necessary to mention this, as it may account, in some degree, for what follows.

There was really nothing the matter with the child, but Mrs. Ordie insisted that there was, and made herself miserable all the day. The surgeon, Mr. Percival, came: he saw little the matter with it either, but he ordered it a warm bath, and sent in some medicine—probably distilled water and sugar. Mrs. Beecher came in again in the evening. Mrs. Ordie hinted that she might as well remain for the night, to be on the spot should baby be taken worse.

The curate's wife laughed. "I think I can promise you that there will be no danger, Louisa. You may cease to torment yourself, and go to sleep in peace."

"If anything does happen, I shall send to call you up."

The Lings kept four servants. Two of these, a man and maid, were with their master and mistress; the other two were at home. And there was also the child's nurse. After Mrs. Beecher left, Mrs. Ordie crept along the corridor to the nurse's room, where the baby slept, and found the nurse undressing herself.

"What are you doing that for?" she indignantly exclaimed. "Of course you will sit up tonight, and watch by baby."

"Sit up for what, ma'am?" returned the nurse.

"I would not leave the child unwatched tonight for anything. My other baby died of convulsions; they may also attack this one. Convulsions are so uncertain: they come on in a moment. I have ordered Martha to sit up in the kitchen and keep hot water in readiness."

"Why, ma'am, there's no cause in the world for it," remonstrated the surprised nurse. "The baby is as well as well can be, and has never woke up since I laid her down at eight o'clock."

"She shall be watched this night," persisted Mrs. Ordie. "So dress yourself again."

"I must say it's a shame," grumbled the nurse, who had grown tired of her mistress's capricious ways, and had privately told the other servants that she did not care how soon she left the situation. "I'd remain up for a week, if there was need of it, but to be deprived of one's natural rest for nothing, ma'am, is too bad. I'll sit myself in the old rocking-chair, if I must stay up," added the servant, half to herself, half to her mistress, "and get a sleep that way."

Mrs. Ordie's eyes flashed anger. The fact was, the slavery of Eastern servants had a little spoiled her for the independence of European ones. She accused the girl of every crime that was unfeeling, short of child murder, and concluded by having the infant's crib carried down to her own room. She would sit up herself and watch it.

The child still slept calmly and quietly, and Mrs. Ordie sat quietly by it. But she began to find it rather dull, and she went to the book-shelves and took down a book. It was then striking eleven. Setting the lamp on a small table at her elbow, she began to read.

She had taken the *Vicar of Wakefield*. She had not opened the book for years, and she read on with interest, all her old pleasure in the tale revived. Nearly half-an-hour had elapsed when she suddenly heard footsteps on the gravel-path outside, advancing towards the house: and she looked off and listened. The first thought that struck her was, that one of the servants had been out without permission, and was coming in at that late hour; which, as her watch, hanging opposite, told her, was twenty-five minutes past eleven. But she had not heard the bell ring.

It must be explained that Enton Parsonage stood back from the high-road and was surrounded by trees. Two iron gates gave ingress to it from the road. They were far apart, for the house was low and long; the kitchens, forming a right angle with the house, projected out, their windows looking sideways on the broad half-circular gravel-path that led from one gate to the other. The entrance-porch was near the kitchens. At the back of the house stood the smaller house of the curate; a narrow pathway leading to it from the parsonage. *That* house faced the side lane, into which lane its small iron gate opened. These gates, the rector's two large ones and the curate's small one, were always locked at sunset, and the premises were then deemed secure. There was no other entrance to them whatever, and all three gates were lofty and spiked at the top, preventing the possibility of any marauder's climbing over. If any friends came to either of the two houses after the gates were locked, they had to ring for admittance.

Mrs. Ordie heard these footsteps in the stillness of the night, and her eyes instantly glanced at her watch. Twenty-five minutes after eleven. Who was it, at this late hour? But, even as the question passed through her mind, an expression of astonishment rose to her face; her eyes dilated, she drew in her breath and listened intently. If ever she heard the footsteps of her husband, she thought she heard them then.

Yes, yes! It was impossible to mistake his sharp, firm step, which she had never heard since she left him in Calcutta. It was very close now, nearly underneath her window. With a cry of joy she arose and opened it.

"George, dear George! I knew your step. What has brought you home?"

There was no answer. The footsteps were still advancing, and Mrs. Ordie leaned out. He had come in at the further gate, had passed along the front of the house, and was now underneath her window. She saw him distinctly in the light cast on the path from the kitchen. There was no mistaking him for any other than Captain Ordie, and he wore his regimentals. He lifted his face, she saw it clearly in the light, and looked at her. Then he went on and stepped inside the porch. She called to him again.

"George, you did not hear me. Don't knock, baby's ill. Wait a moment, and I will let you in."

Closing the window, she sprang to the door. Her lamp was not suitable for carrying, and she would not stay to light a taper: she knew every stair well. But she was awkward at the fastenings of the front-door, and found she could not undo them in the dark, so ran into the kitchen. The cook, sitting up in obedience to her orders, was lying back in a chair, her feet stretched out upon another. She was fast asleep and snoring. A large fire burnt in the grate, and two candles were alight on the ironing-board underneath the window.

"Martha! Martha!" she exclaimed, "rouse yourself. My husband's come."

"What!" cried the woman, starting up in affright, and evidently forgetting where she was. "Who's come, ma'am?"

"Come and open the hall-door. Captain Ordie is here."

She snatched one of the candles from the table, and went on to the door again. The servant followed, rubbing her eyes.

The door was unlocked and thrown open, and Mrs. Ordie drew a little back to give space for him to enter. No one came in. Mrs. Ordie looked out then, holding the candle above her head. She could not see him anywhere.

"Take the light," she said to the maid, and stepped beyond the portico. "George!" she called out, "where are you? The door is open." But Captain Ordie neither appeared nor answered.

"Well, I never knew such an extraordinary thing!"

"Ma'am," said the servant, who began now to be pretty well awake, "I don't understand. Did you say anybody was come?"

"My husband is come. Captain Ordie."

"From Mrs. Beecher's?" asked the woman.

"Mrs. Beecher's, no! What should bring him at Mrs. Beecher's? He must have come direct from Portsmouth."

"But he must have come to the door here from the Beechers'," continued the servant. "He couldn't have come any other way. The gates are locked, ma'am!"

In her wonder at his appearance, this fact had not struck Mrs. Ordie. "One of them must have been left unfastened," she said, after thinking. "That was very careless, Martha. It is your place to see to it, when Richard is out. Papa once turned a servant away for leaving the gates open at night."

"I locked both the gates at sundown," was the woman's reply. "And the key's hanging up in its place in the kitchen."

"Impossible," thought Mrs. Ordie. "Where's Susan?"—alluding to the other servant at home.

"Susan went to bed at ten o'clock, ma'am."

"It is not possible that the gates can have been locked, Martha. The captain came in by the upper one, the furthest from here. I heard him the minute he put his foot on the gravel, and knew his step. You must have thought you locked them. George!" added Mrs. Ordie, in a louder tone. "George!"

There was no answer. No sound whatever broke the stillness of the night.

"Captain Ordie!" she repeated. "Captain Ordie!"

The servant was laughing to herself, taking care that her young mistress did not see her. She believed that Mrs. Ordie had dropped asleep, and had *dreamt* she heard somebody on the gravel.

"I know what it is," cried Mrs. Ordie, briskly. "He has never been here before; and, finding the door was not immediately opened to him, has gone on to Mr. Beecher's, thinking this the wrong house."

She ran down the narrow path as she spoke, which branched off round by the kitchen-window; the maid followed her. It was a light night.

But nothing was to be seen of George Ordie. The curate's house, a small one, presented the appearance of a dwelling whose inmates are at rest; the blinds were drawn before the windows, and all was still. Mrs. Ordie ran over probabilities in her mind, and came to the conclusion that he could not have gone there. The Beechers were early people, and had no doubt been in bed an hour ago. Had her husband knocked there, he would be waiting at the door still, for they had not had time to come down and let him in.

"It could only have been fancy, ma'am," cried Martha.

"Silence," said Mrs. Ordie. "How can it have been fancy? I heard my husband, and saw him."

"Well, ma'am, I argue so from the gates being fast. He couldn't have got over 'em, because of the spikes."

"The gates cannot be fast," returned Mrs. Ordie, "and it is foolish of you to persist in saying so—only to screen your own carelessness."

"I wish you'd just please to look at the gates," retorted Martha.

"I will," said Mrs. Ordie, anxious to convict Martha to her face. "It is an utter impossibility that Captain Ordie can have come in at a high, locked gate, with spikes on the top; he would not attempt to do so. He would have rung the bell."

"That's what I say," answered Martha. "I dreamt t'other night," she muttered, as she followed her mistress, "that a man came down that there path with lovely gownd pieces to sell: I might just as well have riz up the house, and had *him* looked for."

They gained the broad walk, and proceeded round towards the further gate. It was locked. Martha sniffed.

"Why, it is like magic!" uttered Mrs. Ordie.

"I was certain about its being locked, ma'am. And that's why I say it must be fancy."

Mrs. Ordie was indignant. "Is this gate fancy?" she said, shaking it in her anger. "Don't tell me again that my husband is fancy. How could I have seen and heard him if he were not come? Captain Ordie!" she called out, once more. "George! where can you have gone to?"

"Come to the other gate, Martha."

They retraced their steps, Mrs. Ordie looking in all directions for a gleam of scarlet, and reached the other gate. It was locked. Mr. Beecher's gate was locked. Then she went about the garden, and looked and called: but there was no trace of Captain Ordie. The servant walked with her, half amused, half provoked.

"Can he have slipped indoors," murmured Mrs. Ordie, "while we went round to the Beechers?" And she went in to look, taking the opportunity to glance at her child. But Captain Ordie was nowhere to be seen, and she had never been so much perplexed and puzzled in all her life.

"Then he must have gone on, as I thought, to Mr. Beecher's," was her last solution of the enigma. "They were possibly up, and let him in directly. And they are keeping him there till morning, that he may not disturb us, knowing that baby is ill."

"But about the gate," interrupted the servant, returning to her stumbling-block, "how could he have got through it?"

"I know he did get through it, and that's enough," responded Mrs. Ordie, disposing summarily of the difficulty. "Soldiers are venturesome and can do anything. I will go and fetch him. You stop here, Martha, and listen to baby."

Once more Mrs. Ordie sped to the curate's. She knocked at the door, and stood back to look up at the house. "They have put him into their spare bed," she soliloquized; "Mrs. Beecher has kept it made up this fortnight past, expecting their invalid from India. My goodness! I never thought of it: they have no doubt come together, in the same ship. George may have gone to Calcutta; and, finding James Beecher was coming, must have got leave, all in a hurry, and accompanied him."

Picking up some bits of gravel, she threw them at Mrs. Beecher's bedroom-window. This brought forth the curate in his nightcap, peeping through the curtains.

"It is I, Mr. Beecher. Have you got Captain Ordie here?"

"Make haste, Anne," cried the curate, turning his head round to speak to his wife. "It is Mrs. Ordie. Perhaps the child is in a fit."

"My husband," repeated Mrs. Ordie. "He is here, is he not?"

"Yes; directly," answered the curate, imperfectly understanding, but opening the casement about an inch to speak.

"Is she really worse, Louisa?" exclaimed Mrs. Beecher, who now appeared at the window. "I will soon be with you."

The curate, believing the matter to be settled, drew in his nightcap. But Mrs. Ordie's voice was again heard. "Mr. Beecher! I want you."

"Dress yourself, my dear," cried Mrs. Beecher to him, in a flurry. "I dare say they want you to go for Mr. Percival. If the baby is really worse, and it is not Louisa's fancy, I shall never more boast of knowing children. She is calling again."

Mr. Beecher reopened the casement. "I am putting on my clothes, Mrs. Ordie. I am coming."

"But you need not do that. Has your brother arrived?"

"Who?"

"Your brother: James Beecher."

"No. Not yet."

"Some ship is in: it has brought my husband. Tell him I am here."

"We'll be down in a minute," called out Mr. Beecher, and making desperate haste. "Anne, Captain Ordie's come."

"Captain Ordie!" exclaimed Mrs. Beecher.

"Mrs. Ordie says so."

"Then we shall have James here tomorrow. How very unexpected Captain Ordie's arrival must have been to his wife? And to find his child ill!"

Louisa Ordie waited. Mrs. Beecher came down first, in a large shawl, her bonnet tied over her night. cap. They began to speak at cross-purposes.

"Is he coming? Have you told him?" impatiently asked Mrs. Ordie.

"My dear, yes. But he had gone upstairs in slippers, and his shoes were in the back-kitchen. Captain Ordie's arrival must have taken you by surprise."

"I never was so much surprised in my life," answered Mrs. Ordie, standing still, and not offering to stir. "I heard his footstep first, and knew it, even in the distance. I am so glad! He must have come with James Beecher."

"Ay, we shall have James here tomorrow. But, my dear, let us not lose time. Is the child very ill?"

"She is not worse; there is no hurry," answered Mrs. Ordie, planting her back against a tree, as deliberately as if she meant to make it her station for the night, and gazing up at the casement which she knew belonged to their spare bedroom. Mrs. Beecher looked at her in surprise.

"Will he be long?" she resumed. "There's no light."

"He will be here directly," said Mrs. Beecher; "he is finding his shoes. I suppose Kitty put them in some out-of-the-way place, ready for cleaning in the morning."

Another pause, and the curate appeared.

"Oh, Mr. Beecher, *you* need not have got up," was Mrs. Ordie's greeting. "I am sorry to give you all this trouble."

"It is no trouble. Do you want me to go for Mr. Percival?"

"You are very kind, but we shall not require the doctor tonight: at least I hope not. I have been watching her myself: I had her brought down to my own room. Nurse behaved shamefully over it, and I gave her warning.

"Pray let us go on and see how she is," said Mrs. Beecher, never supposing but they had been called up by the state of the child.

"When he comes. You say he will not be long. Had he undressed?"

"Had who undressed?"

"My husband."

Mrs. Beecher stared at her in amazement. "I do not understand you, Louisa. For whom are we waiting here?"

"For *my* husband, of course. You say he is finding his shoes."

Both Mr. and Mrs. Beecher thought her child's illness was turning her crazy. They looked at her, and at one another.

"My dear, you are mystifying us," spoke the wife, drawing her shawl tighter round her shoulders. "Is your husband coming out here, into the garden? Are we to wait here for him?"

"Why, you know he is coming out, and of course I shall wait for him. Only think, he wore his regimentals!"

"His regimentals!"

"Yes. Just as if he were on duty."

"Where is Captain Ordie?" interposed the curate.

"Well, that's a sensible question, from you," laughed Mrs. Ordie. "I suppose he is in your spare bedroom, though I see no light. Or else hunting for his shoes in your kitchen."

"Child," said Mrs. Beecher, taking hold of her tenderly, "you are not well. I told you today what it would be, if you excited yourself. Let us take you home."

"I will not go without my husband. There. And what makes him so long? I shall call to him. Why, you have locked the door!" she exclaimed. "You have locked him in."

"Locked who in, child?" said Mrs. Beecher. "There's no one in the house but Kitty."

"My husband is there. Did he not come to you?"

"No, certainly not. We have not seen him."

"Mr. Beecher," she impatiently uttered, "I asked you, at first, whether my husband had come here, and you said yes."

"My dear young lady, I must have misunderstood you. All I

heard, with reference to Captain Ordie, was, that he had come: I supposed to your house. He has certainly not been to ours."

"Then what were you talking about?" she reproachfully asked of Mrs. Beecher. "It was shameful to deceive me so! You said he had gone upstairs in slippers, and was finding his shoes. You know you did."

"My dear child, I was speaking of Mr. Beecher. I did not know you thought your husband was here. Why did you think so?"

"If he is not here, where is he?" demanded Mrs. Ordie. "You need not look at me as though you thought I was out of my senses. Do you mean to say you have not seen Captain Ordie?"

"We have not, indeed. We went to bed at ten, and heard nothing, until you threw the gravel at the window."

"Where can he be? What can he have done with himself?"

"Did he leave you to come to us? When did he arrive?"

"It was at twenty-five minutes after eleven. I was sitting by baby, reading the *Vicar of Wakefield*. All at once I heard footsteps approaching from the upper gate, and I knew they were my husband's. I looked out, and saw him, and called to him; he did not seem to hear me, but went in to the portico. I ran down to let him in, and to my surprise he was not there, and I thought he must have come on to you."

"Then you have not yet spoken with him?" exclaimed Mr. Beecher.

"Not yet."

"Are you sure it was Captain Ordie? Who opened the gate to him?"

"No one. The gate is locked. There is the strange part of the business."

"My dear Mrs. Ordie! I fear it must be all a mistake. Captain Ordie would not arrive here on foot, even if he landed unexpectedly; and he could not have got through a locked gate. Perhaps you were asleep."

"Nonsense," peevishly replied Mrs. Ordie; "I was as wide awake as I am now. I had come to that part where the fine ladies from town had gone in to neighbour Flamborough's and caught them all at hunt-the-slipper, Olivia in the middle, bawling for fair play. The ballad *Edwin and Angelina* came in a few pages before, and that I skipped. I assure you I was perfectly awake."

"I do not think it possible to have been anything but a delusion," persisted Mr. Beecher.

"How a delusion?" angrily asked the young lady; "I do not know what you mean. If my hearing could play me false, my sight could not. I heard my husband, and saw him, and spoke to him. He was in his regimentals: were they a delusion?"

"This is very strange," said Mrs. Beecher. "He would not be likely to travel in regimentals."

"It is more than strange," was Louisa Ordie's answer, as she looked dreamily about. "He is in the grounds, somewhere, and why he does not come forward, I don't know."

The mystery was not cleared up that night. No Captain Ordie made his appearance. The next day Mrs. Ordie sent for her father, to impart to him the strange circumstance. He adopted his curate's view of the affair; and, indeed, the universal view. Mrs. Ordie was much annoyed at their disbelief; and she actually, in spite of her friends, had Captain Ordie advertised for, in the local papers: he *was* in England, she said, and it would be proved so.

When letters next arrived from India, there was one from Captain Ordie, which gave proof positive that he was not, and had not been in Europe. Mrs. Ordie was perplexed.

The weeks went on, and the time fixed for the departure of Mrs. Ordie and her child drew near. But meanwhile the disastrous news had arrived of the outbreak in India of that dreadful mutiny, and it was deemed advisable to postpone it.

She was sitting one day in a gloomy mood. She had not heard from her husband for some time (his last letter was dated April); and now, as she found, another mail was in, and had brought no news from him. The rising at Delhi, where Captain Ordie was quartered, was known to her, but not, as yet, the details of its more disastrous features. She did not fear his having fallen: had anything happened to him, Mr. Main, or one of her sisters, would have written. They were all at Delhi.

As she thus sat, Mrs. Beecher came in, looking very pale and sad. Dr. and Mrs. Ling had gone off in their pony-carriage to the county town, to pick up news. They were extremely uneasy.

"Another mail has been in these two days!" she exclaimed to Mrs. Beecher. "News travels slower to Enton than anywhere. Have you heard from James Beecher? You don't look well."

"James is come," replied the curate's wife. "He came overland."

"And you have been worrying yourselves that he is dead!" retorted Louisa. "How are things going on, over there?"

"Very badly. They cannot be worse."

"Does he know anything of George?" continued she. "I think he might spare just a minute from his fighting to write to me. What is the matter with you? You have not brought bad news for me?" she added, her fears touched, and rising in excitement. "Oh, surely not! Not *FOR ME!*"

"James's news is altogether very dispiriting," returned Mrs. Beecher, at a loss how to proceed with her task. "My husband is gone to bring Dr. and Mrs. Ling back. We thought you might like them to be at home."

"Has George fallen in battle? Have those half-caste rebels shot him down? Oh——"

"Pray be calm, Louisa!" implored Mrs. Beecher; "if ever you had need of calmness in your life, you have need of it now."

"Is he wounded? Is he dead?" interrupted Mrs. Ordie, with a bitter shriek. "Oh, George! dearest George! and I have been calling you hard names for not writing to me! What is it?"

"There is a great deal to be told, my child. James Beecher was at Delhi in the midst of it."

Louisa suddenly rose and flew from the room. Mrs. Beecher, supposing she had gone to her chamber, went after her; but could not find her there. She had gone out of the house.

A thin man, looking fearfully ill, fair once, but browned by an Eastern sun, was lying on the sofa in the curate's parlour when a young, excited woman came flying in.

"Mr. James Beecher," she uttered, seizing his hands imploringly, "when did it happen? I am Mrs. Ordie."

"Has my sister-in-law told you—anything?" he hesitated.

"Yes, yes. I know the worst. I want particulars."

He had risen into an upright posture, though he could scarcely support himself, and she sat down beside him. He was a church missionary, a widower with children. "Are you sure that you can bear the details?" he asked, believing, from her words, that she knew the general facts.

"I am sure. Omit nothing. You were at Delhi."

"I went there in the spring, to say farewell to some friends, ere I came home. At Delhi I was taken worse, and lay ill there."

"But about the rising?"

"I am coming to it. On the second Monday in May, after breakfast, bad news came in. The 3rd Light Cavalry had dashed in from Meerut, fully armed, and were slaughtering the Europeans. Eighty-five of this regiment had been tried by court-martial at Meerut, for refusing to handle the greased cartridges, and sentenced to imprisonment. Their sentences were read out to them on parade on the previous Saturday, the 9th, and they were sent to gaol. On the 10th, Sunday, the regiment rose, released the prisoners, massacred the European officers, their wives and children, and on the 11th came to Delhi, in open revolt. I struggled up, dressed myself, joined the friends I was staying with, and we waited further news. It came in too soon. The mutineers had gone towards Deriowgunge, shooting all the officers they encountered. The brigadier ordered out the 54th Native Infantry and two guns; and, I believe, a detachment of another regiment; but accounts varied. They met the rebels just outside the Cashmere gate, and it was all up, for the *sepoys* deserted their officers, and shook hands with the *sowars*. Every officer was killed. Treacherous, cowardly wretches! they did not spare one."

She was biting her lips, and striving for calmness, determined to hear all. "Did the officers make no resistance?"

"All that they could make, but they were unarmed," he answered. "The next account that came in was, that the natives had risen and joined the insurrection, were firing the bungalows at Deriowgunge, and ransacking the European residences. The troopers were raging about, destroying life; and when their work was done, the *Goojours*,[1] who had collected in great numbers, as they were sure to do, followed in their wake, and pillaged everything, even to the matting. The bank was rifled."

Mr. Beecher paused, wondering whether he ought to proceed, but her studied calmness deceived him.

"No one knew where to fly for refuge, or what to do: none knew where to put the officers' wives and children. Many were taken to the Flagstaff Tower; but it was thought unsafe and had to be abandoned. Some escaped—many, I hope—in conveyances, or on horseback, or on foot. Some of the officers retreated to the cantonment outside the gates; but the troopers got there when night came, and killed them and their wives and children."

"Were any of *my* family with them?" she asked, still with unnatural composure.

"No. I will tell you. Before mid-day, the ladies of our house, my host's wife and her cousin, escaped to a close hut, or outhouse, and I managed to hobble there with them. I don't know how I did it: but it is astonishing the artificial strength that fear brings out. Others also took refuge there, about half-a-dozen ladies, your two sisters being amongst them, three or four children, and a poor little ensign, as ill and weak as I was. We hoped we were in safety; that the rebels would not think of looking for us there; and some old matting, well wetted, was hung up across the entrance, as if to dry. A *sepoy*, who was really faithful (and there were many such in the city), sat before it to guard it; many a one, raging after prey, did he turn aside with a well-assumed story that his old mother was in there, dying—let her die in peace."

"Was my husband there?"

"Not then. No one came near us all that day: they dared not come, for our sakes; and we bore our suspense and apprehension as we best could, not knowing who was living or who dead,

1. *Goojours*: "A race of peculiar caste, who congregate round Meerut and Delhi. They have been compared to our gipsy tribes, and live by plunder, even in times of peace. Some years ago a regiment was obliged to be raised especially to keep them under."—Wood's note.

of those dearest to us. What a day that was! We had neither food nor drink; the heat of the weather was fearful; and so many of us stowed together, and closely shut up, rendered the air fetid. We thought it could not be less than a hundred and ten degrees. This was not the worst; there were the apprehensions of discovery. We men might brave it, at any rate to appearance, but the poor young women! I believe they would have been glad to die as they cowered there, rather than live to encounter an uncertain fate. I strove to speak comfort to them all, but it was difficult; one or two bore bravely up, and cheered the rest. Late at night, under cover of the darkness, Captain Ordie stole in."

She raised a faint cry at the name. "My husband!"

"He told us what he could of the progress of the day—it was horribly bad, yet I believe he softened it for their ears—and then he began to talk of our own situation. It would be impossible, he said, to keep in the same place of concealment another day, and that we had better join a party who were about to make their escape towards Kurnaul. All seized at the idea eagerly, and wished to start without the delay of an instant. Mrs. Holt, my friend's wife, inquired after her husband, whom she had not seen since morning.

"He is safe, and unharmed," replied Captain Ordie. "You will see him when we are fairly off; but it was not thought well for more than one of us to venture here."

"And my husband?' added Mrs. Main, who had done nothing but clasp her baby to her breast all day, and weep silently. "Is he safe?" Captain Ordie answered evasively," continued Mr. Beecher, "and I knew, by his words and by the turn of his face, that poor Main was gone."

"Go on," groaned Mrs. Ordie. "George's turn comes next."

Mr. Beecher hesitated. "I will finish later," he suggested.

"No, finish now. You cannot leave me in this suspense. It would be cruel."

"Captain Ordie spoke of the plan of departure. The officers had but three horses amongst them, and the ladies and invalids were to take it in turn to ride; two, with a child, on each horse.

All the party were to keep together. At that moment arose a horrible yell, which we knew proceeded from a *sowar*, and one of them appeared at the entrance, tearing down the matting. All the light we had was a night-wick in some oil, but we saw his dark face. The children shrieked; the ladies also, and huddled themselves together in a corner; and Captain Ordie advanced to the entrance, and dealt the man a blow on the temple with the butt-end of his pistol."

"I hope it killed him!" she uttered, her eyes sparkling.

"I think it did, for he lay motionless. Captain Ordie kicked him out of the way, and, throwing himself on his hands and knees, crawled out cautiously to reconnoitre. Alas! we soon heard a struggle outside; two more were upon him."

"And he was struck down! I *know* you are going to tell me so," she uttered, in a low, passionate wailing.

Mr. Beecher sat silent, his countenance full of distress.

"Louisa, my darling, be composed," interrupted Mrs. Beecher, who had come in search of her. "You know the worst now."

"Yes, I know the worst," she moaned. "They killed him, there and then."

"They did," whispered Mr. Beecher. "It was instantaneous."

She turned sick, and shook violently. But, by strong control, spoke again. "Finish the history. What became of you, inside?"

"It was all commotion in a moment, dreadful commotion. The poor terrified women attempted to fly; some succeeded, and I hope escaped. Providentially there were only these two troopers; had more been upon us, none would have been left. The first thing I saw distinctly was, that one of them had caught Mrs. Main's infant, and was tossing it on the point of his bayonet. He next seized her."

"Constance?" panted Mrs. Ordie.

"Yes. And killed her. Killed her instantly. Be thankful."

Mrs. Ordie pressed down her eyelids, as if she would shut out some unwelcome sight. "Constance murdered," she moaned. "And you tell me to be thankful!"

"Be ever thankful," impressively spoke the missionary. "Others met with a worse fate."

"Sarah Ann?" she shivered. "What became of her?"

"I am unable to tell you. I trust she escaped. At the moment of Mrs. Main's death, I fainted on the floor where I was lying, and that must have saved my life. When I recovered, not a creature—living—was to be seen. The children were lying about; they had been put out of their misery; two of the ladies, and the ensign. Poor young fellow! he had told us, in the day, that he had no parents or near friends to mourn him, so the loss of a little griff, if they did kill him, would not count for much."

"Dead? All?"

"All. The two ladies were Mrs. Holt and Mrs. Main. Of the other ladies I saw no trace. I trust," he added, clasping his hands fervently, "that they escaped. We shall hear of many miraculous escapes: I pray that theirs may be of the number."

"Now, Louisa, let me take you home," urged Mrs. Beecher. "You do know the worst."

"I must hear all," was the answer, uttered in a tone of frenzy. " If I thought there was a word, a recital, left untold to me, I must get up in the middle of the night, and come and ask for it."

"You have heard all," said Mr. Beecher—"all that I know. My own escape I will not trouble you with. It was wonderful: and I lost no time in coming home overland."

She leaned back on the sofa and closed her eyes. Mrs. Beecher was thinking of her random words—that she would rather lose everything in the world than her child. But her thoughts had not grasped the dreadful possibility of losing her husband.

"When did this happen?" Mrs. Ordie suddenly asked. "What date?"

"I mentioned it," said Mr. Beecher. "Late on the night of the 11th of May."

She leaned forward breathless, her eyes staring. "How late? The exact hour? Speak!"

"It must have been near half-past eleven. When Captain Ordie came in, we asked him the time (for, strange to say, in our hurried flight, not one of us put a watch about us), and his watch said a quarter-past eleven; and we were talking, after that, perhaps ten minutes. It must have been about twenty-five minutes after eleven when he was killed."

"Listen to that!" shrieked Louisa Ordie, seizing Mrs. Beecher by the arm. "It was the very hour I saw and heard him. How was he dressed?" she rapidly asked.

"In full regimentals."

"There! There! Do you believe me now, Mrs. Beecher? Ah! you all ridiculed me then; but you hear it! It was my husband that came down the path here—appearing to me in the moment of his death."

The reader must judge of this mystery as he pleases.

It happened; at least, to the positive belief of the lady, here called Mrs. Ordie, as her friends can testify. They reason with her in vain. They point out that twenty-five minutes after eleven in Delhi would not be twenty-five minutes after eleven here: they believe that it was, and could have been, nothing but her own vivid imagination, that her thoughts were probably running on her husband through the "George" in the *Vicar of Wakefield*. But Louisa Ordie nevertheless believes, and will believe to the end of time, that it was her husband in the spirit who showed himself to her that unhappy night.

David Garth's Night-Watch

It was the following year, and we were again at Crabb Cot. Fever had broken out at Dr. Frost's, and the school was dismissed. The leaves were falling late that year, for November was nearly half through, and they strewed the ground. But if the leaves were late, the frost was early. The weather had come in curiously cold. Three days before the morning I am about to speak of, the warm weather suddenly changed, and it was now as freezing as January. It is not often that you see ice mingling with the dead leaves of autumn. Both the ice and the leaves have to do with what happened: and I think you often find that if the weather is particularly unseasonable, we get something by which to remember it.

At the corner of a field between our house and North Crabb, stood a small solitary dwelling, called Willow Brook Cottage: but the brook from which it took its name was dry now. The house had a lonely look, and was lonely; and perhaps that kept it empty. It had been unoccupied for more than a year, when the squire, tired of seeing it so, happened to say in the hearing of James Hill, that new bailiff of ours, that he would let it for an almost nominal rent. Hill caught at the words and said he would be glad to rent it: for some cause or other he did not like the house he was in, and had been wanting to leave it. At least, he said so: but he was of a frightfully stingy turn, and we all thought the low rent tempted him. Hill, this working bailiff, was a steady man, but severe upon everyone.

It was during this early frost that he began to move in. One

228

morning after breakfast, I was taking the broad pathway across the fields to North Crabb, which led close by Willow Cottage, and saw Hill wheeling a small truck up with some of his household goods. He was a tall, strong man, and the cold was tolerably sharp, but the load had warmed him.

"Good morning, Master Johnny."

"Making ready for the flitting Hill?"

Hill wheeled the truck up to the door, and sat down on one of the handles whilst he wiped his face. It was an honest, though cross face; habitually red. The house had a good large garden at its side, enclosed by wooden palings; with a shed and some pigsties at the back. Trees overshadowed the palings: and the fallen leaves, just now, inside the garden and out were ankle-deep.

"A fine labour I shall have, getting the place in order!" cried Hill, pointing to some broken palings and the overgrown branches. "Don't think but what the squire has the best of the bargain, after all!"

"You'd say that, Hill, if he gave you a house rent-free."

Hill took the key from his pocket, unlocked the door, and we went in. This lower room was boarded; the kitchen was at the back; above were two fair-sized chambers. One of them looked towards Crabb Ravine; the other was only lighted by a skylight in the roof.

"You have had fires here, Hill!"

"I had 'em in every room all day yesterday, sir, and am going to light 'em again now. My wife said it must be done; and she warn't far wrong; for a damp house plays the mischief with one's bones. The fools that women be, to be sure!—and my wife's the worst of 'em."

"What has your wife done?"

"She had a bit of a accident yesterday, Master Johnny. A coming out with a few things for this place, she stepped upon some ice, and fell; it gave her ankle a twist, and she had to be helped home. I'm blest if she's not a-saying now that it's a bad omen! Because she can't get about and help shift the things in here, she says we shan't have nothing but ill-luck in the place."

I had already heard of the accident. Hill's wife was a little shrinking woman, mild and gentle, quite superior to him. She was a widow when he married her a short time ago, a Mrs. Garth, with one son, David. Miss Timmens, the schoolmistress at North Crab, was her sister. On the previous morning a letter had come from Worcester, saying their mother, Mrs. Timmens, was taken dangerously ill, and asking them to go over. Miss Timmens went; Hill refused for his wife. How could he get along at moving-time without her, he demanded. She cried and implored, but Hill was hard as flint. So she had to remain at home, and set about her preparations for removal; surly Hill was master and mistress too. In starting with the first lot of movables—a few things carried in her arms—the accident occurred. So that, in the helping to move, she was useless; and the neighbours, ever ready to take part in a matrimonial grievance, said it served Hill right. Any way, it did not improve his temper.

"When do you get in here, Hill?"

"Tomorrow, Master Johnny, please the pigs. But for the wife's awk'ardness we'd ha' been in today. As to any help Davvy could give, it's worth no more nor a rat's; he haven't got much more strength in him nor one neither. Drat the boy!"

Leaving Hill to his task, I went on; and in passing Mrs. Hill's dwelling, I thought I'd give a look in to inquire after the ankle. The cottage stood alone, just as this other one did, but was less lonely, for the Crabb houses were round about. Davy's voice called out, "Come in."

He was the handiest little fellow possible for any kind of housework—or for sewing, either; but not half strong enough or rough enough for a boy. His soft brown eyes had a shrinking look in them, his face was delicate as a girl's, and his hair hung in curls. But he was a little bit deformed in the back—some called it only a stoop in the shoulders—and, though fourteen, might have been taken for ten. The boy's love for his mother was something wonderful. They had lived at Worcester; she had a small income, and he had been well brought up. When she married Hill— all her friends were against it, and it was in fact a

230

frightful mistake—of course they had to come to North Crabb; but Davy was not happy. Always a timid lad, he could not overcome his first fear of Hill. Not that the man was unkind, only rough and resolute.

Davy was washing up the breakfast-things; his mother sat near, sorting the contents of a chest: a neat little woman in a green stuff gown, with the same sweet eyes as David and the same shrinking look in them. She left off when I went in, and said her ankle was no worse.

"It's a pity it happened just now, Mrs. Hill."

"I'd have given a great deal for it not to, sir. They call me foolish, I know; always have done; but it just seems to me like an omen. I had a few articles in my arms, the first trifles we'd begun to move, and down I fell on going out at this door. To me it seems nothing but a warning that we ought not to move into Willow Cottage."

David had halted in his work at the tea-cups, his brown eyes fixed on his mother. That it was not the first time he had listened to the superstition, and that he was every whit as bad as she, might plainly be seen.

"I have never liked the thought of that new place from the first, Master Johnny. It is as if something held me back from it. Hill keeps saying that it's a convenient dwelling, and dirt-cheap; and so it is; but I don't like the notion of it. No more does David."

"Oh, I dare say you will like it when you get in, Mrs. Hill, and David, too."

"It is to be hoped so, sir."

The day went on; and its after events I can only speak of from hearsay. Hill moved in a good many of his goods, David carrying some of the lighter things. Luke Macintosh was asked to go and sleep in the house that night as a safeguard against thieves, but he flatly refused, unless someone slept there with him. Hill ridiculed his cowardice; and finally agreed that David should bear him company.

He made the bargain without his wife. She had other views

for David. Her intention was to send the lad over to Worcester by the seven-o'clock evening train; not so much because his bed and bedding had been carried off and there was nothing for him to sleep on, as that his dying grandmother had expressed a wish to see him. To hear then that David was not to go, did not please Mrs. Hill.

It was David himself who carried in the news. She had tea waiting on the table when they came in; David first, for his step-father had stopped to speak to someone in the road.

"But, David, dear—you *must* go to Worcester," she said, when he told her.

"He will never let me, mother," was David's answer. "'He says the things might be stolen if nobody takes care of them: and Macintosh is afraid to be there alone."

She paused and looked at him, a thought striking her. The boy was leaning upon her in his fond manner, his hand in hers.

"Should you be afraid, David? "

"Not—I think—with Luke. We are to be in the same room, mother."

But Mrs. Hill noticed that his voice was hesitating; his small weak hand trembled in hers. There was not a more morally brave heart than David Garth's; he had had a religious training; but at being alone in the dark he was a very coward, afraid of ghosts and goblins.

"Hill," said she to her husband when he stamped in, the lad having gone to wash his hands, "I cannot let David sleep in the other house tonight. He will be too timid."

"Timid!" repeated Hill, staring at the words. "Why, Luke Macintosh will be with him."

"David won't like it. Macintosh is nothing but a coward himself."

"Don't thee be a fool, and show it," returned Hill, roughly. "Thee'll keep that boy a baby for his life. Davy would as soon sleep in the house alone, as not, but for the folly put into his head by you. And why not? He's fourteen."

Hill—to give him his due—only spoke as he thought. That

anyone in the world, grown to fourteen and upwards, could be afraid of sleeping in a house alone, was to him literally incomprehensible.

"I said he must go over to Worcester to see mother, James," she meekly resumed; "you know I did."

"Well, he can't go tonight; he shall go in the morning. There! He may stop with her for a week, an' ye like, for all the good he is to me."

"Mother's looking for him tonight, and he ought to go. The dying—"

"Now just you drop it, for he can't be spared," interrupted Hill. "The goods might be stole, with all the loose characters there is about, and that fool of a Macintosh won't go in of himself. He's a regular coward! Davvy must keep him company—it's not so much he does for his keep—and he may start for Worcester by daylight."

Whenever Hill came down upon her with this resolute decision, it struck her timid forthwith. The allusion to the boy's keep was an additional thrust, for it was beginning to be rather a sore subject. An uncle at Worcester, who had no family and was well to do, had partly offered to adopt the lad; but it was not yet settled. Davy was a great favourite with all the relatives; Miss Timmens, the schoolmistress, doted on him. Mrs. Hill, not venturing on further remonstrance, made the best of the situation.

"Davy, you are to go to Worcester the first thing in the morning," she said, when he came back from washing his hands. "So as soon as you've been home and had a bit o' breakfast, you shall run off to the train."

Tea over, Hill went out on some business, saying he should be in at eight, or thereabouts, to go with Davy to the cottage. As the hour drew near, David, sitting over the fire with his mother in pleasant talk, as they loved to do, asked if he should read before he went: for her habit was to read the Bible to him, or cause him to read to her, the last thing.

"Yes, dear," she said. "Read the ninety-first Psalm."

So David read it. Closing the book when it was over, he sat

with it on his knee, thoughtfully.

"If we could only see the angels, mother! It is so difficult to remember always that they are close around, taking care of us."

"So it is, Davy. Most of us forget it."

"When life's over it will be so pleasant for them to carry us away to heaven! I wish you and I could go together, mother."

"We shall each go when God pleases, David."

"Oh yes, I know that."

Mrs. Hill, remembering this little bit of conversation, word for word, repeated it afterwards to me and others, with how they had sat, and David's looks. I say this for fear people might think I had invented it.

Hill came in, and they prepared to go to the other house. David, his arms full—for, of course, with things to be carried, they did not go out empty-handed—came suddenly back from the door in going out, flung his load down, and clasped his mother. She bent to kiss him.

"Goodnight, my dear one! Don't you and Luke get chattering all night. Go to sleep betimes."

He burst into tears, clinging to her with sobs. It was as if his heart were breaking.

"Are you afraid to go?" she whispered.

"I must go," was his sobbing answer.

"Now then, Davvy!" called back Hill's rough tones. "What the plague are you lagging for?"

"Say goodbye to me, mother! Say goodbye!"

"Goodbye, and God bless you, David! Remember the angels are around you!"

"I know; I know"

Taking up his bundles, he departed, keeping some paces behind Hill all the way; partly to hide his face, down which the tears were raining; partly in his usual awe of that formidable functionary who stood to him as a stepfather.

Arrived at the house. Hill was fumbling for the key, when someone came darting out from the shadow of its eaves. It proved to be Luke Macintosh.

"I was a-looking round for you," said crusty Hill. "I began to think you'd forgot the time o' meeting."

"No, I'd not forgot it; but I be come to say that I can't oblige you by sleeping there," was Luke's reply. "The master have ordered me off with the waggon afore dawn, and so—I'm a-going to sleep at home."

Had I been there, I could have said the master had not ordered Luke off before dawn; but after his breakfast. It was just a ruse of his, to avoid doing what he had never relished, sleeping in the house. Hill suspected as much, and went on at him, mockingly asking if he was afraid of hobgoblins. Luke dodged away in the midst of it, and Hill relieved his anger by a little hot language.

"Come along, Davvy," said he at last; "we must put these here things inside."

Unlocking the door, he went in; and, the first thing, fell against something or other in the dark. Hill swore a little at that, and struck a light, the fire having gone out. This lower room was full of articles, thrown down out of hand; the putting things straight had been left to the morrow.

"Carry the match afore me, Davvy. These blankets must go upstairs."

By some oversight no candles had been taken to the house; only the box of matches. David lighted one match after the other, while Hill arranged the blankets on the mattress for sleeping. This room—the one with the skylight—was to be David's.

"There," said Hill, taking the box of matches from him, "you'll be comfortable here till morning. If you find it cold, you might keep on your trousers."

David Garth stood speechless, a look of horror struggling to his face. In that first moment he dared not remonstrate; his awe of Hill was too great.

"What's the matter now?" asked Hill, striking another match. "What ails you?"

"You'll not leave me here, all by myself?" whispered the unhappy boy, in desperate courage.

"Not leave you here by yourself! Why, what d'ye think is to harm you? Don't you try on your nonsense and your games with me, Master Davvy. I'm not soft, like your mother. Say your prayers and get to sleep, and I'll come and let you out in the morning."

By a dexterous movement, Hill got outside, and closed the door softly, slipping the bolt. The match in his fingers was nearly burnt out; nevertheless, it had shown a last faint vision of a boy kneeling in supplication, his hands held up; his face one of piteous agony. As Hill struck another match to light the staircase, a wailing cry mingled with the sound: entreaties to be let out; prayers not to be left alone; low moans, telling of awful terror.

"Drat the boy! This comes of his mother's coddling. Hold your row, Davvy," he roared out, wrathfully: "you'd not like me to come back and give you a basting."

And Mr. James Hill, picking his way over the bundles, locked the outer door, and betook himself home. That was our respectable bailiff. What do you think of him?

"Did you leave Davy comfortable?" asked Mrs. Hill, when he got back.

"He'll be comfortable enough when he's asleep," shortly answered Hill. "Of all hardened, ungrateful boys, that of yourn's the worst."

"Had Luke come when you got there?" she resumed, passing over the aspersion on Davy.

"He was waiting: he came right out upon us like an apparition." was Hill's evasive answer. And he did not tell the rest.

But now, a singular thing happened that night. Mrs. Hill was in a sound sleep, when a loud, agonized cry of "Mother" aroused her from it. She started up, wide awake instantly, and in terror so great that the perspiration began to pour off her face. In that moment the call was repeated. The voice was David's voice; it had appeared to be in the room, close to her, and she peered into every corner in vain. Then she supposed it must have come through the window; that David, from some cause or other, had come home from Willow Brook, and was waiting to be let in. A dread crossed her of Hill's anger, and she felt inclined to order the boy to go back again.

Opening the casement window, she called to him by name; softly at first, then louder. There was no answer. Mrs. Hill stretched out her head as far as the narrow casement allowed, but neither David nor anyone else could she see; nothing but the shadows cast by the moonlight. Just then the old church clock struck out. She counted the strokes and found it twelve. Midnight. It was bitterly cold: she closed the window at last, concluding David had gone off from fear of being punished. All she could hope was that he would have the sense, that dangerously keen night, to run off to the brick kilns, and get warm there.

But the terror lay upon her yet; she was unable to tell why or wherefore; unless from the strangely appealing agony of the cry; still less could she shake it off. It seemed odd. Hill awoke with the commotion, and found her trembling.

"What have ye got to be affrighted on?" he asked roughly, when she had told her tale. And Mrs. Hill was puzzled to say what.

"You had been a-dreaming of him, that's what it was. You've got nothing else in your mind, day nor night, but that there boy."

"It was not a dream; I am quite positive it was himself; I could not mistake his voice," persisted Mrs. Hill. "He has come away from the cottage, for sure. Perhaps that Luke Macintosh might have got teasing him."

Knowing what Hill knew, that the boy was locked in, he might safely have stood out that he could not have come away from it; but he said no more. Rolling himself round, he prepared to go to sleep again, resentful at having been awakened.

Hill overslept himself in the morning, possibly through the interrupted rest. When he went out it was broad daylight. David Garth's being locked up half-an-hour more or less went for nothing with Hill, and he stayed to load the truck with some of the remainder of his goods.

"Send Davy home at once, James," called out the wife, as he

began to wheel it away. "I'll give him his breakfast, and let him start off to the train."

For, with daylight, and the sight of the door-key, Mrs. Hill could only reverse her opinion, and conclude unwillingly that it might have been a dream. Hill showed her the key, telling her that he had locked the door "for safety." Therefore it appeared to be impossible that David could have got out.

The first thing Hill saw when he and his truck approached the cottage, was young Jim Batley, mounted on the roof and hammering away at the skylight with his freezing hands, Jim, a regular sailor for climbing, had climbed a tree, and thence swung himself on to the tiles. Hill treated him to some hard words, and ordered him to come down and get a licking. Down came Jim, taking care to dodge out of Hill's reach.

"I can't make David hear," said Jim. "I've got to go to Timberdale, and I want him to go along with me."

"That's no reason why you should get atop of my roof," roared Hill. "You look out for a sweet hiding, young Jim. The first time I get hold on you, you shall have it kindly."

"He sleeps uncommon hard," said Jim, "One 'ud think the cold had froze him. I've got to take a letter to my uncle's at Timberdale: we shall find a jolly good hot breakfast when we get there."

Hill condescended to abate his anger so far as to inform Jim Batley that David could not go to Timberdale; adding that he was going off by train to see his grandmother at Worcester, Ordering Jim to take himself away, he unlocked the door and entered the cottage.

Jim Batley chose to stay. He was a tall, thin, obstinate fellow, of eleven, and meant to wait and speak to David. Given to following his own way whenever he could, in spite of his father and mother, it occurred to him that perhaps David might be persuaded to take Timberdale first and the train after.

He amused himself with the dead leaves while he waited. But it seemed that David took a long time dressing. The truck stood at the door; Jim stamped and whistled, and shied a few stones at the topmost article, which was Mrs. Hill's potato saucepan. Presently Hill came out and began to unload, beginning with the saucepan.

"Where's Davy?" demanded Jim, from a safe distance. "Ain't he ready yet?"

"Now if you don't get off about your business I'll make you go," was Hill's answer, keeping his back turned to the boy. "You haven't got nothing to stop here for."

"I'm stopping to speak to Davy."

"Davy was away out o' here afore daylight and took the first train to Worcester. He's a'most there by now."

Young boys are not clever reasoners; but certain contradictory odds and ends passed through Jim's disappointed mind. For one thing, he had seen Hill unlock the door.

"I don't think he's gone out yet. I see his boots."

"What boots?" asked Hill, putting a bandbox inside the door, "Davy's. I see 'em through the skylight; they stood near the mattress."

"Them was a pair of my boots as I carried here last night. I tell ye Davvy's *gone*: can't ye believe? He won't be home for some days neither, for his grandmother's safe to keep him."

Jim Batley went off slowly on his way to Timberdale: there was nothing to stay for, Davy being gone. Happening to turn round, he caught Hill looking after him, and saw his face for the first time. It had turned white as death. The contrast was very remarkable, for it was usually of a deep red.

"Well, I never!" cried Jim, halting in surprise. "Mayhap the cold have took him! Serve him right."

When Hill had got all the things inside he locked himself in, probably not to be disturbed while he arranged them. Mrs. Hill had been waiting breakfast ever so long when she heard the truck coming back.

"Whatever's become of David?" she began. "I expected him home at once."

"David has started for Worcester," said Hill.

"Started for Worcester? Without his breakfast?"

"Now don't you worry yourself about petty things," returned Hill, crustily. "You wanted him to go, and he's gone. He won't starve; let him alone for that."

The notion assumed by Mrs. Hill was, that her husband had started the boy off from the cottage direct to the train. She felt thoroughly vexed.

"He had all his old clothes on. Hill. I would not have had him go to Worcester in that plight for any money. You might have let the child come home for a bit of breakfast—and to dress himself. There was not so much as a brush and comb at the place, to make his hair tidy."

"There's no pleasing you," growled Hill. "Last night you were a'most crying, cause Davvy couldn't be let go over to see your mother; and, now that he is gone, that don't please ye! Women be the very deuce for grumbling."

Mrs. Hill dropped the subject—there could be no remedy— and gave her husband his breakfast in silence. Hill seemed to eat nothing, and looked very pale; at moments ghastly.

"Don't you feel well?" she asked.

"Well?—I'm well enough. What should ail me—barring the cold? It's as sharp a frost as ever I was out in."

"Drink this," she said, pouring him out another cup of hot tea. "It is cold; and I'm sorry we've got it so for our moving. What time shall we get in today, Hill?"

"Not at all,"

"Not at all!" repeated the wife in surprise.

"No, not at all," was Hill's surly confirmation. "What with you disabled, and Davvy o' no use, things is not as forrard as they ought to be. I've got to be off to my work too, pretty quick, or the squire'll be about me. We shan't get in till tomorrow."

"But nearly all our things are in," she remonstrated. "There's as good as nothing left here."

"I tell ye we don't go in afore tomorrow," said Hill, giving the table a thump. "Can't ye be satisfied with that? "

He went off to his work. Mrs. Hill, accepting the change as inevitable, resigned herself, and borrowed a saucepan to cook the potatoes for dinner. She might have spared herself the trouble; her husband did not come in for any. He bought a penny loaf and some cheese, and made his dinner of it inside our home barn, Molly giving him some beer. He had done it before when very busy: but the work he was about that day was in no such hurry, and he might have left it if he would.

"Who is to sleep in the house tonight? "his wife asked him when he got home to tea.

"I shall," said Hill. "I won't be beholden to nobody."

Mrs. Hill, remembering the experience of the past night, quaked a little at finding she should have to sleep in the old place alone, devoutly praying there might be no recurrence of the dream that had thrown her into such mortal terror. She and Davy were just alike—frightened at their own shadows in the dark. When Hill was safe off, she hurried into bed, and kept her head under the clothes.

Hill came back betimes in the morning; and they moved in at once; old Coney's groom, who happened to be out with the dogcart, offering to drive Mrs. Hill. Though her ankle was better and the distance short, she could hardly have walked. Instead of finding the house in order, as she expected, it was all sixes and sevens; the things lying about all over it.

Towards evening, Hannah got me to call at Willow Brook and say she'd go there in the morning for an hour or two, to help put things in order—the mistress had said she might do so. The fact was, Hannah was burning for a gossip, she and Hill's wife being choice friends. It was almost dark; the front room looked tolerably straight, and Mrs. Hill sat by the fire, resting her foot and looking out at the window, the shutters not yet closed.

"I'd be very thankful for her to come. Master Johnny," she said eagerly, hardly letting me finish. "There's a great deal to do; and, besides that, it is so lonesome here. I never had such a feeling in all my life; and I have gone into strange homes before this."

"It does seem lonesome, somehow. The fancy may go off in a day or two."

241

"I don't know, sir: it's to be hoped it will. Master Johnny, as true as that we are sitting here, when I got out of Mr. Coney's dogcart and put my foot over the threshold to enter, a fit of trembling took me all over. There was no cause for it; I mean I was not thinking of anything to give it me. Not a minute before, I was laughing; for the man had been telling me a joking story of something that happened yesterday at his master's. A strange fear seemed to come upon me all at once as I stepped over the threshold, and I began to shake from head to foot. Hill stared at me, and at last asked if it was the cold; I told him truly that I did not know what it was; except that it seemed like some unaccountable attack, for I was well wrapped up. He had some brandy in a bottle, and made me drink a drop. The fit went off; but I have had a queer lonesome feeling on me ever since, as if the house was not one to be alone in."

"And you have been alone, I suppose?"

"Every bit of the time, save when Hill came in to his dinner. I don't remember ever to have had such a feeling before in broad daylight. It's just as if the house was haunted."

Not believing in haunted houses, I laughed. Mrs. Hill got up to stir the fire. It blazed, and cast her shadow upon the opposite wall.

"When dusk came on, I could hardly bear it. But for your coming in, Master Johnny, I should have stood at the door in the cold, and watched for Hill: things don't feel so lonely to one out of doors as in."

So it seemed that I was in for a stay—any way, till Hill arrived. After this, it would not have been very kind to leave her alone; she looked so weak and little.

"I've never liked the thought of moving here from the first," she went on; "and then there came the accident to my foot. Some people think nothing at all of omens. Master Johnny, but I do think of them. They come oftener than is thought for too; only, so few take notice of them. I wish Davy was back! I can't bear to be in this house alone."

"David is at Worcester, I heard Hill say."

"He went yesterday morning, sir. I expected a letter from him today; and it is very curious that none have come. Davy knew how anxious I was about mother; and he never fails to write when he's away from me. Somehow, all things are going crooked and cross just now. I had a fright the night before last, Master Johnny, and I am hardly quit of it yet."

"What was that?" I asked her.

She stared into the fire for a minute or two before she answered me. There was no other light in the room,; I sat back against the wall beside the window—the shutters were still open.

"You might not care to hear it, sir."

"I should if it's worth telling."

Turning from the fire, she looked straight at me while she told it from beginning to end, exactly as I have written it above. The tale would have been just the thing for Mrs. Todhetley: who went in for marvels.

"Hill stood to it that it was a dream, Master Johnny; but the more I think of it, the less I believe it could have been one. If I had only heard the call in my sleep, or in the moment of waking, why of course it might have been a dream; but when I heard it the second time it was *after* I awoke. I heard it as plain as I hear my own voice now; and plainer, too."

"But what else, except a dream, do you fancy it could have been?"

"Well, sir, that's what is puzzling me. But for Hill's convincing me Davy could not have got out of here after he had locked him and Macintosh in for safety, I should have said it was the boy himself, calling me from outside. It sounded in the room, close to me: but the fright I was in might have deceived me. What's that?"

A loud rapping at the window. I am not ashamed to say that coming so unexpectedly it startled me. Mrs. Hill, with a shrill scream, darted forward to catch hold of my arm.

"Let me go. Someone wants to be let in. I dare say it's Hill."

"Master Johnny, I beg your pardon," she said, going back.

"Hill ought to know better than to come frightening me at night like this."

I opened the door, and Miss Timmens walked in: not Hill. The knocking had not been intended to frighten any one, but as a greeting to Mrs. Hill—Miss Timmens having seen her through the glass.

"You know you always were one of the quaking ones, Nanny," she said, scoffing at the alarm. "I have just got back from Worcester, and thought you'd like to hear that mother's better."

"And it is well you are back, Miss Timmens," I put in. "The school has been in rebellion. Strangers, going by, have taken it for a bear garden."

"That Maria Lease is just good for nothing," said Miss Timmens, wrathfully. "When she offered to take my place I knew she'd not be of much use. Yes, sir; it was the thought of the school that brought me back so soon."

"And mother is really better!" cried Mrs. Hill. "I am so thankful. If she had died and I not able to get over to her, I should never have forgiven myself. How is David?"

"Are you getting straight, Nancy?" asked Miss Timmens, looking round the room, and not noticing the question about David.

"Straight! and only moved in this morning! and me with this ankle!"

Miss Timmens laughed. She was just as capable as her sister was the contrary.

"About David?" added Mrs. Hill, "I was so vexed that he went over in his old clothes! It was Hill's fault. Have you brought me a letter from him?"

"How could I bring you a letter from him?" returned Miss Timmens. "A letter from where?"

It was a minute or two before elucidation was arrived at, for both were at cross-purposes. David Garth had not been at Worcester at all, so far as Miss Timmens knew; certainly not at his grandmother's.

To see Mrs. Hill sink back into her chair at this information, and let her hands fall on her lap, and gaze helplessly from her frightened eyes, was only to be expected. Miss Timmens kept asking what it all meant, and where David was, but she could get no answer. So I told her what Mother Hill had just told me—about Hill's sending him off to Worcester. She stared like anything.

"Why, where in the name of wonder can the boy have got to?"

"I see it all," spoke the mother then, in a whisper. "Davy did find his way out of this house; and it was his voice I heard, and not a dream. I knew it. I knew it at the time."

These words would have sounded mysterious to any one given to mystery. Miss Timmens was not. She was a long, thin female, with a chronic redness on her nose and one cheek, and she was as practical as could be. Demanding what Mrs. Hill meant by "not a dream," she stood warming her boots at the fire while she was enlightened.

"The boy is keeping away for fear of Hill tanning him," spoke Miss Timmens, summing up the question. "Don't you think so. Master Ludlow?"

"I should, if I could see how he got out of the cottage, after Hill had locked him in it."

"Luke Macintosh put him out at this window," said Miss Timmens, decisively. "Hill couldn't lock that up. They'd open the shutters, and Luke would pop him out: to get rid of the boy, no doubt. Mr. Luke ought to be punished for it."

I did not contradict her. Of course it might have been so; but knowing Luke, I did not think he would care to be left in the house alone. Unless—the thought flashed over me—unless Luke sent away David that he might be off himself. Amidst a good deal of uncertainty, this view seemed the most probable.

"Where is David?" bemoaned Mrs. Hill; "where is he? And with these bitter cold nights—"

"Now don't you worry yourself, Nanny," interrupted strong-minded Miss Timmens. "I'll see to David; and bring him home, too."

Hill's cough was heard outside. Miss Timmens—who had been in a dead rage at the marriage, and consequently hated Hill like poison—hastened to depart. We went away together, passing Hill by the dried-up brook. He looked stealthily at us, and threw back a surly goodnight to me.

"I'm sure I don't know where I am to look for the boy first," began Miss Timmens, as we went along. "Poor fellow! he is keeping away out of fear. It would not surprise me if Macintosh is taking care of him. The man's not ill-natured."

"I don't understand why Hill should have told his mother David was gone to Worcester, unless he did go." Neither did I.

"David never went to Worcester; rely upon that. Master Ludlow," was her answer. "He is well known at Shrub Hill Station, and I could not have failed to hear of it, for one of the porters lodges in mother's house; besides, David would have come down to us at once. Goodnight, sir. I dare say he will turn up before tomorrow."

She went on towards the schoolhouse, I the other way to Crabb Cot. Mrs. Todhetley and the squire were talking together by the blazing fire, waiting until old Thomas announced dinner.

"Where have you been lingering this cold evening, Johnny?" began the squire. "Don't you get trying the ponds, sir; the ice is not wafer thick yet."

Kneeling on the rug between them, holding my hands to the warmth, I told where I had been, and what I had heard. Mrs. Todhetley, who seemed to have been born with a sympathy for children, went into lamentation over—it was what she said—that poor little gentle lamb, David.

"Macintosh is about somewhere," spoke the squire, ringing the bell. "We will soon hear whether he knows what has become of the boy."

Thomas was ordered to find Macintosh and send him in. He came presently, shy and sheepish, as usual. Standing just inside the door, he blinked his eyes and rubbed his hands one over the other, like an idiot. It was only his way.

"Do you know where David Garth is?" began the squire, who thought himself a regular Q.C. at cross-examining. Luke stared and said "No." The fact was, he had not heard that David was missing.

"What time was it that you put him out of the window the night before last?"

Luke's eyes and mouth opened. He had no more idea what the squire meant than the man in the moon.

"Don't stand there as if you were a born simpleton, but answer me," commanded the squire. "When you and David Garth were put into Hill's new cottage to take care of the things for the night, how came you to let the boy out of it? Why did you do it? Upon what plea?"

"But I didn't do it, sir," said Luke.

"Now don't you stand there and say that to my face, Macintosh. It won't answer; for I know all about it. You put that poor shivering boy out at the window that you might be off yourself; that's about the English of it. Where did he go to?"

"But I couldn't do it, sir," was Luke's answer to this. "I was not in the place myself."

"You were not there yourself?"

"No, sir, I warn't. Knowing I should have to go off with the waggon pretty early, I went down and telled Hill that I should sleep at home."

"Do you mean to say you did not go into Hill's place at all?"

"No, sir, I didn't. I conclude Hill slept there hisself. I know nothing about it, for I don't happen to have come across Hill since. I've kept out of his way."

This was a new turn to the affair. Luke quitted the room, and a silence ensued. Mrs. Todhetley touched me on the shoulder.

"Johnny?"

"Yes!" I said, wondering at the startled look in her eyes.

"I hope Hill did not put that poor child into the house alone! If so, no wonder that he made his escape from it."

★★★★★★

The matter could not rest. One talked, and another talked: and before noon next day it was known all over the place that David Garth had been put to sleep by himself in the empty cottage. Miss Timmens attacked Hill with her strong tongue, and told him it was enough to frighten the child to death. Hill was sullen. He would answer nothing , and all she could get out of him was, that it was no business of hers. In vain she demanded his reasons for saying the boy had gone to Worcester by the early train: whether he sent him— whether he saw him off. Hill said David did go; and then took refuge in dogged silence.

The schoolmistress was not one to be played with. Of a tenacious turn, she followed out things with a will. She called in the police; she harangued people outside her door; she set the parish in a ferment. But David could not be heard of, high or low. Since the midnight hour, when that call of his awoke his mother, and was again repeated, he seemed to have vanished.

There arose a rumour that Jim Batley could tell something. Miss Timmens pounced upon him as he was going by the schoolhouse, conveyed him indoors, and ordered him to make a clean breast of it. It was not much that Jim had to tell: but that little seemed of importance to Miss Timmens, and he told it readily. One thing Jim persisted in—that the boots he saw through the skylight must have been David's boots. Hill had called them his, he said, but they were not big enough—not men's boots at all. Hill was looking "ghastly white," as if he had had a fright, Jim added, when he told him David was gone off to Worcester.

Perhaps it was in that moment that a fear of something worse than had been yet suspected dawned upon Miss Timmens. Tying on her bonnet, she came up to Crabb Cot, and asked to see the squire.

"It is getting more serious," she said, after old Thomas had shown her in. "I think, sir. Hill should be forced to explain what he knows. I have come here to ask you to insist upon it."

"The question is—what does he know?" rejoined the squire.

"More than he has confessed," said Miss Timmens, in her

positive manner. "Jim Batley stands to it that those boots must, from the size, have been David's boots. Now, Squire Todhetley, if David's boots were there, where was David? That is what's lying on my mind, sir."

"What did Jim Batley see besides the boots?" asked the squire.

"Nothing in particular," she answered. "He said the cupboard door stood open, and hid the best part of the room. David would not be likely to run away and leave his boots behind him."

"Unless he was in too great a fright to stop to put them on."

"I don't think that, sir."

"What is it you wish to imply?" asked the squire, not seeing the drift of the argument.

"I wish I knew myself," replied Miss Timmens, candidly. "I am certain Hill has not told all he could tell: he has been deceitful over it from the first, and he must be made to explain. Look here, sir: when he got to Willow Cottage that morning, there's no doubt he thought David was in it. Very well. He goes in to call him; stays a bit, and then comes out and tells young Jim that David has gone to Worcester. How was he to know David had gone to Worcester?—who told him? The boy says, too, that Hill looked ghastly, as if he had been frightened."

"David must have gone somewhere, or he would have been in the room," argued the squire. "He would not be likely to go back after quitting it, and his mother heard him call to her in the middle of the night."

"Just so, sir. But—if Hill did not find him, why should he come out and assert that David had started for Worcester?— Why not have said David had escaped?"

"I am sure I don't know."

"It's the boots that come over me," avowed Miss Timmens; "I can't come to the bottom of them. I mean to come to the bottom of Hill, though, and make him disclose what he knows. You are his master, sir, and perhaps he will tell you without trouble, if you will please to be so good as question him. If he won't, I'll have him brought up before the Bench."

Away went Miss Timmens, with a parting remark that the school must be rampant by that time. The squire sat thinking a bit, and then put on his hat and great-coat, telling me I might come with him and hear what Hill had to say. We expected to find Hill in the ploughed field between his cottage and North Crabb. But Hill was in his own garden; we saw him as we went along. Without ceremony, the squire opened the wooden gate, and stepped in. Hill was raking the leaves together by the shed at the end of the garden.

He threw down the rake when he saw us, as if startled, his red face turning white. Coming forward, he began a confused excuse for being at home at that hour of the day, saying there was so much to do when getting into a fresh place; and that he had not been well for two days, "had had a sickness upon him." The squire, never hard with the men, told him he was welcome to be there, and began talking about the garden.

"It is as rich a bit of land. Hill, as any in the parish, and you may turn it to good account if you are industrious. Does your wife intend to keep chickens?"

"Well, sir, I suppose she will. Town-bred women don't understand far about 'em, though. It may be a'most as much loss as profit."

"Nonsense," said the squire, in his quick way. "Loss! when you have every convenience about you! This used to be the fowl-house in Hopton's time," he added, rapping the side of the shed with his stick. "Why! you've been putting a padlock on it, Hill!"

For the door was fastened with a padlock; a new one, to judge by its look. Hill made no comment. He had taken up the rake again and was raking vigorously at the dead leaves. I wondered what he was shaking for.

"Have you any treasures here, that you should lock it up?"

"Only the watering-can, sir, and a few o' my garden tools," answered Hill. "There's a heap of loose characters about, and nothing's safe from 'em."

Putting his back against the shed, the squire suddenly called on Hill to face him, and entered on the business he had come upon. "Where was David Garth? Did he, Hill, know anything about him?"

Hill had looked pale before; I said so; but that was nothing to the frightful whiteness that took him now. Ears, lips, neck; all turned the hue of the dead. The rake shook in his grasp; his teeth chattered.

"Come, Hill," said the squire; "I see you have something to say."

But Hill protested he had nothing to say: except that the boy's absence puzzled him. The squire put some home questions upon the points spoken of by Miss Timmens, showing Hill that we knew all. He then told him he might take his choice; answer, or go before the magistrates.

Apparently Hill saw the futility of holding out longer. His very aspect would have convicted him, as the squire said: if he had committed murder, he could not have looked more guilty. Glancing shudderingly around on all sides, as though the air had phantoms in it, he whispered his version of the morning's work.

It was true that he *had* gone to the house expecting to find David in it; and it was true that when he entered he found him flown. Not wishing to alarm the boy's mother, he told Jim Batley that David had gone by early train to Worcester: he told the mother so. As to the boots, Hill declared they were his own, not David's; and that Jim's eyes must have been deceived in the size. And he vowed and declared he knew no more than this, or where David could have got to.

"What do you think you deserve for locking the child in the house by himself?" asked the squire, sternly.

"Everything that'll come upon me through it," readily acknowledged Hill. "I could cut my hands off now for having done it; but I never thought he'd be really frightened. It's just as if his ghost had been haunting me ever since; I see him a-following of me everywhere."

"His ghost!" exclaimed the squire. "Do you suppose he is dead?"

"I don't know," said the man, passing his shaking hand across his damp forehead. "I wish to Heaven I had let him go off to his grandmother's that same blessed night!"

"Then you wish me to understand, Hill, that you absolutely know nothing of where the boy may be?"

"Nothing at all, sir."

"Don't you think it might have been as well if you had told the truth from the first?" asked the squire, rather sarcastically.

"Well, sir, one's mind gets confused at times, and I thought of his mother. I could not be off seeing that if anything had happened, it lay on my shoulders for having left him alone, in there."

Whether the squire believed Hill could tell more, I don't know. I did. As we went on to the schoolhouse, the Pater kept silence. Miss Timmens was frightfully disappointed at the result, and said Hill was a shifty scoundrel.

"I cannot tell what to think," the squire remarked to her, "His manner is the strangest I ever saw; it is just as though he had something on his conscience. He said the boy's ghost seemed to haunt him. Did you notice that, Johnny."

"Yes, sir. A queer idea."

"He—he—never could have found David dead in the morning?" cried Miss Timmens, in a low tone, herself turning a little pale. "Dead of fright?"

"That could not be," said the squire. "You forget that David had made his escape before midnight, and was at his mother's, calling to her."

"True, true," assented Miss Timmens. "Anyway, I am certain Hill is somehow or other deceiving us, and he is a born villain for doing it."

But Hill, deceiving us though he had been, could not hold out. In going back, we saw him leaning over the palings waiting for us. But that the man is living yet, I should have said he was going to die there and then, for he looked exactly like it.

252

It seemed that just after we left him, a policeman had made his appearance. Not as a policeman, but as a friend; for he and Hill were cronies. He told Hill confidentially that there was "going to be a row over that there lost boy; that folks were saying that he might have been murdered; that unless Hill could tell something satisfactory about him, he and others might be in custody before the day was over." Whether Hill found himself brought to a point from which there was neither advance nor retreat, or that he inevitably saw that concealment could no longer be maintained, or that he was stricken to despair and felt helpless, I know not. There he stood, his head over the palings, saying he would tell all.

It was a sad tale to listen to. Miss Timmens's last supposition was right—Hill, upon going up to release David Garth, had found him dead. And, so far as the man's experience of death went, he must have been dead for six or seven hours.

"I'd like you to come and see him, sir," panted Hill.

Gingerly stepped the squire in Hill's wake across the garden to the shed. Unlocking the door. Hill stepped back for us to enter. On a mattress on the ground was David, laid straight in his every-day clothes, and covered with a blanket; his pretty hair, which his mother had so loved, carefully smoothed. Hill,— rough, burly, cross-grained Hill,—burst into tears and sobbed like a child.

"I'd give my life to undo it, and bring him back again, squire; I'd give my life twice over, Master Johnny; but I declare before Heaven, I never thought to harm the boy. When I see him the next morning, lying dead, I'd not have minded if the Lord had struck me dead too. I've been a'most mad ever since."

"Johnny," said the squire, in low tones, "go you to South Crabb, and bring over Mr. Cole. Do not talk of this."

The surgeon was at home, and came back with me. I did not quite understand why the squire sent for him, seeing he could do no good.

And the boots were David's, after all; the only things he had taken off. Hill had brought him to this shed the next night; with some vague idea of burying him in the ground under the leaves. "But I couldn't do it," he avowed amid his sobs; "I couldn't do it."

There was an examination. Cole and another making it; and they gave evidence at the inquest. One of them (it was Cole) thought the boy must have died from fright, the other from the cold; and a nice muff this last must have been.

"I did not from the first like that midnight call, or the apparently causeless terror the poor mother awoke in," said Mrs. Todhetley, to me. "The child's spirit must have cried out to her in his death-agony. I have known a case like this before."

"But—"

"Hold your tongue, Johnny. You have not lived long enough to gain experience of these things."

And I held it.

David Garth's Ghost

"Is it true that she's going to marry him, Miss Timmens?"

"True! *I* don't know," retorted Miss Timmens, in wrath. "It won't be for lack of warning, if she does. I told her so last night; and she tossed her head in answer. She's a vain, heartless girl, Hannah Baber, with no more prudence about her than a female ostrich."

"There may be nothing in it, after all," said Hannah. "She is generally ready to flirt, you know."

"Flirt!" shrieked Miss Timmens in her shrillest tone. "She'd flirt with a two-legged wheelbarrow if it had trousers on."

This colloquy was taking place at the private door of the schoolhouse. And you must understand that we have gone back a few months, for at this time David Garth was not dead. Hannah, who had gone down from Crabb Cot on an errand, came upon Miss Timmens standing there to look out. Of course she stayed to gossip.

The object of Miss Timmens's wrath was her niece, Harriet Roe. A vain, showy, handsome, free-natured girl, as you have heard, with bright dark eyes and white teeth—who had helped to work the mischief between Maria Lease and Daniel Ferrar which had led to Ferrar's dreadful death. Humphrey Roe, Harriet's father, was half-brother to Miss Timmens and Mrs. Hill; he had settled in France, and married a Frenchwoman. Miss Harriet chose to call herself French, and politely said the English were not fit to tie that nation's shoes. Perhaps that was why she had now taken up with a cousin, Louis Roe. Not that Louis

Roe was really French: he had been born in France of English parents, and so was next door to it.

A fashionable-looking young man North Crabb considered him, for he wore well-cut coats and a moustache. A moustache was a thing to be stared at in simple country places then. It may have had something to do with Miss Timmens's dislike to the young man. Louis Roe was only a distant relative: a tenth cousin, or so; of whom Miss Timmens had heard before, but never seen. When he appeared unexpectedly one January day at the school-house (it was the January after Daniel Ferrar's death), ostensibly to see Harriet, whom he had known in France, Miss Timmens, between surprise and the moustache, was less gracious than she might have been. From that time to this—March—he had (as Miss Timmens put it) haunted the place, though chiefly taking up his abode at Worcester. Harriet had struck into a flirtation with him at once, after her native fashion: and now it was reported that they were going to be married.

Miss Timmens could not find out that he was doing anything for a living. He talked of his fine "*affaires*" over in France: but when she questioned him of what nature the "*affaires*" were, he either evaded her like an eel, or gave rambling answers that she could make neither head nor tail of. The way in which he and Harriet would jabber French in her presence, not a word of which language could she comprehend, and the laughing that went on at the same time, put Miss Timmens's back up worse than anything, for she thought they were making game of her. She could be tart when she pleased; and when that happened, the redness in the nose and cheek grew redder. Very tart indeed was she, recounting these grievances to Hannah.

"My firm belief, Hannah Baber, is, that he wants to get hold of Harriet for her two-hundred pounds. She has that much, you know: it came to her from her mother. Roe would rather play the gentleman than work. It is the money he's after, not Harriet."

"The money may put him into some good way of business, and they may live comfortably together," suggested Hannah.

"Pigs may fly," returned Miss Timmens. "There's something in that young man, Hannah Baber, that I could not trust. Oh, but girls are wilful!—and simple, at the best, where the men are concerned! They can't see an inch beyond their noses: no, and they won't let others, who have sight, see for them. Look there!" Emerging into the spring sunshine from the withy walk, came the gentleman in question; Harriet Roe in her gay ribbons at his side. Miss Timmens gave her door a bang, regardless of good manners, and Hannah pursued her way.

The road thus paved for it. North Crabb church was not taken by surprise when it heard the marriage banns read out one Sunday morning between Louis Roe, of the parish of St. Swithin, Worcester (he was staying there at the time), and Henriette Adele Marie Roe. Miss Timmens, who had not been taken into confidence, started violently; Mademoiselle Henriette Adele Marie, sitting by her side, held up her head and her blooming cheeks with unruffled equanimity. It was said there was a scene when they got home; Miss Timmens's sister (once Mrs. Garth, but then our bailiff's wife, James Hill) looking in at the school-house to assist at it. Neither of them could make anything of Harriet.

"I'll tell you what it is, Aunt Susan and Aunt Nancy," said the girl passionately, when her temper got roused: "*my mind is made up to marry Louis*; and if you don't drop this magging now and for good; if you attempt to worry me any further, I'll go off to Worcester, and stay with him till the day arrives. There! how would you like that? I will, I declare. It would be thought nothing at all of in my country, with the wedding so near."

This shut them up. Mrs. Hill, a meek, gentle little woman, who had her sorrows, and habitually let Miss Timmens do all the talking when they were together, began to cry. Harriet ate her cold dinner standing, and went off for an afternoon promenade with Monsieur Louis. From that time, even Miss Timmens gave up all thought of opposition, seeing that events must take their course. Harriet's parents were dead; she was over age, and her own mistress in the eye of the law.

"Would you mind taking a turn with me in the withy walk, Harriet Roe?" asked Maria Lease, as they were coming out of church that same night.

Harriet was alone. Louis Roe had gone back to Worcester. The request surprised her considerably. Since Daniel Ferrar's death the past November, Maria had been very distant with her; averting her head if they happened to meet.

"So you have come to your senses, have you, Maria Lease?" was the half insolent, half good-natured answer. "I'll walk down it with you if you like."

"Come to my senses in what way?" asked Maria, in low, subdued, sad tones, as they went towards the withy walk.

"About—*you* know what. You blamed *me* for what happened. As good as laid his death at my door."

"Did you ever hear me say so?"

"Oh, I could see: your manner was enough. As if I either helped it on—or could have prevented it! We used to have just a bit of talking and laughing together, he and I, but that was all."

That's all! And the gold chain was still on Harriet's neck. Maria suppressed a sigh.

"Whether I blamed you for it, Harriet Roe, or whether I blamed myself, is of no moment now. The past can never be recalled or redeemed in this world—its remembrance alone remains. I want to do you a little service, Harriet. Nothing may come of it, but it is my duty to speak."

Amidst the shadows of the withy beds, under the silent stars, Maria spoke, dropping her voice to a whisper. In a sufficiently curious but accidental manner, she had heard something said the previous week about Louis Roe. A stranger, who had known him in France, spoke very much in his disfavour. He said that any girl, if she cared for her future happiness and credit, would be mad to unite herself to him. Maria had asked no particulars; they might not have been given if she had; but the impression of Louis Roe left on her mind was not a good one. All this she quietly repeated to Harriet. It was received in anything but a friendly spirit.

"Thank you for nothing, Maria Lease. Because you lost your own husband—that was to have been—you think you'll try what you can do to deprive me of mine. A slice of revenge, I suppose: but it won't succeed."

"Harriet, you are mistaken," rejoined Maria; and Miss Harriet thought she had never in her life heard so mournfully sad a tone as the words were spoken in. "So much self-reproach fell upon me that bitter evening when he was found dead: reproach that can never be lifted from me while time shall last: that I do not think I can ever again do an ill turn in this life, or give an unkind word. The whole world does not seem to be as sinful in its wickedness as I was in my harsh unkindness; and there's no sort of expiation left to me. If I pass my whole existence laying my hands under other people's feet in humble hope to serve them, it cannot undo the bitterness of my passion when I exposed him before Johnny Ludlow. The exposure was more than he could bear; and he—he put an end to it. I suffer always, Harriet Roe; my days are one prolonged burning agony of repentance. Repentance that brings no relief"

"My goodness!" cried Harriet, her breath almost scared away at hearing this, careless-natured though she was. "I'll tell you what, Maria: I should turn Roman Catholic in your place; and let a priest absolve me from the sin."

A priest absolve her from the sin! The strange anguish on her compressed lips was visible as Maria Lease turned her face upwards in the starlight. ONE Most High and merciful Priest was ever there, who could, and would, wash out her sin. But—what of Daniel Ferrar, who had died in his?

"If there is one person whom I would more especially seek in kindness to serve, it is you, Harriet," she resumed, putting her hand gently on Harriet's arm—and her fingers accidentally touched the chain that Daniel Ferrar had hung round the girl's neck in his perfidy. "Revenge!—from me!"

"The very idea of my giving up Louis is absurd," was Harriet's rejoinder, as they came out of the withy walk. "Thank you all the same, Maria Lease; and there's my hand. I see now that you meant kindly: but no one shall set me against my promised husband."

Maria shook the hand in silence.

"Look here, Maria—don't go and tell your beautiful scandal to sharp Susan Timmens. Not that I care whether you do or not, except on the score of contention. She would strike up fresh opposition, and it might come to scratching and fighting. My temper has borne enough: one can't be a lamb always."

The wedding came off on Easter Tuesday. Harriet wore a bright silk dress, the colour of lilac, with a wreath and veil. When the latter ornaments came home, Miss Timmens nearly fainted. Decent young women in their station of life were married in bonnets, she represented: not in wreaths and veils. But Harriet Roe, reared to French customs, said bonnets could never be admissible for a bride, and she'd sooner go to church in a coal-scuttle. The Batley girls, in trains and straw-hats, were brides-maids. Miss Timmens wore a new shawl and white gloves; and poor little David Garth—who was to die of fright before that same year came to an end—stood with his hand locked in his mother's.

And so, in the self-same church where she had sat displaying her graces before the ill-fated Daniel Ferrar, and by the same young clergyman who had preached to her then, Harriet became the wife of Louis Roe, and went away with him to London.

★★★★★★

The next move in the chain of events was the death of David Garth in Willow Cottage. It occurred in November, when Tod and I were staying at home, and has been already told of. James Hill escaped without punishment: it was said there was no law to touch him. He protested through thick and thin that he meant no harm to the boy; to do him justice, it was not supposed he had: he was finely repentant for it, and escaped with a reprimand.

Mrs. Hill refused to remain in the cottage. What with her innate tendency to superstition, with the real facts of the case, and with that strange belief—that David's spirit had appeared to her in the moment of dying; a belief firm and fixed as adamant—she passed into a state of horror of the dwelling. Not another night could she remain in it. The doctor himself, Cole, said she must not. Miss Timmens took her in as a temporary thing; until the furniture could be replaced in their former house, which was not let. Hill made no objection to this.

For that matter, he seemed afraid of the new place himself, and was glad to get back to the old one. All his native surliness had left him for the time: he was as a subdued man whose tongue has departed on an excursion. You see, he had feared the law might come down upon him. The coroner's inquest had brought in a safe verdict: all Hill received was a censure for having locked the boy in alone: but he could not yet feel sure that the affair would not be taken up by the magistrates: and the parish said in his hearing that his punishment ought to be transportation at the very least. Altogether, it subdued him.

So, as soon as David's funeral was over, and while his wife was still with Miss Timmens, Hill began to move back his goods in a sort of humble silence. Crowds collected to see the transport, much to Hill's annoyance and discomfiture. The calamity had caused intense excitement in the place; and Miss Timmens, who had a very long tongue, and hated Hill just as much as she had loved David, kept up the ball. Hill's intention was to lock up Willow Cottage until he could get Mr. Todhetley to release him from it. At present he dared not ask; all of us at Crabb Cot, from the squire downwards, were bitterly against him for his wicked inhumanity to poor David.

Curious to say—curious because of what was to happen out of it—as Hill was loading the truck with the last remaining things, a stranger came up to the cottage door. Just at the first moment, Hill did not recognize him; he had shaved off his moustache and whiskers, and grown a beard instead. And that alters people.

"How are you, Hill? What are you up to here?"

It was Louis Roe—who had married Mademoiselle Henriette the previous Easter. Where they had been since, or what they had done, was a sort of mystery, for Harriet had written only one letter. By that letter, it was gathered that they were flourishing in London: but no address was given, and Miss Timmens had called her a heartless jade, not to want to hear from her best relatives.

Hill answered that he was pretty well, and went on loading; but said nothing to the other question. Louis Roe—perceiving sundry straggling spectators who stood peering, as if the loading of a handbarrow with goods were a raree-show—rather wondered at appearances, and asked again. Hill shortly explained then that they had moved into Willow Cottage; but his wife found it didn't suit her, and so they were moving back again to the old home.

He went off with the truck, before he had well answered, giving no time for further colloquy. Louis Roe happened to come across young Jim Batley amidst the tag-rag, and heard from him all that had occurred.

"He must be a cruel devil, to leave a timid child all night in a house alone!" was Mr. Roe's indignant comment; who, whatever his shortcomings might be in the eyes of Miss Timmens, was not thought to be hard-hearted.

"His mother, she sees his ghost," went on Jim Batley. "Leastsways, heered it."

Mr. Roe took no notice of this additional communication. Perhaps ghosts held a low place in his creed—and he appeared to have plunged into a reverie. Starting out of it in a minute or two, he ran after Hill, and began talking in a low, business tone.

Hill could not believe his ears. Surely such luck had never befallen a miserable man! For here was Louis Roe offering to take Willow Cottage off his hands: to become his, Hill's, tenant for a short time. The double rent; this, and that for the old house he was returning to; had been weighing upon Hill's mind as heavily as David weighed upon it. The man had saved plenty of money, but he was of a close nature. Squire Todhetley was a generous man; but Hill felt conscious that he had displeased him too much to expect any favour at present.

"What d'ye want of the cottage? " asked Hill, suppressing all signs of satisfaction. "Be you and Harriet a-coming to live down here?"

"We should like to stay here for a few weeks—say till the dead of winter's over," replied Roe. "London is a beastly dull place in bad weather; the fogs don't agree with Harriet. I had thought of taking two or three rooms at Birmingham; but I don't know but she'll like this cottage best—if you will let me have it cheap."

It would be cheap enough. For Hill named the very moderate rent he had agreed to pay the squire. Only too glad was he, to get that. Roe promised to pay him monthly.

North Crabb was electrified at the news. Mr. and Mrs. Roe were coming to stay in the cottage where poor David Garth had just died. No time was lost over it, either. On the following day some hired furniture was put into it, and Harriet herself arrived.

She was looking very ill. And I'm sure if she had appeared with a beard as well as her husband, her face could not have seemed more changed. Not her face only, but her manners. Instead of figuring off in silks and ribbons, finer than the stars, laughing with every one she met, and throwing her handsome eyes about, she wore only plain things, and went along noticing no one. Some people called it "pride;" Miss Timmens said it was disappointment. The first time Tod and I met her, she never lifted her eyes at all. Tod would have stayed to speak; but she just said, "Good morning, gentlemen," and went on.

"I say, Johnny, there's some change there," was Tod's remark, as he turned to look after her.

They had been in the place about a week—and Roe seemed to keep indoors, or else was away, for no one ever saw him—when a strange turn arose, that was destined to set the neighbourhood in an uproar. I was running past the school-house one evening at dusk, and saw Maria Lease sitting with Miss Timmens by firelight. Liking Maria very much—for I always did like her, and always shall—I went bolt in to them. James Hill's wife was also there, in her mourning gown with crape on it, sitting right back in the chimney corner. She had gone back to Hill then, but made no scruple of leaving him alone often; and Hill, who had had his lesson, put up with it. And you would never guess; no, not though you had tried from then till Midsummer; what they were whispering about, as though scared out of their seven senses.

David Garth's ghost was haunting Willow Cottage.

Miss Timmens was telling the story; the others listened with open mouths. She began at the beginning again for my benefit.

"I was sitting by myself here about this time last evening, Master Johnny, having dismissed the children, and almost too tired with their worry to get my own tea, when Harriet Roe came gliding in at the door, looking whiter than a sheet, and startling me beyond everything. 'Aunt Susan,' says she in so indistinct a tone that I should have boxed one of the girls had she attempted to use such, 'would you take pity on me and let me stay here till tomorrow morning? Louis went away this afternoon, and I dare not stop alone in the place all night.' 'What are you afraid of?' I asked, not telling her at once that she might stay; but down she sat, and threw her mantle and bonnet off— taking French leave. I never saw *her* in such a state before," continued Miss Timmens vehemently; "shivering and shaking as if she had an ague, and not a particle of her impudence left in her. 'I think that place must be damp with the willow brook, aunt,' says she; 'it gives me a sensation of cold.'

"'Now don't you talk nonsense about your willow brooks, Harriet Roe,' says I. 'You are not shaking for willow brooks, or for cold either, but from fright. What is it?' 'Well then,' says she, plucking up a bit, ' I'm afraid of seeing the boy.' 'What boy?' says I—'not David?' 'Yes; David,' she says, and trembles worse than ever. 'He appeared to Aunt Nancy; a sign he is not at rest; and he is as sure to be in the house as sure can be. Dying in the way he did, and lying hid in the shed as he did, what else is to be expected' Well, Master Johnny, this all seemed to me very odd—

as I've just observed to Nancy," continued Miss Timmens. "It struck me, sir, there was more behind. 'Harriet,' says I, 'have you *seen* David Garth?' But at first no satisfactory answer could I get from her, neither yes nor no. At last she said she had not seen him, but knew she should if she stayed in the house by herself at night, for that he came again, and was *in* it. It struck me she was speaking falsely; and that she *had* seen him; or what she took for him."

"I know she has; I feel convinced of it," spoke up poor Mrs. Hill, tilting back her black bonnet—worn for David—to wipe the tears from her eyes. "Master Ludlow, don't smile, sir—though it's best perhaps for the young to disbelieve these solemn things. As surely as that we are talking here, my dear boy's spirit came to me in the moment of his death. I feared it might take to haunting the cottage, sir; and that's one reason why I could not stay in it."

"Yes; Harriet has seen him," interposed Maria Lease in low, firm tones. "Just as I saw Daniel Ferrar. Master Johnny, *you* know I saw *him*."

Well, truth to say, I thought she must have seen Daniel Ferrar. Having assisted at the sight—or if not at the actual sight, at the place and time and circumstance attending it—I did not see how else it was to be explained away.

"Where's Harriet now?" I asked.

"She stayed here last night, and went off by rail this morning to her grandmother's at Worcester," replied Miss Timmens. "Mother will be glad of her for a day or so, for she keeps her bed still."

"Then who is in the cottage?"

"Nobody, sir. It's locked up. Roe is expected back tomorrow."

Miss Timmens began to set her tea-things, and I left them. Whom should I come upon in the road, but Tod—who had been over to South Crabb. I told him all this; and we took the broad path home through the fields, which led us past Willow Cottage. The fun Tod made of what the women had been saying, was beyond everything. A dreary dwelling, it looked; cold, and deserted, and solitary in the dusky night, on which the moon was rising. The back looked towards Crabb Ravine and the three-cornered grove in which Daniel Ferrar had taken his own life away; and to the barn where Maria had seen Ferrar after death. In front was the large field, bleak and bare; and beyond, the scattered chimneys of North Crabb. A lively dwelling altogether!—let alone what had happened in it to David Garth. I said so.

"Yes, it is a lively spot!" acquiesced Tod. "Beautifully lively in itself, without having the reputation of being haunted. Eugh! Let's get home to dinner, Johnny."

Mr. and Mrs. Coney and Tom came in after dinner. Old Coney and the squire smoked till tea-time. When tea was over we all sat down to Pope Joan. Mr. Coney kept mistaking hearts for diamonds, clubs for spades; he had not his spectacles, and I offered to fetch them. Upon that, he set upon Tom for being lazy and letting Johnny Ludlow do what it was his place to do. The result was, that Tom Coney and I had a race which should reach the farm first. The night was bright, the moon high. Coming back with the spectacles, a man encountered us, tearing along as fast as we were. And that was like mad.

"Halloa!" cried Tom. "What's up."

Tom had cause to ask it. The man was Luke Macintosh: and never in all my life had I seen a specimen of such terror. His face was white, his breath came in gasps. Without saying with your leave or by your leave, he caught hold of Tom Coney's arm.

"Master, as I be a living sinner, I ha' just seen Davy Garth."

"Seen David Garth? "echoed Tom, wondering whether Luke had been drinking.

"I see him as plain as plain. He be at that end window o' the Willow Cottage."

"Do you mean his ghost, or himself?" asked Tom, making game of it.

"Why, his ghost, in course, sir. It's well known hisself be dead and buried—worse luck! Mercy on us!—I'd ha' lost a month's wages rather nor see this."

Considering Luke Macintosh was so great a coward that he would not go through the ravine after nightfall, this was not much from him. Neither had his conscience been quite easy since David's death: as it may be said that he, through refusing at the last moment to sleep in the house, had in a degree been the remote cause of it. His account was this: Passing the Willow Cottage on his way from North Crabb, he happened to look up at the end window, and saw David standing there all in white in the moonlight.

"I never see nothing plainer in all my born days, never," gasped Luke. "His poor little face hadn't no more colour in it nor chalk. Drat them ghosts and goblins, then! What does they come and show theirselves to decent folk for?"

He was trembling just as Miss Timmens, some three hours before, had described Harriet Roe to have trembled. An idea flashed into my mind.

"Now, Luke, just you confess—who is it that has put this into your head?" I asked. But Luke only stared at me: he seemed unable to understand.

"Someone has been telling you this tonight at North Crabb?"

"Telling me what, Master Ludlow?"

"That David Garth is haunting the cottage. It is what people are saying, Tom," I added to Coney.

"Then, Master Johnny, I never heered a blessed syllable on't," he replied; and so earnestly that it was not possible to doubt him. "Nobody have said nothing to me. For the matter o' that, I didn't stop to talk to a soul, but just put Molly's letter in the window slit—which was what I went for—and turned back again. I wish the woman had ha' been skinned afore she'd got me to go off to the post for her tonight. Plague on me, to have took the way past the cottage! as if the road warn't good enough to ha' served me!—and a sight straighter!"

"Were there lights in the cottage, Luke?" asked Coney. "Did you see the Roes about?"

"There warn't no more sign o' light or life a-nigh the place,

Mr. Tom, no more nor if they'd all been dead and buried inside it."

"It is shut up, Tom," I said. "Roe and his wife are away."

"Lawk a mercy!—not a living creature in it but the ghost!" quaked Luke.

As I have said, this was not much from Luke, taking what he was into consideration; but it was to be confirmed by others. One of the Coneys' maidservants came along, as we stood there, on her way from North Crabb. A sensible, respectable woman, with no nonsense about her in general; but she looked almost as scared as Luke now.

"You don't mean to say *you* have seen it, Dinah ?" cried Tom, staring at her.

"Yes, I have, sir."

"What! seen David Garth?"

"Well, I suppose it was him. It was something at the window, in white, that looked like him, Mr. Tom."

"Did you go on purpose to look for it, Dinah?" asked Tom ironically.

"The way I happened to go was this, sir. James Hill overtook me coming out of North Crabb: he was going up to Willow Cottage to speak to Roe; and I thought I'd walk with him, instead of taking the road. Not but what he's a beauty to walk with, *he* is, after his cruelty to his wife's boy," broke off Dinah: "but company is company on a solitary road at night. When we got to the cottage. Hill knocked; I stayed a minute to say how-d'ye-do to Mrs. Roe, for I've not seen her yet. Nobody answered the door; the place looked all dark and empty. 'They must be out for the evening, I should think,' says Hill: and with that he steps back and looks up at the windows. 'Lord be good to us! what's that?' says he, when he had got round where he could see the end casement. I went to him, and found him standing like a pump, just as stiff and upright, his hands clutched hold of one another, and his eyes staring up at the panes in mortal terror. 'What is it?' says I.

"'It's Davvy,' says he; but the voice didn't sound like Hill's

voice, and it scared me a bit. 'Yes, it's him,' says Hill; 'he have got
on the sheet as was wrapped round him to carry him to the shed.
I—I lodged him again that there window to make the turning;
the stairs was awk'ard,' went on Hill, as if he was speaking again
the grain, but couldn't help himself.—And sure enough, Mr.
Tom—sure enough. Master Ludlow, there was David."

"Nonsense, Dinah!" cried Tom Coney.

"I saw him quite well, sir, in the white sheet," said Dinah.
"The moon was shining on the window a'most as bright as
day."

"It were brighter nor day," eagerly put in Luke Macintosh,
"You'll believe me now, Mr. Tom."

"I'd not believe it if I saw it," said Tom Coney.

"As we stood looking up, me laying hold of Hill's arm," resumed Dinah, as if she had not told all her tale, "there came a
loud whistling and shouting behind. Which was young Jim Batley, bringing some message from them sisters of his to Harriet
Roe. I bade him hush his noise, but he only danced and mocked
at me; so then I told him the cottage was empty, except for
David Garth. That hushed him. He came stealing up, and stood
by me, staring. You should have seen his face change, Mr. Tom.

"Was he frightened?"

"Frightened is hardly the word for it, sir. His teeth began to
chatter, as if he had a fit; and down he went at last like a stone,
face first, howling fearful. We couldn't hardly get him up again
to come away, me and Hill. And as to the ghost, Mr. Tom, it *was*
still there."

"Well, it is a queer tale," acknowledged Tom Coney. "We
made for the road, all three of us then, and I turned on here—
and I didn't half like coming by the barn where Maria Lease saw
Daniel Ferrar," candidly added Dinah. "T'other two went on
their opposite way, Jim never letting go of Hill's coat-tails."

There was no more Pope Joan that night. We carried the
story indoors; and I mentioned also what had been said to Miss
Timmens. The squire and old Coney laughed.

With David Garth's ghost to be seen, it could not be supposed that I, or Tod, or Tom Coney, should stay away from the sight. When we reached the place, some twenty people had collected round the house. Jim Batley had told the tale in North Crabb.

But curious watchers had seen nothing. Neither did we. For the bright night had changed to darkness. A huge curtain of cloud had come up from the south, covering the moon and the best part of the sky, as a pall covers a coffin. If gazing could have brought a ghost to the window, there would assuredly have been one. The casement was at the end of the horse; serving to light the narrow upstairs passage. A huge cherry-tree hid the casement in summer; very slightly its bare branches obscured it now.

A sound, as of some panting animal, came up beside me as I leaned on the side palings. I turned; and saw the bailiff. Some terrible power of fascination had brought him back again, against his will.

"So it is gone. Hill, you see."

"It's not gone, Mr. Johnny," was his answer. "For some of our sights, it'll never go away again. You look well at the right-hand side, sir, and see if you don't see some'at white there."

Peering steadily, I thought I did see something white—as of a face above a white garment. But it might have been fancy."

"Us as saw *him* couldn't mistake it for fancy," was Hill's rejoinder. "There was three on us: me, and Dinah up at Coney's, and that there imp of a Jim Batley."

"Someone saw it before you did, Hill. At least he says so. Luke Macintosh. He was scared out of his senses."

The effect of these words on Hill was such, that I quite believed he was scared out of *his*. He clasped his hands in wild emotion, and turned up his eyes to give thanks.

"It's retribution a working its ends, Mr. Ludlow. See it first, did he! And I hope to my heart he'll see it afore his eyes evermore. If that there Macintosh had not played a false and coward's game, no harm 'ud ha' come to Davvy."

The crowd increased. The squire and old Coney came up, and told the whole assemblage that they were born idiots. Of course,

270

with nothing to be seen, it looked as though we all were that. In the midst of it, making quietly for the backdoor, as though he had come home through Crabb Ravine from Timberdale, I espied Louis Roe. Saying nothing to any one, I went round and told him.

"David Garth's ghost in the place!" he exclaimed. "Why, it will frighten my wife to death. Of course there's nothing of the sort; but women are so foolishly timid."

I said his wife was not there. Roe took a key from his pocket, unlocked the back-door, and went in. He was talking to me, and I stepped over the threshold to the kitchen, into which the door opened. He began feeling on the shelf for matches, and could not find any.

"There's a box in the bedroom, I know," he said; and went stumbling upstairs.

Down he came, after a minute or so, with the matches, struck one, and lighted a candle. Opening the front door, he showed himself, explained that he had just come home, and complained of the commotion.

"There's no such thing in this lower world as ghosts," said Roe. "Whoever pretends to see them must be either drunk or mad. As to this house—well, some of you had better walk in and reassure yourselves. You are welcome."

He was taken at his word. A few came in, and went looking about for the ghost, upstairs and down. Writing about it now, it seems to have been the most ridiculous thing in the world. Nothing was to be found. The narrow passage above, where David had stood, was empty. "As if supernatural visitants waited while you looked for them!" cried the superstitious crowd outside.

It is easier to raise a disturbance of this kind than to allay it, and the ghost-seers stayed on. The heavy cloud in the heavens rolled away by-and-by; and the moon came out, and shone on the casement again. But neither David Garth nor anything else was then to be seen there.

★★★★★★

The night's commotion passed away, but not the rumours. That David Garth's spirit could not rest, but came back to trouble the earth, especially that spot known as Willow Cottage, was accepted as a fact. People would go stealing up there at night, three or four of them arm-in-arm, and stand staring at the casement, and walk round the cottage. Nothing more was to be seen—perhaps because there was no moon to light up the window. Harriet Roe was at home again with her husband; but she did not go abroad much: and her face seemed to wear a sort of uneasy terror. "The fear of seeing *him* is wearing her heart out; why does Roe stop in the place?" said North Crabb: and though Harriet had never been much of a favourite, she had plenty of sympathy now.

It soon came to be known in a gradual sort of way that a visitor was staying at Willow Cottage. A young woman fashionably dressed, who was called Mrs. James; and who was said to be the wife of James Roe, Louis Roe's elder brother. Some people declared that a man was also there: they had seen one. Harriet denied it. An acquaintance of her husband's, a Mr. Duffy, had been over to see them from Birmingham, she said, but he went back again. She was not believed.

What with the ghost, and what with the mystery attaching to its inhabitants. Willow Cottage was a great card just then. If you ask me to explain what mystery there could be, I cannot do so: all I know is, an idea that there was something of the kind, apart from David, dawned upon many minds in North Crabb. Miss Timmens spoke it openly. She did not like Harriet's looks, and said that something or other was killing her. And Susan Timmens considered it her duty to try and come to the bottom of it.

At all sorts of hours, seasonable and unseasonable. Miss Timmens presented herself at Willow Cottage. Rarely alone. Sometimes Mrs. Hill would be with her; or it would be Maria Lease; or one of the Batley girls; and once it was young Jim. Louis Roe grew to feel annoyed at this; he told Harriet he would not have confounded people coming there, prying; and he closed the door against them. So, the next time Miss Timmens went, she found the door bolted in the most inhospitable manner. Harriet threw open the parlour window to speak to her.

"Louis says he won't have any more visitors calling here just now; not even you. Aunt Susan."

"What does he say that for?" snapped Miss Timmens.

"We came down here to be quiet; he has some accounts to go over, and can't be disturbed at them. So perhaps you'll stay away, Aunt Susan. I'll come to the schoolhouse sometimes instead."

It was the dusk of the evening, but Miss Timmens could see the fearful look of illness on Harriet's face. She was also trembling.

"Harriet, what's the matter with you?" she asked, in a kinder tone.

"Nothing."

"*Nothing!* Why, you look as ill as you can look. You are trembling all over."

"It's true I don't feel very well this evening, aunt, but I think it is nothing. I often feel as if I had a touch of ague."

Miss Timmens bent her face nearer; it had a strange concern in it. " Harriet, look here. There's some mystery about this place; won't you tell me what it is? I—seem—to—be—afraid—for—*you*," she concluded, in a slow and scarcely audible whisper.

For answer, Miss Timmens found the window slammed down in her face. An impression arose—she hardly knew whence gathered, or whether it had any foundation—that it was not Harriet who had slammed it, but someone concealed behind the curtain.

"Well I'm sure!" cried she. "It might have taken my nose off."

"It was so cold, aunt!" Harriet called out apologetically through the glass. "Goodnight."

Miss Timmens walked off in dudgeon. Revolving matters along the broad field-path, she liked their appearance less and less. Harriet was looking as ill as possible: and what meant that trembling? Was it caused by sickness of body, or terror of mind? Mrs. Hill, when consulted, summed it up comprehensively: "It is David about the place; *that's* killing her."

Harriet Roe did not make her appearance at the schoolhouse, and the next day but one Miss Timmens went up again. The door was bolted. Miss Timmens knocked, but received no answer. Not choosing to be treated in that way she made so much noise, first at the door and then at the window, that the former was at length unclosed by Mrs. James, in list shoes and a dressing-gown, as if her *toilette* had been delayed that day. The chain was kept up—a new chain that Miss Timmens had not seen before—and she could not enter.

"I want to see Harriet, Mrs. James."

"Harriet's gone," replied Mrs. James.

"Gone! Gone where?"

"To London. She went off there yesterday morning."

Miss Timmens felt, as she would have said, struck into herself. An idea flashed over her that the words had not a syllable of truth in them.

"What did she go to London for?"

Mrs. James glanced over her two shoulders, seemingly in terror herself, and sunk her voice to a whisper. "She had grown afraid of the place, this dark winter weather. Miss Timmens— it's as true as you're there—nothing would persuade her out of the fancy that she was always seeing David Garth. He used to stand in a sheet at the end of the upstairs passage and look at her. Leastways, *she* said so."

This nearly did for Miss Timmens. It might be true; and she could not confute it. "Do *you* see him, Mrs. James?"

"Well, no; I never have. Goodness knows, I don't want to."

"But Harriet was not well enough to take a long journey," contended Miss Timmens. "She never could have undertaken one in her state of health."

"I don't know what you mean by 'state,' Miss Timmens. She would shake a bit at times; but we saw nothing else the matter with her. Perhaps *you* would shake if you had an apparition in the house. Anyway, well or ill, she went off to London. Louis took her as far as the station and saw her away."

"Will you give me her address? I should like to write to her."

Mrs. James said she could not give the address, because she did not know it. Nothing more was to be got out of her, and Miss Timmens reluctantly departed.

"I should hope they've not murdered her—and are concealing her in the house as Hill concealed David," was the comment she gave vent to in her perplexity and wrath.

From that time, nothing could be heard of Harriet Roe. A week went on; nearly two weeks; but she never was seen, and no tidings came of her. So far as could be ascertained, she had not gone away by train: neither station-master nor porter remembered to have seen her. Miss Timmens grew as thin as a ghost herself: the subject worried her night and day. That some ill had happened to Harriet; or been *done* to her, she did not doubt. Once or twice she managed to see Roe; once or twice she saw Mrs. James: speaking to them at the door with the chain up. Roe said he heard from his wife nearly every other day; but he would not show the letters, or give the address: a conclusive proof to the mind of Miss Timmens that neither had any existence. *What had they done with Harriet?* Miss Timmens could not have been in much worse mental trouble had she herself made away with her.

One morning the postman delivered a letter at the schoolhouse. It bore the London post-mark, and purported to be from Harriet. A few lines only—saying she was well and enjoying herself, and should come back sometime—the writing shaky and blotted, and bearing but a slight resemblance to hers. Miss Timmens dashed it on the table.

"The fools, to think they can deceive me this way! That's no more Harriet's writing than it is mine."

But Miss Timmens's passion soon subsided into a grave, settled, awful dread. For she saw that this had been written to delude her into the belief that Harriet was in health and life—

when she might be in neither one nor the other. She brought the letter to Crabb Cot. She took it round the parish. She went with it to the police-station; imparting her views of it to all freely. It was a sham; a blind; a forgery: and *where* was she to look for poor lost Harriet Roe?

That same evening the ghost appeared again. Miss Timmens and others went up to the cottage, intending to demand an interview with Roe; and they found the house shut up, apparently deserted. Reconnoitring the windows from all points, their dismayed eyes rested on something at the end casement; a thin, shadowy form, robed in white. Every one of them saw it; but, even as they looked, it seemed to vanish away. Yes, there was no question that the house was haunted. Perhaps Harriet had died from fright, as poor David died.

Things could not go on like this for ever. After another day or two of discomfort, Mr. Todhetley, as a county magistrate, incited by the feeling in the parish, issued a private mandate for Roe to appear before him, that he might be questioned as to what had become of his wife. It was not a warrant; but a sort of friendly invitation, that could offend no one. Jiff the policeman was entrusted with the delivery of the message, a verbal one, and I went with him.

As if she had scented our errand for herself, and wanted to make a third in it, who should meet us in the broad path, but Miss Timmens. Willow Cottage might or might not be haunted, but I am sure her legs were: they couldn't be still.

"What are *you* doing up here, Jiff?" she tartly asked.

Jiff told her. Squire Todhetley wanted Roe at Crabb Cot.

"It will be of no use. Jiff; the door's sure to be fast," groaned Miss Timmens. "My opinion is that Roe has left the place for good."

Miss Timmens was mistaken. The shutters were open, and the house showed signs of life. Upon knocking at the door—Miss Timmens took off her patten to do it with, and you might have heard the echoes at North Crabb—it was flung wide by Mrs. James.

Mr. Roe? No, Mr. Roe was not at home. Mrs. Roe was.

Mrs. Roe was! "What, Harriet?" cried excited Miss Timmens.

Yes, Harriet. If we liked to walk in and see her, we could do so.

By the kitchen fire, as being biggest and hottest, in a chair stuffed about with blankets, sat Harriet Roe. Worn, white, shadowy, she was evidently just getting over some desperate illness. I stared; the policeman softly whistled; you might have knocked Miss Timmens down with a feather.

"Good patience, child—why, where have you been hiding all this while?" cried she. "And what on earth has been the matter with you?"

"I have been upstairs in my room, Aunt Susan, keeping my bed. As to the illness, it turned out to be ague and low fever."

"Upstairs where?"

"Here."

Jiff went out again; there was nothing to stay for. I followed, leaving Miss Timmens and Harriet to have it out together.

She had really been ill in bed all the time, Mrs. James and Roe attending on her. It did not suit them to admit visitors; for James Roe, who had fallen into some difficulty in London, connected with forged bills, was lying concealed at Willow Cottage. That's why people were kept out. It would not have done by any means for Miss Timmens and her sharp eyes to go upstairs and catch a glimpse of him; so they concocted the tale that Harriet was away. James Roe was safely away now, and Louis with him. Louis had been mixed up in the bill trouble in a lesser degree: but quite enough so to induce him to absent himself from London for a time, and to stay quietly at North Crabb.

"Was it fear or ague that caused you to shake so that last evening I saw you here?" questioned Miss Timmens.

"Ague. I never got out of bed after that night. I could hardly write that letter, aunt, that Louis sent to London to be posted to you."

"And—did you really see David Garth?"

"No, I never saw him," said Harriet. "But, after all the reports and talk, I was timid at being in the house alone—James and his wife had not come then—and that's why I asked you to let me stay at the schoolhouse the night my husband was away."

"But it was told me that you *did* see him."

"I was always frightened for fear I should."

"It strikes me you have had other causes for fright as well, Harriet," cried shrewd Miss Timmens.

"Well, you see—this business of James Roe's has put me about. Every knock that came to the door seemed to me to be somebody coming for *him*. My husband says the ghost is all rubbish and fancy, Aunt Susan."

"Rubbish and fancy, does he?"

"He says that when he came in here with Johnny Ludlow, the night there was that commotion, in going up for some matches, he fell over something at the top of the stairs by the end casement, and flung it behind the rafters. Next day he saw what it was. I had tied a white cloth over a small dwarf mop to sweep the walls with, and must have left it near the window. I remembered that I did leave it there. It no doubt looked in the moonlight just like a white face. And that's what was taken for David's ghost."

Miss Timmens paused, considering matters: she might believe just as much of this as she liked.

"It appeared again at the same place, Harriet, two or three days ago."

That was me, aunt. I saw you all looking up, and drew away again for fear you should know me. Mrs. James was making my bed, and I had crawled there."

There it ended. So far the mystery was over. The explanation was confided to the public, who received it differently. Some accepted the mop version; others clung to the ghost. And Hill never had a penny of his rent. Louis Roe was away; and, as it turned out, did not come back again.

Mrs. James wanted to leave also; and Maria Lease took her place as nurse. Tenderly she did it, too; and Harriet got well. She was going off to join her husband as soon as she could travel: it was said in France. No one knew; unless it was Maria Lease. She and Harriet had become confidential friends.

"Which is the worse fate—yours or mine?" cried Harriet to Maria, half mockingly, half woefully, the day she was packing her trunk. "You have your lonely life, and your never-ending repentance for what you call your harsh sin: I have my sickness and my trouble—and I have enough of that, Maria." But Maria Lease only shook her head in answer.

"Trouble and repentance are our best lot in this world, Harriet. They come to fit us for heaven."

But North Crabb, though willingly admitting that Harriet Roe, in marrying, had not entered on a bed of lilies, and might have been happier had she kept single, would not, on the whole, be shaken from its belief that the ghost still haunted the empty cottage. Small parties made shivering pilgrimages up there on a moonlight night, to watch for it, and sometimes declared that it appeared. Fancy goes a long way in this world.

A Mystery

1

"Look here, Johnny Ludlow," said Darbyshire to me—Darbyshire being, as you may chance to remember, our doctor at Timberdale—"you seem good at telling of unaccountable disappearances: why don't you tell of that disappearance which took place here?"

I had chanced to look in upon him one evening when he was taking rest in his chimney-corner, in the old red-cushioned chair, after his day's work was over, smoking his churchwarden pipe in his slippers and reading the story of *Dorothy Grape*.

"We should like to see that disappearance on paper," went on Darbyshire. "It is the most curious thing that has happened in my experience."

True enough it was. Too curious for any sort of daylight to be seen through it; as you will acknowledge when you hear its details; and far more complicated than the other story.

The lawyer at Timberdale, John Delorane, was a warm-hearted and warm-tempered man of Irish extraction. He had an extensive practice, and lived in an old-fashioned, handsome red-brick house in the heart of Timberdale, with his only daughter and his sister, Hester.

You may have seen prettier girls than Ellin Delorane, but never one that the heart so quickly went out to. She was too much like her dead mother; had the same look of fragile delicacy, the same sweet face with its pensive sadness, the soft brown eyes and the lovely complexion. Mrs. Delorane had died of decline: people would say to one another, in confidence, they hoped Ellin might escape it.

The largest and best farm in the neighbourhood of Timberdale, larger than even that of the Ashtons, was called the Dower Farm. It belonged to Sir Robert Tenby, and had been occupied for many years by one Roger Brook, a genial, pleasant gentleman of large private means apart from his success in farming. Rich though he was, he did not disdain to see practically after his work himself; was up with the lark and out with his men, as a good farmer ought to be. Out-of-doors he was the keen, active, thorough farmer; indoors he lived as a gentleman. He had four children: three boys and one girl, who were all well and comprehensively educated.

But he intended his sons to work as he had worked: no idleness for him; no leading of indolent and self-indulgent lives. "Choose what calling you please," he said to them; "but stick to it when chosen, and do your very best in it." The eldest son, Charles, had no fancy for farming, no particular head for any of the learned professions; he preferred commerce. An uncle, Matthew Brook, was the head of a mercantile house in New York; he offered a post in it to Charles, who went out to him. The second son, Reginald, chose the medical profession; after qualifying for it, he became assistant to a doctor in London to gain experience. William, the third son, went to Oxford. He thought of the Church, but being conscientious, would not decide upon it hastily.

"So that not one of you will be with me," remarked Mr. Brook. "Well, be it so. I only want you to lead good and useful lives, striving to do your duty to God and to man."

But one of those overwhelming misfortunes, that I'm sure may be compared with the falling of an avalanche, fell on Mr. Brook. In an evil hour he had become a shareholder in a stupendous undertaking which had banking for its staple basis; and the thing failed. People talked of "swindling." Its managers ran away; its books and money were nowhere; its shareholders were ruined. Some of the shareholders ran away too; Roger Brook, upright and honourable, remained to face the ruin. And utter ruin it was, for the company was one of unlimited liability.

The shock was too much for him: he died under it. Every shilling he possessed was gone; harpies (it is what Timberdale called them) came down upon his furniture and effects, and swept them away. In less time almost than it takes to tell of, not a vestige remained of what had been, save in memory: Sir Robert Tenby had another tenant at the Dower Farm, and Mrs. Brook had moved into a little cottage-villa not a stone's throw from Darbyshire's. She had about two hundred a-year of her own, which no adverse law could touch. Her daughter, Minnie, remained with her. You will hardly believe it, but they had named her by the romantic name of Araminta.

William Brook had come down from Oxford just before, his mind made up not to be a clergyman, but to remain on the farm with his father. When the misfortunes fell, he was, of course, thrown out; and what to turn his hand to he did not at once know. Brought up to neither profession nor trade, no, nor to farming, it was just a dilemma. At present, he stayed with his mother.

One day he presented himself to Mr. Delorane. "Can you give me some copying to do, sir?" he asked: "either at your office here, or at home. I write a good clear hand."

"What do you mean to do, Master William?" returned the lawyer, passing over the question. The two families had always been intimate and much together.

"I don't know what; I am waiting to see," said William. He was a slender young fellow of middle height, with gentle manners, a very nice, refined face, and a pair of honest, cheery, dark-blue eyes.

"Waiting for something to turn up, like our old friend Micawber!" said the lawyer.

"If I could earn only a pound a-week while I am looking out, I should not feel myself so much of a burden on my mother—though she will not hear me say a word about that," the young man went on. "You would not take me on as clerk and give me that sum, would you, Mr. Delorane?"

Well, they talked further; and the upshot was, that Mr. Delorane did take him on. William Brook went into the office as a clerk, and was paid a pound a-week.

The parish wondered a little, making sundry comments over this at its tea-tables: for the good old custom of going out to real tea was not out of fashion yet in Timberdale. Everyone agreed that William Brook was to be commended for putting his shoulder to the wheel, but that it was a grave descent for one brought up to his expectations. Mr. St. George objected to it on another score.

Years before, there had arrived in England from the West Indies a little gentleman, named Alfred St. George. His father, a planter, had recently died, and the boy's relatives had sent him home to be educated, together with plenty of money for that purpose. Later, when of an age to leave school, he was articled to Mr. Delorane, and proved an apt, keen pupil. Next he went into the office of a renowned legal firm in London, became a qualified lawyer and conveyancer, and finally accepted an offer made him by Mr. Delorane, to return to Timberdale, as his chief and managing clerk. Mr. Delorane paid him a handsome salary, and held out to him, as report ran, hopes of a future partnership.

Alfred St. George had grown up a fine man: tall, strong, lithe and active. People thought his face handsome, but it had unmistakably a touch of the tar-brush. The features were large and well formed, the lips full, and the purple-black hair might have been woolly but for being drilled into order with oils. His complexion was a pale olive, his black eyes were round, showing a great deal of the whites, and at times they wore a very peculiar expression. Take him for all in all, he was a handsome man, with a fluent tongue and persuasive eloquence.

It was Mr. St. George who spoke against William Brook's being taken on as clerk. Not that his objection applied to the young man himself, but to his probable capacity for work. "He will be of no use to us, sir," was the substance of his remonstrance to Mr. Delorane. "He has had no experience: and one can hardly snub Brook as one would a common clerk."

"Don't suppose he will be of much use," carelessly acquiesced Mr. Delorane, who was neither a stingy nor a covetous man. "What could I do but take him on when he asked me to? I like the young fellow; always did; and his poor father was my very good friend. You must make the best of him, St. George: dare say he won't stay long with us." At which St. George laughed good-naturedly and shrugged his shoulders.

But William Brook did prove to be of use. He got on so well, was so punctual, so attentive, so intelligent, that fault could not be found with him; and at the end of the first year Mr. Delorane voluntarily doubled his pay—raising it to two pounds per week.

Timberdale wondered again: and began to ask how it was that young Brook, highly educated, and reared to expect some position in the world, could content himself with stopping on, a lawyer's clerk? Did he mean to continue in the office forever? Had he ceased to look out for that desirable something that was to turn up? Was he parting with all laudable ambitions?

William Brook could have told them, had he dared, that it was not lack of ambition chaining him to his post, but stress of love. He and Ellin Delorane had entered a long while past into the mazes of that charming dream, than which, as Tom Moore tells us, there's nothing half so sweet in life, and the world was to them as the Garden of Eden.

It was close upon the end of the second year before Mr. Delorane found it out. He went into a storm of rage and re-proaches—chiefly showered upon William Brook, partly upon Ellin, a little upon himself.

"I have been an old fool," he spluttered to his confidential clerk. "Because the young people had been intimate in the days when the Brooks were prosperous, I must needs let it go on still, and never suspect danger! Why, the fellow has had his tea here twice a-week upon an average!—and brought Ellin home at night when she has been at his mother's—and I—I—thought no more than if it had been her brother! I could thrash myself!

And where have her aunt Hester's eyes been, I should like to know!"

"Very dishonourable of Brook," assented St. George, knitting his brow. "Perhaps less harm is done than you fear, sir. They are both young, can hardly know their own minds; they will grow out of it. Shall you part them?"

"Do you suppose I shouldn't?" retorted the lawyer.

William Brook was discharged from the office: Ellin received orders to give up his acquaintanceship; she was not to think of him in private or speak to him in public. Thus a little time went on. Ellin's bright face began to fade; Aunt Hester looked sick and sorry; the lawyer had never felt so uncomfortable in his life.

Do what he would, he could not get out of his liking for William Brook, and Ellin was dear to him as the apple of his eye. He had been in love himself once, and knew what it meant; little as you would believe it of a stout old red-faced lawyer; knew that both must be miserable. So much the better for Brook—but what of Ellin?

"One would think it was you who had had your lover sent to time right-about!" he wrathfully began to Aunt Hester, one morning when he came upon her in tears as she sat at her sewing. "I'd hide my face if I were you, unless I could show a better.

"It is that I am so sorry for Ellin, John," replied Aunt Hester, meekly wiping her tears. "I—I am afraid that some people bear sorrow worse than others."

"Now what do you mean by that?"

"Oh, not much," sighed Aunt Hester, not daring to allude to the dread lying latent in her own mind—that Ellin might fade away like her mother. "I can see what a sharp blow it has been to the child, John, and so—and so I can but feel it myself."

"Sharp blow! Deuce take it all! What business had young Brook to get talking to her about such rubbish as love?"

"Yes indeed, it is very unfortunate," said Aunt Hester. "But I do not think he has talked to her, John; I imagine he is too honourable to have said a single word. They have just gone on loving one another in secret and in silence, content to live in the unspoken happiness that has flooded their two hearts."

"Unspoken fiddlestick? What a simpleton you are, Hester!"

Mr. Delorane turned off in a temper. He knew it must have been a "sharp blow" to Ellin, but he did not like to hear it so stated to his face. Banging the door behind him, he was crossing the hall to the office—which made a sort of wing to the house—when he met William Brook.

"Will you allow me to speak to you, sir?" asked the young man in a tone of deprecation. And, though the lawyer had the greatest mind in the world to tell him no and send him headforemost out again, he thought of Ellin, he thought of his dead friend, Roger Brook; so he gave a growl, and led the way into the dining-room.

In his modest winning way, William Brook spoke a little of the trouble that had come upon their family—how deeply sorry he was that Ellin and he should have learnt to care for one another for all time, as it was displeasing to Mr. Delorane—

"Hang it, man," interrupted the lawyer irascibly, too impatient to listen further—"what on earth do you propose to yourself? Suppose I did not look up upon it with displeasure?—are you in a position to marry her?"

"You would not have objected to me had we been as we once were—prosperous, and—"

"What the dickens has that to do with it?" roared the lawyer. "Our business lies with the present, not the past."

"I came here to tell you, sir, that I am to leave for New York tonight. My brother Charles has been writing to me about it for some time past. He says I cannot fail to get on well in my uncle's house, and attain to a good position. Uncle Matthew has no sons: he will do his best to advance his nephews. What I wish to ask you, sir, is this—if, when my means shall be good and my position assured, you will allow me to think of Ellin?"

"The man's mad?" broke forth Mr. Delorane, more put about than he had been at all. "Do you suppose I should let my only child go to live in a country over the seas?"

"No, sir, I have thought of that. Charles thinks, if I show an aptitude for business, they may make me their agent over here. Oh, Mr. Delorane, be kind, be merciful: for Ellin's sake and for mine! Do not send me away without hope!"

"Don't you think you possess a ready-made stock of impudence, William Brook?"

The young man threw his earnest, dark-blue eyes into the lawyer's. "I feared you would deem so, sir. But I am pleading for what is dearer to me and to her than life: our lives will be of little value to us if we must spend them apart. Only just one ray of possible hope, Mr. Delorane! It is all I ask.'

"Look here; we'll drop this," cried the lawyer, his hands in his pockets, rattling away violently at the silver in them, his habit when put out, but nevertheless calming down in temper, for in spite of prejudice he did like the young man greatly, and he was not easy as to Ellin. "The best thing you can do is to go where you are going—over the Atlantic: and we'll leave the future to take care of itself. The money you think to make may turn out all moonshine, you know. There; that's every word I'll say and every hope I'll give, though you stop all day bothering me, William Brook."

And perhaps it was as much as William Brook had expected any way, it did not absolutely forbid him to hope. He held out his hand timidly.

"Will you not shake hands with me, sir—I start tonight—and wish me God speed."

"I'll wish you better sense; and—and I hope you'll get over safely," retorted Mr. Delorane: but he did not withhold his hand. "No correspondence with Ellin, you understand, young man; no underhand love-making."

"Yes, sir, I understand; and you may rely upon me."

He quitted the room as he spoke, to make his way out as he came—through the office. The lawyer stood in the passage and looked after him: and a thought, that had forced itself into his mind several times since this trouble set in, crossed it again. Should he make the best of a bad bargain: give Brook a chief place in his own office and let them set up in some pleasant lit-tle home near at hand? Ellin had her mother's money: and she would have a great deal more at his own death; quite enough to allow her husband to live the idle life of a gentleman—and William was a gentleman, and the nicest young fellow he knew. Should he? For a full minute Mr. Delorane stood deliberating—yes, or no; then he took a hasty step forward to call the young man back. Then, wavering and uncertain, he stepped back again, and let the idea pass.

"Well, how have you sped?" asked Mr. St. George, as William Brook reappeared in the office. "Any hope?"

"Yes, I think so," answered William. "At least, it is not abso-lutely forbidden. There's a line in a poem my mother would repeat to us when we were boys—'*God and an honest heart will bear us through the roughest day.*' I trust He, and it, will so bear me and Ellin."

"Wish I had your chance, old fellow!"

"My chance!" repeated William.

"To go out to see the world; to go out to the countries where gold and diamonds are picked up for the stooping—instead of being chained, as I am, between four confined walls, condemned to spend my life over musty parchments."

William smiled. "I don't know where you can pick up gold and diamonds for the stooping. Not where I am going."

"No, not in New York. You should make your way to the Australian gold-fields, Brook, or to the rich Californian mines, or to the diamond mountains in Africa, and come back—as you would in no time—with a sack of money on your shoulders, large enough to satisfy even Delorane."

"Or lose my health, if not my life, in digging, and come home without a shirt to my back; a more common result than the oth-er, I fancy," remarked William. "Well, goodbye, old friend."

St. George, towering aloft in his height and strength, put his arm around William's shoulder and walked thus with him to the street-entrance. There they shook hands, and parted. Ellin Delorane, her face shaded behind the drawing-room curtain from the October sun, watched the parting.

There was to be no set farewell allowed to her. She understood that. But she gathered from Aunt Hester, during the day, that her father had not been altogether obdurate, and that if William could get on in the future, perhaps things might be suffered to come right. It brought to her a strange comfort. So very slight a ray, no bigger than one of the specks that fall from the sky, as children say, will serve to impart a most unreasonable amount of hope to the troubled heart.

Towards the close of the afternoon, Ellin went in her restlessness to pay a visit to her friend Grace at the Rectory, who had recently become Herbert Tanerton's wife, and sat talking with her till it was pretty late. The moon, rising over the tops of the trees, caused her to start up with an exclamation.

"What will Aunt Hester say?"

"If you don't mind going through the churchyard, Ellin," said Grace, "you would cut off that corner, and save a little time." So Ellin took that route.

"Ellin!"

"William!"

They had met face to face under the church walls. He explained that he was sparing a few minutes to say farewell to his friends at the rectory. The moon, coming out from behind a swiftly passing cloud, for it was rather a rough night, shone down upon them and upon the graves around them. Wildly enough beat the heart of each.

"You saw papa today," she whispered unevenly, as though her breath were short.

"Yes, I saw him. I cannot say that he gave me hope, Ellin, but he certainly did not wholly deny it. I think—I believe—that—if I can succeed in getting on, all may be well with us yet."

William Brook spoke with hesitation. He felt trammelled; he could not in honour say what he would have wished to say. This meeting might be unorthodox, but it was purely accidental; neither he nor Ellin had sought it.

"Goodbye, my darling," he said with emotion, clasping her

hands in his. "As we have met, there cannot be much wrong in our saying it. I may not write to you, Ellin; I may not even ask you to think of me; I may not, I suppose, tell you in so many words that I shall think of you; but, believe this: I go out with one sole aim and end in view—that of striving to make a position sufficiently fair to satisfy your father."

The tears were coursing down her cheeks; she could hardly speak for agitation. Their hearts were aching to pain.

"I will be true to you always, William," she whispered. "I will wait for you, though it be to the end of life."

To be in love with a charming young lady, and to have her all to yourself in a solitary graveyard under the light of the moon, presents an irresistible temptation for taking a kiss, especially if the kiss is to be a farewell kiss for days and for years. William Brook did not resist it; very likely did not try to. In spite of Mr. Delorane and everyone else, he took his farewell kiss from Ellin's lips.

Then they parted, he going one way, she the other. Only those of us—there are not many—who have gone through this parting agony can know how it wrings the heart.

But sundry superstitious gossips, hearing of this afterwards, assured Ellin that it must be unlucky to say farewell amidst graves.

★★★★★★

The time went on. William Brook wrote regularly to his people, and Minty whispered the news to Ellin Delorane. He would send kind remembrances to friends, love to those who cared for it. He did not dislike the work of a mercantile life, and thought he should do well—in time.

In time. There was the rub, you see. We say "in time" when we mean next Christmas, and we also say it when we mean next century. By the end of the first year William Brook was commanding a handsome salary; but the riches that might enable him to aspire to the hand of Miss Delorane loomed obscurely in the distance yet. Ellin seemed strong and well, gay and cheerful, went about Timberdale, and laughed and talked with the world, just as though she had never had a lover, or was not waiting for somebody over the water. Mr. Delorane thought she must have forgotten that scapegrace, and he hoped it was so.

It was about this time, the end of the first year, that a piece of good luck fell to Mr. St. George. He came into a fortune. Some relative in the West Indies died and left it to him. Timberdale put it down at a thousand pounds a-year, so I suppose it might be about five hundred. It was thought he might be for giving up his post at Mr. Delorane's to be a gentleman at large. But he did nothing of the kind. He quitted his lodgings over Salmon's shop, and went into a pretty house near Timberdale Court, with a groom and old Betty Huntsman as housekeeper, and set up a handsome gig and a grey horse. And that was all the change.

As the second year went on, Ellin Delorane began to droop a little. Aunt Hester did not like it. One of the kindest friends Ellin had was Alfred St. George. After the departure of young Brook, he had been so tender with Ellin, so considerate, so in-dulgent to her sorrow, and so regretful (like herself) of William's absence, that he had won her regard. "It will be all right when he comes back, Ellin," he would whisper: "only be patient."

But in this, the second year, Mr. St. George's tone changed. It may be that he saw no hope of any happy return, and deemed that, for her own sake, he ought to repress any hope left in her.

"There's no more chance of his returning with a fortune than there is of my going up to the moon," he said to Tod con-fidentially one day when we met him striding along near the Ravine.

"Don't suppose there is—in this short time," responded Tod.

"I'm afraid Ellin sees it, too: she seems to be losing her spir-its. Ah, Brook should have done as I advised him—gone a little farther and dug in the gold-fields. He might have come back a Crœsus then. As it is—whew! I wouldn't give a copper sixpence for his chance."

"Do you know what I heard say, St. George?—that you'd like to go in for the little lady yourself."

The white eye-balls surrounding St. George's dark orbs took

a tinge of yellow as they rolled on Tod. "Who said it?" he asked quietly.

"Darbyshire. He says you are in love with her as much as ever Brook was."

St. George laughed. "Old Darbyshire? Well, perhaps he is not far wrong. Anyway, love's free, I believe. Were I her father, Brook should prove his eligibility to propose for her, or else give her up. Good-day, Todhetley; good-day, Johnny."

St. George went off at a quick pace. Tod, looking after him, made his comments. "Should not wonder but he wins her. He is the better man of the two—"

"The better man!" I interrupted.

"As to means, at any rate: and see what a fine upright free-limbed fellow he is! And where will you find one more agreeable?"

"In tongue, nowhere; I admit that. But I wouldn't give up William Brook for him, were I Ellin Delorane."

That St. George was in love with her grew as easy to be seen as is the round moon in harvest. Small blame to him. Who could be in the daily companionship of a sweet girl like Ellin Delorane, and not learn to love her, I should like to know? Tod told St. George he wished he had his chance.

At last St. George spoke to her. It was in April, eighteen months after Brook's departure. Ellin was in the garden at sunset, busy with the budding flowers, when St. George came to join her, as he sometimes did, on leaving the office for the day. Aunt Hester sat sewing at the open glass-doors of the window.

"I have been gardening till I am tired," was Ellin's greeting to him, as she sat down on a bench near the sweetbriar bush.

"You look pale," said Mr. St. George. "You often do look pale now, Ellin: do you think you can be quite well?"

"Pray don't let Aunt Hester overhear you," returned Ellin in covert, jesting tones. "She begins to have fancies, she says, that I am not as well as I ought to be, and threatens to call in Mr. Darbyshire."

"You need someone to take care of you; someone near and

dear to you, who would study your every look and action, who would not suffer the winds of heaven to blow upon your face too roughly," went on St. George, plunging into Shakespeare. "Oh, Ellin, if you would suffer me to be that one—"

Her face turned crimson; her lips parted with emotion; she rose up to interrupt him in a sort of terror.

"Pray do not continue, Mr. St. George. If—if I understand you rightly, that you—that you—"

"That I would be your loving husband, Ellin; that I would shelter you from all ill until death us do part. Yes, it is nothing less than that."

"Then you must please never to speak of such a thing again; never to think of it. Oh, do not let me find that I have been mistaking you all this time," she added in uncontrollable agitation: "that while I have ever welcomed you as my friend—and his—you have been swayed by another motive!"

He did not like the agitation; he did not like the words; and he bit his lips, striving for calmness.

"This is very hard, Ellin."

"Let us understand each other once for all," she said—"and oh, I am so sorry that there's need to say it. What you have hinted at is impossible. Impossible: please not to mistake me. You have been my very kind friend, and I value you; and, if you will, we can go on still on the same pleasant terms, caring for one another in friendship. There can be nothing more."

"Tell me one thing," he said: "we had better, as you intimate, understand each other fully. Can it be that your hopes are still fixed upon William Brook?"

"Yes," she answered in a low tone, as she turned her face away. "I hope he will come home yet, and that—that matters may be smoothed for us with papa. Whilst that hope remains it is simply treason to talk to me as you would have done," she concluded with a spurt of anger.

"Ellin," called out Aunt Hester, putting her head out beyond the glass-doors, "the sun has set; you had better come in."

"One moment, Ellin," cried Mr. St. George, preventing her:

"will you forgive me?"

"Forgive and forget, too," smiled Ellin, her brow smoothing itself. "But you must never recur to the subject again."

So Mr. St. George went home, his accounts settled—as Tod would have said: and the days glided on.

★★★★★★

"What is it that ails Ellin?"

It was a piping-hot morning in July, in one of the good old hot summers that we seem never to get now; and Aunt Hester sat in her parlour, its glass-doors open, adding up the last week's bills of the butcher and the baker, when she was interrupted by this question from her brother. He had come stalking upon her, rattling as usual, though quite unconsciously, the silver in his trousers pockets. The trousers were of nankeen: elderly gentlemen wore them in those days for coolness.

"What ails her!" repeated Aunt Hester, dropping the bills in alarm. "Why do you ask me, John?"

"Now, don't you think you should have been a Quaker?" retorted Mr. Delorane. "I put a simple question to you, and you reply to it by asking me another. Please to answer mine first. What is it that is the matter with Ellin?"

Aunt Hester sighed. Of too timid a nature to put forth her own opinion upon any subject gratuitously in her brother's house, she hardly liked to give it even when asked for. For the past few weeks Ellin had been almost palpably fading; was silent and dispirited, losing her bright colour, growing thinner; might be heard catching her breath in one of those sobbing sighs that betoken all too surely some secret, ever-present sorrow. Aunt Hester had observed this; she now supposed it had at length penetrated to the observation of her brother.

"Can't you speak?" he demanded.

"I don't know what to say, John. Ellin does not seem well, and looks languid: of course this broiling weather is against us all. But—"

"But what?" cried the lawyer, as she paused. "As to broiling weather, that's nothing new in July."

"Well, John—only you take me up so—and I'm sure I shouldn't like to anger you. I was about to add that I think it is not so much illness of body with Ellin as illness of mind. If one's mind is ransacked with perpetual worry—"

"Racked with perpetual worry," interrupted Mr. Delorane, unconsciously correcting her mistake. "What has she to worry her?"

"Dear me! I suppose it is about William Brook. He has been gone nearly two years, John, and seems to be no nearer coming home with a fortune than he was when he left. I take it that this troubles the child: she is losing hope."

Mr. Delorane, standing before the open window, his back to his sister, turned the silver coins about in his pockets more vehemently than before. "You say she is not ailing in body?"

"Not yet. She is never very strong, you know."

"Then there's no need to be uneasy."

"Well, John—not yet, perhaps. But should this state of despair, if I don't use too strong a word, continue, it will tell in time upon her health, and might bring on—bring on—"

"Bring on what?" sharply asked the lawyer.

"I was thinking of her mother," said poor Aunt Hester, with as much deprecation as though he had been the Great Mogul: "but I trust, John, you won't be too angry with me for saying it."

Mr. Delorane did not say whether he was angry or not. He stood there, fingering his sixpences and shillings, gazing apparently at the grass-plat, in reality seeing nothing. He was recalling a past vision: that of his delicate wife, dying of consumption before her time; he seemed to see a future vision: that of his daughter, dying as she had died.

"When it comes to dreams," timidly went on Aunt Hester, "I can't say I like it. Not that I am one to put faith in the foolish signs old wives talk of—that if you dream of seeing a snake, you've got an enemy; or, if you seem to be in the midst of a lot of beautiful white flowers, it's a token of somebody's death. I am not so silly as that, John. But for some time past Ellin has dreamt perpetually of one theme—that of being in trouble about William Brook. Night after night she seems to be searching for him: he is lost, and she cannot tell how or where."

Had Aunt Hester suddenly begun to hold forth in the known tongue, it could not have brought greater surprise to Mr. Delorane. He turned short round to stare at her.

"Seeing what a wan and weary face the child has come down with of late, I taxed her with not sleeping well," continued Aunt Hester, "and she confessed to me that she was feeling a good bit troubled by her dreams. She generally has them towards morning, and the theme is always the same. The dreams vary, but the subject is alike in all—William Brook is lost, and she is searching for him."

"Nonsense! Rubbish!" put in Mr. Delorane.

"Well, John, I dare say it is nonsense," conceded Aunt Hester meekly: "but I confess I don't like dreams that come to you persistently night after night and always upon one and the same subject. Why should they come?—that's what I ask myself. Be sure, though, I make light of the matter to Ellin, and tell her her digestion is out of order. Over and over again, she says, they seem to have the clue to his hiding place, but they never succeed in finding him. And—and I am afraid, John, that the child, through this, has taken up the notion that she shall never see him again."

Mr. Delorane, making some impatient remark about the absurdity of women in general, turned round and stood looking into the garden as before. Ellin's mind was getting unhinged with the long separation, she had begun to regard it as hopeless, and hence these dreams that Brook was "lost," he told himself, and with reason: and what was he to do?

How long he stood thus in perfect silence, no sound to be heard but the everlasting jingling of the loose silver, Aunt Hester did not know; pretty near an hour she thought. She wished he would go; she felt very uncomfortable, as she always did feel when she vexed him—and here were the bills waiting to be added up. At length he turned sharply, with the air of one who has come to some decision, and returned to the office.

"I suppose I shall have to do it myself," he remarked to Mr. St. George.

"Do what, sir?"

"Send for that young fellow back, and let them set up in some little homestead near me. I mean Brook."

"Brook!" stammered St. George.

"Here's Ellin beginning to fade and wither. It's all very well for her aunt to talk about the heat! *I* know. She is pining after him, and I can't see her do it; so he must come home."

Of all the queer shades that can be displayed by the human countenance, about the queerest appeared in that of Mr. St. George. It was not purple, it was not green, it was not yellow; it was a mixture of all three. He gazed at his chief and master as one gazes at a madman.

"Brook can come into the office again," continued Mr. Delorane. "I don't like young men to be idle; leads 'em into temptation. We'll make him head clerk here, next to you, and give him a couple of hundred a-year. If—what's the matter?"

For the strange look on his manager's face had caught the eye of Mr. Delorane. St. George drew three or four deep breaths.

"Have you thought of Miss Delorane, sir—of her interests—in planning this?" he presently asked.

"Why, that's what I do think of; nothing else. You may be sure I shouldn't think of it for the interest of Brook. All the same, I like the young man, and always shall. The child is moping herself into a bad way. Where shall I be if she should go into a decline like her mother? No, no; she shall marry and have proper interests around her."

"She could do that without being sacrificed to Brook," returned St. George in a low tone. "There are others, sir, of good and suitable position, who would be thankful to take her—whose pride it would be to cherish her and render every moment of her life happy."

"Oh, I know that; you are one of 'em," returned Mr. Delorane carelessly. "It's what all you young sparks are ready to say of a pretty girl, especially if she be rich as well. But don't you see, St. George, that Ellin does not care for any of you. Her heart is fixed upon Brook, and Brook it must be."

Of course this news came out to Timberdale. Some people blamed Mr. Delorane, others praised him. Delorane must be turning childish in his old age, said one; Delorane is doing a good and a wise thing, cried another. Opinions vary in this world, you know, and ever will, as proved to us in the fable of the old man and his ass.

But now—and it was a strange thing to happen—the very next day Mr. Delorane received a letter from William Brook, eight closely written pages. Briefly, this was its substance. The uncle, Matthew Brook of New York, was about to establish a house in London, in correspondence with his own; he had offered the managership of it to William, with a small share of profits, guaranteeing that the latter should not be less than seven hundred a-year.

"And if you can only be induced to think this enough for us to begin upon, sir, and will give me Ellin," wrote the young man, "I can but say that I will strive to prove my gratitude in loving care for her and I trust you will not object to her living in London. I leave New York next month, to be in England in September, landing at Liverpool, and I shall make my way at once to Timberdale, hoping you will allow me to plead my cause in person."

"No no, Master William, you won't carry my daughter off to London," commented Mr. Delorane aloud, when he had read the letter—not but that it gratified him. "You must give up your post, young man, and settle down by me here, if you are to have Ellin. I don't see, St. George, why Brook should not make himself into a lawyer, legal and proper," added he thoughtfully. "He is young enough—and he does not dislike the work. You and he might be associated together after I am dead: 'Brook and St. George.'"

Mr. St. George's face turned crusty: he did not like to hear his name put next to Brook's. "I never feel too sure of my own future," he said in reply. "Now that I am at my ease in the world, tempting visions come often enough across me of travelling out to see it."

Mr. Delorane wrote a short, pithy note in answer to the appeal of William Brook, telling him he might come and talk to him as soon as he returned. "The young fellow may have left New York before it can reach him," remarked the lawyer, as he put the letter in the post; "but if so, it does not much matter."

So there was Timberdale, all cock-a-hoop at the prospect of seeing William Brook again, and the wedding that was to follow. Sam Mullet, the clerk, was for setting the bells to ring beforehand.

★★★★★★

Some people think September the pleasantest month in the year, when the heats of summer have passed and the frosts of winter have not come. Never a finer September than we had that autumn at Timberdale; the skies looked bright, the leaves of the trees were putting on their tints of many colours, and the land was not yet quite shorn of its golden grain.

All the world was looking out for William Brook. He did not come. Disappointment is the lot of man. Of woman also. When the third week was dragging itself along in expectancy, a letter came to Mrs. Brook from William. It was to say that his return home was somewhat delayed, as he should have to take Jamaica *en route*, to transact some business at Kingston for his uncle. He should then proceed direct from Kingston by steamer to Liverpool, which place he hoped to reach before the middle of October. "Tell all my friends this, that they may not wonder at my delay," the letter concluded; but it contained no intimation that he had received the answer written by Mr. Delorane.

A short postscript was yet added, in these words:

"Alfred St. George has, I know, some relatives living in, or near Kingston—planters, I believe. Tell him I shall call upon them, if I can make time, to see whether they have any commands for him."

Long before the middle of October, Ellin Delorane became

obviously restless. A sort of uneasy impatience seemed to have taken possession of her: and without cause. One day, when we called at Mr. Delorane's to take a message from home, Ellin was in the garden with her outdoor things on, waiting to go out with her aunt.

"What a ridiculous goose you are!" began Tod. "I hear you have taken up the notion that Sweet William has gone down in the Caribbean Sea."

"I'm sure I have not," said Ellin. "Aunt Hester must have told you that fable when she was at Crabb Cot yesterday."

"Just so. She and the mater laid their gossiping caps together for the best part of an hour—and all about the foolishness of Miss Ellin Delorane."

"Why, you know, Ellin," I put in, "it is hardly the middle of October yet."

"I tell myself that it is not," she answered gravely. "But, some-how, Johnny, I don't—don't—expect—him."

"Now, what on earth do you mean?"

"I wish I knew what. All I can tell you is, that when his mother received that letter from William last month, saying his return was delayed, a sort of foreboding seized hold of me, an apprehension that he would never come. I try to shake it off, but I cannot. Each day, as the days come round, only serves to make it stronger."

"Don't you think a short visit to Droitwich would do you good, Ellin?" cried Tod, which was our Worcestershire fashion of recommending people to the lunatic asylum.

"Just listen to him, Johnny!" she exclaimed, with a laugh.

"Yes, 'just listen to him'—and just listen to yourself, Miss El-lin, and see which talks the most sense," he retorted. "Have you got over those dreams yet?"

Ellin turned her face to him quickly. "Who told you any-thing about that, Aunt Hester?"

Tod nodded. "It's true, you know."

"Yes, it is true," she slowly said. I have had those strange dreams for some weeks now; I have them still."

"That William Brook is lost?"

"That he is lost, and that we are persistently searching for him. Sometimes we are seeking for him in Timberdale, sometimes at Worcester—in America, in France, in places that I have no knowledge of. There always seems to be a sadness connected with it—a sort of latent conviction that he will never be found."

"The dreams beget the dreams," said Tod, "and I should have thought you had better sense. They will soon vanish, once Sweet William makes his appearance: and mind, Miss Ellin, that you invite me to the wedding."

Ellin sighed—and smiled. And just then Aunt Hester appeared attired in her crimson silk shawl with the fancy border, and the primrose feather in her Leghorn bonnet.

A day or two went on, bringing no news of the traveller. On the nineteenth of October—I shall never forget the date—Mr. and Mrs. Todhetley and ourselves set off in the large open phaeton for a place called Pigeon Green, to spend the day with some friends living there. On this same morning, as it chanced, a very wintry one, Mr. St. George started for Worcester in his gig, accompanied by Ellin Delorane. But of this we knew nothing. He had business in the town; she was going to spend a few days with Mary West, formerly Mary Coney.

Ellin was well wrapped up, and Mr. St. George, ever solicitous for her comfort, kept the warm fur rug well about her during the journey: the skies looked grey and threatening, the wind was high and bitterly cold. Worcester reached, he drove straight through the town, left Ellin at Mrs. West's door, in the Foregate Street, and then drove back to the Hare and Hounds Inn to put up his horse and gig.

2

I shall always say, always think, it was a curious thing we chanced to go that day, of all days, to Pigeon Green. It is not chance that brings about these strange coincidences.

There's a divinity that shapes our ends,

Rough-hew them how we will."

Pigeon Green, a small colony of a dozen houses, formed a triangle, as may be said, with Timberdale and Evesham, being a few miles distant from each. Old Mr. and Mrs. Beele, life-long friends of the squire, lived here. Their nephew had brought his newly-married wife from London to show her to them, and we were all invited to dinner. As the squire did not care to be out in the dark, his sight not being what it used to be, the dinner-hour was fixed for two o'clock. We started in the large open phaeton, the squire driving his favourite horses, Bob and Blister. It was the nineteenth of October. Mrs. Todhetley complained of the cold as we went along. The lovely weather of September had left us; early winter seemed to be setting in with a vengeance. The easterly wind was unusually high, and the skies were leaden.

On this same wintry morning Mr. St. George left Timberdale in his gig for Worcester, accompanied by Ellin Delorane. St. George had business to transact with Philip West, a lawyer, who was Mr. Delorane's agent in Worcester. Philip West lived in the Foregate Street, his offices being in the same house. Ellin was very intimate with his wife, formerly Mary Coney, and was invited to spend a few days with her. It was Aunt Hester who had urged the acceptance of this invitation seeing that Ellin was nervous at the non-arrival of her lover, William Brook, was peeping into the newspapers for accounts of shipwrecks and other calamities at sea. So they set off after breakfast, Ellin well wrapped up, in this stylish gig of Mr. St. George's. There are gigs and gigs, you know, and I assure you some gigs were yet fashionable vehicles in those days.

It was bitterly cold. St. George, remarking that they should have snow as soon as the high wind would let it come down, urged his handsome grey horse to a fleet pace, and they soon reached Worcester. He drove straight to Foregate Street, which lay at the other end of the town, set down Ellin, and then went back again to leave his horse and gig at the Hare and Hounds in College Street, the inn at which he generally put up, retracing his steps on foot to Mr. West's.

And now I must return to ourselves.

After a jolly dinner at two o'clock with the Beeles, and a jolly dessert after it, including plenty of fresh filberts and walnuts, and upon that a good cup of tea and some buttered toast, we began to think about getting home. When the phaeton came round, the squire remarked that it was half-an-hour later than he had meant to start; upon which, old Beele laid the fault of its looking late to the ungenial weather of the evening.

We drove off. Dusk was approaching; the leaden skies looked dark and sullen, the wind, unpleasantly high all day, had increased to nearly a hurricane. It roared round our heads, it whistled wildly through the trees and hedges, it shook the very ears of Bob and Blister; the few flakes of snow or sleet beginning then to fall were whirled about in the air like demons. It was an awful evening, no mistake about that; and a very unusual one for the middle of October.

The squire faced the storm as well as he could, his coat-collar turned up, his cloth cap, kept for emergencies in a pocket of the carriage, tied down well on his ears. Mrs. Todhetley tied a knitted grey shawl right over her bonnet. We, in the back seat, had much ado to keep our hats on: I sat right behind the squire, Tod behind Mrs. Todhetley. It was about the worst drive I remember. The wild wind, keen as a knife, stung our faces, and seemed at times as if it would whirl us, carriage and horses and all, in the air, as it was whirling the sleet and snow.

Tod stood up to speak to his father. "Shall I drive, sir?" he asked. "Perhaps you would be more sheltered if you sat here behind."

Tod's driving in those days was regarded by the squire with remarkable disparagement, and Tod received only a sharp answer—which could not be heard for the wind.

We got along somehow in the teeth of the storm. The route lay chiefly through by-ways, solitary and unfrequented, not in the good, open turnpike-roads. For about a mile, midway between Pigeon Green and Timberdale, was an ultra dreary spot; dreary in itself and dreary in its associations. It was called Dip

Lane, possibly because the ground dipped there so much that it lay in a hollow; overgrown dark elm-trees grew thickly on each side of it, their branches nearly meeting overhead. In the brightest summer's day the place was gloomy, so you may guess how it looked now.

But the downward dip and the dark elm trees did not constitute all the dreariness of Dip Lane. Many years before, a murder had been committed there. The squire used to tell us of the commotion it caused, all the gentlemen for miles and miles round bestirring themselves to search out the murderers. He himself was a little fellow of five or six years old, and could just remember what a talk it made. A wealthy farmer, belated, riding through the lane from market one dark night, was attacked and pulled from his horse. The assailants beat him to death, rifled his pockets of a large sum, for he had been selling stock, and dragged him *through the hedge,* making a large gap in it.

Across the field, near its opposite side, was the round, deep stagnant piece of water known as Dip Pond (popularly supposed to be too deep to have any bottom to it); and it was conjectured that the object of the murderers, in dragging him through the hedge, was to conceal the body beneath the dark and slimy water, and that they must have been disturbed by someone passing in the lane. Anyway, the body was found in the morning lying in the field a few yards from the gap in the hedge, pockets turned inside out, and watch and seals gone. The poor frightened horse had made its way home, and stayed whinnying by the stable-door all night.

The men were never found. A labourer, hastening through the lane earlier in the evening, with some medicine from the doctor's for his sick wife, had noticed two foot-pads, as he described them, standing under a tree. That these were the murderers, then waiting for prey, possibly for this very gentleman they attacked, no one had any doubt; but they were never traced. Whoever they were, they got clear off with their booty, and—the squire would always add when telling the story to a stranger—with their wicked consciences, which he sincerely hoped tormented them ever afterwards.

But the most singular fact in the affair remains to be told. From that night nothing would grow on the spot in the hedge over which the murdered man was dragged, and on which his blood had fallen. The bloodstains were easily got rid of, but the hedge, though replanted more than once, never grew again and the gap remained in it still. Report went that the farmer's ghost haunted it—that, I am sure, you will not be surprised to hear, ghosts being so popular—and might be seen hovering around it on a moonlit night.

And amidst the many small coincidences attending the story (my story) which I am trying to place clearly before you, was this one: that the history of the murder was gone over that day at Mr. Beele's. Some remark led to the subject as we sat round the dessert-table, and Mrs. Frank Beele, who had never heard of it, inquired what it was. Upon that, the squire and old Beele recounted it to her, each ransacking his memory to help the other with fullest particulars.

To go on with our homeward journey. Battling along, we at length plunged into Dip Lane—which, to its other recommendations, added that of being inconveniently narrow—and Tod, peering outwards in the gloomy dusk, fancied he saw some vehicle before us. Bringing his keen sight to bear upon it, he stood up to reconnoitre, and made it out to be a gig, going the same way that we were. The wind was not quite so bad in this low spot, and the snow and sleet had ceased for a bit.

"Take care, father," said Tod: "there's a gig on ahead."

"A gig, Joe?"

"Yes, it's a gig: and going at a strapping pace."

But the squire was going at a strapping pace also, and driving two fresh horses, whereas the gig had but one horse. We caught it up in no time. It slackened speed slightly as it drew close to the hedge on that side, to give us room to pass. In a moment we saw it was St. George's gig, St. George driving.

"Halloa!" called Tod, as we shot by, and his shout was loud enough to frighten the ghost at the gap, which lively spot we were fast approaching, "there's William Brook! Father, pull up: there's William Brook!"

Brook was sitting with St. George. His coat was well buttoned up, a white woollen comforter folded round his neck and chin, and a low-crowned, wide-brimmed hat pulled down over his brows. I confess that but for Tom's shout I should not have recognized him—muffed up in that way.

Anxious to get home, out of the storm, the squire paid no heed to Tod's injunction of pulling up. He just turned his head for a moment towards the gig, but drove on at the same speed as before. All we could do was to call out every welcome we could think of to William Brook as we looked back, and to pull off our hats and wave them frantically.

William Brook pulled off his, and waved it to us in return. *I saw him do it.* He called out something also, no doubt a greeting. At least, I thought he did; but the wind swept by with a gust at the moment, and it might have been St. George's voice and not his.

"Johnny, lad, it's better than nuts," cried Tod to me, all excitement for once, as he fixed his hat on his head again. "How glad I am—for Nelly's sake. But what on earth brings the pair of them—he and St. George—in Dip Lane?"

Another minute or so, and we reached the gap in the hedge. I turned my eyes to it and to the pond beyond it in a sort of fascination; I was sure to do so whenever I went by, but that was seldom; and the conversation at the dessert-table had opened the wretched details afresh. Almost immediately afterwards, the gig wheels behind us, which I could hear above the noise of the wind, scorned to me to come to a sudden standstill. "St. George has stopped," I exclaimed to Tod. "Not a bit of it," answered he; "we can no longer hear him." Almost close upon that, we passed the turning which led out of the lane towards Evesham. Not heeding anything of all this, as indeed why should he, the squire dashed straight onwards, and in time we gained our homestead, Crabb Cot.

The first thing the squire did, when we were all gathered

round the welcome fire, blazing and crackling with wood and coal, and the stormy blasts beat on the window-panes, but no longer upon us, was to attack us for making that noise in Dip Lane, and for shouting out that it was Brook.

"It was Brook, father," said Tod. "St. George was driving him."

"Nonsense, Joe," reprimanded the squire. "William Brook has not landed from the high seas yet. And, if he had landed, what should bring him in Dip Lane—or St. George either!"

"It was St. George," persisted Tod.

"Well, that might have been. It looked like his grey horse. Where was he coming from, I wonder?"

"Mr. St. George went to Worcester this morning, sir," interposed Thomas, who had come in with some glasses, the squire having asked for some hot brandy-and-water. "Giles saw his man Japhet this afternoon, and he said his master had gone off in his gig to Worcester for the day."

"Then he must have picked up Brook at Worcester," said Tod, in his decisive way.

"May be so," conceded the squire, coming round to reason. "But I don't see what they could be doing in Dip Lane."

The storm had disappeared the following morning, but the ground was white with a thin coating of snow; and in the afternoon, when we started for Timberdale to call on William Brook, the sky was blue and the sun shining. Climbing up from the ravine and crossing the field beyond it to the high-road, we met Darbyshire, the surgeon, striding along as fast as his legs would carry him.

"You seem to be in a hurry," remarked the squire.

"Just sent for to a sick patient over yonder," replied Darbyshire, nodding to some cottages in the distance. "Dying, the report is; supposed to have swallowed poison. Dare say it will turn out to be a case of cucumber."

He was speeding on when Tod asked whether he had seen William Brook yet. Darbyshire turned to face him, looking surprised.

"Seen Brook yet! No; how should I see him? Brook's not come, is he?"

"He got home last night. St. George drove him from Worcester in his gig," said Tod, and went on to explain that we had passed them in Dip Lane. Darbyshire was uncommonly pleased. Brook was a favourite of his.

"I am surprised that I have not seen him," he cried; "I have been about all the morning. St. George was in Worcester yesterday, I know. Wonder, though, what induced them to make a pilgrimage through Dip Lane!"

Just, you see, as the rest of us had wondered.

We went on towards Mrs. Brook's. But in passing Mr. Delorane's, Aunt Hester's head appeared above the Venetian blind of the dining-room. She began nodding cordially.

"How lively she looks," exclaimed the squire. "Pleased that he is back, I take it. Suppose we go in?"

The front-door was standing open, and we went in unannounced. Aunt Hester, sitting then at the little work-table, making herself a cap with lace and pink ribbons, got up and tried to shake hands with all three of us at once.

"We are on our way to call on William Brook," cried the squire, as we sat down, and Aunt Hester was taking up her work again.

"On William Brook!—why, what do you mean?" she exclaimed. "Has he come?"

"You don't mean to say you did not know it—that he has not been to see you?" cried the squire.

"I don't know a thing about it; I did not know he had come; no one has told me," rejoined Aunt Hester. "As to his coming to see me—well, I suppose he would not feel himself at liberty to do that until Mr. Delorane gave permission. When did he arrive? I am so glad."

"And he is not much behind his time, either," observed Tod.

"Not at all behind it, to speak of, only we were impatient. The truth is, I caught somewhat of Ellin's fears," added Aunt Hester, looking at us over her spectacles, which she rarely wore higher than the end of her nose. "Ellin has had gloomy ideas about his never coming back at all; and one can't see a person perpetually sighing away in silence, without sighing a bit also for company. Did he get here this morning? What a pity Ellin is in Worcester!"

We told Aunt Hester all about it, just as we had told Darby-shire, but not quite so curtly, for she was not in a hurry to be off to a poisoned patient. She dropped her work to listen, and took off her spectacles, looking, however, uncommonly puzzled.

"What a singular thing—that you should chance to have been in Dip Lane just at the time they were!—and why should they have chosen that dreary route? But—but—"

"But what, ma'am?" cried the squire.

"Well, I am thinking what could have been St. George's motive for concealing the news from me when he came round here last night to tell me he had left Ellin safely at Philip West's," replied she.

"Did he say nothing to you about William Brook?"

"Not a word. He said what a nasty drive home it had been in the teeth of the storm and wind, but he did not mention William Brook. He seemed tired, and did not stay above a minute or two. John was out. Oh, here is John."

Mr. Delorane, hearing our voices, I suppose, came in from the office. Aunt Hester told him the news at once—that William Brook was come home.

"I am downright glad," interrupted the lawyer emphatically. "What with one delay and another, one might have begun to think him lost: it was September, you know, that he original-ly announced himself for. What do you say?"—his own words having partly drowned Aunt Hester's—"St. George drove him home last night from Worcester? Drove Brook? Nonsense! Had St. George brought Brook he would have told me of it."

"But he did bring him, sir," affirmed Tod: and he went over the history once more. Mr. Delorane did not take it in.

"Are these lads playing a joke upon me, squire?" asked he.

"Look here, Delorane. That we passed St. George in Dip Lane

is a fact; I knew the cut of his gig and horse. Someone was with him; I saw that much. The boys called out that it was William Brook, and began shouting to him. Whether it was he, or not, I can't say; I had enough to do with my horses, I can tell you; they did not like the wind, Blister especially."

"It was William Brook, safe enough, sir," interposed Tod. "Do you think I don't know him? We spoke to him, and he spoke to us. Why should you doubt it?"

"Well, I suppose I can't doubt it, as you speak so positively," said Mr. Delorane. "The news took me by surprise, you see. Why on earth did St. George not tell me of it? I shall take him to task when he comes in. Anyway, I am glad Brook's come. We will drink his health."

He opened what was in those days called the cellaret—and a very convenient article it was for those who drank wine as a rule—and put on the table some of the glasses that were standing on the sideboard. Then we drank health and happiness to William Brook.

"And to someone else also," cried bold Tod, winking at Aunt Hester.

"You two boys can go on to Mrs. Brook's," cried the squire "I shall stop here a bit. Tell William I am glad he has surmounted the perils of the treacherous seas."

"And tell him he may come to see me if he likes," added the lawyer. "I expect he did not get a note I wrote to him a few months back, or he'd have been here this morning."

Away we went to Mrs. Brook's. And the first thing that flabbergasted us (the expression was Tod's, not mine) was to be met by a denial of the servant's. Upon Tod asking to see Mr. William, she stared at us and said he was not back from his travels.

"Come in," called out Minty from the parlour; "I know your voices." She sat at the table, her paint-box before her. Minty painted very nice pieces in water-colours: the one in process was a lovely bit of scenery taken from Little Malvern. Mrs. Brook was out.

"What did I hear you saying to Ann about William—that he

had come home?" she began to us, without getting up from her work—for we were too intimate to be upon any ceremony with one another. "He is not come yet. I only wish he was."

"But he is come," said Tod. "He came last night. We saw him and spoke to him."

Minty put down her camel-hair pencil then, and turned round. "What do you mean?" she asked.

"Mr. St. George drove William home from Worcester. We passed them in the gig in Dip Lane."

Minty retorted by asking whether we were not dreaming; and for a minute or two we kept at cross-purposes. She held to it that they had seen nothing of her brother; that he was not at Timberdale.

"Mamma never had a wink of sleep last night, for thinking of the dreadful gale William must be in at sea. Your fancy misled you," went on Minty, calmly touching up the cottage in her painting—and Tod looked as if he would like to beat her.

But it did really seem that William had not come, and we took our departure. I don't think I had ever seen Tod look so puzzled.

"I wish I may be shot if I can understand this!" said he.

"Could we have been mistaken in thinking it was Brook?" I was beginning; and Tod turned upon me savagely.

"I swear it was Brook. There! And you know it as well as I, Mr. Johnny. Where can he be hiding himself? What is the meaning of it?"

It is my habit always to try to account for things that seem unaccountable; to search out reasons and fathom them; and you would be surprised at the light that will sometimes crop up. An idea flashed across me now.

"Can Brook be ill, Tod, think you?—done up with his voyage, or something—and St. George is nursing him at his house for a day or two before he shows himself to Timberdale?" And Tod thought it might be so.

Getting back to Mr. Delorane's, we found him and the squire sitting at the table still. St. George, just come in, was standing by, hat in hand, and they were both tackling him at once.

"*What* do you say?" asked St. George of his master, when he found room for a word. "That I brought William Brook home here last night from Worcester! Why, what can have put such a thing into your head, sir?"

"*Didn't* you bring him?" cried the squire. "Didn't you drive him home in your gig?"

"That I did not. I have not seen William Brook."

He spoke in a ready, though surprised tone, not at all like one who is shuffling with the truth, or telling a fable, and looked from one to another of his two questioners, as if not yet understanding them. The squire pushed his spectacles to the top of his brow and stared at St. George. He did not understand, either.

"Look here, St. George: do you deny that it was you we passed in Dip Lane last night—and your grey horse—and your gig?"

"Why should I deny it?" quietly returned St. George. "I drew as close as I could to the hedge as a matter of precaution to let you go by, squire, you were driving so quickly. And a fine shouting you greeted me with," he added, turning to Tod, with a slight laugh.

"The greeting was not intended for you; it was for William Brook," answered Tod, his voice bearing a spice of antagonism; for he thought he was being played with.

St. George was evidently at a loss yet, and stood in silence. All in a moment, his face lighted up.

"Surely," he cried impulsively, "you did not take that man in the gig for William Brook!"

"It was William Brook. Who else was it?"

"A stranger. A stranger to me and to the neighbourhood. A man to whom I gave a lift."

Tod's face presented a picture. Believing, as he did still, that it was Brook in the gig, the idea suggested by me—that St. George was concealing Brook at his house out of good-fellowship—grew stronger and stronger. But he considered that, as it had come to thus, St. George ought to say so.

"Where's the use of your continuing to deny it, St. George?" he asked. "You had Brook there, and you know you had."

"But I tell you that it was not Brook," returned St. George. "Should I deny it, if it had been he? You talk like a child."

"Has Brook been away so long that we shouldn't know him, do you suppose?" retorted quick-tempered Tod. "Why I as a proof that it was Brook, he shouted back his greeting to us, taking off his hat to wave it in answer to ours. Would a strange man have done that?"

"The man did nothing of the kind," said St. George.

"Yes, he did," I said, thinking it was time I spoke. "He called back a greeting to us, and he waved his hat round and round. I should not have felt so sure it was Brook but for seeing him without his hat."

"Well, I did not see him do it," conceded St. George. "When you began to shout in passing the man seemed surprised. 'What do those people want?' he said to me; and I told him you were acquaintances of mine. It never occurred to my mind, or to his either, I should imagine, but that the shouts were meant for me. If he did take off his hat in response, as you say, he must have done it, I reckon, because I did not take off mine."

"Couldn't you hear our welcome to him? Couldn't you hear us call him 'Brook'?" persisted Tod.

"I did not distinguish a single word. The wind was too high for that."

"Then we are to understand that Brook has not come back; that you did not bring him?" interposed the squire. "Be quiet, Joe; can't you see you were mistaken? I told you you were, you know, at the time. You and Johnny are forever taking up odd notions, Johnny especially."

"The man was a stranger to me," spoke St. George. "I overtook him trudging along the road, soon after leaving Worcester; it was between Red Hill and the turning to Whittington. He accosted me, asking which of the two roads before us would take him to Evesham. I told him which, and was about to drive on when it occurred to me that I might as well offer to give the man a lift: it was an awful evening, and that's the truth: one that nobody would, as the saying runs, turn a dog out in. He thanked me, and got up; and I drove him as far as—"

"Then that's what took you round by Dip Lane, St. George?" interrupted Mr. Delorane.

"That's what took me round by Dip Lane," acquiesced St. George, slightly smiling; "and which seems to have led to this misapprehension. But don't give my humanity more credit than it deserves. Previously to this I had been debating in my own mind whether to take the round, seeing what a journey was before me. It was about the wildest night I ever was out in, the horse could hardly make head against the wind, and I thought we might feel it less in the small and more sheltered by-ways than in the open road. Taking up the traveller decided me."

"You put him down in Dip Lane, at the turning that leads to Evesham," remarked the squire.

"Yes, I put him down there. It was just after you passed us. He thanked me heartily, and walked on; and I drove quickly home, glad enough to reach it. Who he was, or what he was, I do not know, and did not ask."

Tod was still in a quandary; his countenance betrayed it. "Did you notice that he resembled William Brook, St. George?"

"No. It did not strike me that he resembled any one. His face was well wrapped up from the cold, and I did not get a clear view of it: I am not sure that I should know it again. I should know his voice, though," he added quickly.

Poor Aunt Hester, listening to all this in dismay, felt the disappointment keenly: the tears were stealing down her face. "And we have been drinking his health, and—and feeling so thankful that he was safely back again!" she murmured gently.

"Hang it, yes," added Mr. Delorane. "Well, well; I dare say a day or two more will bring him. I must say I thought it odd that you should not have mentioned it to me, St. George, if he had come."

"I should have thought it very odd, sir," spoke St. George.

"Will you take a glass of wine?"

314

"No, thank you; I have not time for it. Those deeds have to be gone over, you know, sir, before post-time," replied St. George; and he left the room.

"And if ever you two boys serve me such a trick again—bringing me over with a cock-and-bull story that people have come back from sea who haven't—I'll punish you," stuttered the squire, too angry to speak clearly.

We went away in humility; heads down, metaphorically speaking, tails between legs. The squire kept up the ball, firing away sarcastic reproaches hotly.

Ted never answered. The truth was, he felt angry himself. Not with the squire, but with the affair altogether. Tod hated mystification, and the matter was mystifying him utterly. With all his heart, with all the sight of his eyes, he had believed it to be William Brook: and he could not drive the conviction away, that it was Brook, and that St. George was giving him house room.

"I don't like complications," spoke he resentfully.

"Complications!" retorted the squire. "What complications are there in this? None. You two lads must have been thinking of William Brook, perhaps speaking of him, and so you thought you saw him. That's all about it, Joe."

The complications were not at an end. A curious addition to them was at hand. The squire came to a halt at the turning to the ravine, undecided whether to betake himself home at once, or to make a call first at Timberdale Court, to see Robert Ashton.

"I think we'll go there, lads," said he: "there's plenty of time. I want to ask him how that squabble about the hunting arrangements has been settled."

So we continued our way along the road, presently crossing it to take the one in which the Court was situated: a large handsome house, lying back on the right hand. Before gaining it, however, we had to pass the pretty villa rented by Mr. St. George, its stable and coach-house and dog-kennel beside it. The railway was on ahead; a train was shrieking itself at that moment into the station.

St. George's groom and man-of-all-work, Japhet, was sweeping up the leaves on the little lawn. Tod, who was in advance of us, put his arms on the gate. "Are you going to make a bonfire with them?" asked he.

"There's enough for't, sir," answered Japhet. "I never see such a wind as yesterday's," he ran on, dropping his besom to face Tod, for the man was a lazy fellow, always ready for a gossip. "I'm sure I thought it 'ud ha' blowed the trees down as well as the leaves."

"It was pretty strong," assented Tod, as I halted beside him, and the squire walked on towards the Court. "We were out in it—coming home from Pigeon Green. There was one gust that I thought would have blown the horses right over."

"The master, he were out in it, too, a coming home from Worcester," cried Japhet, taking off his old hat to push his red hair back. "When he got in here, he said as he'd had enough on't for one journey. I should think the poor horse had too; his coat were all wet."

Tod lifted up his head, speaking impulsively. "Was your master alone, Japhet, when he got home? Had he anyone with him?"

"Yes, he were all alone, sir," replied the man. "Miss Delorane were with him when he drove off in the morning, but she stayed at Worcester."

Had Tod taken a moment for thought he might not have asked the question. He had nothing of the sneak in him, and would have scorned to pump a servant about his master's movements. The answer tended to destroy his theory of Brook's being concealed here, and to uphold the account given by Mr. St. George.

Quitting the railings, we ran to catch up the squire. And at that moment two or three railway passengers loomed into view, coming from the train. One of them was Ellin Delorane.

She came along briskly, with a buoyant step and a smiling face. The squire dropped us a word of caution.

"Now don't go telling her of your stupid fancy about Brook, you two: it would only cause her disappointment." And with the last word we met her.

"Ah ha, Miss Ellin!" he exclaimed, taking her hands. "And so the truant's back again!"

"Yes, he is back again," she softly whispered, with a blush that was deep in colour.

The squire did not quite catch the words. She and he were at cross-purposes. "We have but now left your house, my dear," he continued. "Your aunt does not expect you back today; she thought you would stay at Worcester till Saturday."

Ellin smiled shyly. "Have you seen him?" she asked in the same soft whisper.

"Seen whom, my dear?"

"Mr. Brook."

"Mr. Brook! Do you mean *William* Brook? He is not back, is he?"

"Yes, he is back," she answered. "I thought you might have seen him: you spoke of the return of the truant."

"Why, child, I meant you," explained the squire. "Nobody else. Who says William Brook is back?"

"Oh, I say it," returned Ellin, her cheeks all rosy dimples. "He reached Worcester yesterday."

"And where is he now?" cried the squire, feeling a little at sea.

"He is here, at Timberdale," answered Ellin. "Mr. St. George drove him home last night."

"There!" cried Tod with startling emphasis. "There, father, please not to disparage my sight anymore."

Well, what do you think of this for another complication? It took me aback. The squire rubbed his face, and stared.

"My dear, just let us understand how the land lies," said he, putting his hand on Ellin's shoulder. "Do you say that William Brook reached Worcester yesterday on his return, and that St. George drove him home here at night?"

"Yes," replied Ellin. "Why should you doubt it? It is true."

"Well, we thought St. George did drive him home," was the squire's answer, staring into her face; "we passed his gig in Dip Lane and thought that it was Brook that he had with him. But

317

St. George denies this. He says it was not Brook; that he has not seen Brook, does not know he has come home; he says the man he had with him was a stranger, to whom he was giving a lift."

Ellin looked grave for a moment; then the smiles broke out again.

"St. George must have been joking," she cried; "he cannot mean it. He happened to be at Worcester Station yesterday when Mr. Brook arrived by the Birmingham train: we suppose he then offered to drive him home. Any way, he did do it."

"But St. George denied that he did, Ellin," I said.

"He will not deny it to me, Johnny. Gregory West, returning from a visit to some client at Spetchley, met them in the gig together."

The squire listened as a man dazed. "I can't make head or tail of it," cried he. "What does St. George mean by denying that he brought Brook? And where *is* Brook?"

"Has no one seen him?" questioned Ellin.

"Not a soul, apparently. Ellin, my girl," added the squire, "we will walk back with you to your father's, and get this cleared up. Come along, boys."

So back we went to turn the tables upon St. George, Tod in a rapture of gratification. You might have thought he was treading upon eggs.

We had it out this time in Mr. Delorane's private office; the squire walked straight into it. Not but that "having it out" must be regarded as a figure of speech, for elucidation seemed farther off than before, and the complications greater.

Mr. Delorane and his head-clerk were both bending over the same parchment when we entered. Ellin kissed her father, and turned to St. George.

"Why have you been saying that you did not drive home William Brook?" she asked as they shook hands.

"A moment, my dear; let me speak," interrupted the squire, who never believed any one's explanation could be so lucid as his own. "Delorane, I left you just now with an apology for having brought to you a cock-and-bull story through the misleading fancies of these boys; but we have come back again to tell you the story's true. Your daughter here says that it was William Brook that St. George had in his gig. And perhaps Mr. St. George"—giving that gentleman a sharp nod—"will explain what he meant by denying it?"

"I denied it because it was not he," said Mr. St. George, not appearing to be in the least put out. "How can I tell you it was Brook when it was not Brook? If it had been—"

"You met William Brook at the Worcester railway-station yesterday afternoon," interrupted Ellin. "Mrs. James Ashton saw you there; saw the meeting. You *were* at the station, were you not?"

"I was at the station," readily replied St. George, "and Mrs. James Ashton may have seen me there, for all I know—I did not see her. But she certainly did not see William Brook. Or, if she did, I didn't."

"Gregory West saw you and him in your gig together later, when you were leaving Worcester," continued Ellin. "It was at the top of Red Hill."

St. George shook his head. "The person I had in my gig was a stranger. Had Gregory West come up one minute earlier he would have seen me take the man into it."

"William *has* come," persisted Ellin.

"I don't say he has not," returned St. George. "All I can say is that I did not know he had come and that I have not seen him."

Who was right, and who was wrong? Any faces more hopelessly puzzled than the two old gentlemen's were, as they listened to these contradictory assertions, I'd not wish to see. Nothing came of the interview; nothing but fresh mystification. Ellin declared William Brook had arrived, had been driven out of Worcester for Timberdale in St. George's gig. We felt equally certain we had passed them in Dip Lane, sitting together in the gig; but St. George denied it *in toto*, affirming that the person with him was a stranger.

And perhaps it may be as well if I here say a word about the routes. Evesham lay fifteen miles from Worcester; Timberdale not much more than half that distance, in a somewhat different direction, and on a different road. In going to Timberdale, if when about halfway there you quitted the high-road for byways you would come to Dip Lane. Traversing nearly the length of the lane, you would then come to a by-way leading from it on the other side, which would bring you on the direct road to Evesham, still far off. Failing to take this by-way heading to Evesham, you would presently quit the lane, and by dint of more by-ways would gain again the high-road and soon come to Timberdale. This is the route that Mr. St. George took that night.

We went home from Mr. Delorane's, hopelessly mystified, the squire rubbing up his hair the wrong way; now blowing us both up for what he called our "fancies" in supposing we saw William Brook, and now veering round to the opposite opinion that we and Ellin must be alike correct in saying Brook had come.

Ellin's account was this: she passed a pleasant morning with Mary West, who was nearly always more or less of an invalid. At half-past one o'clock dinner was served; Philip West, his younger brother Gregory, who had recently joined him, and Mr. St. George coming in from the office to partake of it. Dinner over, they left the room, having no time to linger. In fact, Gregory rose from table before he had well finished. Mary West inquired what his haste was, and he replied that he was off to Spetchley; someone had been taken ill there and wanted a will made. It was Philip who ought to have gone, who had been sent for; but Philip had an hour or two's business yet to do with Mr. St. George. Mrs. West told St. George that she would have tea ready at five o'clock, that he might drink a cup before starting for home.

Later on in the afternoon, when Ellin and Mrs. West were sitting over the fire, talking of things past and present, and listening to the howling of the wind, growing more furious every hour, James Ashton's wife came in, all excitement. Her husband, in medical practice at Worcester, was the brother of Robert Ashton of Timberdale. A very nice young woman was Marianne Ashton, but given to an excited manner. Taking no notice of Mrs. West, she flew to Ellin and began dancing round her like a demented Red Indian squaw.

"What will you give me for my news, Ellin?"

"Now, Marianne!" remonstrated Mrs. West. "Do be sensible, if you can."

"Be quiet, Mary: I am sensible. Your runaway lover is come, Ellin; quite safely."

They saw by her manner, heard by her earnest tone, that it was true. William Brook had indeed come, was then in the town. Throwing off her bonnet, and remarking that she meant to remain for tea, Mrs. James Ashton sat down to tell her story soberly.

"You must know that I had to go up to the Shrub Hill Station this afternoon," began she, "to meet the Birmingham train. We expected Patty Silvester in by it; and James has been since a most unearthly hour this morning with some cross-grained patient, who must needs go and be ill at the wrong time. I went up in the brougham, and had hardly reached the platform when the train came in. There was a good deal of confusion; there always is, you know; passengers getting out and getting in. I ran about looking for Patty, and found she had not come: taken fright at the weather, I suppose. As the train cleared off, I saw a figure that seemed familiar to me; it was William Brook; and I gave a glad cry that you might have heard on the top of St. Andrew's spire. He was crossing the line with others who had alighted, a small black-leather travelling-bag in his hand. I was about to run over after him, when a porter stopped me, saying a stray engine was on the point of coming up, to take on the Malvern train. So, all I could do was to stand there, hoping he would turn his head and see me. Well: just as he reached the opposite platform, Mr. St. George stepped out of the stationmaster's office, and I can tell you there was some shaking of hands between the two. There's my story."

"And where is he now?"

"Oh, they are somewhere together, I suppose; on their way

here perhaps," rejoined Mrs. James Ashton carelessly. "I lost sight of them: that ridiculous stray engine the man spoke of puffed up at the minute, and stopped right in front of me. When it puffed on again, leaving the way clear, both he and St. George had vanished. So I got into the brougham to bring you the news in advance, lest the sudden sight of William the deserter should cause a fainting-fit."

Ellen, unable to control herself, burst into glad tears of relief. "You don't know what a strain it has been," she said. And she sat listening for his step on the stairs. But William Brook did not come.

At five o'clock punctually the tea was brought in, and waited for some little time on the table. Presently Mr. West appeared. When they told him he was late, he replied that he had lingered in the office expecting Mr. St. George. St. George had left him some time before to go to the Shrub Hill Station, having business to see to there, and had promised to be back by tea-time. However, he was not back yet. Mr. West was very glad to hear of the arrival of William Brook, and supposed St. George was then with him.

Before the tea was quite over, Gregory West got back from Spetchley. He told them that he had met St. George just outside the town, and that he had a gentleman in his gig. He, Gregory West, who was in his brother's gig, pulled up to ask St. George whether he was not going home earlier than he had said. Yes, somewhat, St. George called back, without stopping: when he had seen what sort of a night it was going to be, he thought it best to be off as soon as he could.

"Of course it was William Brook that he had with him, Gregory" exclaimed Mary West, forgetting that her brother-in-law had never seen William Brook.

"I cannot tell," was the only answer the young lawyer could give. "It was a stranger to me: he wore a lightish-coloured overcoat and a white comforter."

"That's he," said Mrs. James Ashton. "And he had on new tan-coloured kid gloves: I noticed them. I think St. George might have brought him here, in spite of the roughness of the night. He is jealous, Ellin."

They all laughed. But never a shadow of doubt rested on any one of their minds that St. George was driving William Brook home to Timberdale. And we, as you have heard, saw him, or thought we saw him, in Dip Lane.

3

I scarcely know how to go on with this story so as to put its complications and discrepancies of evidence clearly before you. William Brook had been daily expected to land at Liverpool front the West Indies, and to make his way at once to Timberdale by rail, *via* Birmingham and Worcester.

In the afternoon of the 19th of October, Mrs. James Ashton chanced to be at the Worcester Station when the Birmingham train came in. Amidst the passengers who alighted from it she saw William Brook, whom she had known all her life. She was not near enough to speak to him, but she watched him cross the line to the opposite platform, shake hands there with Mr. St. George, and remain talking. Subsequently, Gregory West had met St. George leaving Worcester in his gig, a gentleman sitting with him; it was therefore assumed without doubt that he was driving William Brook to Timberdale, to save him the railway journey and for companionship.

That same evening, at dusk, as we (not knowing that Brook had landed) were returning home from Pigeon Green in the large phaeton, amid a great storm of wind, and slight sleet and snow, Mrs. Todhetley sitting with the Squire in front, Tod and I behind, we passed St. George's gig in Dip Lane; and saw William Brook with him—as we believed, Tod most positively. We called out to Brook, waving our hats; Brook called back to us and waved his.

But now, Mr. St. George denied that it was Brook. He said the gentleman with him was a stranger to whom he had given a lift of three or four miles on the road, and who bore no resemblance to Brook, so far as he saw. Was it Brook, or was it not?

asked every one. If it was Brook, what had become of him? The only one point that seemed to be sure in the matter was this—William Brook had not reached Timberdale.

The following, elaborated, was Mr. St. George's statement.

He, as confidential clerk, soon to be partner, of Mr. Delorane, had a good deal of business to go through that day with Philip West at Worcester, and the afternoon was well on before it was concluded. He then went up to the station at Shrub Hill to inquire after a missing packet of deeds, which had been des-patched by rail from Birmingham to Mr. Delorane and as yet could not be heard of. His inquiries over, St. George was travers-ing the platform on his way to quit the station, when one of the passengers, who had then crossed the line from the Birmingham train, stopped him to ask if he could inform him when the next train would leave for Evesham. "Very shortly," St. George re-plied, speaking from memory but even as he spoke a doubt arose in his mind. "Wait a moment," he said to the stranger; "I am not sure that I am correct"—and he drew from his pocket a time-table and consulted it. There would not be a train for Evesham for more than two hours, he found, one having just gone.

The stranger remarked that it was very unfortunate; he had not wanted to wait all that time at Worcester, but to get on at once. The stranger then detained him to ask, apologizing for the trouble, and adding that it was the first time he had been in the locality, whether he could get on from Evesham to Cheltenham. St. George told him that he could, but that he could also get on to Cheltenham from Worcester direct. "Ah," remarked the stranger, "but I have to take Evesham on my way." No more passed, and St. George left him on the platform. He appeared to be a gentleman, spoke as a cultured man speaks, St. George added when questioned on these points: and his appearance and attire tallied with that given by Mrs. Ashton. St. George had not observed Mrs. James Ashton on the opposite platform; did not know she was there.

Perceiving, as he left the station, how bad the weather was getting, and what a wild night might be expected, St. George rapidly made up his mind to start for home at once, without waiting for tea at Philip West's or going back at all to the house. He made his way to the Hare-and-Hounds through the back streets, as being the nearest, ordered his gig, and set off—alone— as soon as it was ready. It was then growing dusk; snow was falling in scanty flakes mixed with sleet, and the wind was roaring and rushing like mad.

Gaining the top of Red Hill, St. George was bowling along the level road beyond it, when some wayfarer turned round just before him, put up his hand, and spoke. By the peculiar-coloured coat—a sort of slate—and white comforter, he recognized the stranger of the railway-station; he also remembered the voice. "I beg your pardon a thousand times for stopping you," he said, "but I think I perceive that the road branches off two ways yonder: will you kindly tell me which of them will take me to Evesham? there seems to be no one about on foot that I can inquire of." "That will be your way," St. George answered, pointing with his whip. "But you are not thinking of walking to Evesham tonight, are you?" he added. "It is fifteen miles off."

The stranger replied that he had made up his mind to walk, rather than wait two hours at Worcester station: and St. George was touching his horse to move on, when a thought struck him.

"I am not going the direct Evesham road, but I can give you a lift part of the way," he said. "It will not cut off any of the distance for you, but it will save your legs three or four miles." The stranger thanked him and got up at once, St. George undoing the apron to admit him. He had the same black bag with him that St. George had noticed at the station.

St. George had thus to make a detour to accommodate the stranger. He was by no means unwilling to do it; for, apart from the wish to help a fellow-creature, he believed it would be less rough in the low-lying lands. Driving along in the teeth of the furious wind, he turned off the highway and got into Dip Lane. We saw him in it, the stranger sitting with him. He drove on after we had passed, pulled up at the proper place for the man to descend, and pointed out the route. "You have a mile or two of these by-ways," he said to him, "but keep straight on and they will bring you out into the open road. Turn to your left then, and you will gain Evesham in time—and I wish you well through your walk."

Those were St. George's exact words—as he repeated them to us later. The stranger thanked him heartily, shook hands and went on his way, carrying his black bag. St. George said that before parting with the traveller, he suggested that he should go on with him to Timberdale, seeing the night was so cold and wild, put up at the Plough-and-Harrow, where he could get a comfortable bed, and go on to Evesham in the morning. But the stranger declined, and seemed impatient to get on.

He did not tell St. George who he was, or what he was; he did not tell his name, or what his business was in Worcestershire, or whether he was purposing to make a stay at Evesham, or whither he might be going when he left it: unless the question he had put to St. George, as to being able to get on to Cheltenham, might be taken for an indication of his route. In fact, he stated nothing whatever about himself; but, as St. George said, the state of the weather was against talking. It was difficult to hear each other speak; the blasts howled about their ears perpetually, and the sharp sleet stung their faces. As to his bearing the resemblance to Brook that was being talked of, St. George could only repeat that he did not perceive it; he might have been about Brook's height and size, but that was all. The voice was certainly not Brook's, not in the least like Brook's, neither was the face, so far as St. George saw of it: no idea of the kind struck him.

★★★★★★

These were the different statements: and, reading them, you have the matter in a nutshell. Mrs. James Ashton continued to affirm that it was William Brook she saw at the station, and could not be shaken out of her belief. She and William had played together as children, they had flirted together, she was pleased to declare, as youth and maiden, and *did* anybody suppose she could mistake an unknown young man for him in broad daylight? An immense favourite with all the world, Marianne Ashton was fond of holding decisively to her own opinions; all her words might have begun with capital letters.

I also maintained that the young man we saw in St. George's gig in Dip Lane, and who wore a warm great-coat of rather an unusual colour, something of a grey—or a slate—or a mouse, with the white woollen comforter on his neck and the soft low-crowned hat drawn well on his brows, was William Brook. When he took off his hat to wave it to us in response, I saw (as I fully believed) that it was Brook; and I noticed his gloves. Mrs. Todhetley, who had turned her head at our words, also saw him and felt not the slightest doubt that it was he. Tod was ready to swear to it.

To combat this, we had Mr. St. George's cool, calm, decisive assertion that the man was a stranger. Of course it outweighed ours. All the probabilities lay with it; he had been in companionship with the stranger, had talked with him face to face: we had not. Besides, if it had been Brook, where was he that he had not made his way to Timberdale? So we took up the common-sense view of the matter and dismissed our own impressions as fancies that would not hold water, and looked out daily for the landing of the exile. Aunt Hester hoped he was not "lost at sea:" but she did not say it in the hearing of Ellin Delorane.

******

The days went on. November came in. William Brook did not appear; no tidings reached us of him. His continued non-appearance so effectually confirmed St. George's statement, that the other idea was exploded and forgotten by all reasonable minds. Possibly in one or two unreasonable ones, such as mine, say, a sort of hazy doubt might still hover. But, doubt of what? Ay, that was the question. Even Tod veered round to the enemy, said his sight must have misled him, and laid the blame on the wind. Both common sense and uncommon said Brook had but been detained in Jamaica, and might be expected in any day.

The first check to this security of expectation was wrought

by a letter. A letter from New York, addressed to William Brook by his brother there, Charles. Mrs. Brook opened it. She was growing vaguely uneasy, and had already begun to ask herself why, were William detained in the West Indies, he did not write to tell her so.

And this, as it proved, was the chief question the letter was written to ask. Charles Brook wrote to his brother:

"If you have arrived at home—as we conclude you must have done, having seen in the papers the safe arrival of the *Dart* at Liverpool—how is it you have not written to say so, and to inform us how things are progressing? The uncle does not like it. 'Is William growing negligent?' he said to me yesterday."

The phrase "*how things are progressing*," Mrs. Brook understood to apply to the new mercantile house about to be established in London. She sent the letter by Araminta to Mr. Delorane.

"Can William have been drowned at sea?" breathed Minty.

"No, no; I don't fear that; I'm not like that silly woman, Aunt Hester, with her dreams and her fancies," said Mr. Delorane. "It seems odd, though, where he can be."

Inquiries were made at Liverpool for the list of passengers by the *Dart*. William Brook's name was not amongst them. Timberdale waited on. There was nothing else for it to do. Waited until a second letter came from Charles Brook. It was written to his mother this time. He asked for news of William; whether he had, or had not, arrived at home.

The next West Indian mail-packet, steaming from Southampton, carried out a letter from Mr. St. George, written to his cousin in Kingston, Jamaica, at the desire of Mr. Delorane: at the desire, it may with truth be said, of Timberdale in general. The same mail also took out a letter from Reginald Brook in London, who had been made acquainted with the trouble. Both letters were to the same purport—an inquiry as to William Brook and his movements, more particularly as to the time he had departed for home, and the vessel he had sailed in.

In six or eight weeks, which seemed to some of us like so many months, Mr. St. George received an answer. His relative,

Leonard St. George, sent rather a curious story. He did not know anything of William Brook's movements himself, he wrote, and could not gain much reliable information about them. It appeared that he was to have sailed for England in the *Dart,* a steamer bound for Liverpool, not one of their regular passenger-packets. He was unable, however, to find any record that Brook had gone in her, and believed he had not: neither could he learn that Brook had departed by any other vessel. A friend of his told him that he feared Brook was dead. The day before the *Dart* went out of port, a young man, who bore out in every respect the description of Brook, was drowned in the harbour.

Comforting news! Delightfully comforting for Ellin Delorane, not to speak of Brook's people. Aunt Hester came over to Crabb Cot, and burst into tears as she told it.

But the next morning brought a turn in the tide; one less sombre, though uncertain still. Mrs. Brook, who had bedewed her pillow with salt tears, for her youngest son was very dear to her heart, received a letter from her son Reginald in London, enclosing one he had just received from the West Indies. She brought them to Mr. Delorane's office during the morning, and the squire and I happened to be there.

"How should Reginald know anything about it!" demanded St. George, in the haughty manner he could put on when not pleased; and his countenance looked dark as he gazed across his desk at Mrs. Brook, for which I saw no occasion. Evidently he did not like having his brother's news disputed.

"Reginald wrote to Kingston by the same mail that you wrote," she said. "He received an introduction to some mercantile firm out there, and this is their answer to him."

They stated, these merchants, that they had made due inquiries according to request, and found that William Brook had secured a passage on board the *Dart;* but that, finding himself unable to go in her, his business in Kingston not being finished, he had, at the last moment, made over his berth and ticket to another gentleman, who found himself called upon to sail unexpectedly: and that he, Brook, had departed by the *Idalia,* which left two days later than the *Dart* and was also bound for Liverpool.

Reginald wrote from London:

I have ascertained here, dear mother, that the *Idalia* made a good passage and reached Liverpool on the 18th of October. If the statement which I enclose you be correct, that William left Jamaica in her, he must have arrived in her at Liverpool, unless he died on the way. It is very strange where he can be, and what can have become of him. Of course, inquiries must now be made in Liverpool. I only wish I could go down myself, but our patients are all on my hands just now, for Dr. Croft is ill.

The first thought, flashing into the mind of Mr. Delorane, was, that the 18th of October was the eve of the day on which William Brook was said to have been seen by Mrs. James Ashton. He paused to consider, a sort of puzzled doubt on his face.

"Why, look you here," cried he quickly, "it seems as though that *was* Brook at Worcester Station. If he reached Liverpool on the 18th, the probabilities are that he would be at Worcester on the 19th. What do you make of it?"

We could not make anything. Mrs. Brook looked pale and distressed. The squire, in his impulsive good-nature, offered to be the one to go, off-hand, to make the inquiries at Liverpool. St. George opposed this: he was the proper person to go, he said; but Mrs. Delorane reminded him that he could be ill spared just then, when the assizes were at hand. For the time had gone on to spring.

"I will start tonight," said the squire, "and take Johnny with me. My time is my own. We will turn Liverpool upside down but what we find Brook—if he is to be found on earth."

★★★★★★

That the squire might have turned Liverpool "upside down" with the confusion of his inquiries was likely enough, only that Jack Tanerton was there, having brought his own good ship, the *Rose of Delhi,* into port but a few days before. Jack and William

330

Brook had been boys together, and Jack took up the cause in warm-hearted zeal. His knowledge of the town and its shipping made our way plain before us. That is, as plain as a way can be made which seems to have neither inlet nor outlet.

The *Idalia* was then lying in the Liverpool docks, not long in again from the West Indies. We ascertained that William Brook had come in her the previous autumn, making the port of Liverpool on the 18th of October.

"Then nothing happened to him halfway?" cried the squire to the second mate, a decent sort of fellow who did all he could for us. "He was not lost, or—or—anything of that sort?"

"Why no," said the mate, looking surprised. "He was all right the whole of the voyage and in first-rate spirits—a very nice young fellow altogether. The *Idalia* brought him home, all taut and safe, take our word for that, sir; and he went ashore with the rest, and his luggage also: of which he had but little just a big case and the small one that was in his cabin."

All this was certain. But from the hour Brook stepped ashore, we were unable to trace anything certain about him. The hotels could not single him out in memory from other temporary sojourners. I think it was by no means a usual occurrence in those days for passing guests to give in their names. Any way, we found no record of Brook's. The railway porters remembered no more of him than the hotels—and it was hardly likely they would.

Captain Tanerton—to give Jack his title—was indefatigable; winding himself in and out of all kinds of places like a detective eel. In some marvellous way he got to learn that a gentleman whose appearance tallied with Brook's had bought some tan-coloured kid gloves and also a white comforter in a shop in Bold Street on the morning of the 19th of October. Jack took us there that we might question the people, especially the young woman who served him. She said that, while choosing the gloves, he observed that he had just come off a sea-voyage and found the weather here very chilly.

He wore a lightish greatcoat, a sort of slate or grey. She was setting out the window when he came in, and had to leave it to serve him; it was barely eight o'clock, and she remarked that he was shopping betimes; he replied yes, for he was going off directly by train. He bought two pair of the gloves, putting one pair of them on in the shop; he next bought a warm knitted woollen scarf, white, and put that on. She was quite certain it was the 19th of October, and told us why she could not be mistaken. And that was the last trace we could get of Brook in Liverpool.

Well, well; it is of no use to linger. We went away from Liverpool, the squire and I, no better off than we were when we entered it. That William Brook had arrived safely by the *Idalia,* and that he had landed safely, appeared to be a fact indisputable: but after that time he seemed to have vanished into air. Unless, mark you, it was he who had come on to Worcester.

The most concerned of all at our ill-luck was Mr. St. George. He had treated the matter lightly when thinking Brook was only lingering over the seas; now that it was proved he returned by the *Idalia,* the case was different.

"I don't like it at all," he said to the squire frankly. "People may begin to think it was really Brook I had with me that night, and ask me what I did with him."

"What could you have done with him?" dissented the squire.

"Not much—that I see. I couldn't pack him up in a parcel to be sent back overseas, and I couldn't bury him here. I wish with all my heart it had been Brook! I won't leave a stone unturned now but what I find him," added St. George, his eyes flashing, his face flushing hotly. "Any way, I'll find the man who was with me."

St. George set to work. Making inquiries here, there, and everywhere for William Brook, personally and by advertising. But little came of it. A porter at the Worcester railway-station, who had seen the traveller talking with St. George on the platform, came forward to state that they (the gentleman and Mr. St. George) had left the station together, walking away from it side by side, down the road. St. George utterly denied this. He admitted that the other might have followed him so closely as to impart a possible appearance of their being together, but if so, he was not conscious of it. Just as he had denied shaking hands with the stranger, which Mrs. James Ashton insisted upon.

Next a lady came forward. She had travelled from Birmingham that afternoon, the 19th of October, with her little nephew and niece. In the same compartment, a first-class one, was another passenger, bearing, both in attire and person, the description told of—a very pleasant, gentlemanly young man, nicelooking, eyes dark blue. It was bitterly cold: he seemed to feel it greatly, and said he had recently come from a warmer climate. He also said that he ought to have got into Worcester by an earlier train, but had been detained in Birmingham, through missing his luggage, which he supposed must have been put out by mistake at some intermediate station. He had with him a small black hand-bag; nothing else that she saw. His great-coat was of a peculiar shade of grey; it did not look like an English-made coat; his well-fitting kid gloves were of fawn (or tan) colour, and appeared to be new. Once, when the high wind seemed to shake the carriage, he remarked with a smile that one might almost as well be at sea; upon which her little nephew said: "Have you ever been to sea, sir?"

"Yes, my little lad," he answered; "I landed from it only yesterday."

The only other person to come forward was a farmer named Lockett, well known to us all. He lived on the Evesham Road, close upon the turning, or by-way, which led up from Dip Lane. On the night of the storm, the 19th of October, he went out about ten o'clock to visit a neighbour, who had met with a bad accident. In passing by this turning, a man came out of it, walking pretty sharply. He looked like a gentleman, seemed to be muffled up round the neck, and carried something in his hand; whether a black bag, or not, Mr. Lockett did not observe. "A wild night," said the farmer to him in salutation. "It is that," answered the other. He took the road to Evesham, and Mr. Lockett saw him no more.

St. George was delighted at this evidence. He could have hugged old Lockett. "I knew that the truth would be corroborated sooner or later," he said, his eyes sparkling. "That was the man I put out of my gig in Dip Lane."

"Stop a bit," cried Mr. Delorane, a doubt striking him. "If it was the same man, what had he been doing to take two or three hours to get into the Evesham Road? Did he bear any resemblance to William Brook, Lockett?—you would have known Brook."

"None at all that I saw. As to knowing Brook, or anyone else, I can't answer for it on such a night as that," added the farmer after a pause. "Brook would have known me, though, I take it, daylight or dark, seeing me close to my own place, and all."

"It was the other man," affirmed St. George exultantly, "and now we will find him."

An advertisement was next inserted in the local newspapers by Mr. St. George, and also in the *Times*.

"Gentleman Wanted. The traveller who got out of the Birmingham train at Worcester railway-station on the 19th of last October, towards the close of the afternoon, and who spoke to a gentleman on the platform respecting the trains to Evesham and to Cheltenham, and who was subsequently overtaken a little way out of Worcester by the same gentleman and given a few miles' lift in his gig, and was put down in a cross-country lane to continue his walk to Evesham: this traveller is earnestly requested to give an address where he may be communicated with, to Alfred St. George, Esquire, Timberdale, Worcester. By doing so, he will be conferring a great favour."

For two long weeks the advertisements brought forth no reply. At the end of that time there came to Mr. St. George a post-letter, short and sweet.

Tell me what I am wanted for.—R.W.

It was dated Post Office, Cheltenham. To the Post Office, Cheltenham, St. George, consulting with Mr. Delorane, wrote a brief explanation. That he (R.W.) had been mistaken by some people who saw him that night in the gig, for a gentleman named Brook, a native of Timberdale, who had been missing since about that time. This, as R.W. might perceive, was not pleasant for himself, St. George; and he begged R.W. to come forward and set the erroneous idea at rest, or to state where he could be seen. Expenses, if any, would be cheerfully paid.

This letter brought forth the following answer:—

Dear Sir,

I regret that your courtesy to me that stormy night should have led to misapprehension. I the more regret it that I am not able to comply with your request to come forward. At present that is impossible. The truth is, I am, and have been for some months now, lying under a cloud, partly through my own credulous fault, chiefly through the designing faults of another man, and I dare not show myself. It may be many more months yet before I am cleared: that I shall be, in time, there exists no doubt, and I shall then gladly bear personal testimony to the fact that it was I myself who was with you. Meanwhile, perhaps the following statement will suffice: which I declare upon my honour to be true.

I was hiding at Crewe, when I received a letter from a friend at Evesham, bidding me go to him without delay. I had no scruple in complying, not being known at all in Worcestershire, and I started by one of the Liverpool trains. I had a portmanteau with me containing papers principally, and this I missed on arriving at Birmingham. The looking for it caused me to lose the Worcester train, but I went on by the next. Upon getting out there, I addressed the first person I saw after crossing the line—yourself. I inquired of you when the next train would start for Evesham. Not for two hours, you told me: so I set off to walk, after getting some light refreshment. Barely had I left Worcester when, through the dusk of evening, I thought I saw that the road before me branched off two ways. I did not know which to take, and ventured to stop a gig, then bowling up behind me, to ask.

As you answered me I recognized you for the gentleman to whom I had spoken at the station. You offered to take me a few miles on my road, and I got into the gig. I found that you would have to go out of your way to do this, and I expressed concern; you laughed my apologies off, saying you should probably have chosen the way in any case, as it was more sheltered. You drove me as far as your road lay, told me that after I got out of the cross-lanes my way would be a straight one, and I left you with hearty thanks—which I repeat now. I may as well tell you that I reached Evesham without mishap—in process of time.

The storm was so bad, the wind so fierce, that I was fain to turn out of the lane close upon leaving you, and shelter myself for an hour or two under a hay-rick, hoping it would abate. How it was possible for mortal man to see enough of me that night in your gig to mistake me for someone else, I am at a loss to understand. I remember that carriage passing us in the narrow line, the people in it shouted out to you: it must have been they, I conclude, who mistook me, for I do not think we saw another soul. You are at full liberty to show them this letter: but I must ask you not to make it absolutely public. I have purposely elaborated its details. I repeat my sacred declaration that every word of it is true—and I heartily regret that I cannot yet testify to it personally.

R W.

This letter set the matter at rest. We never doubted that it was genuine, or anything but a plain narrative of absolute facts. But the one great question remained—where was William Brook?

It was not answered. The disappearance, which had been a mystery at the beginning, seemed likely to remain a mystery to the end.

★★★★★★

Another autumn had come round. Ellin Delorane, feeble now, sat in the church-porch, the graveyard lying around her under the hot September sun, soon herself to be laid there. Chancing to take that way round from buying some figs at Salmon's for Hugh and Lena, I saw her, and dashed up the churchyard path.

"You seem to have set up a love for this lively spot, Ellin! You were sitting here the last time I passed by."

"The sun is hot yet, and I get tired, so I come across here for a rest when out this way," she answered, a sweet smile on her wan face and a hectic on her thin cheeks. "Won't you stay with me for a little while, Johnny?"

"Are you better, Ellin?" I asked, taking my place on the opposite bench, which brought my knees near to hers, for the porch was not much more than big enough for a coffin to pass through.

She gently shook her head as she glanced across at me, a steadfast look in her sad brown eyes. "Don't you see how it is, Johnny? That I shall never be better in this world?"

"Your weakness may take a turn, Ellin; it may indeed. And— *he* may come back yet."

"He will never come back: rely upon that," she quietly said. "He is waiting for me on the Eternal shores."

Her gaze went out afar, over the gravestones and the green meadows beyond, almost (one might fancy) into the blue skies, as if she could see those shores in the distant horizon.

"Is it well to lose hope, Eileen mavourneen?"

"The hope of his returning died out long ago," she answered. "Those dreams that visited me so strangely last year, night after night, night after night, seemed to take *that* from me. Perhaps they came to do it. You remember them, Johnny?"

"I cannot think, Ellin, how you could put faith in a parcel of dreams!"

"It was not in the dreams I put faith—exactly. It was in the mysterious influence—I hope I don't speak profanely—which caused me to have the dreams. A silent, undetected influence that I understood not and never grasped—but it was there. Curious dreams they were," she added, after a pause; "curious that they should have come to me. William was always lost, and I, with others, was always searching for him—and never, never found him. They lasted, Johnny, for weeks and months; and almost from the time of their first setting-in, the impression, that I should never see him again, lay latent in my heart."

"Do they visit you still?"

"No. At least, they have changed in character. Ever since the night that he seems to have been really lost, the 19th of October. How you look at me, Johnny!"

"You speak so strangely."

"The subject is strange. I was at Worcester, you know, at Mary West's, and we thought he had come. That night I had the pleasantest dream. We were no longer seeking for him; all the anxiety, the distress of that was gone. We saw him; he seemed to be with us—though yet at a distance. When I awoke, I said in my happiness, 'Ah, those sad dreams will visit me no more, now he is found.' I thought he was, you see. Since then, though the dreams continue, he is never lost in them. I see him always; we are often talking, though we are never very close together. I will be indoors, perhaps, and he outside in the garden; or maybe I am toiling up a steep hill and he stands higher up. I seem to be *always going towards him* and he to be waiting for me. And though I never quite reach him, they are happy dreams. It will not be very long first now."

I knew what she meant—and had nothing to say to it.

"Perhaps it may be as well, Johnny," she went on in speculative thought. "God does all things for the best."

"Perhaps what may be as well?"

"That he should never have come back to marry me. I do not suppose I should have lived long in any case; I am too much like mamma. And to have been left a widower—perhaps—no, it is best as it is."

"You don't give yourself a chance of getting better, Ellin—cherishing these gloomy views."

"Gloomy! They are not gloomy. I am as happy as I can be. I often picture to myself the glories of the world I am hastening to; the lovely flowers, the trees that overshadow the banks of the pure crystal river, whose leaves are for the healing of the nations, and the beautiful golden light shed around us by God and the Lamb. Oh, Johnny, what a rest it will be after the weary sorrow here—and the weakness—and the pain!"

"But you should not wish to leave us before your time."

"I do not wish it; it is God who is taking me. I think if I had a wish it would be to stay here as long as papa stays. For I know what my death will be to him. And what it will be to you all, she generously added, holding out her hands to me, as the tears filled her eyes.

I held them for a minute in mine. Ellin took up her parasol, preparatory to moving away; but laid it down again.

"Johnny, tell me—I have often thought I should like to ask you—what do you think could have become of William? Have you ever picked up an idea, however faint, of anything that could tend to solve the mystery?

It was a hard question to answer, and she saw my hesitation.

"I cannot admit that I have, Ellin. When looking at the affair in one light, I whisper to myself, 'It might have been this way;' when looking at it in another, I say, 'It might have been that.' Difficulties and contradictions encompass it on all sides. One impediment to elucidation was the length of time that elapsed before we began the search in earnest. Had we known from the first that he was really lost, and gone to work then, we might have had a better chance."

Ellin nodded assent. "Marianne Ashton still maintains that it was William she saw that day at the railway-station."

"I know she does. She always will maintain it."

"Has it ever struck you, Johnny, in how rather remarkable a way any proof that it was he, or not he, seems to have been withheld?"

"Well, we could not get at any positive proof, one way or the other."

"But I mean that proof seems to *have been withheld*," repeated Ellin. "Take, to begin with, the traveller's luggage: but for its be-ing lost (and we do not know that it was ever found), the name, sure to have been on it, would have told whether its owner was William Brook, or not. Then take Marianne Ashton: had she gained the platform but a few seconds earlier, she would have met the traveller face to face, avoiding all possibility of mistake either way.

"Next take the meeting of the two gigs that evening when Gregory West was returning from Spetchley. Gregory, a stranger to Worcester until recently, did not know William Brook; but had Philip West himself gone to Spetchley—as he ought to have done—he would have known him. Again, had Philip's groom, Brian, been there, he would have known him: he comes from this neighbourhood, you know. Brian was going with the gig that afternoon, but just as it was starting Philip got a message from a client living at Lower Wick, and he had to send Brian with the answer, so Gregory went alone. You must see how very near proof was in all these moments, yet it was withheld."

Of course I saw it. And there was yet another instance: Had the squire only pulled up when we passed the gig in Dip Lane, instead of driving on like the wind, we should have had proof that it was, or was not, Brook.

"If it was he," breathed Ellin, "it must have been that night he died. He would not, else, keep away from Timberdale."

My voice dropped to a lower key than hers. "Ellin! Do you really think it was he with St. George?"

"Oh, I cannot say that. If any such thought intrudes itself, I drive it away. I do not like St. George, but I would not be unjust to him."

"I thought St. George was one of your prime favourites."

"He was never that. He used to be very kind to me, especially after William went away, and I liked him for it. But latterly I have taken a most unreasonable dislike to him—and really without any justifiable cause. He worries me—but it is not that."

"Worries you!"

"In pressing me to be his wife," she sighed. "Of course I ought to be grateful: he tells me, he tells papa, that with a new life and new scenes, which he would carry me to, my health might be re-established. Poor papa! Only the other day he said to me, 'My dear, don't you think you might bring yourself to try it,' and I was so silly as to burst into tears. The tears came into papa's eyes too, and he promised never to suggest it to me again."

The tears were trickling down her cheeks, now as she spoke. "What a world of crosses and contradiction it is!" she cried, smiling through them as she rose. "And, Johnny, all this is between ourselves, remember."

Yes, it was between ourselves. We strolled across the churchyard to a tomb that stood in a corner facing the western sun. It was of white marble, aromatic shrubs encircling it within ornamental railings, and an inscription on it to her who lay beneath—"Maria, the beloved wife of John Delorane."

Ellin lingered on through the frosts of winter. Except that she grew thinner and weaker and her cheeks brighter, there really did not seem to be much the matter. Darbyshire saw her every day, other medical men occasionally, but they could not save her. When the snowdrops were peeping from the ground, and the violets nestled in their mossy shelters, and the trees and hedges began to show signs of budding, tokens of the renewal of life after the death of winter, Ellin passed away to that other life, where there is no death and the flowers bloom forever. And another inscription was added to the white tombstone in the churchyard—"Ellin Maria, the only child of John and Maria Delorane."

"You should have seen St. George at the funeral," said Tom Coney to us, as we turned aside after church one hot summer's day to look at the new name on the grave, for we were away from Crabb Cot when she died. "His face was green; yes, green—hold your tongue, Johnny!—green, not yellow; and his eyes had the queerest look. You were right, Todhetley; you used to say, you know, that St. George was wild after poor Ellin."

"Positive of it," affirmed Tod.

"And he can't bear the place now she's gone out of it," continued Tom Coney. "Report says that he means to throw up his post and his prospects, and run away for good."

"Not likely," dissented Tod, tossing his head. "A strong man like St. George does not die of love nowadays, or put himself out of good things, either. You have been reading romances, Coney."

But Tom Coney was right. When the summer was on the wane St. George bade a final *adieu* to Timberdale. And if it was his love for Ellin, or her death, that drove him away, he made no mention of it. He told Timberdale that he was growing tired of work and meant to travel. As he had a good income, Timberdale agreed that it was only natural he should grow tired of work and want to travel. So he said *adieu*, and departed: and Mr. Delorane speedily engaged another head-clerk in his place, who was to become his partner later.

St. George wrote to Mr. Delorane from Jamaica, to which place he steamed first, to take a look at his cousins. The letter contained a few words about William Brook. St. George had been instituting inquiries, and he said that, by what he could learn, it was certainly William Brook who was drowned in Kingston harbour the day before he ought to have sailed for England in the *Dart*. He, St. George, felt perfectly assured of this fact, and also that if any man had sailed in the *Idalia* under Brook's name, it must have been an impostor who had nefariously substituted himself. St. George added that he was going "farther afield," possibly to California: he would write again from thence if he arrived without mishap.

No other letter ever came from him. So whether the sea swallowed him up, as, according to his report, it had swallowed his rival, none could tell. But it would take better evidence than that, to convince us William Brook had not come home in the *Idalia*.

And that is all I have to tell. I know you will deem it most unsatisfactory. Was it William Brook in the gig, or was it not? We found no trace of him after that stormy night: we have found none to this day. And, whether that was he, or was not he, what became of him? Questions never, as I believe, to be solved in this life.

There was a peculiar absence of proof every way, as Ellin remarked; nothing but doubt on all sides. Going over the matter with Darbyshire the other evening, when, as I have already told you, he suggested that I should relate it, we could not, either of us, see daylight through it, any more than we saw it at the time of its occurrence.

There was the certainty (yes, I say so) that Brook landed at Liverpool the evening of the 18th of October; he would no doubt start for home the morning of the 19th, by rail, which would take him through Birmingham to Worcester; there was also what the shop woman in Bold Street said, though hers might be called negative testimony, as well as the lady's in the train. There was Mrs. James Ashton's positive belief that she saw him arrive that afternoon at Worcester by the Birmingham train, *shake hands* with St. George and talk with him: and there was our recognition of him an hour or two later in St. George's gig in Dip Lane—

"Hold there, Johnny," cried Darbyshire, taking his long clay pipe from his mouth to interrupt me as I went over the items. "You should say *supposed* recognition."

"Yes, of course. Well, all that points to its having been Brook: you must see that, Mr. Darbyshire. But, if it was in truth he, there's a great deal that seems inexplicable. Why did he set off to *walk* from Worcester to Timberdale—and on such a night!— why not have gone on by rail? It is incredible."

"Nay, lad, we are told he—that is, the traveller—set off to walk to Evesham. St. George says he put him down in Dip Lane; and Lockett, you know, saw somebody, that seems to answer the description, turn from the lanes into the Evesham road."

I was silent, thinking out my thoughts. Or, rather, not daring to think them out. Darbyshire put his pipe in the fender and went on.

"If it was Brook and no stranger that St. George met at Worcester Station, the only possible theory I can form on that point is this, Johnny: that St George then proposed to drive him home. "He may have said to him, 'You walk on, and I will get my gig and overtake you directly:' it is a lame theory, you may say, lad, but it is the only one I can discern, and I have thought of the matter more than you suppose. St. George started for home earlier than he had meant to start, and this may have been the reason: though *he* says it was because he saw it was going to be so wild a night. Why they should not have gone in company to the Hare-and-Hounds, and started thence in the gig together, is another question."

"Unless Brook, being done up, wished not to show himself at Worcester that day—to get on at once to Timberdale."

Darbyshire nodded: the thought, I am sure, was not strange to him. "The most weighty question of all remains yet, lad: if St. George took up Brook in his gig, what did he do with him? *He* would not want to be put down in Dip Lane to walk to Evesham."

He caught up his churchwarden pipe, relighted it at the fire, and puffed away in silence. Presently I spoke again.

"Mr. Darbyshire, I do not like St. George. I never did. You may not believe me, perhaps, but the first time I ever saw his face—I was a little fellow—I drew back startled. There was something in its expression which frightened me."

"One of your unreasonable dislikes, Johnny?"

"Are they unreasonable? But I have not taken many such dislikes in my life as that one was. Perhaps I might say *any* such."

"St. George was liked by most people."

"I know he was. Anyway, my dislike remained with me. I never spoke of it; no, not even to Tod."

"Liking him or disliking him has nothing to do with the main question—what became of Brook. There were the letters too, sent by the traveller in answer to St. George's advertisements."

"Yes, there were the letters. But—did it ever occur to you to notice that not one word was said in those letters, or one new fact given, that we had not heard before? They bore out St. George's statement, but they afforded no proof that his statement was true."

"That is, Mr. Johnny, you would insinuate, putting it genteelly, that St. George fabricated the answers himself."

"No, not that he did, only that there was nothing in the letters to render it impossible that he did."

"After having fabricated the pretty little tale that it was a stranger he picked up, and what the stranger said to him, and all the rest of it, eh, Johnny?"

"Well"—I hesitated—"as to the letters, it seemed to me to be an unaccountable thing that the traveller could not let even one person see him in private, to hear his personal testimony; say Mr. Delorane, or a member of the Brook family. The squire went hot over it: he asked St. George whether the fellow thought men of honour carried handcuffs in their pockets. Again, the stranger said he should be at liberty to come forward later, but he never has come."

Darbyshire smoked on. "I'd give this full of gold," he broke the silence with, touching the big bowl of the clay pipe, "to know where Brook vanished to."

My restless fingers had strayed to his old leaden tobacco jar, on the table by me, pressing down its heavy lid and lifting it again. When I next spoke he might have thought the words came out of the tobacco, they were so low.

"Do you think St. George had a grudge against Brook, Mr. Darbyshire?—that he wished him out of the way?"

Darbyshire gave me a look through the wreathing smoke. "Speak out, lad. What have you on your mind?"

"St. George said, you know, that he stopped the gig in Dip Lane at the turning which would lead to Evesham, for Brook— I mean the traveller—to get out. But I thought I heard it stop before that. I was almost sure of it."

"Stop where?"

"Just about opposite the gap in the hedge; hardly even quite as far as that. We had not reached the turning to Evesham ourselves when I heard this. The gig seemed to come to a sudden standstill. I said so to Tod at the time."

"Well?"

"Why should he have stopped just at the gap?"

"How can I tell, lad?"

"I suppose he could not have damaged Brook? Struck him a blow to stun him—or—or anything of that?"

"And if he had? If he (let us put it so) *killed* him, Johnny, what did he do with—what was left of him? What could he do with it?"

Darbyshire paused in his smoking. I played unconsciously with the jar. He was looking at me, waiting to be answered.

"I suppose—if that pond had been dragged—Dip Pond—if it were to be dragged now—that—that—nothing would be found—"

"Hush, lad," struck in Darbyshire, all hastily. "Walls have ears, people tell us: and we must not even whisper grave charges without sufficient grounds; grounds that we could substantiate."

True: and of course he did right to stop me.

★★★★★★

But we cannot stay rebellious thought: and no end of gruesome ideas connected with that night in Dip Lane steal creepingly at times into my mind. If I am not mistaken they steal also into Darbyshire's.

All the same they may be but phantoms of the imagination, and St. George may have been a truthful, and innocent man. You must decide for yourselves, if you can, on which side the weight of evidence seems to lie. I have told you the story as it happened, and I cannot clear up for you what has never yet been cleared for Timberdale. It remains an unsolved mystery.

A Soldier's Career
From a Record of the Past

I do not know whether the following sketch will prove of much interest to the general reader, since it refers to time and events that are past. The incidents related in it are authentic, though they savour strongly of romance.

In the year 1833, a handsome young lad of seventeen, whom it will not do to call here by his full name, went out to India as a cadet. It is his career—and it was but a short one—that is about to be told. He was a high-spirited, noble boy, though wild, thoughtless, and everlastingly in scrapes; and had caused his guardians no end of trouble and expense. But they could not help admiring the lad, with all his faults; and his mother, while she would call him her unlucky boy, called him likewise her darling Harry. Henry Lynn was the name given him in baptism; there's no necessity to suppress that. He was the younger of two sons; and a profitable living, in the gift of the family, was destined for him.

So, by way of preparation, the child, at nine years old, was sent to Dr. Bringemon's great academy in London, where he picked up notions quite at variance with those of his sober father and mother. At twelve years old he had fallen in love with a soldier's coat, and told his sisters privately that they should never make a parson of *him*. At fourteen, ere the mourning he wore for his father was soiled, he wrote word home that he would be a captain in India. He was sent for to the Hall. His mother cried, his guardians talked of a birch-rod, but Master Harry held to his own will. He lavished love upon his mother, but he laughingly defied his guardians; and the upshot of the business was that Henry Lynn G—— was posted as a gentleman cadet, and at seventeen set sail for India.

It would seem that he liked the life he found there, for, some five or six years afterwards, when, by the death of his brother, he succeeded to the family estate, and it was supposed he would sell out and go home to enjoy it, he made no change at all, save paying off his debts, and launching forth into fresh expenses— which he had been quite ready to do before. Few men were so universally liked as Harry Lynn. Impetuous, open-hearted, generous, and handsome as he had been in boyhood, so he remained in manhood.

Now, do you know much about that race of men called the Sikhs? Few do, save that they are people inhabiting certain tracts of land in India. Nobody had ever heard of them till about two hundred years ago, speaking in round numbers, when they came to light as natives of Hindostan; a peaceful, submissive race of men, inoffensive as are our Quakers. Their religion was a mixture of Mahometanism and Hindooism, neither entirely one nor the other, which brought down upon them persecutions from the bigots of both creeds; and towards the termination of the empire of Delhi these persecutions became so excessive that the Sikhs were compelled to rise in arms against their oppressors. It takes but little, when once the train is laid, to change a peaceful race of men to one of cruelty; and the Sikhs were goaded to become such. They established certain chieftaincies amongst themselves, called Missuls, and, with time, rose to greatness. Some of them took possession of that portion of India which, being watered by the five branches of the Indus, is called the Punjab, or Land of Five Waters; whilst others settled themselves on the opposite, or eastern, side of the Sutlej.

It is more than three-parts of a century now, that the Sikhs of the Punjab, on the western side of the Sutlej, were first governed by Runjeet Singh—a man of great ability who established his kingdom, called by the name of its capital, Lahore, on a sure foundation. But power begets the love of power, and Runjeet Singh cast his eye to the Sikhs on the east of the Sutlej, and thought he should like to govern *them*. His hopes were fruitless, for they had been taken under the protection of the British Government; and the chances of a war with that formidable power Runjeet Singh knew better than to hazard.

On the contrary, he entered into a treaty with the British authorities, which proved of advantage to both parties. Years wore on, and the kingdom of Lahore increased in importance. On the termination of the continental wars, when Napoleon was sent to St. Helena, numerous European soldiers, men and officers, passed over to India, and enlisted into the service of Runjeet Singh. Under the example and training of these brave men, the army of Runjeet Singh became almost equal to our own. It carried its conquests into Afghanistan, and amongst other provinces that fell before its prowess was the beautiful Vale of Cashmere, so celebrated in song. But Runjeet Singh died in the course of time, and, with his death, all the jealousies and ill feeling of the Sikhs towards the British, which he had kept under, broke out with irresistible bitterness, and there was little peace in the Punjab afterwards. Not that these animosities and petty wars concern us here.

In the same year that Harry Lynn obtained his captaincy he went about exploring the country. Amongst other places that he visited was Lahore, and when he left it he performed an exploit that officers have borne the character for being expert at—from a captain bold of Halifax and ghostly memory, down to those of our own times—he "ran away with a maid, who"—did *not* hang herself, but went with him to his quarters at Calcutta.

She was one of the loveliest creatures possible to be imagined, as some few men, then living at Calcutta, can remember now; but that was no justification for the step taken by Captain Lynn. Her mother, a Sikh, had married one of those European officers who had joined Runjeet Singh's army, a handsome Frenchman; and this child, Agee, their only one, was strikingly like her father, so that her beauty was of the European, not Asiatic, cast. The Frenchman died when she was an infant, and her mother married again, a Sikh. All trace, nearly all remembrance, of the lady's early alliance was lost, and Agee was brought up in the customs, habits, and religion of her mother's land. During the visit of Captain Lynn at Lahore he became acquainted with her, a lovely girl just blossoming into womanhood; a powerful attachment sprang up between them, and the result was—as I have told you above. Such was the history of the girl, and the particulars of the affair, as they became known, bit by bit, to Captain Lynn's circle of friends at Calcutta.

He enshrined her in a secluded homo at Calcutta; he surrounded her with all sorts of expensive luxuries; he lavished every proof of affection upon her save one—marriage. And that she could not now expect.

Yet this Indian girl must not be judged as we should judge one reared in our own land of propriety and civilization. She knew not that she was committing any grave offence; modest, gentle, innocent in mind as she was before, so she remained. The very few friends admitted by Captain Lynn recognized this, and involuntarily accorded her a respect quite at variance with the position.

★★★★★★

We must now go on to the autumn of 1845. In her Calcutta home, in a luxurious apartment of it, richly furnished with articles peculiar to an Eastern life, sat this young girl we have been speaking of, Agee. She was in evening dress, enhancing, if that were possible, her surpassing beauty. Her robe was of muslin sprigged with silver, silver ornaments were on her neck and arms, and were interlaced with her dark hair. Young and lovely, she looked fitted to adorn society; a nameless grace pervaded her presence, a sweet, modest refinement shone forth in her every look and action. Poor girl! hers was an unhappy fate. Calcutta railed at her greatly, especially those ladies in it who had sisters to marry, and who would have given their heads to get Harry Lynn. None thought of compassion; it was all censure; yet she merited far more of the one than of the other, and she was very unhappy.

She had not understood these matters when she left Lahore, poor maiden; she understood them too well now. Perhaps the consciousness was especially present to her this evening, for her pale delicate features wore a look of pain, and tears gathered frequently in her eyes. The room was redolent of a sweet perfume, emitted from burning pastilles; it was open to the terrace, and the breezy fans intervening kept up a delightful motion. Outside, stretched at his ease on a large bench, his heels higher than his head, and lazily blowing clouds into the air from his cigar, was one of the handsomest men in all Calcutta, and in manners one of the most prepossessing—and the two don't always go together. You guess of course that it was Harry Lynn. He was quite as deep in thought as Agee inside, and it may be that his reflections, occurring in disjointed interludes, were, like hers, not agreeable, for a contraction, as of perplexity or anger, sat on his otherwise open brow.

"I was a fool—that's what I was!—and awfully to blame. I ought not to have brought her away with me or saddled myself like this for years. How the deuce it's to be broken through now I can't see. By Jove! I shall be worn to a skeleton with all this planning and perplexity. I have no sleep at night for worrying over it.

"My mother writes me that it's time I married! and thinks me an ungrateful dog never to have run over to England. Ungrateful! no, no, not that, dearest mother. Thoughtlessness was born with me, and will never leave me. It is time I married; in a year I shall count thirty summers, and a fellow gets confirmed in bachelor habits after that. I wish I *could* marry. Maria Grame is the dearest and loveliest girl I have ever known, but it's of no use telling the old colonel I think so till Agee's disposed of. Maria cannot know anything about her, that's clear, for she's too correct a girl to have listened to my semi-lovemaking if she did. Wish I could make it wholly!"

Captain Lynn broke off for a moment to shake the ashes from

his cigar.

"We might be married here; I would get leave of absence and take her to England; my dear mother's old heart would be delighted; and Maria but where's the use of planning if one can't execute? *What's to be done with Agee?* I can't turn her over as one does a ballet-dancer. If I could see any way to send her back to Lahore, with a few thousands settled on her but there's none to be seen. She would rebel at the first hint of parting, and as to force and stratagem awkward both; and the end not gained perhaps. The worst is she's so innocent and unsuspicious, so different from this sort of thing in general, that there's no knowing how to deal with her. This all comes of my own folly. Devil take the cigar! it's gone out."

Rising, and throwing his cigar away, Harry Lynn stepped into the room, and spoke, his tone betraying somewhat of the irritation of his thoughts.

"Agee! how fond you are of those pastilles. The smell of them is quite overpowering."

"I will not light anymore; these are nearly out," she answered in perfect English, for she had been an apt scholar under his tuition.

"Oh, light as many as you please," he returned, in a kinder and more careless tone. "I am going to dress."

"To dress!" she exclaimed.

"There's a party at Colonel Grame's tonight. I promised to be there."

She leaned back on the ottoman, her whole attitude bespeaking disappointment, if not despair. "How many nights—weeks—months have you thus spoken: leaving me to this home-solitude; to my dreary thoughts!"

"Now, Agee, don't be unreasonable," he remonstrated. "I am sure you, of all people, cannot complain of neglect. But society has also claims on me."

"It had the same claims when I was first here," she answered mournfully, "and you did not leave me then."

He soothed her, but he evaded a direct answer, and strode out of the room. He was never otherwise than affectionate, though he had tired of her in accordance with the nature of man. When he returned, he was in full dress, and, wishing her goodnight, left for Colonel Grame's, gaily whistling some bars from the last new opera that had found its way from our shores to Calcutta.

Agee sat on where she was. Musical instruments, on which she was a finished performer, were at hand, books in French and English lay on the tables; but she neglected all, and never moved from her attitude of despair. Late in the evening, a middle-aged woman, dressed in a fashion peculiar to Lahore, glided in.

"Ever thus, lady," she said in their native language, "ever cast down! You would be better and happier in your own land than here; and—the time has come when you must indeed return to it."

Agee looked up with a deepening colour, for the words were peremptorily spoken.

"Listen!" cried the woman, earnestly, as she bent to her mistress. "This bosom pillowed your head in its infancy; you were the solace of this poor heart in your childhood, and when you left us, I thought it would have broken. Your mother died; and I, who felt myself more to you than she had ever been, set out to seek you. Far, far I travelled; through hunger, and thirst, and heat, and weariness; along plains of sand, over deserts, through rivers, across mountains; with no guide to direct me, save instinct the same instinct that will take a bird to its nest! and when I was well-nigh wearied out of life, I found you. What motive had I, think you, except *love?*"

"Dayah!" cried the young lady, rousing herself, "I know your love for me. I know you have been to me all that a mother can be—more than mine was: that you have remained here in this strange land, away from ties and kindred, for my sake. I know all this."

"Then, remembering it, dear lady, you may be sure I would be silent forever, rather than speak a word to give you pain. Yet I must say that word this night."

"Say on," she faintly cried.

"You have clung to this Englishman longer than is well. You—"

"Not so," interrupted Agee, her pale cheek flushing. "We shall cling to each other so long as our years shall last."

"No, no, lady," returned the woman; "he seeks to deceive, if he says that. There is a fair girl of the north ready to supplant you; one whose eyes are of the beautiful hue of the heavens; whose hair is as sunny threads of gold. I have seen her. This very day, in public, he was by her side."

"What of her?" shivered Agee.

"She is to be his wife: it is no secret in Calcutta. And you, lady, will be put away, estranged from him more effectually than if you had never known him. It is their custom, these Europeans."

Agee did not answer. She rose and stood there, motionless and rigid. It seemed as if the woman's gaze, bent on her, had turned her into stone, like the Ægie of old. Was *this* the cause of his changed affection—that he loved another?

The attendant looked round, and bringing her face in closer contact with that of her mistress, proceeded in a cautious whisper—

"I have heard again today. The Sikhs waver no longer; they are united and determined, and the war is coming on rapidly. In three moons from this, lady, they will have possession of India."

But still there was no answer. It was as if the young girl heard not.

"The *akalio*[1] are urging them on now," proceeded the old nurse, "so any thought of peace is fruitless. You must not stay here: the land will be overrun with blood, from one end of it to the other."

"You have had news?" asked Agee, at length. "Who was your messenger?"

"He who always is. He is true to me and swift. He returns the day after tomorrow, not earlier, for he must have time for

---

1. Wandering priests. A fanatic race of men, possessing unbounded influence in the Punjab, especially over the native chieftains.

rest. Leave this false Englishman at once, dearest lady; our people must not find you here with him. I will conduct you back to our own land; and let the two years you have passed out of it be blotted from remembrance."

A step was heard, and the speaker bent down her ear to listen. It was that of Captain Lynn, and she drew away as noiselessly as she had entered. Agee sank down and buried her face in her hands.

It was for this, then, that the unhappy girl had followed him! It was for this she had relinquished her beloved native land, envying the very winds that blew towards it; her dearest friends; her fair fame, though she knew it not; her childhood's language—only to be cast aside for another; one to be as much loved and more honoured than she had been!

Captain Lynn came on, whistling; rather a habit of his. But his step was slow, and the tune—if it might be called one—was melancholy as the Dead March in *Saul*. She rose in an outburst of passionate sobs when he entered, and throwing herself at his feet, wildly clasped his knees.

"Oh, send me not away from you" she besought in agony. "This northern girl cannot love you as I have loved. Will she tend you in sickness—bear with your wayward moods in health?—would she give up home, mother, reputation for you as I did, and endure silently the scorn and neglect of the world?"

"Agee, what mean you?" he asked in agitation.

"You are false to me!" she exclaimed; "you are about to turn me adrift that you may wed the fair girl of the north. I have not deserved it of you."

"Stay, Agee!" he interrupted. "Whence you derived this information, I know not. That my name has been coupled with this English lady's is, I believe, true; but it will never be coupled with hers again. From this night I go to her house no more."

"More deceit! more deceit!" she wailed, lifting her hands wildly. "You are mocking me now!"

"No; on a soldier's honour. I have bid *adieu* to Maria Grame forever."

The fact was, Colonel Grame, finding that the attentions of Captain Lynn at his house were daily becoming more particular, had that night intimated to him that, "under existing circumstances," his friendship with his daughters had better cease. Whether, when he lingered with Maria for a moment in parting, Captain Lynn had whispered a hope that a more favourable future might yet dawn for them, cannot be known; if so, he would not be likely to speak of it to the Asiatic girl.

2

It was the following December. Captain Lynn had transferred his quarters to Umballah, where a great portion of the British army was now collected. Preparations were being made for battle, but much uncertainty was experienced regarding the movements of the Sikhs. Some days, news would be brought that they were about to cross the Sutlej; others, that they were crossing it; again, that they were retreating and would not cross at all. But these various details need not be given here.

Captain Lynn, to his most excessive annoyance, had been followed to Umballah by the young Sikh woman, Agee—not to his quarters, of course, but to the town. He had peremptorily enjoined her to remain at Calcutta until his return. The old nurse or attendant, Dayah, had accompanied her thither, and this woman never ceased to urge upon her mistress the expediency of her quitting any place that contained Captain Lynn. One evening, she glided into Agee's presence, her face pale, her mouth compressed, and approached with a dread whisper—

"Lady, you *must* leave him now: the hour has come. A few days will see him and his companions mown down; earth shall hold them no more."

Agee's lips turned white as marble.

"They are crossing the Sutlej," continued the woman in a still lower whisper, as if she feared the very walls would hear her, "an army of from sixty to a hundred thousand strong. What can their handful of British troops effect against it?—and that handful not yet conveyed thither?"

"When heard you this?" murmured Agee.

"He came this evening; he is swift and sure of foot, and has outstripped the European news-scouts by some hours; but their great chieftain[2] will know it ere tomorrow's sun be up. He little suspects the fate that is in store for him! They are fine of limb, these northern soldiers, tall and straight; but ere long they must measure their length upon the earth. As the grass falls before the scythe, so must they fall before their fierce and powerful foe."

"And Captain Lynn?" shivered Agee, from between her bloodless lips.

"He must share the fate of his comrades what should hinder it? Why, even did you turn apostate to your oath, lady, and betray to him what I have now told you, which you know you may not do, it could not serve him; he would still go to battle with the rest. You must escape with me."

But Agee, with an impatient gesture, turned away and ventured forth into the night. Captain Lynn was leaving his quarters to join a carouse of some of his brother-officers, got up on the spur of the moment, when he came full upon her, stealing up.

"You are on the eve of being ordered out to battle," she whispered. "You must not go."

"Not go" he exclaimed, wondering what she was talking of.

"Sickness must be your excuse," she eagerly explained. "A man unable to rise from his bed cannot be expected to go out and fight."

"Are you in your right mind, Agee?" he asked, laughing lightly.

"You would never leave the battlefield with life."

"Then I must die on it, child."

"You can make a joke even of this!"

"No, not a joke. Though that's a good one of yours about sickness. An Englishman does not know what fear is," he said, drawing himself unconsciously to his full height; "and for the chances of war, we must all share them, and trust to Providence."

"Dayah is curious in herbs and medicines," she persisted, in a

---

2. Governor-General.

despairing whisper, "many of our women are so. A potion from her would render you incapable of marching with the rest; and to the world you would seem sick unto death."

"That's quite enough, Agee," he said, half peevishly, half laughingly. "You don't understand these things, child. And you promised me yesterday to leave this place! I was in hopes you were gone."

"You seem strangely anxious to harm my countrymen," she exclaimed, still reverting to the war.

"Not at all. I wish to my soul they were other than yours, but I must do my duty."

★★★★★★

Thirteen of them were present; the ominous number; and they sat around the convivial table of night. Not with the luxurious appurtenances usual in polished Europe; the rich plate, the glittering crystal, the numerous lights; such things pertain not to a half-civilized land or to a time of war and tumult; but the gay jest, the sparkling remark, and the merry song went round all the same. Gallant, gallant officers they were, true-hearted Englishmen, in the flower of early manhood! And they knew not that the shadow of grim *DEATH* was upon them, his dart pointed at the heart of *all*.

"The information is so imperfect, so contradictory," observed Major Challoner, the only grey-headed man at the board: "if we lance the full tilt of belief into a report one day, it is contradicted the next."

"In my opinion our march will be useless," cried handsome Lieutenant Bell. "I don't believe the Sikhs are coming forward at all."

"They dare not cross," burst forth the hot-headed young Irishman, Dan Ennis.

"I hope to goodness they may!" exclaimed little Parker, who had certainly been smuggled into the army, for he was under height, or looked it. "The glory of routing 'em right and left!"

"They may prove a more formidable enemy than we think for," remarked the cautious old major who had spoken first.

"Not they," replied Harry Lynn, contemptuously. "An inorganised rabble never proved formidable. The wine stands with you, Henderson."

"For my part," resumed Major Challoner, as he thoughtfully filled his glass, "I think Sir Henry—"

"Well, major?" cried one; for the major had brought his sentence to a standstill.

"What's that in the shade? There! by the entrance? Who's eavesdropping?"

Every head was turned round at the exclamation of Major Challoner. A figure, clad from head to foot in a long black garment, with a cowl drawn over the face, if it had a face; in short, a dim, shapeless form, stood there in the obscurity.

"What do you want? Who are you? "roared out Major Challoner in his mother-tongue; indeed, he could speak no other.

"Beware!" was uttered by the figure in Hindostanee; a language familiar to some of them only; but the voice was as a strange unearthly sound, ringing with startling distinctness through the depths of the room. "You sit here, mocking at the Sikhs, but know that the moment you march upon them you are doomed—doomed! They are crossing the Sutlej now, a hundred thousand strong. You will be cut off in your early lives; your fair British homes you will never see again: not one of you but will be struck down; not one will be left alive to mourn the rest! Pray to the Lord for your souls: as sure as that you go out against the Sikhs, your destruction cometh: and they have need of prayer who rush into His presence uncalled by Him."

Surprise kept the officers silent. Lieutenant Parker, who had more ready bravery in him than many a man twice his size, was the first to start from his seat and rush after the form; others followed: but it was already gone. They looked outside, and could see no trace of it; but there were many ins and outs of buildings close by that might favour concealment.

"What was it all?" cried Major Challoner, who had not understood a word.

"Oh, a trick of one of the fellows," said Henderson: "nothing else."

"I don't know," cried the young Irishman, dubiously. "I hate such tricks. I can fight a host of men hand to hand, and glory in it: but for these ghosts and warnings and omens, I wish the fiend had them all."

"Did you ever see a ghost, Ennis?" asked Captain Lynn, winking at the rest, for the lieutenant's superstitious tendencies were well known in the regiment. "What are ghosts like?"

"Which of us was to die, eh?" cried Major Challoner.

"Every one of us," cried Bell, making a joke of it. "We had better have a batch of will-making, and go to prayers afterwards."

"All, eh? That's rather too good a jest," returned the major.

"You and all, major," nodded Quicksilver Peacock, as he was designated amongst his comrades, from the mercurial tendency he possessed of never being still. "By George! the black fellow, ghost or no ghost, must think we have tolerable swallows! I should like to get at *his* with my good sword."

"Thirteen as brave fellows as ever drew breath!" laughed Parker. "A pretty go if we are to make food forthwith for the vultures!"

"And be sent to our accounts with all our imperfections—"

"If you go on like this, I won't stop with you," interrupted the young Irishman.

They did go on; and enjoyed their laugh at him: but there was scarcely one heart, brave though they all were, on which the incident had not struck an uncomfortable feeling, a sort of chill. It was as if they had seen the shadow of Death, which stalked on before.

3

The Sikhs advanced unconscious of the mocking disbelief of their British adversaries, and encamped themselves before the gates of Ferozepore, an army sixty thousand strong. That they did not make themselves masters of the town was a matter of astonishment then, and will ever remain such.

By command of the governor-general, Sir Henry Hardinge, all the troops that could be mustered together at Umballah marched out to meet this force and to succour Ferozepore. They were headed by the commander-in-chief, General Sir Hugh Gough, and were accompanied by Sir Henry, who, laying aside his dignity as Governor of India, took upon himself a command in the army under Sir Hugh. The marches were forced, about thirty miles per day. Both men and officers endured all sorts of hardship and privation without a murmur: the most painful to be borne perhaps was that arising from the want of water, there being none to be found on the route. On December 18, after some days' march, they reached the village of Moodkee about one hour after noon, and proceeded to encamp there, trusting the next day's march would bring them to Ferozepore.

But we civilians, in our peaceful country, talk as we may, cannot form any adequate idea of the hardships undergone by the soldiers on these Indian plains in time of war; the unconscious British trooper who has never been out of his own island would scarcely believe in them. Long marches in the burning sun, over roads heavy with sand, which, flying to the eyes, goes halfway towards entailing blindness; or trailing painfully through the tangled jungle and brushwood, with no water, no refreshment, to cool their parched lips. We know not what intense thirst is; the cravings of real hunger; the pain of continued and heavy toil. Sometimes, nay often, it happened, through this period of the Sikh war, that when the men had arrived at the end of their march, it would be two hours before the tents and baggage came up, and until they did come there was no chance of refreshment. So the troops, all in a state of physical exhaustion painful to witness, still more painful to bear, would sink down on the ground, utterly prostrated, beneath the burning rays of an Indian sun, or, worse still, under torrents of rain. Was it a matter of surprise that the hospitals were overflowing?

But to return to these men we are speaking of. They arrived at Moodkee, exhausted with their march and with physical privations, and had barely taken up their station before its walls, when the Sikhs bore down upon them and opened a tremendous fire. But weary and unfit for contest as they were, the men had the spirit of Britons, and rushed forward to meet their powerful enemy. They repulsed and routed them for the time, but with a fearful loss both of men and officers.

They were burying their dead the next day, calling over the muster-rolls, succouring the wounded, and consoling the dying, when Captain Lynn and little Parker ran against Lieutenant Ennis.

"I say!" cried the Irishman, "it's beginning to work itself out. We were thirteen, you know, that night at Umballah, and five are already gone."

"Four," responded Harry Lynn.

"Wrong, Captain, they have just found poor Henderson."

"Dead?"

"Stark and cold. He was under a heap of slain."

On the 21st, the army marched out of camp, leaving it standing, and neared Ferozepore, after a march of sixteen miles. Here they met with General Sir John Littler, commanding about five thousand men. The Sikhs were at hand, and the whole body of our troops were at once formed into four divisions and arranged in fighting order. But again, as in the recent battle of Moodkee, were the unfortunate men hurried into action unfit for the contest, hungry, thirsty, and weary.

The Battle of Ferozeshah, as it was called, began under a mutual assault of cannon; but the light artillery of the British was of little avail against the heavy guns of the Sikhs, so the firing was ordered to cease and the infantry to advance. The Sikh army was strongly entrenched among the jungle and brushwood, rendering the approach of our infantry not only difficult but dangerous. They advanced in line, and charged with the bayonet, but the firing of the enemy was redoubled: *and the Sikhs had laid mines, which were now fired underneath our soldiers' feet.* Hundreds were thus shattered to pieces; officers, men, and horses were indiscriminately blown up.

The action soon raged fearfully, the slaughter being terrible;

the heavy cannonade of the Sikhs kept up a continuous roar, overwhelming with destruction the ill-fated Europeans: but the latter were gallant fellows, cheering on each other with their indomitable breasts of valour, carrying much and overcoming much. The atmosphere seemed alive with bullets; the roll of the musketry grew deeper and deeper; the shouts and noise of the combatants increased the confusion; above the roar of the tempest would be heard the voices of the commanding offic-ers: "Men of the —— Europeans, prepare to charge. Charge!" and, mingling painfully with the tumult, rose the shrieks of the wounded and the groans of the dying.

Night put a stop to the slaughter. Some of the troops retired to bivouac at a little distance, but considerable numbers of each contending party intermingled on the plain together.

But oh! what a night it was! The air cutting cold; no tents, no covering, no food for the exhausted soldiery, who had been sixteen hours under arms, and, worse than all, *no water!* Many a wounded man died that night for want of it. There was very little medical assistance, for the numbers wounded were too great to allow of much, and the shades of darkness were upon the earth. And so there they lay, poor fellows, groaning in their agony; no linen to bandage up their wounds, no pillow to lay their beating heads upon, save the dead bodies that crowded there and the horses that were slain. It was a ghastly sight, that field of battle, as seen by the glimmering of some solitary torch; it would be more ghastly still in the coming moonlight.

The forms of the dead lay stiffened and rigid as they had fall-en, the sharp expression of anguish yet conspicuous on the livid, upturned faces. Officers and men, Sikhs and British, had fallen there together, peaceful towards each other in death, though they were not so in life. Ah! they were equal now: the officers, some perchance of noble family, who had been reared luxuri-ously, and the men, who, it may be, had never known a home, or an asylum worthy the name. The one class had received no more care than the other in dying: there was no wife or mother to soothe their agonies of body, no priest to administer calmness to the soul: equal as they would be in the next world, so had been the last scene of their lives in this.

But striking more painfully still upon the heart of the beholder, himself hitherto spared, came the incessant cries of the departing—of those who *might* have been saved; the vain cry that went up around for *WATER*; and the anguished, unanswered calls for assistance, the sharp, eager question of were they to be left there, among the dead, to die!

In a part of the field, near to the camp of the governor-general, reclining on the ground in their arms, was a group of officers. When you last saw some of these it was at that convivial night-meeting at Umballah. *All* were not there of that thirteen: five had been slain at Moodkee and three more in that day's carnage. Leaving five: but two of those five were wounded, it was thought mortally.

"I say!" cried Lieutenant Bell, who had been nursed in blue and silver at his mother's apron-string, and had never known a care in the world, except that of his handsome face, "we were all calling out for a taste of the battlefield, but I don't admire such rough work as this."

"Rough enough," commented Major Challoner. "But there's the glory, you know, Bell."

"Egad, I'd rather have another sort of glory, than what's to be got fighting with these demons of Sikhs. If they were but an honourable, open foe, meeting you hand to hand, it would be something like. Who would have laid a powder-magazine under our feet, to blow us up wholesale, save these sneaking cowards of heathens?"

"All stratagems are fair in war, they say."

"Stratagems be shot!" muttered the lieutenant wrathfully. "I think those prolific-brained enthusiasts who rave so much of the glories of war, major, exciting us on to become soldiers, might put in a little about its horrors. What was that cry? "

"Only a death-shriek," said Major Challoner.

"Ugh! "shivered the young man. "How ghastly the heaps of slain look in the moonlight! "

"Why, yes," cried the major. "One who faints at the sight of blood had best go away from a field when the battle's over. I freely admit that it wants the excitement of engagement to keep one's spirit above zero."

"Do you know," resumed the lieutenant, "the scene has several times today put me in mind of a war-description of Byron? It's in a short poem, or fragment, of his, called *The Devil's Drive.* Do you know it?"

"Not I," growled Major Challoner, "poetry's not in my line: never read a verse in my life. It may be in yours."

"It is a glance at the Battle of Leipsic. He watches the red blood running in such streams from the mountains of slain, that the field *'looks like the waves of Hell.'* The 'he' being the devil, you know."

"Ah," cried the major, "very likely. It partakes more of the devil's work than angels'."

"Hark at the moans of those poor wretches, dying for water! Ugh!" shivered the young man again, "how damp it is!"

"And bitter cold. Lynn, how are you?"

A groan was the only answer Major Challoner received. Captain Lynn had been dangerously wounded in the leg with grape-shot.

"How's the pain?"

"Oh, don't talk about the pain," murmured poor Harry Lynn. "If I could only have some water!" Hundreds echoed the cry that night, in vain.

Major Challoner moved away on a work of succour. Exhausted though he might be, and necessary as repose was to him, he could not hear those wails for help around and lie down to his own rest. There came up to the spot soon afterwards, making his way over the prostrate bodies, the young Irishman, Ennis.

"Lynn! Bell!" he cried eagerly, "by all that's true, I have seen it again!"

"Seen what?" asked Captain Lynn, rousing himself momentarily from his agony.

"That bird of ill-omen: the black form—ghost, banshee, or

whatever it might be—which appeared to us that night at Umballah."

"Don't be a fool," retorted Bell, savagely, disturbed out of the sleep into which he was falling. "Your superstitious absurdities are not wanted tonight, Ennis; we've horrors enough without them."

"I swear I saw it! I swear it by the Blessed Virgin! The same black, shapeless figure. It's dodging about the field, as if it were seeking something amongst the dead."

"I wish you were dodging amongst the dead!" growled the handsome lieutenant. "Why did you not stop in Ireland along with your banshees, if you are so fond of them? Your teeth are chattering now."

"With cold," answered Ennis, hastily. "But I must go back: I am on the staff, in the place of poor Bellassis. Lynn, can I change your position before I go?"

Towards the hour of midnight, Captain Lynn, between his paroxysms of pain, had dropped into an uneasy doze, when some movement aroused him. The dark shape spoken of by Lieutenant Ennis was bending over him.

Doubting if he were awake, or whether it was not a delusion of the imagination, caused by the conversation of his brother-officers, he rubbed his eyes and gazed up at it, when the figure drew back the dark cowl and disclosed to his astonished sight the features of the young Asiatic.

"Good heavens, Agee! What brought—how came you here?"

"I told you I would share your fate, whatever it might be," she whispered. "*You* talked of separation, and I let you talk, keeping to my own resolve. I assumed this disguise that night at Umballah, hoping to frighten you from marching against the Sikhs. And when I found it was useless, and you left, I followed in the track of the regiment; but I could not come up with it until this night."

"It was not your voice that spoke to us that night at Umballah!" exclaimed Captain Lynn, bewildered with her words.

"It was my voice, but I spoke through a small bone instrument, in use among the Sikhs, something like a ring; so that none could recognise it to be the voice of a woman. I have come now to save you. I will find you a sure asylum amongst my countrymen. Rise, and follow me."

"I shall never rise again," was his reply. "I am severely wounded."

"Wounded!" she uttered, in an accent of deep horror. "But you must not stay in this spot: it is certain destruction."

"Destruction anywhere for me. Why in this spot more than in another?"

"I have wandered amongst the Sikhs unmolested this night," she whispered, "speaking my own tongue. They have just found out the place where your chiefs are encamped, and are hastening back to fire on it. This is in the direct line. You must not remain here."

"To fire on the camp!" he screamed. "Bell!"

But the young lieutenant slept heavily. "Bell! Bell!" continued Captain Lynn.

"What are you about to do?" cried Agee, wildly. "Would you betray me—what I have told you?"

"Betray *you!* No, no, I don't mean that. Sink down here by my side, Agee; the light does not give here, in the shade of the hillock."

He pulled her down with one hand, and managed, though he could not stir his maimed leg, to stretch out the other till it touched the lieutenant, who partially aroused himself.

"Bell! Bell! fly to the camp. The enemy are upon them, opening their guns. Bell, I say!"

"What guns? "cried the sleepy lieutenant, raising himself into a sitting posture. "Guns! Where are our scouts and sentinels then? Have we none out?"

"Are you a coward?" reiterated Captain Lynn; "every moment that you waste is worth a Jew's ransom. Fly for your life, and arouse the staff. Would you have the camp destroyed?"

The lieutenant, fully aroused now to the sense of the words, started up in haste to do his mission. Captain Lynn turned to that dark figure by his side.

"Now, Agee! quick! you can make your escape."

"As I have clung to thee in life, so will I in death," she murmured. "What, think you, will existence be for me henceforth, that you should wish me to remain in it?"

"This is madness!" he exclaimed in much excitement. "Agee —"

Boom!—boom!—boom! rolled the thunder of the Sikhs' heavy gun. It had commenced its work of destruction. Captain Lynn, supporting himself on his elbow as he best could, turned his head to look after his messenger. Even in that very moment, as he gazed, a shot overtook the young lieutenant. With a wild, piercing cry, that reached and rung in the ear of Captain Lynn, he leaped some feet into the air. It was the last cry that ever came from poor William Bell. He was shot right through the heart.

Captain Lynn, amidst all the smoke and the dismay and the confusion that now reigned around, was conscious of a start and a moan beside him: but not for a few minutes was he aware that the unhappy young lady who lay there had received her death-wound.

"Oh, Agee! this is fearful!" he cried, almost beside himself with horror. "And I am helpless—helpless!" he despairingly wailed, wildly throwing his arms up, in vain efforts to move; "I cannot bear you hence to safety and succour!"

"There is no succour for me," she returned in hollow tones, "my soul is fleeing. But oh, Henry! which dost thou think is more welcome to me—to live on in perpetual dread that thou wilt desert me for another, or to sink quietly to death thus by thy side?"

The camp, so startlingly aroused from its temporary security, sallied out against the Sikhs, but not until fearful havoc had been committed. The whole of the staff, with the exception of Captain Hardinge, were killed or disabled. Sir Henry ordered Her Majesty's 80th Foot and the 1st European Light Infantry to the attack, who drove back the enemy and spiked their gun.

What were the reflections of Captain Lynn as he lay there through the night, with the dead body of the young girl resting against him? Not such as can tend to soothe the conscience of a dying man. He felt that the career bestowed on him from above was over, and how had he worked it out? He saw things clearly now: the near approach of death dashed away the scales from his eyes, and denuded his conscience of its worldly sophistries. The recollection of the life he had led came pressing on his brain. He knew that it was not one that fitted him to stand at that Judgment-bar whither he was hastening, to which *her* spirit had already flown: and, it may be, in those closing hours, in his soul's sharp tribulation, that he wailed forth an agonized petition for renewed days, like unto one we read of—not that he might return to his years of vanity, but that he might strive to redeem the past. But no: the sun went not back for him.

With daylight the battle was renewed. The conflict raged with redoubled fury, and the slaughter on both sides was great. Victory appeared at length to favour the British, and the en-gagement, it was thought, was over. Our troops began to collect their wounded and bury their dead, when, suddenly, a force of the enemy, thirty thousand strong, consisting of cavalry and their camel-corps with swivels, bore down upon them. The infantry drove them back at the point of the bayonet, amidst showers of round and grape.

The British forces were certainly at this moment in a critical position: *all their ammunition teas expended, and they had not a single gun werewith to answer the enemy.* Thirty thousand fresh troops and a heavy cannonade brought to bear upon our exhausted and, as far as artillery went, defenceless soldiers! Yet strange to say, at sight of some threatening manoeuvres, the Sikhs fled, leaving the British in possession of the field and of much of their artillery! And thus, in this strange manner, ended the sanguinary Battle of Ferozoshah. You don't want to hear of many such, do you?

"A well! a well!" broke forth, in shouts of exultation, from some hundreds of British voices soon after the fighting was over. It was really true: they had discovered one in front of the village they had taken. Bitter disappointment! the water was putrid, it having been half filled with their dead by the Sikhs. Nevertheless, it was greedily partaken of: general officers, poor soldiers, all pressed round to drink. "Horrible" shudders the dandy, sipping his claret at home. It *was* horrible; but when you, my dear sir, shall have experienced the blessings of a forced march under an Indian sun, winding up with a hot engagement of some six-and-twenty hours at its end, without a drop of moisture having gone into your parched lips, you will not turn away from even putrid water.

Two only remained out of the thirteen officers of Umballah memory, Captain Lynn and the young Irishman, and they were wounded unto death. Major Challoner and Captain Peacock had that day fallen. The Asiatic girl, when she pretended to foretell their doom, knowing nothing of it, gave a pretty good guess at the extent of the carnage. They, the two yet living, had been drawn aside from the dead, and were lying close to each other, amidst a whole crowd of wounded; and the agony of their wounds was even as nothing compared with that arising from their distressing thirst.

"Lynn," cried the Irishman, who retained his superstition to the last, "we can sympathise with Dives now, when he asks for Lazarus to dip the tip of his finger in water and come and cool his tongue. It has been an unlucky fight for us: there was no escaping our fate."

"We have earned laurels, you know," returned Captain Lynn, with half-mocking bitterness on his lip. Poor Harry Lynn! take it for all in all, his was a cruel fate, and his heart was full.

"And lost life," retorted Ennis. "For my part, I *expected* the bullet that struck me, after what I saw yesterday. You matter-of-fact Anglicans don't stoop to believe in death-warnings. Perhaps I may sec it again before I die: but it must make haste."

A paler shade, if that could be, came over the face of Captain Lynn, and he pressed his hands upon his temples. He was about to speak, about to tell Ennis that he need have no fear of seeing "it" again, when a wild shouting noise in the distance stopped his words.

"What's all that?" inquired Lieutenant Ennis of a soldier who approached carrying something in his hand. It was a man belonging to Captain Lynn's corps.

"We have been rummaging over the Sikh entrenchment, sir," was the reply, "and in it we have found the mess stores which they had captured, intended for the Bengal Native Infantry. There was a lot of beer in it—so glorious! It is being dealt out, and I have brought you some."

The officers raised their earnest eyes, their parched, eager lips, and a rush of joy, almost frantic in its excess, illumined their dying features.

"God be thanked!—He is with us still, Lynn," reverently spoke Ennis as he fell back, after drinking of the sweetest draught he had ever yet tasted. "We can now die in peace. God be thanked!"

"Amen," responded Harry Lynn.

An Interlude

Adam Grainger Part 2 Chapter 4

The handsome house of Adam Grainger was ablaze with light. And the house really was a handsome one, commodious also, in spite of the disparaging remarks he had made on it, since visions of wealth were breaking upon him. But Margaret made the most of it tonight: opened all available rooms and decorated them with flowers.

The baby, Walter, had been taken to church in the morning, and christened: afterwards Mr. Grainger and his wife dined quietly, with George Little for their only guest. At first they had meant to give a dinner-party. But so many friends had to be asked: or, rather, there were so many whom they wished to ask: that the idea was abandoned and an evening party decided on.

In the principal room, in the rich silk dress the reader has already heard of, stood Mrs. Grainger, receiving her guests. Perhaps she had never in her life looked so well. Somewhat fragile still from her long illness, that but enhanced her charms; the excitement was giving to her cheeks a lovely flush, delicately beautiful.

The silk was of pearl grey hue, gleaming with richness; it was much trimmed with some costly lace that Margaret happened to have by her; a blush rose peeped from its bosom's folds; another rose nestled in her soft brown hair. Margaret was conscious that she looked well tonight—and it was what she especially wished to do.

Not perhaps so much as a tribute to her vanity, as because one was coming in whose eyes she would be glad to look well.

A slight feeling of mortification—it might be wrong to say resentment—had lain in her heart ever since the rejection of her hand by Captain Hoare. For, that Captain Hoare, or his father for him, had rejected her hand when he discovered she would not have a large fortune, was a fact indisputable. Margaret Channing had never loved Captain Hoare; but she did not like the slight put upon her; it pricked like a thorn; and now that he and she were about to meet again, she naturally wished him to see her at her best.

Their encounter that morning—for the first time since the old days that seemed to Margaret so long ago—was one of those curious coincidences we sometimes observe in life. As Mrs. Grainger's own small christening party was entering the church, a larger and a gayer party was quitting it. For an instant some little confusion occurred; the inner porch was narrow, and a gentleman accidentally stepped on Mrs. Grainger's gown. He turned to apologize, and there was a mutual recognition. It was Captain Hoare. Major Hoare now.

"Miss Channing!" he exclaimed in the moment's impulse. "But, I beg your pardon"—catching sight of the baby, following in Margaret's wake—"no longer Miss Channing, I presume?"

A few words of explanation ensued. Major Hoare had been in India with his regiment for some few years, was home on leave, but would shortly go out again. A child of his had just been christened. But there was really no time for anything like detail; the clergyman waited at the font for this second baby, and Margaret could not linger.

"I should like to come and see you and Mr. Grainger if you will allow me," cordially spoke the major in the hurry of parting: and Margaret said they should be very glad. "It must be today," he resumed: "we go to Scotland tomorrow on a visit to my wife's family. And I shall be occupied, I fear, all day—I have so much to do. Would you mind my calling in the evening? Some people with you? Oh, that's nothing. Farewell until then. Ah, here is my wife. She has heard of you."

For the first time Margaret observed a lady standing behind

him. A little woman, who had a plain and homely, yet an attractive face. A faint colour tinged her own: he had talked of her, then, to his wife!

"Until this evening, then," said Major Hoare. And as he led his wife to one of the fine carriages, waiting with their powdered servants in attendance on them, Margaret saw that she was lame.

"A good woman, but not a handsome one," she decided in her mind, as she went forward to the font. "And no doubt a good wife."

The evening had come; and there stood Margaret in a blaze of light. A little joking had passed between her and her husband. "I don't know that I do care to see that man here," he said to her with mock severity. "He was my rival once, you know."

"Are you jealous, Adam?" she asked, laughing.

"Very jealous indeed," he answered, his eyes dancing with merriment.

However, here they were, expecting Major Hoare; and quite prepared, Adam as well as his wife, to receive him with cordial suavity.

The guests were coming in quickly. Adam was making himself as busy with them as his wife. He looked well—as he always did: a good-looking man, a gentleman, and one with whom the world was prospering.

But a somewhat curious incident occurred that night which shall be related. It is strictly true, and Margaret will remember it to her dying day. Often and often in later years did she recall it to her mind, and always with an uncertain, unsatisfied feeling of doubt. Was it only a piece of folly, a coincidence? Or was it what it purported to be, a warning touching events unforeseen?

Some more people were entering; a gentleman and lady. Margaret moved a step or two forward to welcome them. They were old friends of Mr. and Mrs. Grainger, the Reverend Charles Anderson and his sister; rather elderly people, who had come all the way from their residence ten miles off. It may as well be mentioned, *en passant,* that this fact, their distant home, caused their intercourse with the Graingers to be limited. Quite six months had elapsed since the last meeting, for Miss Anderson had been an invalid as well as Mrs. Grainger; and they had not heard one syllable of the expected rise in Mr. Grainger's fortunes, or knew that he was becoming connected with any speculation whatever.

But, moving onwards by the side of Miss Anderson, came a strange lady, whom Margaret had never seen. She was a remarkable-looking woman: her height alone would have made her so; for, as it struck Margaret and many of the others present, she was the tallest woman in the civilized world—in fact, almost a giantess.

"My dear," said Miss Anderson to Margaret, "we have taken the liberty of bringing with us our friend, Mrs. Dale." And by that name she introduced the tall woman.

"Just come over from the West Indies; landed only yesterday morning at Southampton, reached us at night," Miss Anderson took occasion presently to mention in a whisper, when a seat had been found for Mrs. Dale. "Her husband and Charles were at school together when they were boys, and they have always kept up a correspondence. Mrs. Dale will stay a week with us, and then go on to some relatives in Norfolk."

"What an extraordinary height she is!" whispered back Margaret.

Miss Anderson smiled. "Do you know she quite startled us when she came in last night. The room was but dimly lighted, for Charles's eyes, as you know, are not strong, and she looked like some huge phantom walking in. We had heard that Dale married a remarkably tall wife; but had no idea she could be anything like this. She seems a very nice woman, her manner notably quiet and retiring, and her voice gentle."

"Yes, I think I like her look," assented Margaret, glancing across at Mrs. Dale to examine her more critically. Her face was smooth and pale; her brown eyes were large, luminous, and set very deep in the head. In years she might have been somewhat past thirty. But Mrs. Grainger's thoughts soon wandered from her: her duties, as hostess, were relaxing.

"So you have got back!" she said, as George Little approached. For that gentleman had quitted the dinner-table before the cloth was well removed, to go about some of his multifarious engagements in the city, connected with the Trebeddon mines. "I am glad you are not late. Mr. Little, Miss Anderson."

"A pleasant-looking little man," remarked the clergyman's sister, as Little passed on. "Who is he? I don't remember to have seen him here before."

"No, I don't think you have. We have not known him very long. Adam and he are particularly intimate. He stood to baby today. Adam and I were the other sponsors. You see—"

"Major and Lady Janet Hoare."

Margaret's words ceased at the announcement, and her face slightly flushed once more as she turned it to the entrance. Had Major Hoare brought his wife? Yes, there she was; Lady Janet. The same little limping woman that Margaret had seen in the morning, with the same plain, homely face, and the same sweet expression on it.

"Will you pardon the intrusion and our lack of ceremony?" courteously asked Major Hoare, as he took Mrs. Grainger's hand. "Janet said she should like to accompany me, and we could not altogether help coming out together, as we are on our way to another party."

In her honest Scotch fashion, so true and simple. Lady Janet was holding out her hand. Margaret shook it. Some difference existed between Lady Janet Hoare's place in the world and Mrs. Grainger's; but not an iota of its consciousness was there in Lady Janet's manner; no, nor in her heart. Plain she might be, and unattractive, as the world counts attraction; but, unless Margaret's judgment was strangely at fault, her whilom would-be lover had gained a prize in the matrimonial lottery.

"How nice, how very nice she is!" exclaimed Margaret enthusiastically to Major Hoare, as Lady Janet moved away.

"I am glad you think so. I did not choose her for her beauty."

"Oh, but she has that which is better than beauty. Goodness. I am sure of it. She carries it in her countenance."

"She admires your beauty," returned the major, smiling; "she said so as we left the church this morning. I had often spoken of you to her."

"Had you?" replied Margaret, as she played absently with one of her bracelets.

"And I think she was somewhat curious to see you."

"Why—what did you tell her of me?" came the hasty question.

"I have told her before now that at one time of my life there was no living person I esteemed so highly as Margaret Channing."

A pause. He laid a stress on the word esteem. Margaret rallied her wits. "How she must have laughed at that!"

"Laughed? Indeed no. There was nothing to laugh at in it—or to cry either. I am sure she would be glad to make a friend of you, Mrs. Grainger: only it cannot be. You dwell at one end of the globe, and we at the other. We only return from Scotland to embark again."

"Lady Sophia is dead, I think," observed Margaret. "I read of it in the papers."

"Yes; and my father has become an invalid."'

"Have you many children? "

"Only two, living. A boy of four years old, and the little girl who was christened today."

"A little girl, was it. What have you named her?"

"Margaret."

"Margaret!" she could not help the quick echo of the name, or her tone of surprise.

"After my wife's sister," explained Major Hoare. "Margaret Janet the child is named; but she will be called Margaret."

"I am sure they are nice children."

"Passably so—as children go," laughed the major. "And you, Mrs. Grainger—how many have you? "

"Four. Two boys and two girls. Shall you take the baby to

India?"

"That is a question that is puzzling us. My wife wishes to take her, naturally; but we are in doubt about the climate. Few children can stand it well——What an immense woman!"

Margaret followed the direction of his eyes. Standing in an adjoining room within view, was Mrs. Dale. She did look immense—towering up like a column.

"Yes, her height amazes me," replied Margaret.

"It is quite a misfortune to be so tall as that. I am sure she could not walk along the street without being followed by the boys."

"Who is she?"

"A stranger to me and Mr. Grainger. She came here tonight with some friends. Her home, I fancy, is in the West Indies."

"Well, she might spare some of her height, and be none the worse for it. What a pretty house you have here!" added Major Hoare, quitting the topic and glancing about the rooms, and the well-dressed company filling them.

"Yes, it is pretty. I am not sure but I shall regret to leave it."

"Are you about to leave it?"

"Shortly. We must move into a larger."

"You find this too small, then?"

"No, I cannot say we do. But—but Mr, Grainger expects to come into a good deal of property," she added briefly, putting the matter so for convenience' sake. "And that will necessitate a different style of living."

"He is lucky. We are anything but rich. Lady Janet will have a good fortune later; but she has not very much at present. And I am no richer than I used to be," he added, laughing. "You may remember how poor that was."

"I suppose we all have enough for our wants," remarked Margaret. "Wants increase with means."

"That's true enough. If——Is that the baby?"

For at this juncture, all the company having arrived, or supposed to have arrived, the nurse came in to parade the baby, as by arrangement, once through the rooms. Not an infant in long clothes; but a fine baby of some months old, who sat up in Jemima's arms to look about him, and had the sleeves of his short white frock tied up with blue ribbons. Jemima, who had lived with Mrs, Grainger ever since she required a nurse, was a staid, most respectable-looking woman, plainly attired.

"I am not sure that it is at all an orthodox proceeding," said Margaret, alluding with a smile to the child's appearance. "He ought to be in bed and asleep, instead of exhibiting himself to the world. The custom of showing off a baby applies to dinner-time, not evening."

"And not always then. Why did you delay his christening so long?"

"On account of my illness. I have been laid up for many months, and no one knew whether I should live or die. He was baptized, but not christened. You have not given a christening dinner today?"

Major Hoare shook his head. "My wife is a Presbyterian, and rather a strict one; she does not like a christening to be made a worldly festival. The people stayed luncheon with us. Breakfast, they called it."

But Margaret felt that one individual had engaged her attention sufficiently. She might not linger with him longer, and moved away amidst her guests, halting for a few minutes to enjoy a talk with Lady Janet.

By-and-by, Major Hoare and his wife made their *adieux*. A carpet *quadrille* was begun in one of the rooms, Margaret sitting down to play for it. Dancing had not been one of the projected amusements; but it is always welcome to the young. And the evening passed on.

"Would you like your fortune told?"

Mrs. Dale, who put the question, was seated at the table in the little card-room, slowly shuffling one of the packs of cards. Most of the people were at supper. Margaret, looking about to see that none were neglected, had come upon Mrs. Dale alone in the card-room.

"Oh, I beg your pardon; I am so sorry," she said, speaking

warmly in her good feeling at witnessing what she thought was neglect. "Has no one offered to take you in to supper?"

"Nay, it is my own fault," was the answer. "I stay here by choice. Mr. Grainger and one or two more gentlemen were good enough to think of me; but I declined to go in. I never take supper."

"Will you not take just a glass of wine—and some jelly?"

"Nothing, thank you. My last meal invariably consists of a cup of arrow-root, which I take while undressing, and I know that will be ready for me on our return to the Vicarage. What a pleasant evening it has been!"

"It is very good of you to say so; but I fear you have found it dull," replied Margaret. "You have not danced, or played at cards, or—or talked much. All the while you seem to have been sitting still, looking on at others."

"I never dance. Fancy one of my height jigging about a room!" added the tall lady, with a brief smile. "And I rarely play at cards: they send me to sleep. I do not even know the moves at whist—if that is the right word to give it."

"Well, I wish we could have amused you better. And to find you here all by yourself! It seems most inhospitable."

But Mrs. Dale shook her head to the last remark, and a bright smile of gratitude went out of her face to Margaret. The latter could not help fancying that she must be inured to neglect, that any little attention struck upon her as strange. She was still toying with the cards, slowly and abstractedly.

"Would you like your fortune told?"

Margaret, to whom the question was suddenly put, laughed merrily in answer. "Can you tell fortunes?" she rejoined.

"Yes," said Mrs. Dale. "It is all I can do with the cards. I was taught the art by an old Indian woman."

"The art!" repeated Margaret, still laughing. "You are investing it with quite a serious entourage. Do the fortunes you tell come true?"

"I fear they do," said Mrs. Dale.

"You shall tell mine, then. I should like to have the future truly foretold."

Now, in saying this, Margaret Grainger spoke lightly, and meant lightly; attaching as much real importance to her words, and also to the proposal, as she might have given to some game played with her children. Nevertheless she entered into it cordially, eagerly hoping the "fortune" would be a good one. Perhaps in the like case there are few of us but could own, in spite of our more sober senses, to an innate, semi-feeling of—what can we call it? Belief? Expectation? Some latent doubt whether the mysterious necromancy will not open out a leaf of the future to us.

Mrs. Dale bowed her head in acknowledgment of the permission, and at once passed the pack of cards across the table to Margaret. But ere they could be taken up, she laid her detaining hand upon them, and spoke; some sudden thought apparently occurring to her.

"Before beginning, I must inquire whether you will hear all the cards say, good or bad?"

"Undoubtedly," replied Margaret, surprised at the question. "How could it be my fortune unless I heard it?"

"Friends have reproached me before now, when the cards have not been favourable, with having imparted to them the ill that the cards held. Therefore I like to inquire beforehand."

"Oh, please tell me *everything*, good or bad," said Margaret with warm eagerness.

"So be it. But I hope your fortune will be a good one. Shuffle the cards well, and then cut them into three."

Margaret did as desired. Mrs. Dale took up the three heaps one at a time, threw out some of the cards, and placed the rest in rows before her. Then she sat in perfect stillness, looking at them. The hum of voices from the distant supper-room came distinctly to Margaret's ear.

"I do not like their aspect," said Mrs. Dale at length, lifting her head from the cards. "Will you shuffle and cut again."

Margaret obeyed, doing just as before: and once more Mrs. Dale bent over the rows of cards, apparently seeing what did not please her. This process was repeated again, and yet again. The fourth and final time, more of the cards were spread out by Mrs. Dale; and then she began to speak,

"You bade me tell you all, Mrs. Grainger."

"Certainly. All."

"Well, the cards are not propitious. I have rarely seen them worse. Misfortune is undoubtedly about to overtake your house. Each time it has come up most prominently."

In spite of her belief that this must be "all nonsense," Margaret felt an unpleasant twinge. "Of what nature is the misfortune?" she asked.

A pause of hesitation. "I cannot altogether tell."

"Perhaps I am going to be ill again?"

"Oh no; I see no sickness. Sickness appears to have been in the house, though, lately."

"Yes, I am only just recovering from a long illness. Possibly you knew that?"

Mrs. Dale raised her eyes and looked at Margaret. "I did not know it," she answered. And in truth she did not.

"There is great trouble in store," she resumed, all her attention once more given to the cards. "It is not upon yourself individually that it will fall, but upon the house generally. It seems to be connected with business affairs—with money."

"A sign how little she knows; we are going to be richer than we have ever been," thought Margaret. "Will it be very dreadful trouble?" she added aloud, suppressing the mocking tone that rose to her lips.

"I fear it will be. And it will continue long—long. In fact, I can see no end to it."

At this moment. Miss Anderson, who had come out of the supper-room to look for her friend and visitor, entered the room. Margaret extended her finger warningly; a saucy smile upon her lips.

"Hush, please. You don't know what you may interrupt if you speak. I am having my fortune told." Upon which. Miss Anderson, echoing the smile, sat down, and looked on. Mrs. Dale had not taken her eyes off the cards. For all that appeared, she was unconscious of the addition to the company.

"You will quit this dwelling-house," she went on. "And—"

"That's true," interrupted Margaret. "We shad shortly leave it for a better."

"And you will quit it in the midst of woe and wailing," continued the oracle, hardly pausing at all. "Shall I go on?"

"Of course."

For some moments she did not go on; but kept looking in silence at the cards; now putting her forefinger upon one, with a light touch, now upon another, as if they required especial consideration,

"You are intimate with a dark man. He comes to the house a great deal."

"A dark man?" repeated Margaret, running over in her mind their various acquaintances. "I wonder if she means Little?—he has dark hair and eyes."

Mrs. Dale waited for the answer.

"A gentleman who is dark does come here frequently. He is an intimate friend of my husband's; not particularly so of mine."

"I have said that the threatened evil concerns the house generally, including your husband; not yourself alone," spoke Mrs. Dale. "This dark man is in some way connected with it. Either he will share it; that is, it will fall upon him as well as on you: or else he will be concerned in bringing it upon you, I think it is the latter."

"Why, he is the truest friend my husband possesses." returned Margaret. "Quite like a benefactor."

"We may be thinking of two dark men, then," resumed Mrs. Dale, after again examining the cards. "One man; the one I mean, who is here conspicuously," pointing to the knave of clubs, "will bring your husband no good. You have shuffled the cards well each time. Is it not so?"

"Yes."

"But you have not been able to shuffle this man away from

383

your husband. See; here he is still, at your husband's back: and it has been so each time the cards were turned up."

"Do you make my husband the king of hearts?"

"I make him what he is. I took notice of his complexion."

"That you might tell his fortune—or mine?" laughed Margaret.

"The idea that I should do anything of the kind never entered my mind until we were sitting here alone just now. I only proposed it to while away your time until your visitors came in from supper. And I should not have thought of it then but for seeing and handling the cards on the table."

"I was only joking," said Margaret.

"Rely upon it, this dark man—though it may not be the one you are thinking of—is bringing your house no good," continued Mrs. Dale, once more touching the offending card. "He seems to have a load of business upon his head."

"What else do the cards say?"

"Very little. With the exception of this one sweeping evil, they say almost nothing: that seems to be so great that all minor events are lost in it. I never saw cards show so little of events as these."

"It is not at all a good fortune, I must say."

Mrs. Dale gave no assent. In her heart she deemed it to be one of the worst she had ever foretold.

"I wonder if you believe in it?" cried Margaret.

"There it lies," was the answer—spreading her open hands above the pack. "The cards show nothing but misfortune."

"I wish you would tell me its nature. I might guard against it."

"I cannot tell that—save that it seems to be connected with business matters: with the bustle of out-of-door life. It appears to me that you will soon be entering on some long, dark, dreary road, from which there is no outlet. A narrow, dismal lane that we have to go down sometimes in life, plunging into its gloom from the cheerfulness of sunshine, is a type of it. And I can see no turning out of it, and no ending."

"And you believe that it will be so?"

"I do; for the cards show it. Some notable evil of some kind is coming on. Perhaps not very quickly; not just yet. And—that is all."

"And a very unsatisfactory 'all' it is," laughed Margaret. "What do you think, Miss Anderson?"

"I? My dear, I have always believed implicitly in fortune-telling since I was promised a lord for my husband. That is twenty-five years ago; and he has not come yet."

Miss Anderson spoke, of course, jestingly. In her opinion the whole matter was a jest altogether. She could as soon have believed in conjuring as in fortune-telling. And Margaret laughed again at the "promised lord."

"And I dare say this long lane of trouble will come just as much for me as the lord came for you," she said. "Nevertheless," turning graciously to Mrs. Dale, "I am very much obliged to you for the pains you have taken to amuse me. I think I should like to learn fortune-telling myself."

"Would you like to have a wish?" asked Mrs. Dale.

"Oh yes."

"Then shuffle the cards again."

The cards had not yet been disturbed, but lay as they were placed. Margaret gathered them up.

"Now what shall I wish?" she thought to herself, as she shuffled them. "I'll wish that this wretched rubbish may not come true."

"Well," said Mrs. Dale. "Are you ready?"

"Quite. I have wished."

"Then cut."

Some more manipulations with the cards, and Mrs. Dale pronounced the fiat. Again Fate was adverse.

"Shall I have my wish?" asked Margaret.

"No."

But now some people came pouring in from the supper-room. Mrs. Dale quietly mixed the cards together, just as though she were preparing to take a hand at whist. And the "fortune-telling" was over.

"But, my dear Margaret, you and your husband are too happy and prosperous to fear reverses," remarked Miss Anderson as she rose. "If every man were but as well off and as secure in his position as he is! Look at my poor brother! Having only two hundred a-year to make both ends meet upon—and with this fear of a disabling throat coming on!"

"Would you please play another set of *quadrilles* for us, Mrs. Grainger?"

"Nay," interposed a gentleman, "I think it is time Mrs. Grainger danced a *quadrille* herself. Someone else will play."

Margaret, all light-heartedness again, stood up, though she knew she was hardly strong enough to dance, especially after the day and night's exertions. But excitement carries off fatigue wonderfully; and no one was more active in the dance than she, no one more joyously happy. The promised ill-fortune had quite gone out of her mind, proving how little impression it had made there.

She remembered it again when she was undressing. The company gone, she went upstairs, leaving the servants to put the rooms somewhat straight. The fatigue was telling upon her now. Sitting down by her dressing-room fire while she brushed out her hair, after drinking some warm wine-and-water, mixed for her, the evening's incidents passed through her mind, and amidst them the one in which Mrs. Dale had taken a prominent share.

"What do you think, Adam?" she cried, her husband just then entering the room. "I have had my fortune told!"

"Had your fortune told!" echoed Mr. Grainger.

"And it was the most lugubrious, miserable fortune you ever heard. That tall Mrs. Dale told it with the cards."

"What did she promise you?"

"Everything that's bad, I think. At any rate, nothing that was good. She said some frightful misfortunes were about to overtake us; and that she could see no end to them."

"Good soul!" cried Mr. Grainger.

"But I must say she told it well, Adam. Her manner was excellent; so quiet and impressive. You might have taken her for a real fortune-teller."

"She had need do something well: to make up for her unfortunate height. I thought at first she must have mistaken this for Carnival time, and come out upon stilts."

"What a gentle voice she has!"

"Yes; that's in her favour. And so she promised you ill luck, did she?"

"Dreadful luck. It was to come to you as well as to me; and to be connected with business and money —and with a dark man. The singular thing was, that she should believe in it herself."

"Nonsense, Margaret!"

"She appeared to."

"That's another thing."

"You don't think there can be anything in it, do you, Adam?"

Mr. Grainger, who was taking off his coat, turned to his wife in sheer amazement.

"*Do I think there can be anything in it!*" he repeated, his tone a mixture of astonishment, reproof, and mockery. "Anything in what?"

"In what the cards said."

"In what she said, you mean. I think there's a great deal in it. I shouldn't wonder but you and I are about to be tossed up to the moon in a blanket. Oh, Margaret!"

Mrs. Grainger burst into laughter. Had she entertained any little *soupçon* of uneasiness, his light manner effectually dispelled it. All her common sense came back to her. She was as ready to ridicule Mrs. Dale's pastime as he.

"Do you intend to sit brushing your hair all night, Margaret?"

"Not quite. I was thinking what dolorous fortunes I could promise, if I learned to tell them."

"Because it will be daylight soon," added he, alluding to the hour.

"And oh, what oceans of good luck! Dukes and lords—as

Mary Anderson said; and gold and diamonds, and all kinds of bright things."

Thus, in careless joking, the night's incident passed away, and was thought of no more. Ay, and it died out of remembrance; for months had elapsed, if not years, ere it recalled itself again to memory.

The intelligent reader will of course ridicule this little episode. As before stated, it occurred: occurred exactly, and word for word, as it is written. For that reason it has been given here. And, though it lapsed from Margaret Grainger's mind at the time, in the insignificance to which it was entitled, it recurs to her now at odd moments; and will so recur to her until the last.

"All Soul's Eve"

1

One of the pleasantest spots in that part of France is the little commune of St. Eloi, so named after its church. It lies in the north, not many miles from Calais. One summer's day, years ago, two strange ladies were set down by the morning diligence at its only inn, or *auberge*, over whose door was written, *Ici on loge à pied et à cheval*.

The landlady came forward, in a blue petticoat and white braces; *sabots* on her feet and a long broom in her hand. "What did *mesdames* please to require?"

"*Nous êtes viens*—tell her, Clara—*pour avoir trouver* some apartments," began the elder lady, in a tumult of confusion.

"*Mesdames sont Anglaises?*" interrupted the woman.

"*Oui*," hastily answered the elder lady; "that is, *Irlandaises*—it's all the same—and *nous besoin des appartements. Vous comprends?* Why don't you explain, Clara, standing there as silent as a post?"

"Dear mamma, if you will allow me a moment to speak." And the young lady explained, in perfect French, that her mother, being in delicate health, required quiet, pure country air, and pure country milk; and that a friend had recommended St. Eloi. Could the landlady tell them of apartments?

"Never was asked for such a thing before," responded the hostess. But at that moment a very handsome young man, tall and slender, rode up, sprang from his horse, tossed the bridle to the landlady, and spoke.

"I'll leave him here for five minutes, *dame*. Just put him in the stable as he is: while I go into Duterte's on an errand for my mother.'

"Master Francis," cried the landlady, "these good English ladies want apartments. Do you believe there is such a thing to be had?"

The young man raised his hat to the ladies. "Could he have the honour of being of service to them?"

"Tell him, Clara—I can see he is a gentleman—he may be of more use to us than that ill-dressed landlady," cried Mrs. Fitzgerald. And the young lady, blushing proceeded to do so.

The young man considered. "Truly, I don't know," he said. "I fear—— This spot is so very small and retired, you see, that visitors rarely come to it, consequently no accommodation has ever been provided. Let me see—Madame Coe has a commodious house: what do you think of *la mère Coe, dame?*" turning to the landlady.

"Well, you have a talent for getting out of difficulties, Master Francis! Mother Coe has done nothing but grumble at the loneliness of her big house, since her daughters married, and at the easy life Babette leads of it. She might like somebody in it for company. Suppose you were to go and see, Master Francis?"

"What a civil, gentlemanly young man!" exclaimed the lady, looking after him as he moved away. "I always took young Frenchmen to be nothing but monkeys. Ask who he is, Clara?"

He was the young gentleman at the *château*, the landlady answered, François Latange, and owned a good bit of property in the commune—that is, his father did. Monsieur Latange was very old now, turned seventy, and sat in the chimney-corner all day, sucking *tablettes*.[1] Madame Latange was not fifty yet; a scolding, never-quiet *dame*, who ruled despotically the house, and the village, and especially Master Francis He was the only child, heir to all; but *Madame* had a niece who lived with her, Mademoiselle Anastasie, a *demoiselle* of six-and-twenty with a vinegar face and

---

1. A sweetmeat made of treacle and butter, answering somewhat to the English "bull's-eye," much patronised by French people of all ages.

a cherry-coloured *coiffure*, who looked after the kitchen sharper than *Madame* did, and scolded the servants twice to her once.

Master Francis was betrothed to Mademoiselle Anastasie, and they were to be married when he was twenty-one: that would be in another year. The landlady *hoped* it would be a prosperous *ménage*: *Madame* had brought it all about: but some people had a notion that Master Francis was too fond of admiring pretty faces to put up exclusively with the plain one of Mademoiselle Anastasie.

She was interrupted by the return of Master Francis himself. He had seen Madame Coe (except in conversations of ceremony, like the present, that gentlewoman was familiarly styled *la mère Coe* , and thought matters might be arranged. Would the ladies allow him the honour of escorting them to her house?

Matters were arranged. Madame Coe was not less pleased to have her solitary rooms occupied, and to afford an increase of employment to her lazy maid Babette, than the ladies were to agree to her very reasonable terms. And in a few days they arrived finally with their luggage from Calais, and took up their abode in St. Eloi.

It was quite an event to the village, and everyone fell in love with Clara, who really was a very lovable young lady, with her charming beauty and her modest manners. Mrs. Fitzgerald at times got laughed at, and that was when she insisted on plunging wholesale into French. At first, a few styled them "English heretics," but they proved to be staunch Roman Catholics, with not a taint of heresy about them. Madame Latange did not take quite kindly to them. She hated and despised the English. But she condescendingly invited them to spend an occasional day at the *château*, where Clara had to make friends with Mademoiselle Anastasie. Master Francis and Miss Clara got on very well together. But we are coming to that by-and-by.

2

The time arrived for the *tirage au sort* of that year for the department of the Pas de Calais. Every French male subject, on approaching his twenty-first year, has to draw lots whether he shall be a soldier or not. There is no exception the prince's son and the beggar's must alike hazard their chance. But when once the drawing is over, the equality ends; for while the poor, if they fall, have no chance but to serve; the rich, should they have been unlucky, provide a substitute

Heavily rose the morning, and heavily rose the hearts in St. Eloi, on the day fixed for the *tirage*. Many a mother, sick with anxious suspense, saw her boy depart for Calais, with a wailing prayer to the Virgin that a high number might fall to him. They were mostly peasants' sons who went from St. Eloi; and they started to walk, in their clean blue blouses and greased Sunday shoes; started with heavy steps and still more heavy hearts: but Master Francis Latange, for *his* time had now come, rode forth from his father's house, well mounted, followed by his servant It may indeed be said that what was as death to them was sport to him. Suppose he did fall? Well, what of that? a substitute was ready. Twenty substitutes had he needed them.

As he came to *la mère Coe's* house, he looked up at certain of its windows. A young, anxious face was at one of them; and Master Francis leapt off his horse; which Paul, the groom, rode up and held.

"Just a word, Clara, my dearest," he said, as he entered, "to bid me God-speed."

"Now why did you come in, Francis?" she asked, in quite a cold sort of voice, though she was trembling with delight. "It is wrong."

"Bah, Clara! I know now who it was that busied herself to tell you that rubbish about my mother. It came through that interesting cousin of mine, Mademoiselle Anastasie."

"It is of no consequence who it was, Francis. If—if—it is really so"—Clara seemed to hesitate for words—"that Madame Latange forbids your visits here, we cannot continue to receive you."

"We'll talk of that another time: my horse won't stand. Farewell, my love," he whispered, snatching also another sort of farewell. "There, Clara, my own! that's what I came in for."

He was outside almost as he spoke, vaulting on his horse, and the blushing face of Clara peeped again from the window. He detected it, hidden though it nearly was by the curtain, and he smiled and bowed gallantly, riding away bareheaded till he was beyond her view.

"I wouldn't give my old clay pipe for Mam'selle Anastasie's chance now," cogitated old Paul, shrewdly, as he trotted after his young master. "But I'm not going to split upon him to *Madame*."

Ah! those anxious hearts those anxious faces, standing, that afternoon, at their cottage doors! The day had turned out wretchedly cold, and pouring with rain. Francis Latange was back early.

"Oh, Master Francis," cried a woman, from the first door he came to, "what about my poor boy? His number—"

"First-rate, Mother Gris," interrupted the young man cheerily, riding on without stopping. "Ninety-six, I think."

"Thank the good God!" murmured the mother, falling upon her knees on the threshold, and drawing out her beads.

"Master Francis—a moment, sir!" implored an aged man, staggering across the road. "Has my grandson fallen?"

"I cannot tell you, Joseph," answered the young horseman, in a kindly tone; doubly kind, because he knew the news that was in store for the poor old man. "I did not get at all the numbers you know."

"I feel he is down," moaned the old man, " though you won't tell it me, sir. Who is to work for me, in my years, when Jean shall be gone! His brother does nothing for me."

"Don't meet sorrow halfway, my poor Joseph. You shan't want a crust and a roof, even if Jean can has to go."

"The saints protect him for a kind heart!" muttered the aged man, gazing after the horseman. "But—oh, Mother of Mercy, help me and my poor boy! I know he has fallen."

Mrs. Fitzgerald saw Master Francis coming, and threw her window up. "What speed?" she called out, as Clara glided to her side.

"*Tombé*." replied the young man, partly checking his horse; "my number was seventeen. So I can go for a soldier, now, as soon as I please." And Clara's very lips turned white as he cantered on.

The next morning, as Clara was making the breakfast, Madame Coe came in. "I have news to tell you, Miss Clara," she began, "and I'll tell it before *Madame* your mamma comes down—I know I did not want my mother to ferret into my private affairs when I was a *demoiselle*. There was a great dispute up at the *château* last night."

"A dispute!" repeated Clara.

"Between Master Francis and his mother. Mam'selle Adèle, who was up there yesterday doing some dress-making, told me. It seems they were talking about the substitute for Master Francis, and that brought up other matters. *Madame* began to speak of his marriage, and Master Francis stopped her, quite carelessly like, and said he did not intend to carry out the marriage, for he thought he and Mam'selle Anastasie would not suit each other."

Clara changed colour. "And the joke of it was, that Mam'selle Anastasie had got her ear to the partition, along with *mam'selle* and heard it," continued the Mother Coe, in perfect glee. "Then *Madame* set-to, and wrangled with him; and Master Francis brought out that he liked somebody else better—and of course, my dear, *we* know who that is. Upon which *Madame's* rage ran sky high, and she gave him a flat box on both his ears. He is to serve his seven years. *Madame* will not buy him a substitute. In her passion she swore it."

"But his father?" Clara shivered, much shocked and bewildered.

"His father! My dear, you might as well speak of a block of wood. Whatever *Madame* decrees, is law. She tamed the spirit out of her old husband years ago."

"But the property is his—the estate, the money; it is not hers."

"Just as much his as it is mine, for any manner of use," persisted Dame Coe. "He dare not ask for a *sou*, that old man, and he never has one. He might as well ask *Madame* for her head as for money to buy his son off, unless she chose to give it. No, Miss Clara. Femme Latange has not sworn to many things in her life, but she has to this. Poor Master Francis must serve."

Mademoiselle Adèle's report was substantially correct. Master Francis had declined to marry Mam'selle Anastasie, and when his mother defiantly urged the contract, he said the contract might go and be hanged—to speak politely. So then she boxed his ears. Upon which, Master Francis, his cheeks tingling with pain, and himself with anger, boldly avowed there was only one woman in the world should call him husband, and that was Clara Fitzgerald.

Madame danced about the room with rage, and finally fell on her knees and *swore* that he should serve his seven years as a soldier; she would find him no substitute. At the end of that period he would come back glad enough to take to himself his deserving cousin Anastasie.

Oh, he would serve, Francis replied with bravado, and glad to do so; anything to get away from home tyranny. But he thought Mademoiselle Anastasie need not trouble herself to wait for him.

Everyone said that before the time came for the calling out of the new recruits, *Madame* would grow cool and reasonable: she never would permit her fine son, of whom she was so proud, to serve as a soldier. It is probable that these were precisely *Madame's* own intentions. But one early day, long before *Madame* or St. Eloi expected it, an order descended on the village like a clap of thunder. The new recruits were to join forthwith: *for war had broken out with Russia.*

War! Francis Latange to go forth and be shot at: *Madame* came to her senses at once: and she ordered the horses to the lumbering, window-rattling old family coach, that she might jog off to Calais to see about the substitute.

"Spare yourself the trouble, mother," said Francis. " I shall serve my time."

"We are at war," shrieked *Madame*. "You'll get killed."

"I dare say I shall. And not be sorry, either. Anything for a quiet life. You might have purchased a substitute *before* the war broke out, but none shall say that Francis Latange shirked his duty now."

"The grief will kill me," wailed *Madame*.

"Oh no, it won't," returned Francis. "You and Mam'selle Anastasie will just go on as much alive as ever, looking after the eggs, and blowing up the servants."

Madame melted into tears. "Francis, you are ungrateful. Won't you reflect that you are very dear to me: the day-star of my life, the apple of my eye?"

"Well, mother, you have taken the wrong way to show it; treating me as a child, and magging the peace out of me."

"I *will get* you a substitute, my son," she passionately broke forth. " Or, if you must go to the war, you shall have your commission."

"Listen mother," he answered. "You have suffered my name to stand enrolled, these many weeks, as one of the ranks, and as such I will serve. Do you fear I am a coward? Would I like the reproach of being one cast at me?"

The village all turned out to see the recruits depart; there was not a dry eye in it. Francis Latange went with the rest, and his mother flung herself down on her knees in the mud of the road, to pray the Virgin for his safe return. Mam'selle Anastasie was behind her, also on her knees, telling her beads. This was nothing extraordinary for that moment of painful emotion at St. Eloi.

Francis had stolen a meeting with Clara Fitzgerald the evening before. He had not seen much of her lately; for Clara had refused to meet him in opposition to his mother. But now that he was going away, perhaps forever, she was as anxious as he for a parting interview. She had learnt to love him deeply, passionately; and when the last moment of farewell came, her anguish rose in convulsive sobs.

"Do not grieve so, Clara," he whispered, fondly laying her head upon his shoulder. "I may be back sooner than you think.

If the war should abruptly end, as many prophesy it will, they may then send a substitute for me, and I will come home. But rest assured of one thing, Clara: that when I do come, be it sooner or later, it shall be to win you for my wife. God protect you, my love, forever and forever."

But the war did not come to an end and the months dragged themselves slowly on. A letter now and then found its way from Francis to his father, and to Clara Fitzgerald. These letters gave the leading incidents in the progress of the allied armies, the landing in the Crimea, the Battle of the Alma, and the long and terrible siege of Sebastopol. The summer of 1855 came round, and the troops were still *before* Sebastopol, not in it

It would really seem, at least it did to the village, that Mrs. Fitzgerald was going to be a fixture at St. Eloi. But Mrs. Fitzgerald was not rich, and she was unwilling to quit a locality where she saved no inconsiderable portion of her income. With the exception of a week or two's absence occasionally, she had now been two years at St. Eloi.

July came in; and with it the news of the disastrous battle of the 17th and 18th of June before Sebastopol when the allied armies were repulsed in their attempt to take the Malakhof and the Redan. It was rumoured that the loss of the French was frightful, and St. Eloi trembled for the safety of its children. But they had to wait many days yet for the details and the names of the fallen.

The official returns came at last, and *Monsieur le Commissure de Police*, who in his own august person did duty for the *maire*, *préfet* and the rest of the authorities in a larger town, stood in his *bureau*, ready to read over the list of the slain. The poor villagers were crowding in: those who had relatives at the war in dread fear, those who had not, from sympathy and curiosity. The *commissaire* was opening his mouth to begin, when a movement amongst his audience took place; they were pushing each other back, treading on toes, and humbly squeezing themselves into nothing, to make way for a feeble old gentleman who was entering

It was Monsieur Latange. He had actually come out of his chimney-corner, and walked down from his *château*. *Monsieur le Commissaire* stepped forth, bowing, from behind his desk, and installed his guest in his own office-chair.

"Attention!" shouted the *commissaire*. And he proceeded to read out the list in his most official voice.

"'For the commune of St. Eloi. Return of those killed in the engagement of the 18th of June, before Sebastopol:

"'Jean-Marie Dubuis.

"'Robert Eloi Hans.

"'Paul Vanderwelde.

"'François Latange.'

"*C'est tout mes amis, grâce à Dieu!*" concluded the *commissaire*, taking off his spectacles.

There was a moment of dead silence, and then a burst of sobs and smothered cries arose from the listeners, in the midst of which the poor old proprietor fell heavily from his chair. They picked him up, and *M. le Commissaire* went to the pump, in the yard behind his *bureau*, and fetched some water. It restored him: but the hope of his old age was gone. Père Latange had truly loved his son.

Madame Latange was a changed woman from that day. It was not only her happiness, but the *pride* of her existence, that had left her with her son's life. She never knew until now how entirely her hopes had been concentrated in that son's future. *Madame* spent a little fortune in masses for his soul—for which the priests prayed their best. And she ordered a handsome tombstone to be placed in the cemetery to his memory. Mademoiselle Anastasie consoled herself by accepting the addresses of a neighbouring farmer: who, having become possessed of the notion that she would now be the inheritor, had hastened to offer them.

But the grief of Clara Fitzgerald! None saw its outward signs, save in her now invariably languid manner and pallid cheek. Babette set that down to her mother's illness. For Mrs. Fitzgerald had been seized with rheumatic-fever; and lay a martyr to suffering and fractiousness. And the weeks flew on again.

BOOM! boom! boom! The heavy bell of St. Eloi's Church, never heard but on state occasions, or when a fire happened in the commune, suddenly tolled out at evening twilight. *Boom! boom! boom!*

Clara started in nervousness from the chair she occupied in Babette's kitchen. Anxiety on her mother's account, combined with her own secret sorrow, was beginning to tell on her nerves and health.

"Babette! hark! It must be a fire."

"Sit yourself down again, Miss Clare, and look to your saucepan," responded Babette. "You are forgetting the *fête* of tomorrow: All Saints' Day. The bell's thundering out for that."

Clara resumed her place on the wooden chair by the stove, and went on stirring the arrowroot in the saucepan. Mrs. Fitzgerald, more peevish than ever, now she was recovering, fancied none of these messes, unless they were prepared by her daughter. So Clara made frequent visits to Babette's kitchen, to the complete satisfaction of that valuable domestic, who invariably treated her to a dish of gossip.

"My faith! isn't *la patronne* going to be smart tomorrow!" she began, in a half-whisper, jerking her head in the direction of Madame Coe's *salle-à-manger*, where that lady was snugly ensconced, her feet and her petticoats over an open charcoal *chauffrette*. "She has been having her purple velvet bonnet done up with green ribbons and grapes, and she has a new cloth mantle; one of those round grey things just come up. What are you going to wear new tomorrow, Miss Clara?"

"I?" answered Clara, languidly. "Nothing."

"Nothing!" retorted Babette. "But you are going to church?"

"Of course," answered the young lady.

"And as if folks went there in old clothes tomorrow! I wouldn't show my face at church on All Saints' Day in a cap I had worn before, if I knew I should get a sweetheart by it You have not been here on the First of November, Miss Clara?"

"No, we have been in England both years. Mamma receives her rents then. I have never been in France on the day of All Saints."

"Then it's kept in this village, I can tell you, *mademoiselle!* The grand bell, that's stunning us now, begins at five in the morning, and never leaves off all day. And the church is kept open till ten at night. You should see the candles that are burnt in it after dark. Hundreds of them."

"Why, yes!" interrupted Clara, in sudden recollection; "to-morrow night is the Eve of All Souls! The night when we pray for the dead!"

"And wherever were your wits, *mademoiselle*, that you have only just thought of that?" asked Babette, with that familiarity of manner characteristic of French servants: who, however, with all their freedom of speech, do not lose sight of respect.

"Is it the custom here to kneel in the cemetery and pray on the Day of the Dead?" questioned Clara.

"I should think it is the custom everywhere," answered Babette, indignation in her tone at the superfluous question. "Dry or wet, we all go if we have any dead to pray for; and those who've not go for company. That arrowroot's thickening, Miss Clara."

"Do you go, Babette?"

"What should hinder me?" asked Babette. "And *la patronne*," with another jerk of the head towards the *salle-à-manger*, "gives me two hours tomorrow afternoon for church. But there's one thing I would not do, *mademoiselle*; and that is, go out to pray tomorrow night."

"Why not?" asked Clara.

"Catch me stirring abroad after dark on All Souls' Eve! Why, you know, Miss Clare, that the spirits come out of purgatory then, and appear to you."

"Superstitious people say so, Babette. But it is not true."

"Oh, well—if you know better than those who have seen them. *I have seen them,*" concluded Babette, resolutely.

"You may have fancied so."

"I saw my sister's husband. She, hard-hearted creature! had got married again, so, of course, it was no use its appearing to *her*. I was scuttering along in the dark to the church—it's six years ago this same blessed November—and there I beheld something without form, a fluttering of wings like, just before me, high in the air. I knew it was my poor brother-in-law's soul, released for that night out of purgatory, and I fell flat down on my face in a pool of water, and never dared to get up again till some passers-by led me home. You may well fancy, *mademoiselle*, that I have not put myself outside the door since on All Souls' Eve. But oh, my heart, Miss Clare! have you heard what Madame Latange is going to do?"

"No," answered Clara, rousing up at the name.

"Master Francis's tombstone is completed, and in the cemetery. The most superb slab, they say: a white urn, a willow on black marble that you may see your face in, and gold letters for the inscription. It must have cost money, though, that tablet."

The spoon had dropped into the arrowroot, and lay there. Babette's voice fell to a still lower key.

"She is going to church tomorrow night at seven, and when the candles are burnt out—she's to have some dozens, they say, all alight together—she goes off straight to the cemetery, to pray over this new stone. She *is*, Miss Clara."

"But it is not the custom to pray in the cemetery tomorrow night," debated the young lady, forgetting the spoon and the arrowroot.

"Never was yet," responded Babette. "But *Madame* lays his death at her own door, and she thinks to expiate some of his time in purgatory, poor young gentleman, by praying-in the Day of the Dead. She'll kneel in the cemetery until the clocks have told midnight."

"All alone?" shivered Clara.

"Not she. Plenty of *commères* will go with her for the novelty of the thing I wouldn't be one: and risk seeing his spirit—which is certain to appear. Do you notice how thin she's grown?"

Clara replied by a faint moan. Her face was hidden in her

hands.

"She's like a shadow, compared with what she was when Master Francis was at home; and as to her dead-alive old husband—There's your arrow-root all gone, Miss Clare!" screamed out Babette, by way of conclusion. "And *now you* must begin some more! I'll put on a handful of braises and get up the fire."

All Saints' Day is the greatest religious *fête*, excepting Easter, in the Catholic calendar. The church decorations, the music, the rich robes of the priests, and the brilliancy of the ladies' toilets, are perfect on the *fête* of Toussaint. A strange contrast does the following day present, All Souls'; or, as the French emphatically express it, the *Jour des Morts*. There are no gaudy colours in dress then; no decorations. The world attires itself in sombre black; the glittering tints in the priests' robes are replaced by black and white; the church is hung with black, and nothing meets the eye, inside it, but deaths' heads, and cross-bones, and skulls elevated on poles; whilst in the bowed, craped heads of the hushed congregation you behold real mourners.

People in the large towns do not go to the cemetery, to kneel on the damp earth and pray, quite so universally as they once did; but in the small rural communes, such as St. Eloi, none omit it. The superstition, that the souls of the deceased come out of purgatory after dark on All Souls' Eve and hover in the air, waiting to appear to any of their relatives who may venture abroad, is most religiously believed by the lower orders; and by a good many of their betters also. The supposed object of their appearing is to remind these their relatives to pray for them on the *Jour des Morts:* and with the first glimmer of that sombre day's dawn, the poor spirits wing their flight back to purgatory.

4

All Saints' Day at last! and a very fine one. It was to be an eventful day, take it for all in all. Breakfast over, Clara left her mother to the care of the French nurse and prepared to go out.

"Have you seen her, Miss Clara" whispered Babette, as she traversed the passage to open the house-door for the young lady.

"Seen whom?"

"*La patronne*," answered Babette, with one of her favourite side-nods towards the staircase. "She'll be down by-and-by, as fine as an empress, in her brown satin gown; and she's putting white net sleeves over her old wrists, and there's a pair of straw-coloured gloves lying on the commode by her bonnet and new cloak. Won't some cats have tails!"

"Open the door, Babette. I shall be late at mass."

"Not so late as she'll be. When she comes out *en grande tenue*, she's always an hour at her toilet. But for the love of all the saints, *mademoiselle*," continued the unceremonious Babette, running her eyes over Clara, "why did you keep on your old mourning today? And all the commune so elegant!—and you with those lovely dresses in your *garde-robe!* I'm sure that uncle of *Madame* your mamma's has had the mourning worn for him these six months. It's getting to look quite rusty."

"Oh, what matters it—black or white?" uttered Clara, the grieved feeling in her heart finding vent, as the woman spoke about *mourning.* "Don't keep me here, Babette I want to go—"

Babette moved her back from against the door; and Clara, passing out, found herself face to face with Madame Latange, with whom she had held no intercourse since the departure of Francis. She would willingly have shrunk away now, but Babette had shut the door.

"Don't look so scared, young lady," said the latter, in a kindly tone, to Clara's very great astonishment. "I am not going to reproach you. *He* is gone; and to indulge ill-feeling will not bring him back again. Perhaps I might have liked you better, but you see I had set my mind on his marrying Anastasie. She was just the wife for him, for she would have kept the *château* together, and things in the kitchen from going to rack and ruin, and checked Francis in his generous fits."

Madame paused, but Clara did not answer.

"She has been ungrateful, has Anastasie. Actually gone and promised to marry a man who is at mortal enmity with me—Farmer Brun. He won a lawsuit from me last year. Since then, my dear, it has crossed my mind that you might have made him as good a wife as she; so let us be friends. We'll go to mass together."

Clara went. Walking into church side by side with *Madame*, to the wondering astonishment of all the gazers in it.

"Mother," said Clara, as she sat by her mother's bedside that evening, when the shades of night were gathering, "you have no objection to my accompanying Madame Latange to pray tonight?"

"Madame Latange!"

"I told you, dear mother, I met her this morning, and how pleasant she was. She is coming to see you, when tomorrow is over."

"What good's Madame Latange to do me?" querulously interrupted Mrs. Fitzgerald. "I don't like her. Breaking off her acquaintance with us, as she did, without reason!"

"She goes tonight to pray for her son; in the church and at his tombstone. May I make one of those who join her?"

"What, in the cemetery? Nonsense. You'll catch your death."

"Oh no, I shall be well wrapped up. We knew poor Francis"— Clara's voice trembled. "Let me make one to pray for the repose of his soul."

"I don't see why its repose need trouble you," returned Mrs. Fitzgerald. "Quite the contrary. I had used to think he was inclined to flirt with you, and that you encouraged him. There's nothing so unladylike for a young girl as flirting, Clara."

"Well, mamma, you will not have that to complain of again," sighed Clara. " I may go with *Madame?*"

"Now, I don't want to be teased. My arms are in excruciating pain, and it's nothing to me whether you go or not. But if you catch rheumatic-fever in the cemetery, there'll be nobody to nurse you, recollect."

A goodly company of *commères*, as Babette had expressed it, went forth that night with Madame Latange. The great bell boomed out incessantly: the church was crowded with devout groups, bowed in silence before their many candles, the grease

404

from which guttered down on the stone floor; and the priests, for the last time that long day, sang over their monotonous chants. A little before nine, the last candle offered up by Madame Latange had expired.

The cemetery lay beyond the village. It was a dreary walk to it at all times, between the two straight rows of poplars. The stout hearts of some of the *commères* failed; and they turned home on leaving the church. Mademoiselle Anastasie, who was a very coward, had been brought by her aunt against her will.

"For the love of Heaven, don't go, my aunt," she implored, with chattering teeth; "wait till daylight. The shades will have returned to purgatory then, and we can all join you, and pray in peace. Should *he* appear to us, I should just die of fright."

Madame Latange's only answer was the taking of Mam'selle Anastasie by the arm, and marching her off towards the cemetery. Her serving man, Paul, walked first with a blazing torch, and the group of courageous *commères* huddled close behind, holding on to one another.

"But is *Madame* herself not afraid to behold the spirit of poor Master Francis?" ventured Paul, who by no means admired the position assigned him in the march.

"My eyes have ached to see him so long that they would rejoice in the sight," replied his mistress, with valiance.

"*Igh!—igh!—igh!*" burst out Mam'selle Anastasie, in a succession of shrill screams. "What's that looking over the hedge?"

Considerable confusion ensued. Cries of horror. Everyone laying hold of everyone else's clothes.

"I tell you what it is, ladies," said the unfortunate torchbearer standing stock still, "if you are to frighten one like this, I can't go on in advance. *Madame* must forgive me when I say I'd rather lose my place first."

"Courage," commanded Madame Latange. " If you all walk linked, and bend your eyes on the ground, there'll be no danger of seeing anything As for Mademoiselle Anastasie, should she frighten us again, I shall leave her in the hedge by herself till we come back."

The threat imposed silence on Mademoiselle Anastasie, and the procession resumed its march. It came to the gate of the cemetery, and bore on through its cold grass to the corner, where stood the tablet to the memory of Francis Latange.

It was a handsome erection of black marble: a white urn and drooping willow carved on it.

Francois Latange,

Fils unique de Pierre Latange et de Francoise de Brie.

Tué devant Sébastopol le 18 de Juin, 1855, agé de 22 ans.

Priez pour lui.

They sank on their knees around the stone, and the sobs of the *mother* broke forth aloud. Clara Fitzgerald's head was pressed on the cold marble, her grief was silent; but many wept in concert with *Madame*. And so they knelt, and sobbed, and prayed, their faces hidden: a strange group to look on, in that dark night, in that lonely graveyard!

Paul's torch was coming to an end. Rising, he proceeded to light another. This little diversion caused *la mère Coe* to look up. Being middle-aged and stout, she was getting tired of her kneeling position. The cramp was coming into her legs

A hideous shriek! an unearthly howl! and Madame Coe, from whom they proceeded, flung her arms round the legs of the startled Paul, and buried her face against them, and howled interminably. Whatever had taken *la mère Coe?*

"There he is! his own spectre!" she burst forth, her voice shrill with terror. "I knew it would appear."

Paul raised his torch; the unhappy devotees looked as high in the air as its light would allow. Standing close by his own tombstone, his head bending forward as if to read its inscription, was the spectre of Francis Latange. Thin, worn, his cheeks pale, his eyes sunk, there it was, with only one arm, and in a faded old suit of rentals. No doubt the clothes he had died in.

What had been the screams of the Mother Coe to those which now ensued? Not a saint in the calendar but was invoked with every variety of terrified aspiration; and the wretched group started to their feet and rushed away, pell-mell, out of the haunted cemetery. Paul, dropping his torch, and ungallantly shaking off the ladies, flew off in front; the ghost went after them; some choking, some praying, and the rest yelling. The noise penetrated nearly all the way to St. Eloi.

Clara Fitzgerald did not fly with the rest. In rising, her foot caught in a tuft of grass, and she was thrown heavily down again. Her companions were then at a distance, and she remained, clasping the marble stone, overcome with faintness and extremity of terror. The ghost came striding back again, in very unghostly fashion. It took up the flickering torch, and held it to her face.

"Clara," it gently said—and, with the words, Clara began to suspect it was no ghost, but real flesh and blood—"do I frighten *you?*"

But she was too terrified still to answer: and her teeth chattered, and her frame shook.

"I have still one arm left," he said, digging the torch in the earth, so that it still gave its light, and passing his arm round Clara. "Those terrified women must have taken me for my own spectre, for I see you have my death recorded here. Some mistake in the returns."

"But is it really you?" she said, bursting into tears. "We thought you were dead."

"So I was nearly, Clara. They took me up for dead last June, in the storming of the Malakhof. I have come home to recruit my strength, come home for good: a one-armed man is useless as a soldier. Perhaps you too will reject me now."

Her tears flowed on. Delicious tears!

"Oh, Clara," he whispered, as he held her to him, "though I have only one arm left, it shall be found powerful to protect you through life—my cherished wife. I said I would come home to you, my darling. None knew the fervent prayer I offered up for it, save God. He heard and blessed it."

★★★★★★

"But did you drop from the clouds?" demanded Madame Latange, in the midst of her tears, when Francis got home.

"No, mother, I dropped from the diligence. We were invalided home, *via* Marseilles, and I reached Calais today. There I got a *banquette* place in the six-o'clock diligence. The first face I saw here was Père Duterte's; when he recovered from his wonder, he volunteered the information that a company had just started to pray for me in the cemetery. So I thought I'd go after it, and send Duterte up here first to break the news to my father. How you all screamed!"

"But you are so piteously thin and ill, Francis! And your one arm! It is dreadful!"

"Never mind, mother. I shall get strong again. And for my lost arm—it might have been worse."

"*François, mon cher*," uttered the old man, with imploring eyes, "you will not go away again?"

"Never, father. I have sown my wild oats, and have come home to settle. If my mother will allow me."

"Yes, I will, my son," she replied, with a pointed meaning in her tone. "Mademoiselle Anastasie's going to settle herself also, Francis. With Farmer Brun."

"It is not fixed; there's nothing decided; I'm not obliged to have him, now my cousin is come home," eagerly interrupted Mademoiselle Anastasie. "And I think Farmer Brun an old bear."

"You should have discovered that before," said Madame Latange.

"*She will* make you a dutiful daughter, mother dear," whispered Francis, "though she is an English girl. Will you not try her?"

"I suppose I shall have to do so, my son. You may go tomorrow, with my love, and fetch her to dinner."

"A nice wife she'll make!" called out Mam'selle Anastasie, red with spite. "She'll never look after the eggs. They'll be half lost—you'll see! And I know she could not make an omelette if she tried."

"I'll teach her," said *Madame.*

"*Grâce à Dieu!*" cried old Pere Latange.

Gina Montani

1

In one of the sunniest spots of sunny Tuscany, that favoured department of Italy, may still be seen the ruins of a strong, ancient-built castle, or palace, surrounded by extensive grounds now run to waste; and which was, a century or two ago, one of the proudest buildings in that balmy land.

It was on an evening of delicious coolness, there so coveted, that a cavalier issued on horseback from the gates of the castle, which was then at the acme of its pride and strength. Numerous retainers stood on either side by the drawbridge, their heads bared to the evening sun, until the horseman should have passed; but he went forth unattended: and then the men resumed their caps, and swung-to the drawbridge, as he urged his horse to a quick pace. It was the lord of that stately castle, the young inheritor of the lands of Visinara. His form, tall and graceful, was bent occasionally to the very neck of his horse, in acknowledgment of the homage that was universally paid him, though he sat his steed proudly, as if conscious that such bearing befitted the descendant of one of Italia's noblest families. In years he had numbered scarcely more than a quarter of a century, and yet on his beautiful features might be traced a shade, which told of perplexity and care.

Turning down a narrow and not much frequented way which branched off from the main road, a mile or two distant from his residence, he at length came in view of one of those pretty places, partly mansion, partly cottage, and partly temple, at that period to be seen in Italy; but which we *now* meet with rarely, save in pictures. Fastening the bridle of his charger to a tree, he walked towards the house, and passing down the colonnade which ran along the south side of it, entered one of the rooms through the open window.

A lady, young and beautiful, sat there alone. She had delicate features, and a fair, open countenance, the complexion of which resembled more that of an English than an Italian one, inasmuch as a fine, transparent colour was glowing on the cheeks. The expression of her eyes was mild and sweet, and her hair, of a chestnut brown, fell in curls upon her neck, according to the fashion of the times. She started visibly at sight of the count, and her tongue gave utterance to words, but what she apparently knew not.

"So you have returned, *signor?*"

"At last, Gina," was the count's answer, as he stole his arm round her slender waist, and essayed to draw her affectionately towards him.

"Unhand me, Count di Visinara!" she impetuously exclaimed, moving away; and her whole form trembled with agitation.

He stood irresolute; aghast at the reception from her, who was his early and dearest love.

"Are you out of your senses?" was his exclamation.

"No, but I soon shall be. Better for insanity to fall upon me, than experience the wretchedness of these last few days."

"My love, my love, what mean you"

"*My love!* call you *me* your love, Count di Visinara! Be silent, hypocrite! I know you now. Cajoled that I have been in listening to you so long!"

"Gina!"

"And so the honourable Count di Visinara has amused his leisure hours in making love to Gina Montani!" she cried, vehemently. "The lordly chieftain who—"

"Be silent, Gina!" he interrupted. "Before you continue your strange accusations, tell me the origin of them. My love has never wandered from you."

"Yet you are seeking a wife in the heiress of Delia Ripa!" was her quick retort. "Ah, Sir Count, your complexion changes now!"

Gina Montani was right: the flush of excitement on his face had turned to paleness.

"Your long and repeated journeys, for days together, are now explained," she continued. "It was well to tell me business took you from home."

"I have had business to transact with the Prince of Della Ripa," he replied, boldly, recovering his equanimity.

"And to combine business with pleasure," she answered, with a curl of her delicate lip, "you have been wont to linger by the side of his daughter."

"And what though I have sometimes seen the Lady Adelaide?" he rejoined. "I have no love for her."

Gina was silent for awhile, as if struggling with her strong emotion, and then spoke calmly.

"My mother has enjoined me, times out of mind, not to suffer your continued visits here, for that you would never speak of marriage. You never will, Giovanni."

"Turn to my faith, Gina," he exclaimed, with emotion, "and I will marry thee tomorrow."

"They say you are about to marry Adelaide of Della Ripa," she replied, passing by his own words with a gesture.

"They deceive you, Gina."

"*You* deceive me," she answered, passionately; "you upon whose veracity I would have staked my life. And this is to be my reward!"

"You are like all your sex, Gina—when their jealousy is aroused, goodbye to reason. One and all are alike."

"Can you say that in this case my suspicions are unfounded?"

"Gina," he answered, as he once again would have drawn her to his heart, "let us not waste the hours in vain recriminations. *I have no love for Adelaide of Delia Ripa.*"

411

He spoke with the emphasis of truth, and she suffered herself to believe him. How credulous is the heart of a woman when she loves!

They sat in the garden when the heat of the sun had passed; her hand in his, her ear bent to his honeyed words. In one sense they were true enough, those whispers, for his love was all hers; and once more they were happy together as of old.

But this was not to last. As the weeks and the months flew on, the visits of the count grew few and far between. He made long stays at the territory of Della Ripa, and people told it as a fact, no longer disputable, that he was about to make a bride of the Lady Adelaide.

They had come strangers into Tuscany, the Signora Montani and her daughter, but a year or two before. The *signora* was in deep grief for the loss of her husband, she was also in ill health, and they lived the most secluded life, making no acquaintances. They were scarcely known by name or by sight; and, save the Count di Visinara, no visitors were ever found there. The *signora* was of northern extraction, and of the Reformed faith, and had reared her daughter in the principles of the latter, which of itself would cause them to court seclusion, at that period, in Italy. And the Lord of Visinara, independent and haughty as he was by nature and by position, would not have dared to take Gina Montani to be his wedded wife.

2

It was on a calm moonlight night that a closely-wrapped-up form stood in the deep shade of a grove of cypress-trees, within the gates of the Castle of Visinara, anxiously watching.

Parties passed and repassed, and the figure stirred not; but now there came one, the very echo of whose footsteps had command in it, and the form advanced stealthily, and glided out of its hiding-place, right upon the path of the Lord of Visinara. He stood still, and faced the intruder.

"Who are you?—and what do you do here?"

"I came to bid you farewell. Sir Count; to wish you joy of

your marriage!" And, throwing back the mantle and hood, Gina Montani's fragile form stood out to view.

"You here, Gina!"

"Ay; I have struggled long—long. Pride, resentment, jealousy—I have struggled fiercely with them; but all are forgotten in my unhappy love."

He drew her closely to him, as in their happy days.

"You depart tomorrow morning on your way to bring home your bride. I have seen your preparations—I have watched the movements of your retainers. No farewell was given me—no word offered of consolation—no last visit vouchsafed."

It would seem that he could not gainsay her words, for he made no reply.

"Know you how long it is since we met?" she continued; "how long—"

"Reproach me not," he interrupted. "I have suffered more than you. And, for a farewell visit, I did not dare to trust myself"

"And so this is to be the end of your enduring love, that you said was to be mine, and only mine, till death!"

"And before Heaven I spoke the truth. I have never loved—I never shall love but you. Yet, Gina, what would you have me do? I may not speak to you of marriage; and it is necessary to my position that I wed."

"*She* is of your own rank, therefore you have wooed her?"

"And of my own faith. Difference of rank may be overcome; of faith, never."

"Oh, that the time had come when God's children shall be all of one mind, of one faith!" she uttered. "In later ages, this peace may be upon the earth."

"Would it were, Gina! Or that you and I had never met him!"

"What, do *you* wish it!" she retorted. "You, who voluntarily sever yourself from me!"

"I have acted an honourable part, Gina," he cried, striding to and fro, in his agitation.

413

"*Honourable*, did you say?"

"Ay, honourable. You were growing too dear to me, and I could not speak of marriage to you."

There was a long pause. She was standing against one of the cypress-trees, the moon, through an opening above, casting its light upon her pure face, down which were coursing tears of anguish.

"So henceforth we must be brother and sister," he whispered.

"Brother and sister," she repeated, in a moaning voice, pressing the cold tree against her aching temples.

"After awhile, Gina, when time shall have subdued our feelings. Until then we may not meet."

She was startled by the words into sudden pain. "Will you not! come here? Shall we never see you here?"

"Nay, Gina, I must not do so great wrong to the Lady Adelaide."

"So great wrong!" she exclaimed, in amazement.

"Not real wrong, I am aware. But I shall undertake at the altar to love and cherish her; and though I cannot do the one, I will the other. Knowing that I cannot love her, I would be doubly careful of her feelings."

"I see, I see," interrupted the young lady, indignantly; "*her* feelings must be respected, whilst mine—"

"And for my own sake," he added, in a whisper.

"And my poor sick mother, to whom your visits have been as a balm?—But I see: I see. Farewell, Giovanni."

"One word yet, Gina," he said, detaining her. "You will probably hear of me much—foremost in the chase, gayest in the ballroom, last at the banquet—the gay, fortunate Lord of Visinara; and when you do so, remember that that gay lord wears about him a secret chain, suspected by and known to none—a chain, some links of which will remain entwined around his heart to his dying day, though the gilding that made it precious must from this time moulder away. Know you what the chain is, Gina?"

The suffocating sobs were rising in her throat, and she made no answer.

"*His love for you*. Fare thee well, my dearest and best. Nay, another instant; it is our last embrace in this world."

3

It was a princely cavalcade that bore the heiress of Della Ripa to her new territories, and all eyes looked out upon it. The armour of the warlike retainers of the house of Visinara sparkled in the sun, and the more peaceful servitors were attired with a gorgeousness that would have done honour to an Eastern clime. The old chief of Della Ripa, than whom one more fierce and brave never existed in all Italy, had that morning given his daughter's hand to Giovanni of Visinara; and as she neared the castle that was henceforth to be her home, every point from which a view of the procession could be obtained was seized upon.

"By my patron saint, but it is a goodly sight!" exclaimed one of a group of maidens, gathered at a window beneath which the bridal cavalcade was prancing. "Only look at Master Pietro, the *seneschal*."

"And at the steel points of the halberds,—how they shine in the crimson of the setting sun."

"Nay, rather look at these lovely dames that follow—the Lady Adelaide's tire-women. By the sacred relics! if her beauty exceed that of her maidens, it must be rare to look upon. See the gold and purple of their palfreys' horsecloths waving in the air."

"Hist! hist! it is the Count of Visinara in his emblazoned carriage! How haughtily he sits; but the Visinara is a haughty race. And—yes—see—by his side—oh, how lovely! Signora Montani, look! That face might win a kingdom."

Gina Montani, who stood in the corner of the lattice, shielded from view by its massive frame, may possibly have heard, but she answered not.

"Say what you will of his pride, he is the handsomest man that ever lived," exclaimed a damsel, enthusiastically. "Look at him now—he sits bareheaded, his plumed cap resting on his

415

knee—where will you find a face and form like that?"

"What is *she* like?" interrupted an old *duenna*, snappishly, who, standing behind, could not as yet obtain a view of the coveted sight; "we know enough of his looks, let us hear something of hers. But you girls are ever the same: if a troop of sister angels came down from heaven, and a graceless cavalier appeared at the other side, you would turn your backs to the angels and your eyes upon him. Is she as handsome as the young Lady Beatrice, the count's sister, who married away a year agone?"

"Oh, mother, she is not like her. Beatrice of Visinara had a warm countenance, with eyes black as the darkest night, and brilliant as a diamond aigrette."

"And are the wife's not black?" screamed out the *duenna*. "They ought to be: her blood is pure Italian."

"They are blue as heaven's sky, and her face is dazzling to behold from its extreme fairness, and her golden hair droops in curls almost to her waist—it is a band of diamonds, you observe, that confines it from the temples. But you can see her now, mother: remember you one half so lovely?"

"*Dio mio!*" uttered the woman, startled at the beautiful vision that now came within her sight; "the Lord of Visinara has not sacrificed his liberty for nothing."

"Mark you her rich white dress, mother, with its corsage of diamonds, and the sleeves looped up to the elbow with lace and jewels? And over it, nearly hiding her fair neck, is a mantle of blue velvet, clasped by a diamond star. And see, she is taking her glove off, and her hand is raised to her cheek—small and delicate it is too, as befitteth her rank and beauty. And—look!—he lays his own upon it as she drops it, but she would draw it from him to replace the glove. Now he bends to speak to her, and she steals a glance at him with her blushing cheeks and her eyes full of love. And now he is bowing to the people—hark how they shout, 'Long life to the Lady Adelaide—long life and happiness to the Count and Countess of Visinara!'"

"She is very beautiful, Bianca; but—"

"Ay, what? You are a reader of countenances, *madra mia*; what see you there?"

"That she is proud and self-willed. And woe be to any who may hereafter look upon her handsome husband with an eye of favour, for she loves him."

"Can there be a doubt of that?" echoed Bianca: "has she not married him? And look at his attractions: see this goodly lot of cavaliers speeding on to join his banquet; can any there compare with him?"

"*Chi é stracco di bonaccie, si mariti,*" answered the old lady. "Have you, Bianca, yet to learn that the comeliest mates oftentimes bring anything but love to the altar?"

Bianca made a grimace, as if she doubted. "It would have come sure enough, then," she said, aloud; "for none could be brought into daily contact with one so attractive and not learn to love him."

"And who should this be in a saintly habit, following the bridal equipage on his mule? Surely the spiritual director of the Lady Adelaide—the Father Anselmo it must be, that we have heard speak of. A faithful man, but stern, it is told; and so his countenance would betray. Bend your heads in reverence, my children: the holy man is bestowing his blessings."

"How savage I should be were I the Lady Beatrice, not to be able to come to the wedding," broke in the giddy Bianca. "She reckoned fully upon it, they say, and had caused her dress to be prepared—one to rival the bride's in splendour."

"She has enough to do with her newly-born infant," mumbled the good *duenna*. "Gaiety first, care afterwards; a christening usually follows a wedding. Come, girls, there's nothing more to see."

"Nay, mother mine, some of these dames that follow, guests for the banquet, lack not beauty."

"Pish!" uttered a fair young girl, who had hitherto been silent; "it would be waste of time to look at their faces after the Lady Adelaide's."

"Who is that going away? The Signora Montani? Why, it has not all passed, *signora*. She is gone, I declare! What a curious girl

417

she seems, that."

"Do you know what they say?" cried little Lisa, Bianca's cousin.

"What do they say?"

"That her mother is a descendant of those dreadful people over the sea, who have no religion, the heretics."

The pious *duenna* boxed her niece's ears.

"You sinful little monkey, to utter such heresy!"she cried, when anger allowed her to speak.

"They do say so!" sobbed the young lady, dancing about with the passion she dared not otherwise vent. "And people *do* say," she continued, out of bravado, and smarting under the pain, "that they are heretics themselves: or else why do they never come to mass?"

"The old Signora Montani is nearly bedridden: how could she get to mass?" laughed Bianca.

"Don't answer her, Bianca. If she says such a thing here again—if she insinuates that the Signora Gina, knowing herself to be in such league with the Evil One, would dare to put her head inside a faithful house such as this, I will cause her to do public penance—the wicked little calumniator!" concluded the good *duenna*, adding a few finishing strokes upon Lisa's ear.

4

Long lasted the bridal banquet, and merrily it sped. Ere its conclusion, and when the hours were drawing towards midnight, the young Lady Adelaide, attended by her maidens, was conducted to her dressing chamber, according to the custom of the times and of the country.

She sat down in front of a large mirror whilst they disrobed her. They took the circlet of diamonds from her head, the jewels from her neck and arms, and then removed the elegant bridal dress; and there she sat, in a dressing-robe of cambric and lace, while they brushed out and braided her beautiful hair.

As they were thus engaged, the lady's eyes ran round and round the costly chamber. The furniture and appurtenances were of the most *recherché* description: it had been the count's pleasure so to decorate it for his bride. One article in particular attracted her admiration. It was a small, but costly cabinet of malachite marble, exquisitely mounted in silver, and had been a present to the count from a Russian despot. In the inner part was a fixed mirror, encircled by a large frame of silver, and on the projecting slab stood open essence-bottles of pure crystal in silver frames, emitting various perfumes. As she continued to look at this novelty—the marble called malachite was even more rare and costly in those days than it is in ours—she perceived lying by the side of the scent-bottles, a piece of folded paper. Wondering what it could be, she desired one of the ladies to bring it to her. It proved to be a sealed letter, and was addressed to herself.

The conscious blush of love rose to her cheeks, for she deemed it was some communication or present from her husband. She opened it, and the contents instantly caught her eye, in the soft, pure light which the lamps shed over the apartment:—

To the Lady Adelaide, Countess of Visinara.
You fancy yourself the beloved of Giovanni, Count of Visinara, but retire not to your rest this night, lady, in any such vain imagining. The heart of the count has long been given to another, and you know, by your love for him, that such passion—that of first love—can never change its object. Had he met you in earlier life, it might have been otherwise. He marries you, for your lineage is a high one, and she, in the world's eye and in that of his own haughty race, was no fit mate for him.

★★★★★★

The bridegroom was still at the banquet, for some of his guests drank deeply, when a hasty summons came to him. Quitting the hall, he found standing outside two of his bride's attendants.

"Sir Count, the Lady Adelaide—"

"Has retired?" he observed, finding they hesitated, yet feeling somewhat surprised at so speedy a summons.

"Nay, *signor*, not retired, but—"

"But what? Speak out."

"We were disrobing the Lady Adelaide, Sir Count, when she saw in the chamber a note addressed to her. And—and—she read it, and fainted, in spite of the essence we poured on her hands and brow."

"A note!—fainted!" ejaculated the count.

"It was an insulting letter, *signor,* for Irene, the youngest of the Lady Adelaide's attendants, read the first line or two of it aloud, before we could prevent her, it having fallen, open, to the floor. Our lady is yet insensible, and the Signora Lucrezia desires us to acquaint you, my lord."

Without another word he turned from them, and, passing through the various corridors, entered the dressing-chamber. The Lady Adelaide was still motionless, but a faint colouring had begun to appear in her face.

"What is this, *signora?*" demanded the count of the chief attendant, Lucrezia.

"It must be owing to this letter, Sir Count, which was waiting for her on the cabinet," was the lady's reply, holding out the open note. "The Lady Adelaide fainted while she was perusing it."

"Fold it up," interrupted the count, "and replace it there." And Lucrezia did as she was bid.

"You may now go," said Giovanni to the attendants, advancing to support his bride himself, as she revived. "When the countess has need of you, you shall be summoned."

"You have read that letter?" were the first connected words of the Lady Adelaide.

"Nay, my love, surely not without your permission. Will you that I read it?"

She motioned in the affirmative.

A guilty, glowing colour came over his face as he read. From whom did it come? That it alluded to Gina Montani there was no doubt. He felt sure, or thought he did, that Gina had no act or part in so dishonourable a trick. Yet what may not be expected from a jealous woman? Now came his trial.

"Was it not enough to make me ill?" demanded Adelaide. And he stammered something by way of answer.

"Giovanni," she exclaimed, passionately, "deceive me not. Tell me what I have to fear: how much of your love is left for me— if any." He tried to soothe her. He told her an enemy must have done this: and he mentioned Gina Montani, though not by name. He said that he had sometimes visited her house, but not to love, and that the letter must allude to this.

"You *say* you did not love her!" she cried, resentment in her tone, as she listened to the tale.

For a single second he hesitated. But for her own sake he felt it to be his duty to lull her suspicions. The flush of shame rose to his brow for he deemed a falsehood dishonourable.

"In truth I did not. My love is yours, Adelaide."

"Why did you visit her? "

"I can hardly tell you. I hardly know myself; want of thought— or of occupation probably."

"You surely did not wrong her?" was the next whispered question as she turned her face from him.

"Wrong *her!* Did you know her, you could not admit the possibility of the idea," he answered, resentment in his tone now. "She is of gentle birth, has been carefully reared, and is as innocent as you are."

"Who is she?—what is her name?"

"Adelaide, let us forget the subject. I have told you I loved her not: and I should not have mentioned this at all, but that I can think of nothing else to which that diabolical letter can have alluded. Believe me, my own wife"— and he drew her to him as he spoke—"that I have not done you so great an injury as to marry where I could not love."

"Oh," she exclaimed, wringing her hands, "that this cruel news had not been given me! Giovanni," she continued, vehemently, and half sinking on her knees before him, "deceive me not. If there be aught of truth in this accusation, let me depart. I am your wife but in name; a slight ceremony only has passed

421

between us, and we both know how readily, with such influence as ours, the Church at Rome would dissolve that. Suffer me to depart ere I shall be indeed your wife."

"Adelaide," he replied, mournfully, as he held her, "I thought you loved me."

"I do—I do. None can know how passionately. My very life is bound up in yours; but it is because I so love you, that I could not brook a rival."

"You have no rival, Adelaide. You never shall have one."

"I mean not a rival in the vulgar acceptation of the term," she replied, a shade of haughtiness mingling with her tone—"but one in your heart—your mind. This I could not bear."

"Adelaide, hear me. Some enemy, wishing to do me a foul injury, has thrust himself between us: but, rely on it, they are but false cowards who stab in the dark. I have sought you these many months; I have striven to gain your love; I have now made you mine. Talk not of separation, Adelaide."

She burst into a passionate fit of weeping.

"Adelaide," he whispered, as he fondly clasped her to his heart, "believe that I love you; believe that you have no rival, and that I will give you none. I have made you my wife—the wife of my bosom: you are, and ever shall be, my only love."

Sweet words! And the Lady Adelaide suffered her disturbed mind to yield to them, resolutely thrusting away the dreadful thought that the heart of her attractive husband could ever have been given to another,

5

Months elapsed, and the Lady Adelaide was the happiest of the happy, although now and again the remembrance of that anonymous letter would flit into her mind like a dream. That most rare felicity was indeed hers, of passionately idolising one from whom she need never be separated by night or by day. But how was it with him? Love is almost the only passion which cannot be called forth or turned aside at will, and though the Count di Visinara treated his wife, and ever would so treat her, with the most anxious affection, though he strove with all his might and main to love her, his rebellious heart was still true to Gina Montani.

But now the count had to leave home on business; to remain away fifteen days. In those earlier times women could not accompany their lords everywhere, as they may in these; and when Giovanni rode away from his castle gates, the Lady Adelaide sank in solitude upon the arm of one of her costly sofas, all rich with brocaded velvet; and though not a tear dimmed her eye, or a line of pain marked her forehead, to tell of suppressed feelings, it seemed to her that her heart was breaking.

It was on the morrow. News was brought to the countess that one craved admission to her—a maiden, young and beautiful, the *servitor* said; and the Lady Adelaide ordered her to be admitted.

Young and beautiful indeed, and so she looked, as, with downcast eyes, the visitor was ushered in. You know her, reader, though the Lady Adelaide did not. She began to stammer out an incoherent explanation: that news had reached her of the retirement of one of the Lady Adelaide's attendants, and of her wish to fill the vacant place. "What is your name?" inquired the countess, already taken, as the young are apt to be, with the prepossessing manners and appearance of her visitor.

"*Signora*, it is Gina Montani."

"And in whose household have you resided?"

A deep shade rose to Gina's face. "Madam, as yet only in my mother's. But she is dead and I am alone in the world. I have heard much of the Countess of Visinara's gentleness and worth, and I should wish to serve her."

Some further conversation, a few preliminary arrangements, and Gina Montani was installed at the castle as one of the countess's maids in waiting. A somewhat contradistinctive term, be it understood, to a *waiting-maid*; these attendants of high-born gentlewomen being then made, in a great degree, their companions.

Gina speedily rose in favour. Her manners were gentle and

unassuming; and there was ever a sadness about her which, coupled with her great beauty, rendered her eminently interesting.

6

The Lady Adelaide stood at the eastern window of the purple-room—so called from its magnificent hangings—watching eagerly for the appearance of her husband, it being the day and hour of his expected return. So had she stood since the morning. Ah! what pleasure is there in this world like that of watching for a beloved one? At the opposite end of the apartment sat her ladies, engaged upon some fancy work, then in vogue.

"Come hither, Lucrezia," said the lady at length. "Discern you yon groups of trees in the distance, through which glimpses of the highway may be distinguished? See you aught?"

"Nothing but the road, my lady. And yet, now I look attentively, there seems to be a movement, as of a body of horsemen. It should be the count, madam, and his followers."

"I think it is, Lucrezia," said the Lady Adelaide, calmly, not suffering her emotion to appear in the presence of her maidens, for that haughty girl brooked not that others should read her deep love for Giovanni. "You may return to your embroidery."

The Count di Visinara rode at a sharp trot towards his home, followed by his retainers. When near enough to see his wife at the window, he quickened the pace to a gallop, after taking off his plumed cap, and waving his hand towards her in the distance. She pressed her heart to still its throbbing, as she heard him rattle over the drawbridge.

She was turning to leave the apartment to welcome him, when he entered, so great haste had he made. Without observing that she was not alone, he threw his arms round her, fondly drew aside her fair golden curls, and kissed her repeatedly. She drew back, the glowing crimson overspreading her face; and then the count turned and saw they were not alone. At the extreme end of the apartment, out of hearing, but within sight, were the damsels seated over their embroidery.

"Gina," murmured one of the girls, still pursuing her work,

"what has made you turn so pale? You are as white as Juliette's dress."

"Is the Signora Montani ill?" demanded Lucrezia, sharply; for she liked not Gina.

"A sudden pain—a spasm in my side," gasped poor Gina. "It is over now."

"Is he not an attractive man?" whispered another of the ladies in Gina's ear.

"He?"

"The Count di Visinara. I suppose you never saw him before They are well matched for beauty, he and the Lady Adelaide."

"Pray attend to your work, and let this gossiping cease," exclaimed Lucrezia, angrily.

Giovanni and his wife remained at the window, their backs towards the damsels. She suffered her hand to remain in his—they could not see *that*—and conversed with him in a confidential tone. Then she began chattering to him of her new attendant, saying how lovely she was, how pleasing and sad and gentle. In the midst of this, a servant announced the mid-day meal.

"Now you shall see my favourite," she exclaimed, as he took her hand to conduct her to the banquet-hall. "I will stop as I pass them, to look at their work, and you shall tell me if you do not think her very beautiful."

"Scarcely, Adelaide, when beside you."

"She is about my age," ran on Adelaide, whose spirits were raised to exuberance. But it had never entered the mind of that haughty lady to imagine the possibility of the Lord of Visinara, *her husband*, looking upon any attendant of hers with real admiration. Or she might not have discussed their personal merits.

"How goes on the work, Lucrezia?" demanded the Lady Adelaide, halting close to her attendants.

"Favourably, madam," answered the *signora*, rising from her seat.

"That is a beautiful part that you are engaged upon, Gina. Bring it forward, that we may exhibit our handiwork to my lord."

Gina Montani, without raising her eyes, and trembling inwardly and outwardly, rose, and advanced with the embroidery. The Signora Lucrezia, detecting her curious agitation, was regarding her, covertly.

"Is it not a handsome pattern?" exclaimed Adelaide, her thoughts now really occupied with the beauty of the work. "And I was so industrious while you were away, Giovanni. I did a good portion of this myself—I did, indeed; all the shadings of the rosebuds are my doing, and those interlaces of silver."

But, raising her pretty face to his, eager for his meed of approbation, Adelaide was startled at its look. It had turned to a frightful pallor.

"Oh, Giovanni, you are ill! My husband, what is it? Giovanni—"

"It is nothing," interrupted the count, leading her hurriedly from the room. "I rode hard, and the sun was hot. A cup of wine will restore me."

But not less awake to this emotion of the count's than she had been to Gina's, was the Signora Lucrezia, and she came to the conclusion that there was some unaccountable mystery at the bottom of it. Which mystery she forthwith, as a matter of course, determined to do all in her power to solve.

7

Days passed. The count had not yet seen Gina alone, though he had sought for the opportunity; but one morning when he entered the embroidery-room—so-called—Gina sat there alone, sorting silks. He did not observe her at first, and, being in search of his wife, called to her.

"Adelaide?"

"The Lady Adelaide is not here, *signor,*" was Gina's reply, as she rose from her seat.

"Gina," he said, advancing cautiously, and speaking in an under tone, "what in the name of all that was foolish brought you here—an inmate of my house—the attendant of the Lady Adelaide?"

"You shall hear the truth," she gasped, leaning against the wall for support. "I have lived all these months in my dreary home, unseeing you, uncared for, knowing only that you were happy with another. Giovanni, can you picture what I endured? My mother died—you may have heard of it—and her relations sent to ask me to go into their distant country, and would have comforted me; but I would not go. I remained on here, alone, to be near you. Oh, it was long, long! I struggled much with my unhappy passion. My very soul was wearing away with despair. I would see you pass sometimes at a distance with your retainers—and that was heaven to me. Then came a thought into my mind; I wrestled with it, and would have driven it away—but there it was, ever haunting me. It may be that my better angel sent it there; it may be that the Evil One, who is ever tempting us for ill, urged it on."

"What mean you?" he inquired.

"It suggested," she continued, in a low voice, "that if but to see you at a distance and at rare intervals, could almost compensate for my life of misery, what bliss would be mine were I living under the roof of your own home, liable to see you perhaps even once a day. Hence you find me numbered amongst your wife's waiting-maids. And blame me not, Giovanni," she hastily concluded, seeing him about to interrupt her; "you are the cause of all, for you sought and gained my love. And such love! I think none can have ever known such. It is the one task of my life to suppress it. The fiercest jealousy of the Lady Adelaide torments my heart—and yet I must suppress it. Giovanni, you have brought this anguish upon me; so blame me not."

"It is a dangerous proceeding, Gina. I was becoming reconciled to our separation; but now—it will be dangerous for both of us."

"Ay," she answered, bitterly, "you had all. Friends, revelry, a wife of rare beauty, the chase, the bustle of an immense household—in short, what had you not to aid your mental struggles? I but my home of solitude, and the jealous pictures, self, but ever inflicted, of your happiness with the Lady Adelaide."

"I still love you, Gina," he repeated. "But you know that I can show it not."

"Do I ask you to show it?—think you I would permit you to show it?" she reiterated quickly. "No, no; I did not come here to sow discord in your household. Suffer me to live on unnoticed, as of these last few days, but, oh! drive me not away from you."

"Gina, Gina, this will never do. I mistrust my own powers of endurance; ay, and of concealment."

"You can think of me but as the waiting-maid of your lady," she interrupted, in a tone of bitterness. "In time you will solely regard me as such."

"There would be another obstacle," he added, his voice sinking to a whisper. "How could you live in my household, and not conform to the usages of our faith? Believe me, Gina, it is a plan that will never answer."

She burst into tears: beseeching him not to drive her away. And to the tears he, against his better judgment, yielded.

"But you understand," he said, somewhat sternly, "that from this moment all confidence ceases between us: we must be to each other as strangers."

"Even so," she acquiesced. "Yet if you deem that my enduring affection deserves requital, give me at times a look as of old; a smile, unperceived by others, but acknowledged by, and too dear to, my own heart. I ask no more than that. It will be a token that you have not driven away all remembrance of our once youthful love, though it is at an end forever."

He smiled sadly now in answer, and they parted by different doors. He to seek his wife, she the solitude of her chamber. And no sooner had the sound of their footsteps died away in the gallery, than out of a closet in the room stepped the Signora Lucrezia, her eyes and mouth wide open, and her hair standing on end.

"May all the saints reject me if ever I met with such a plot as this !" she ejaculated. "I knew there was something underhand about her, but who would have suspected this! So the innocent-faced madam is nothing but a she-wolf in sheep's petticoats!

That dreadful letter is explained now. May I die unabsolved if ever I met with the like of this! It is her fault, the wicked one; not his. She must have bewitched him with her false face. If my baby mistress did but know it! *Her* rival—and she showering down favours on her! A pretty life the count will lead between the two, dear good man I—and neither of them fit to tie his shoes. I'll keep my eyes and ears open: there will be an explosion some day, or my name is not Lucrezia Andrini."

PART THE SECOND

1

There was much bustle and commotion in the Castle of Visinara. Servitors ran hither and thither, the tire-maidens stood in groups to gossip with each other, messengers were despatched in various directions, and skilful leeches and experienced nurses were brought in. Then came a long silence. Voices were hushed and footsteps muffled; the apartments of the countess were darkened, and naught was heard save the issued whisper, or the stealthy tread of the sick-chamber. The Lady Adelaide was ill.

Hours elapsed—hours of intolerable suspense to the Lord of Visinara; and then were heard deep, heartfelt congratulations; but they were spoken in a whisper, for the lady was still in danger, and had suffered almost unto death. There was born an heir to Visinara.

And as Giovanni, Count of Visinara, bent over his child, and embraced its young mother, he felt repaid for all he had suffered in voluntarily severing himself from Gina Montani. From that time he forgot her; or something very like it. And for this he could not be condemned, for it lay in the line of honour and of duty. Yet it was another proof, if one were wanting, of the fickle nature of man's love. It has been well compared to words written on the sands.

Many weeks elapsed ere the Lady Adelaide was allowed to join in the gaieties and festal meetings of the land. A two days' fete, given at the Capella Palace, was the signal for her reappearance in the world. It was to be of great magnificence, and she consented to attend it on the morning of the second day.

She placed herself in front of the large mirror in her dressing-chamber whilst she was prepared for the visit, the same mirror before which she had sat on the evening of her wedding-day. The Signora Lucrezia and Gina were alone present. The former was arranging her fair silken tresses, whilst Gina handed the *signora* the articles required for the task. The count entered, dressed.

"Giovanni," exclaimed Adelaide, "Lucrezia thinks that I should wear something in my hair—a wreath, or my diamond coronet; but I feel tired already, and wish the dressing was over. Need I be teased with ornaments?"

"My sweet wife, wear what you best like. *You* need no superficial adorning."

"You hear, Lucrezia: make haste and finish. You may put aside the diamond casket, Gina. Oh, there's my darling!" continued the countess, hearing the baby pass the door with its nurse. "Call him in."

The count himself opened the door, and took his infant.

"The precious, precious child!" exclaimed Adelaide, bending over the infant, which he placed on her knees. "Giovanni," she added, looking up eagerly to her husband's face, "do you think there ever was so lovely a babe sent on earth?"

He smiled at her earnestness—men are never so rapturously blind in the worship of their first-born as women. But he stooped down, and fondly pressed his lips upon her forehead, while he played with the little hand of the infant. She yielded to the temptation of suffering her face to rest for a moment close to his.

"But it grows late," resumed the young mother. "Take the baby to its nurse, Lucrezia;" and she kissed it fifty times as she resigned it.

The count had chanced to draw behind his wife: and there stood Gina. He was struck by the pallid sorrow of her countenance. Ill-fated Gina! and he had been so absorbed these weeks in his new happiness!

A rush of pity, mingled perhaps with self-reproach, penetrated his heart. In that moment he remembered her last words at the interview in the embroidery-room, and gave her a look—the look she had coveted.

It was not to be mistaken. Love—love, pure and tender—gleamed from his eyes; and Gina answered him with a smile which told her thanks. Had anyone been looking on, they could scarcely fail to become aware of their mutual love, or of a secret understanding between them.

And one was looking on. In the large glass before her the Lady Adelaide had distinctly seen the reflection of all that took place Her countenance became white as death, and her anger was terrible.

"You may retire for the present," she said, in a calm, subdued tone, to the startled Gina, upon whose mind flashed somewhat of the truth. "Tell the Signora Lucrezia not to return until I call for her."

To describe the scene that ensued would be difficult. The shock to the young wife's feelings had been very great. That her husband was faithless to her, not only in deed but in heart, she never doubted. It was in vain he endeavoured to explain all; she listened to him not. To her, he seemed to be uttering falsehoods, which but increased his treachery. Gina had once spoken of her fierce jealousy: but what was hers compared with the Lady Adelaide's? In the midst of her explosion of passion, Lucrezia, who had misunderstood her lady's prohibitory message, entered, and stood aghast: until admonished from the room again by a haughty wave of the count's hand.

He departed for the Capella *fête* alone. His wife refused to go. "Mercy! mercy!" she moaned in anguish, as she remained alone in her apartments. "To be thus requited by Giovanni—whom I so loved! My husband—my own husband! Is it possible that a man can be guilty of treachery so deep? Would that I had died ere I knew his faithlessness. To introduce her into our home, into my very presence, an attendant on my person. That I should be so degraded! Sure a wife, young and beautiful, was never treated as I have been. Lowered in the eyes of my own servants; insulted by him who ought to have guarded me from insult; laughed at—ridiculed by *her!* Oh! terrible! terrible!"

The Lady Adelaide had taken up a wrong and exaggerated view of the case. Rising as she spoke the last words, she unlocked the bright green cabinet, that of malachite marble already spoken of, and took from thence a small box of silver gilt. Touching the secret spring of this, she drew forth a letter, opened, and read it:

To the Lady Adelaide, Countess of Visinara.

You fancy yourself the beloved of Giovanni, Count of Visinara; but retire not to your rest this night, lady, in any such vain imagining. The heart of the count has long been given to another; and you know, by your love for him, that such passion—that of first love—can never change its object. Had he met you in earlier life, it might have been otherwise. He marries you, for your lineage is a high one, and she, in the world's eye and in that of his own haughty race, was no fit mate for him.

"Ay," she shuddered, "it is explained now. So, Gina Montani was this beloved one. I am his by sufferance—she, by love. Holy Mother, have mercy on my brain! I *know* they love—I see it all too plainly. And I could believe his deceitful explanation, and trust him. I told him I believed it on our wedding-night. *He did not know why he went to her house; habit, he supposed, or want of occupation.* Oh, shame on his false words! Shame on my own credulity!"

None of us can forget the *stanzas* in Collins's *Ode to the Passions*:—

Thy numbers, Jealousy, to nought were fixed,
Sad proof of thy distressful state:
Of differing themes the veering song was mixed,
And now it courted love—now, raving, called on hate."

And calling, indeed, upon hate, as she strode her chamber in a frenzy near akin to madness, was the Lady Adelaide, when her attendant, Lucrezia, entered.

"My dear lady," she exclaimed, bursting into tears, false as those of a crocodile, "my dear, dear young lady, I cannot know that you are thus suffering, and keep away from your presence. Pardon me for intruding upon you against orders."

The Lady Adelaide smoothed her brow, and the lines of her face resumed their haughtiness, as she imperiously motioned Lucrezia to quit the room. The heart most awake to the miseries of life wears to the world the coldest surface; and it was not in the Lady Adelaide's nature to betray aught of her emotions to any living being; save, perhaps, to her husband.

"Nay, my lady, suffer me to remain yet a moment. At least, while I disclose what I know of that viper."

The Lady Adelaide started; but she suppressed all excitement, and set herself to listen. Lucrezia began her tale—an exaggerated account of the interview she had been a witness to between the Lord of Visinara and Gina Montani. The countess listened to its conclusion, and a low moan escaped her.

"What think you now, madam, she deserves?"

"*To die!*" burst from the pale lips of the unhappy lady.

"To die," acquiesced Lucrezia, calmly. "No other punishment would meet her guilt; and no other, that I am aware of, could be devised to bring you security for the future."

"Oh! tempt me not," cried the lady, wringing her hands. "I spoke hastily."

"And wisely, madam," put in Lucrezia. "Give but the orders."

"How can I?" demanded the Lady Adelaide, once more pacing the room, in her anguish; "how could I ever rest afterwards, with so great a guilt upon my soul?"

"It will be no guilt, lady."

"Lucrezia!"

"I have made it my business to inquire much about this girl— to ascertain her history. I thought it my duty to do so, and very soon I should have laid the whole matter before you."

"Well?"

"You may destroy her, madam, as you would destroy that little bird there in its golden cage, without sin and without compunction."

"Oh, Lucrezia, Lucrezia I once more I say unto thee, tempt me not. Wicked and artful though she is, she is still one of God's creatures."

"Scarcely, my lady." answered the bigoted woman, with a gesture which spoke of deep scorn for the culprit. "I have cause to believe—good cause," she repeated, lowering her voice, and looking round, as if she feared the very walls might hear the fearful words she was about to utter, "that she is one of those lost creatures who are enemies to our faith and to Heaven: a descendant of the Saxons, and an apostate."

"*What* say you?" gasped the Lady Adelaide.

"That we have been harbouring a heretic, madam," continued Lucrezia, her passion rising. "No wonder that evil has fallen upon this house."

"Go to the cell of Father Anselmo," shivered the Lady Adelaide, "and pray his holiness to step hither. This doubt shall at once be set at rest."

2

Gina Montani, her head aching with suspense and anxiety, was shut up alone in her chamber, when she received a summons to attend her mistress. Obeying at once, she found the confessor, Father Anselmo, sitting there, by the side of the countess. He cast his eyes steadfastly upon Gina, as if examining her features.

"Never, my daughter, never!" he said, at length, turning to the countess. "I can take upon myself to assert that this damsel of thine has never once appeared before me to be shriven."

"Examine her," was the reply of the lady.

"Daughter," said the priest, turning to Gina, "for so I would fain call thee, what faith is it that thou professest?"

Gina raised her hand to her burning temples. She saw that all was discovered. But when she removed it, the perplexity in her face had cleared away, and her resolution was taken.

"The truth, the truth," she murmured; "for good, or for ill, I will tell it now. I am not a Roman Catholic," she answered timidly.

The Lady Adelaide crossed herself, as if for protection from the words: she had been reared in all the bigotry and superstition of the times. Gina grasped the arm of the chair against which she was standing. She was endeavouring to steel her heart to bravery; but in those days, and in that country, such a scene was a terrible ordeal.

"Dost thou not worship the One True God?" asked the priest, looking with compassion upon the sad and unhappy girl.

"I worship the One True God," replied Gina, solemnly, joining her hands in a reverent attitude. "But we—we—do not recognise the Pope."

"And yet, child, to him it is given to mediate between man and heaven? Hast thou yet to learn," continued the priest, troubled and aghast, "that in the next world there is a place of torture kept for unbelievers—a gulf of burning flames, to be extinguished never?"

"We are told there is such a place," she answered, struggling with her tears, for the interview was becoming too painful. "May the infinite love and mercy of God keep both you and me from it!"

"Thou art bold," he cried. "Whence hast thou imbibed these doctrines?"

"My mother wedded with an Italian," answered Gina; "but she was born on the free soil of England, and reared in its Reformed Faith."

"And this mother of thine, child: where may she be?"

"She is dead," gasped Gina, bursting into tears. "I have no guide now but my Bible."

Now, it is well known that in those ages in Italy the Bible was regarded as a very unfit book to be read indiscriminately by the people. The priest shook his head. To the Lady Adelaide and to Lucrezia, Gina's confessions brought absolute horror.

"She is hopeless," gasped the former.

"I fear me so, my daughter. At least, at present," added the priest; some benevolent idea crossing his mind that perhaps he might by his teachings redeem her. "Fetch me thy Bible, child," he said to Gina. "I will take care of it for a time."

She took it out of a pocket underneath her gown. An English Bible. The priest could not read it.

"Dost thou speak this language, then, daughter?"

"It is familiar to me as my own," replied Gina.

"Oh, father, father!" cried the Lady Adelaide, sinking at his feet, after Gina had been despatched to her chamber, and giving vent involuntarily to sobs of agony, "she has dared to come between me and my husband—he has known her long, it seems. If she should taint him with this dreadful heresy?"

Father Anselmo did not like the suggestion. Giovanni of Visinara was a true servant of his church and a liberal benefactor. In his perplexity, he made for the moment no rejoinder.

"It will not be a crime to remove her, father," faltered the Lady Adelaide.

"*Crime!*" repeated the priest. "Canst thou connect the word with any such procedure? It is on the contrary, a measure needful to be taken."

But the probability is that the speaker never supposed that any measure, more stringent than that of removing her from the castle, was contemplated.

"To remove her in any way," persisted the lady, in a whisper. "Yet the world might call it by—by an ugly name."

"Certainly, in *any way*," assented the father. "By force, if necessary."

"Thou wilt then grant me absolution beforehand, holy father," implored the Lady Adelaide, the tears streaming from her eyes.

"For all that thou canst do, my child," he smiled. "Thou hast not been used to these troublous duties; thy life has been one of peace and sunshine."

"Oh true, true! I have been too happy. My waiting woman,

Lucrezia, says she has a plan, holy father, to—to—to effect it, by which all scandal may be avoided. She waits only for my orders."

"Thou canst give them, my daughter."

And the Lady Adelaide, believing that she had received sanction for the worst, for so terrible a deed that she had not dared to allude to it in words—and in that reticence may have lain the fatal misapprehension—summoned Lucrezia to her when the priest had departed.

3

The castle was wrapped in silence, it being past the hour at which the household retired to repose. Gina Montani was in her nightdress, though as yet she had not touched her hair, which remained in long curls, as she had worn it in the day. Suspense and agitation caused her movements to be slow, to linger; and she sat at her dressing-table in a musing attitude, her head resting on her hand, wondering what would be the ending to all that the day had brought forth. She had dismissed her attendant an hour ago.

With a deep sigh she rose to continue her preparations for rest, when the door softly opened, and the Signora Lucrezia appeared.

"You need not prepare yourself for bed," observed Lucrezia, in a low, distinct whisper; "another sort of bed is preparing for you."

"What do you mean?" demanded the startled girl.

"That you are this night to die."

Gina shrieked.

"I may tell you," interrupted the lady, "that screams and resistance will be wholly useless. Your doom is irrevocable, therefore it may save you trouble to be silent."

"You are speaking falsely to me. I have done nothing to deserve death."

"Equivocation will be alike unavailing," repeated Lucrezia. "And if you ask what you have done—you have dared to step with your ill-placed passion between my lord and the Lady Adelaide: you have brought discredit upon the faith of this house and of the land."

"I have disturbed no one's faith," returned Gina. "I wish to disturb none. It is true that I love Giovanni, Count di Visinara, but I loved him long ere he saw the Lady Adelaide."

"What!" cried the *signora*, her brow darkening, "do you dare to avow your shame to my face?"

"It is no shame," answered Gina, sadly; "there is nothing of guilt in such a love as mine."

"Follow me," repeated Lucrezia. "You have no time to waste in lamentations."

"By whose orders do I die?" demanded the indignant girl. "Not by *his*; and no one else has a right to condemn me."

Lucrezia expected this, and was prepared. Alas, that the Lord of Visinara should that day have inadvertently left his signet-ring behind him!

"Do you know this ring?" demanded Lucrezia, holding out the jewel.

"Too well. It is the Count of Visinara's."

"You may then know who has condemned you."

"But the count is at the Capella Palace. He is not yet back from the *fêtes*."

"Not back!" returned Lucrezia, scornfully. "Heard you not the clatter of the men? Some of them had imbibed largely of the Capella wine, I trow. I bring this ring from him I say: a proof that he has condemned you."

"Oh, Giovanni!" wailed Gina, as she sank prostrate on the floor in her anguish, and no longer doubting, "this from you!" All idea of resistance vanished with the thought that it was him she so loved who doomed her to destruction. "How long is it since he returned?"

"I came not to waste the moments in idle words," said Lucrezia, brazening out her falsehoods. "It is sufficient for you to know that he has returned, and has given the orders that you seem inclined to resist."

"Implore him to come to me for one moment, for a last farewell,"

"I may not ask it. He is with the Lady Adelaide."

"First, my happiness, then, my life; both sacrificed to appease the Lady Adelaide! Oh, Giovanni! false, but dear Giovanni—"

"I have no orders to call those who will use violence," interrupted the *signora*, "but I must do so if you delay to follow me."

"I am about to dress myself," returned Gina.

"The dress you have on will serve as well as another. And better: for a nightgown bears some resemblance to a shroud—"

"One moment for prayer," was the next imploring petition.

"Prayer for you!" broke contemptuously from the *signora*.

"A single moment for prayer," reiterated the victim. "If I am, indeed, about to meet my Maker, I stand fearfully in need of it; for I have of late worshipped one, more perhaps than I have him."

"Prayer for you, you heretic!" contemptuously retorted Lucrezia, who, in her own way, was very much of a saint.

Yet still Gina repeated it. "A few moments for prayer—in mercy!"

"Then pray away where you are going," was the impatient answer. "You will have time enough, and to spare—minutes, and hours. Perhaps days."

The *signora* evidently took a strange pleasure in urging on the death of Gina Montani. What could be the reason? Women in general are not so frightfully cruel. The truth was, that she herself loved the count. The giddy Bianca had said, when watching the bridal cavalcade, that none could be brought into daily contact with one so attractive as he, and not learn to love him. So had it proved with Lucrezia. Being the favourite attendant of her mistress, she was much with her, and consequently daily and frequently in the company of Giovanni. He had many a gay word and passing jest for her, for he was by nature a gallant, free-spoken man; and this had brought forth its result. Whilst he never gave a thought to her but as of one who waited on his wife, he became to her heart dangerously dear; and her jealousy of Gina, arising first of all from the interview she had witnessed in the embroidery-room, now at least equalled that of the Lady Adelaide.

Pushing the unfortunate girl on before her, Lucrezia silently passed onwards to the more remote parts of the castle. She bore a lantern in her hand which emitted a dim, uncertain light. At length they came to a passage a little beyond the chapel, far removed from the habited apartments; and in the middle of this were two male forms, busily occupied at work of some description. A lantern, similar to the one Lucrezia carried, was hanging high up against the opposite wall; another stood on the ground. Gina stopped and shivered; but Lucrezia touched her arm, and she walked on.

They were nearing the men, who were habited as monks, probably for disguise, their faces shielded beneath cowls, when the *signora* halted and pressed her hand upon her brow, as if in thought. Presently she turned to Gina. A second lie was in her mouth; but how was the ill-fated young lady to know it?

"*He* sent you a message," she whispered. "It is his last request to you. Will you receive it?" The unhappy victim looked up eagerly.

"He requests, then, by his love for you—by the remembrance of the happy moments you once spent together, that you neither resist nor scream."

Her heart was too full to speak; but she bowed her head in acquiescence. Lucrezia moved to go on.

"How is my life to be taken? By the dagger? By blows?"

"By neither—by *nothing*. Not a hair of your head will be touched."

"Ah! I might have guessed. It is by poison."

"It will be taken by nothing, I tell you. Why do you not listen to me?"

"You speak in riddles," said Gina, faintly. "But I will bear my fate, whatever it may be."

"And in silence? *He* asks it by your mutual love."

"All, all, for his sake," she answered. "Tell him, that as I have loved, so will I obey him to the last."

Lucrezia walked on, and Gina followed. Whether she understood the manner of her death, might be a question; but, faithful
to the imagined wish of her lover, she uttered neither remonstrance nor cry. The clock was upon the stroke of one, when
smothered groans of fear and anguish told that her punishment
had begun; she understood it then: but no louder sound broke
the midnight silence, or carried the appalling deed to the inhabitants of the castle. An hour passed before all was completed;
they were long in doing their deed of vengeance; and when
it was over, Gina Montani had been removed from the world
forever.

"Madam, she is gone!" was the salutation of Lucrezia, her
teeth chattering, and her face the hue of a corpse, when she
entered the chamber of her mistress.

The Lady Adelaide had not retired to rest. She was pacing her
apartment in unutterable misery. The social conditions of life,
its forms and objects, were to her as nothing since her terrible
awaking to reality.

Morning had dawned before the return of the Lord of Visinara. The festivities had lasted long. He was fatigued both in
body and mind, and, throwing himself upon a couch, sank to
sleep. An unusual disturbance and commotion aroused him.
The household, struck with amazement and terror, were telling
a strange tale: one that, for the moment, drove the life-blood
from his heart. The wicked dealing of Gina Montani had been
brought to light on the previous day. What these wicked deal-
ings consisted of, no one professed to be able to define, except
that Gina had confessed in the presence of the good Father
Anselmo that she was in league with the Evil One. And the Evil
One had appeared in the night, and had run away with her—a
just reward.

In those times, a reputed visit of his Satanic Majesty *in propriâ
persona* would have been likely to obtain more credence than
it could in these; but it would probably be going too far to say
that the Lord of Visinara participated in the belief of his horror-

stricken household: neither could he trace any positive foundation for the assertion. Gina was gone. To say the least of it, Satan or no Satan, her disappearance was mysterious in the extreme. The maid who waited on her testified that she assisted Gina to undress on the previous night. In proof of which, the garments she had taken off were found in the chamber. The remainder of her clothes were also in their places undisturbed; the only article missing being a nightdress, which the attendant in question said she saw her put on; and her bed had not been slept in.

Giovanni spoke to his wife, but she observed a cold, haughty silence, confessing to nothing: it was quite useless to question her. The house was searched and searched, and the neighbourhood, for miles round, scoured; but no trace or tidings of her whatever could be obtained. And yet, strange to say, in passing on that first morning through the remote corridors, the count fancied he heard her voice pronounce his name in a tone of imploring agony. Whether this was but fancy, or whether she had indeed called to him, he never knew, then or later. He searched himself in every nook and corner but nothing came of it.

After a time, peace was once more restored between him and his wife: but the perfect bliss of her once secure love for him had ceased forever. As to Lucrezia, she seemed to have acquired a scared kind of look and manner; was more devout at prayers than before, and offered up no end of candles.

And so the time passed on.

4

It was the hour of midnight. In the nursery at the castle sat the head nurse, holding on her lap the dying heir of Visinara, now some eight or ten months old. Until about nine days previously, he had been a fine, healthy child, but from that time a wasting fever had attacked him. It had left him pale and cold; ill unto death.

The Lady Adelaide, her eyes blinded with tears, knelt beside him, gazing on his colourless face. The count himself was gently rubbing his little hands, to try and excite some warmth in them.

"Do you not think he looks a little, a very little better?" de-manded the lady, anxiously.

The nurse hesitated. She did not think so, but she was unwill-ing to say what she thought.

"His hands—are they any warmer, Giovanni?"

The count shook his head. The Lady Adelaide pressed her lips upon the infant's damp forehead, and burst into renewed tears.

"You will be ill, Adelaide," said her husband. "This incessant watching is bad for you. Let me persuade you to take an hour's rest."

She motioned in the negative.

"Indeed, madam, but you ought to do so," interposed Lu-crezia, who was present. "These many nights you have passed without sleep; and your health so delicate!"

"Lie down—lie down, my love," he interposed, "if only for a short time."

And at length she was induced to comply, the nurse under-taking to let her know if there should be the slightest change in the child. Giovanni passed his arm round his wife to lead her from the chamber, for she was painfully weak; but they had scarcely gone ten steps from the door, when a prolonged, shrill scream, as of one in unutterable terror, reached their ears. They rushed back again.

The nurse sat, her dilating eyes fixed on one corner of the room, her face rigid with horror. It was she who had screamed.

"My child! my child!" groaned the Lady Adelaide.

"Nurse, what in the name of terror is the matter?" exclaimed the count, perceiving no alteration in the infant. "You look as if you had seen a spectre!"

"I have seen one," shuddered the nurse.

"What *have* you been dreaming of?" he returned, angrily.

"As true as that we are all assembled here, my lord," contin-ued the nurse, solemnly, "I saw the spirit of Gina Montani! "

A change came over the Lord of Visinara's countenance, but

443

he spoke not. The Lady Adelaide clung to her husband in fear; while Lucrezia, who had been listening in perplexed arrangement, darted into the midst of the group, and laid hold of the nurse's chair.

"What absurdity!" exclaimed the count, recovering himself "How could such an idea enter your head?"

"Were it the last word I had to speak, my lord," continued the woman, "and to my dying day, I will maintain what I assert. I saw Gina Montani. She stood in a nightdress, there, where the lamp casts its shade."

"Nonsense," repeated the count, abstractedly. But Lucrezia was white, and shook convulsively.

At this moment, a wild, frantic sob burst from the Lady Adelaide. The child was dead!

5

Many months again slipped by, with little to distinguish them save the decreasing strength of the Lady Adelaide. She had been wasting slowly away ever since the shock given to her heart at discovering her husband's love for Gina Montani. She loved him passionately, and she *knew* her love must be unrequited; for the affections once bestowed, as his had been, can never be recalled and given to another. The illness of the mind wrought upon the body. She became worse and worse; and after the birth of a second child, it was evident that she was sinking rapidly.

She lay upon the stately bed in her magnificent chamber, about which were scattered many articles consecrated to her girlhood, or to her happy bridal, and, as such, precious. Seated by the bedside was her husband, one of his hands clasping hers. In the other hand he held a cambric handkerchief, with which he occasionally wiped her languid brow.

"Bear with me a little longer, my husband. But a short time."

"Bear with you, Adelaide!" he repeated. "Would to Heaven you might he spared to me!"

"It is impossible," she sighed, pressing his hand upon her

wasted bosom.

"Adelaide"—he hesitated, after a while—"I would ask you a question. A question which, if you can, I entreat that you will answer."

She looked at him inquiringly, and he resumed, in a low voice: "What became of Gina Montani?"

Even amidst the pallid hue of death, a hectic colour flushed her cheeks at the words. She gasped with agitation before she could speak.

"Bring not up that subject now; the only one that came between us to disturb our peace; the one to which I am indebted for my death. I am lying dying before you, Giovanni, and you can think but of her."

"My love, why will you so misunderstand me?"

"These thoughts excite me dreadfully," she continued. "Let us banish them, if you would have peace visit me in dying."

"May your death be far away yet," he sighed.

"Ah! I trust so! A little longer—a few days with you and my dear child!" And the count clasped his hands together as he silently echoed her prayer.

"Will you reach me my lazuli casket?" she continued. "I have put a few trinkets into it, to leave as tokens of remembrance. I must show you how I wish them bestowed."

He rose from his seat, and looked about the room; but he could not find the jewel-case.

"The small one, Giovanni," she said; "not my diamond casket. I thought it was in the mosaic cabinet. Or perhaps they may have taken it into my dressing-room."

He went into the adjoining apartment, and had found the missing casket, when a wild shriek from her lips smote upon his ear. In an instant he had gained the bedside, and was supporting her. The attendants came running in.

"My dearest Adelaide! What is it that excites you thus?"

But his inquiries were in vain. She lay in his arms sobbing convulsively, and clinging to him in some terrible fear. Broken words came from her at length.

"I looked up—when you were away—and saw—there, in that darkened recess—*her*. I did—I did, Giovanni !"

"Whom?" he said, becoming very pale.

"Her—Gina Montani. She was in white—a long dress it seemed Oh! Giovanni, leave me not again."

"I will never leave you, Adelaide. But, this—it must have been a fancy—an illusion of the imagination. We had just been speaking of her."

"You remember," she sobbed, "the night our child died—nurse saw her also. It may—"

The lady's voice failed her, and her husband started, for a rapid change was taking place in her countenance.

"I am dying, Giovanni," she uttered, clinging to him, and trembling to the utmost extent of nervous terror. "Oh, support me! A doctor—a priest—Father Anselmo—where are they? He would give me absolution, he said: then why does the remembrance come back again now? It would not have been done without my sanction. Giovanni, my husband—protect and love our child—desert him never. Giovanni, where are you? My sight is going—Giovanni—"

Her voice died away, and the count bowed his head down in his anguish, whilst the attendants pressed forward to look at her countenance. The Lady Adelaide had passed from amongst the living.

6

It was many years after the death of the Lady Adelaide, that several workmen were engaged making some extensive alterations in the Castle of Visinara, preparatory to the second marriage of its lord, who was about to espouse the lovely Elena di Capella. They were taking down the walls of a remote passage, or corridor, leading out of the chapel.

Standing, looking on, was the count, still to all appearance youthful, though he was in reality some years past thirty. By his side stood a fair boy of seven years old. It was the heir of Visinara. He was an open-hearted, engaging child, with a smiling countenance, on which might be traced his father's features, whilst he had inherited his mother's soft blue eyes and her sunny hair.

"What a long while you are !" exclaimed the child boyishly impatient to see the walls come down. "You should hit harder."

"The walls are very thick, Alberto," observed his father. "All these niches, which have been blocked up, and in the olden time contained statues, have to come down also."

"They are taking down a niche now, are they not, papa?" "Not yet. They are removing the wall which has been built before it. It appears fresher, too, than the rest; of more recent date."

"It seems extraordinarily fresh. Sir Count," observed one of the workmen. "The materials are old, but it has certainly been rebuilt within a few years—within ten, I should say."

"Not it," laughed the count. "These corridors have not been touched during my lifetime."

"This portion of them has, my lord, you may rely upon it." As the workman spoke, the remainder came down with a tremendous crash, leaving the niche exposed to view. There was no statue there—but the corpse of the unfortunate Gina Montani, standing upright in her nightdress, was revealed to their sight. It was nearly as fresh as if she had departed but yesterday, having been excluded from the air. The features, it is true, were scarcely to be recognised, but the hair—the long brown curls falling on her neck—was the same as ever. This was her horrible death, then—to be walled up alive. The Count di Visinara grew sick and faint as he gazed. Before he had time to collect his startled thoughts, the child was pulling at his arm.

"Papa, take me away. What is that dreadful thing there? You look white and cold, too, not as you always do. Oh, what is it? Dear dear papa, take me from here."

The workmen were affrighted, and shook with fear—perhaps more frightened though less shocked than the count. But one of them, partially recovering himself, touched the corpse with an implement he had been using for his work, and down it came, a heap of dust.

The Lord of Visinara turned, and with steps that tottered under him, bore his child back to the castle.

7

You may hear in Italy, unto this day, various versions of this tradition. One will tell you that the Lord of Visinara offered moneys and treasures, even to the half of his possessions, unto the fathers of the church, if they would lay the troubled spirit of Gina Montani; but that, although the monks tried hard, they could not do it. Another version goes, that the church did not try, because she had died a heretic. However that may have been, all agree in one respect—that the ghost was not laid. That it never would be, and never could be, but still wanders to haunt the descendants of the Lady Adelaide.

Several of these descendants still exist in Tuscany, though greatly reduced in station. And the accredited belief is, that whenever death is going to remove one of them, the spirit of the ill-fated Gina Montani appears and shows itself to them when they are dying.

Fred Temple's Warning

You cannot relate two narratives at the same time; any more than you can be in two places at once. If you are at this precise hour and minute in Africa, it stands to reason that you cannot be in Asia. After I had told you something about Oxford the beginning of the year, I ought to have gone on with this account that I'm going to write now; but Janet Carey intervened and crossed my life, and she had to cross my papers.

When we got back to Oxford for the Easter Term—which does not begin, as everybody knows, until Easter's over—things went on quietly. The fret and worry introduced during the last term was over; over for good: and we just minded our business and were as staid as the severest dean or tutor could wish. Tod stuck fairly well to his studies, only varying them—and not too much—with boating and riding.

Fred Temple and I grew better acquainted that term: I liked him, and he liked me. He was one of the best looking men I ever saw; and a rare good fellow. Slingsby Temple, the elder brother, was a dark little man, reserved, and proud as Lucifer; Fred was taller, and had affable ways; his every look and movement bespoke the gentleman, and his face was beautiful, fresh and fair to look upon, with perfect features and dark blue eyes. It sounds like the description of a woman's face: but it's true; and I still see it sometimes before my mind's eye just as plainly as I used to see it then.

Their place, Templemore, was in one of the remote counties. Long Webster (who was built like a lamp-post and had come up as servitor at Magdalen's) knew all about them. Old Webster was Perpetual Curate down there, and dined regularly at Templemore twice a year, Mr. Temple was dead, and Slingsby Temple would come into Templemore when he was twenty-five; not before. His mother had it to live in until then: she was a lord's daughter and the Hon. Mrs. Temple.

"The curious thing in that family is that the heads of it never live to be old," said Webster, one day that he and I and Tod had to run to a shed for shelter in an unseasonable thunderstorm, and we happened to get talking of the Temples. "At about thirty they drop off."

"Drop off!" said Tod, taking him up. "How's that? Do they go off of themselves?"

Webster (who was not half a bad fellow, and more industrious than a working bee) shook his head in denial. "Something takes them off: sometimes it's natural illness, fever, or that; sometimes it's accident; but they never get beyond thirty. They have all married young; and just as the little ones are coming on, off they die. The late Temple was shot by accident when he was out shooting."

"Leaving these two?"

"Leaving these two, and three more," replied Webster. "There's a younger brother, and there's one girl: the other girl died."

"I should try and break the spell, were I Slingsby," cried Tod. "Is Templemore a nice place?"

"Very. And has plenty of money to keep it up. Mrs. Temple has never gone out of widow's weeds yet, though it's ever so many years since he died. It was a great blow to her; people thought she'd have died of it herself but for her pride."

"Is she proud?"

Webster threw his long neck back at the question. "Proud! Well, we have known some proud people down yonder, but we never knew one like Mrs. Temple. The heir is the same—Slingsby."

"He's awfully reserved," said Tod.

"And proud, too, with a pride rarely seen," added Webster:

"and it will grow upon him as he gets older. Pride such as that is not to be coveted: but I think it helps to keep a young man straight. The rain's over."

We exchanged the shed for the wet grass, soaking with the heavy shower, and went back: I thinking of what Webster had said, for it interested me.

That Easter term, a fresh man had entered at Queen's: one MacRae. A Scotchman; as may be guessed by his name: and by his speech, too, if you had heard it, for it had the Scotch ring in it. He was a plain man in all senses of the word, but he was liked very well; a hard reader, he, and steady as Old Time. I need not have brought in his name at all but for one peculiarity—he believed in second sight. Nay, more: he said he possessed it: possessed it himself.

When this belief of his first crept out, he was roasted finely; but it made no impression upon him at all. He just went on in his civil, quiet way, and cared no more for the ridicule than eels do for skinning. MacRae would look steadily at the fellows with his deep-set eyes, Turning attentively, a half smile on his wide and projecting mouth; mid tell them at the first break that they were welcome to laugh at him as much as they liked, and at second sight also, for they did not understand it. So the roasting ceased by degrees: when mockery falls harmless, where's the fun of it?

One evening some few of us, including MacRae, were at the Temples' rooms in Trinity, with Fred. Slingsby was off, star-gazing: he had one great hobby besides his pride, and that was astronomy. Somebody started a little quiet chaffing at Mac: but the only result that came of it was, his telling us some stories that would have made your hair stand on end. Mac called them his experiences, and said they were solemn ones.

One of the stories I particularly remember; and I'll give it here that you may judge of their nature. He said he was nearing his home in the Highlands one evening on foot after some days' absence, and had got to within twenty yards of his door, when a funeral procession suddenly issued from it. He declared that at the moment he believed it to be a real funeral coming forth, the personages real personages; and he stood back against the fence in dismay, wondering who had died during his absence. It was only when he found the procession passed him without noise, their footsteps making no echo, that the truth flashed over him that it was a vision of Second Sight. He watched them wind by in the moonlight; the coffin and all the followers, his father and a crowd of his brothers being among them—for they numbered a baker's dozen.

He watched the procession glide, glide on, with the regularity of silent clock-work; watched it until it was out of sight; and he said you might just have wrung the wet out of his hair. He went in, and found his father, mother, sister, and all the young fry of brothers—Mac was the eldest—at their supper of oatmeal porridge. Mac called it parritch: and he did not in the least, mind giving these homely details: but the family had come into money since then. He said he looked round on them all, his heart failing him and inwardly wondering which of them it was that would have to go; but he held his peace as to what he had seen. It turned out to be the youngest of all: and in little more than a week's time the same procession he had seen as a phantasm filed out of the house in reality, to bear him to his grave.

We could have stood those tales decently: but what nobody liked was another thing—Mac deliberately avowed that he had occasionally foreseen the death of some particular person in whose company he might chance to be: it had happened to him three or four times. This was not at all a comfortable idea. Fancy! for anything we knew to the contrary, the foresight might come to him while he was talking to us. It might be one of us that he saw was doomed to go! You may laugh; and I daresay are laughing: but it was not a thing that any of us relished. The singular part of it was, that Mac himself so implicitly believed it all. There could be no mistake in that: any more than you could mistake the pain and earnestness in his voice when he said how miserable this gift of Second Sight made him, and how he had prayed to be delivered from it.

That's all I have to say in this paper about MacRae. It was through him that I and Fred Temple got talking together as we did talk. Mac had just concluded another of his dreadful experiences, when Slingsby Temple came in with his night telescope, and we separated. Slingsby generally acted as a wet blanket on Fred's visitors: and when they had dispersed, he would go on at Fred for making himself common with undesirable gownsmen: meaning the gownsmen who had not the state and pride of the Temples.

On the following afternoon, it chanced that I and Fred Temple met, and we turned off together for a stroll by the river. Naturally enough we began to speak of Mac's tales of the previous night, and then passed on to talk of superstition generally: a subject that would never have entered our minds but for Mac. Fred had rather a habit of mocking at many things in a good-natured way; and, of all topics in the world, I should have expected him to mock at this. But he did not: he was more silent than usual: and it was only when I found he was letting me have all the talk to myself, he just answering Yes or No, as might be, that I turned to look at him.

"You don't *believe* in it, Temple!"

For a minute or so he did not answer. He had a bit of the growing clover between his lips, and his nice blue eyes looked straight out at the sky.

"I don't believe all the things Mac treated us to," returned he. "They are not credible; and how Mac himself can put the faith in them that he evidently does put, is incomprehensible. But I think more people are imbued with a spice of superstition than their friends would give them credit for. There are whole families who hold belief in some superstition or other; a ghost, or what not."

"Of course. Just as some houses are said to be haunted. Remember the tale about one of the Lords Lyttelton."

"Our family has a tale attaching to it," he went on, twirling the clover about with his lips.

"Yours has!—Oh I know," I thoughtlessly added, as the recollection of what Webster had once said flashed up. "The head of your family always dies young."

"That's fact, Johnny: not superstition. Why it should be so, I don't know, but for the past hundred years not one of the reigning Temples has lived to be much past thirty. The collateral branches, brothers and sisters, and that, live long enough: but not the possessor of Templemore."

"What did you mean, then?"

"Well, amidst the people that enrol a ghost in their family archives, we boast of one. When any of the Temples are going to die, the laic runs that they are called."

"Called!"

"Called by the head of the family, who has last departed. You are staring, Johnny," he added with a half smile, biting the clover to bits: "you don't understand, I suppose."

"Not quite."

"Well, I'll make it plain. My father died several years ago: the superstition rife amid us is, that when any of us, his children, come to die, he will first of all appear to and beckon us."

"But you don't believe it, Temple!"

"Perhaps, in a case such as this, no one absolutely believes or disbelieves," he returned. "You see, until the warning comes to our own individual selves, we can't speak to it personally: no one, I believe man or woman, gives another unlimited credit for seeing an apparition: and after it has come, you know, we don't live to assert our belief in it."

Was he joking? I thought and said so.

"No I am not," said Fred. "We Temples are all, so to say, brought up in the superstition, because we hear of it when we are young. You can't shut people's mouths, servants' and dependents' and neighbours'; and children always get hold of exactly what they ought not to."

"Has the warning ever come in your time?"

"Yes; twice. Said to have come, at least. A day or two before my father died he had been out shooting partridges. It was the 4th of September. Coming home at dusk with the head-keeper,

454

they we passing through a coppice, talking of the birds, when my father suddenly stopped, and put his hand upon the keeper's arm. 'Who's that Patterson?' said he. Patterson looked in the direction that his masters eyes had taken, but could see nothing at all but the tree. 'Where, sir?' he asked: 'what is it?' There was no answer, and upon looking at his master he saw that his eyes had a wild stare in them and his face had turned ghastly. Patterson has said many a time since that he felt as queer as could be, and did not like to speak again. 'He's gone,' said my father in another minute, loosing hold off the man's arm: 'Patterson, that was my father standing there, he looked at me, and had his right arm lifted; I thought he beckoned with it.'

"Patterson, knowing of the superstition, felt worse at this: he says came into his mind with the words. But he thought—and said—that some intruder might have been pushing himself into the coppice; and he beat about a bit, but could see no one. Of course, he did not speak of the incident: he knew his place better than that: and the next morning the man thought his master seemed to have forgotten all about it, for he was in high spirits, full of some friends who were coming that day to stay at Templemore, and giving orders for a grand day's shooting for the following one. Patterson got all things in readiness, and the party, a large one, went out early. Before ten o'clock had struck, Johnny, my father was brought home with his death-wound."

"How dreadful!"

"I saw them bring him in. I was a little fellow of five, and I shall never forget the bustle and the grief. I shall never forget my mother s cries. She was in weak health: the baby was not a month old. Johnny, if I ever want to be sobered I think of that day."

"Was your father dead?"

"No; but it was known that he could not live. Someone of them, in getting through a hedge, had let his gun go off and the charge entered my father's body. He was quite sensible until he died; which was about twelve hours after he was shot; and he disclosed the fact of having seen, or thought he had seen, his father on the previous evening in the coppice. Patterson spoke of it afterwards, and there was a good deal of talk about it in the neighbourhood."

It almost seemed to me that I could see that past day, its confusion, and its troubles. Temple broke the silence.

"Since then it has been said that my father has appeared to give this warning in his turn. My little sister—the one who was the baby when he died—had scarlet fever when she was about eight years old. You must know, Johnny, that just before my father's death he had caused his portrait to be painted, life size. It was done by only a local artist, but the likeness was wonderful: it was himself on canvas. They painted him standing up, a roll of paper in his hand. Everybody agreed that it was a living likeness; and many a friend, entering the drawing-room where it was hung, has started back with an unpleasant sensation, believing for the moment that they saw himself.

"Thus you will understand that we children grew up with a perfect knowledge of his person; and the child, Ella, knew him by sight as well as though she had known him in reality. Well, Ella had had scarlet fever, and was supposed to be getting well. One morning, however, upon my mother's going to the room, the nurse reported that Miss Ella had had a good night, but that she thought she must have been dreaming, for she said she had seen her papa. Ella, who still seemed better, took up the words and said she did see papa. He had stood at the end of the room by the drawers where the night-light was, and he seemed to want her to go to him."

"Was she frightened when she saw this?" I struck in, interested in the tale.

"Not in the least. I see what you are thinking of, Ludlow; but the superstition had never been allowed to reach the child's ears. She evidently thought no more of having seen her papa, or fancied she saw him, than she would have thought had he been living. They told her she had only dreamt it; they told her, I believe, that the doctor called in the night, and was standing there—which was not true; they told her all sorts of tales to take her thoughts off. All of no use: it was papa, and nobody else, she persisted, and she wished he'd come again and talk to her. Some unfavourable symptoms set in, and before the week had worn itself out, Ella was dead."

"It seems very odd, Temple."

"Well, it does," he answered. "Down with us, the public call it the Temple Superstition. But you see now why it is hard to disbelieve; and, being men of the world and of the enlightened nineteenth century equally hard to believe. I have just related the exact facts without colouring; as you would have known them were you one of us. You'll not repeat this, Johnny."

"Certainly not."

"Slingsby would go wild if it got about here. It is not exactly the thing one would like talked of in this place."

"Does he believe in it?"

"No. He says he does not. He is an exclusive-natured fellow you know, and looks down upon ghosts and fancies as beneath the Temples.—And by Jove! here comes Slingsby! Is he after me, wonder? Have you seen any papers today, Ludlow! It's thought the ministers must go out."

★★★★★★

The weeks went on, one week after another; and the term and it duties with them. I did not see so much of Fred Temple as at first At leisure times he seemed to keep to himself: or, at least, not to b available for me. We were just as good friends as ever, only less together.

Going in to the stationer's, headforemost, one day, after some paper, I nearly upset an old lady in a brown bonnet, who was coming out the shop. Begging her pardon, I drew aside to let her pass, when voice behind called me by my name.

"Johnny Ludlow! Grandmamma, it's Johnny Ludlow." It was Mabel Smith. And but for Mabel, I think I should not have re-membered the old lady: who was Mrs. Golding.

"Very happy to meet you again, sir," said the old lady, her face amiable as ever. "I hoped to have had the pleasure of seeing you at my house; but I suppose you find it too far. I and Mabel have talked of you sometimes."

I made the best excuse I could—busy; reading hard. In truth, had forgotten all about the old lady and her invitation: and I suppose Mabel had left weeks ago.

"Are you here still, Mabel? Or have you come back again?"

"I have been here all the while," said Mabel. "The children at home took measles last April, and papa wrote word I had better not go home. Every week, every week after Easter Term came in, grandmamma and I looked for you, Mr. Ludlow: but you never came. You don't care to come?"

"But I do care, and I will come," I answered, amid the pricks of conscience—for the old lady was a nice old lady; and I had been taught in my early years that it is next door to a sin to ne-glect the old or slight their wishes. "I'll be sure to come one of these days, Mabel."

Mabel gave me the address again, and I helped Mrs. Golding into her fly, which had a restless horse, and Mabel after her; and they drove away.

There was a change in Mabel Smith that struck me. She was hardly like the same. The sallow, sickly face had a tinge of bright colour, the keen dark eyes had a pleasant light in them, the thin shrill voice was softer than I had ever heard it. It was a marvel-lous improvement. Deformed and undersized poor Mabel al-ways would be; but her muslin dress was made with frillings and furbelows which rendered the defect less conspicuous; and her straw hat was a gay one, with a wreath of flowers round it. Mabel was coming out !

I walked over the next Saturday afternoon, and readily found the house at the end of about two miles and a half. It was a very pretty place: a small villa with a grass-plot and flower-beds be-fore it, enclosed by iron palisades painted green, and a low green gate in the middle.

I asked for Mrs. Golding. The maid-servant, a neat girl, shut me into a drawing-room, and said she would tell her mistress. The furniture was bright and good, and the glass-doors opened to the back garden. Before the window was another grass-plot, with shrubs round it, and beyond lay fruit-trees and vegetables. I stood at the window, looking out.

And you might just have knocked me down with a feather. Not often in my life had I been so surprised as then. Strolling about amid the trees beyond the lawn, with no eyes for anybody but themselves, were Mabel Smith and Fred Temple.

I rubbed my eyes; I pinched my arms: was I awake or dreaming? Yes, it was Fred himself, his slender figure bending down to her, his fair, refined face bright as life's morning.

"My mistress's respects to you, sir, and she will be down in a few minutes to welcome you, and she is very glad you are come," said the maid, entering, and who seemed to have caught some of the old-fashioned formality. "My mistress has not been well today, and she went to lie down after her dinner. Would you please to take a seat, sir; or would you like to go in the garden and eat some fruit? The strawberries are ripe."

"Thank you, I will go into the garden. I think I see Mr. Frederick Temple there?"

"Oh yes, sir, it's Mr. Temple. He comes over to see his aunt."

His aunt! Surprise the second: and a huge surprise too. What was there in common between the high and mighty Temples of Templemore. and this obscure old lady in the brown satin bonnet?

They did not see me till I was close upon them. Mabel's face flushed to a bright rose colour, and for the time it lasted she looked almost beautiful. Fred turned as red as brick-dust.

"What, have you really come to see us, Mr. Ludlow!" cried Mabel. "I did not expect it."

"I said I would, you know. Mrs. Golding is not well, I hear."

"It has been very warm, and the heat takes grandmamma's strength away. There she is!"

Mrs. Golding, in a black silk gown and lace cap with lilac ribbons, was standing at the window. I went to her at once. She welcomed me very heartily; and after a bit I spoke of Fred's being her nephew.

"Oh dear no, he is not my nephew," she said with a smile. "We are but very distant relatives, though it pleases Mr. Temple to call me aunt. Some young men have pleasant ways with them, you know sir; and I'm sure I like to hear him say it. His grandmother and I were first cousins in the old days, so the relationship is not much now. The Temples have never had any knowledge of me till one day this term the young gentleman came over and found me out. It was very pretty of him, I thought, Mr. Ludlow, and I begged him to come whenever he could."

They were in view, Fred and Mabel, through an opening in the tree. Was it a case of *love!* Nothing I ever saw looked so much like it. And yet, it was scarcely believable. Putting aside the disparities in their condition, there was that wonderful disparity between themselves: Fred Temple with his beauty of face and form, his distinguished air and bearing, every look, every movement bespeaking the high-bred gentleman; and poor Mabel with her thin, querulous face, and her misshapen figure! That she should fall in love with him, opportunity being given for it, was more than likely: but how could his fancy have been taken by her? It was just one of those things that are incomprehensible; that can never be understood in this world.

"The tea is ready, ma'am."

Mrs. Golding got up at the maid's announcement, and took her stick. I gave her my arm: and the maid waited respectfully outside for us to pass into the other room.

"Go and tell Miss Mabel, Hannah," said the old lady. "I think she is in the garden with Mr. Temple. And give my respects to Mr. Temple and say I hope he will take a dish of tea with me."

The tea was laid on a white cloth in the other room, with bread-and-butter, biscuits, and two glass dishes of strawberries. "We take tea early," said the old lady, as she sat down in her place. "I am always ready for it myself, and I know it is more convenient to Mr. Temple who has to get back to Oxford."

Fred came in first: Mabel followed in a minute or two. She stood at the table, and began to wet the cups. The old lady told us she had never made tea herself: when her granddaughter was not with her, Hannah had to do it.

"You'd be better without that tippet, child. Take it off."

"I like it on, thank you, grandmamma."

Mabel went red as she said it. I thought I knew why, and why she wanted to keep the cape on. It was a frilled muslin cape the same as her dress, and it served in a measure to hide her deformity.

Fred eat nothing, and hardly talked at all. I made up for him in the former department, for the bread-and-butter and strawberries were all delicious. The old lady said she liked to see us enjoy ourselves; and that her cook was an excellent hand at bread-making.

"You are getting tired of strawberries, I expect," she said to Fred.

"No, aunt, I'm not: but I have a headache this afternoon."

"It is the heat," she answered. "You should bring an umbrella over with you, my dear, when you come, to keep the sun off."

Which made us both laugh. Umbrellas had not come into fashion for men then, except in the rain.

We went away together. Fred put his arm into mine in turning from the gate. "Field way, or road way, Johnny?"

"Field way, I should say, if there is one."

"Oh, there is one. It is the route I always take."

Upon the intimate terms we were, it was impossible to ignore the topic that lay uppermost in both our minds. Which of us spoke first I don't remember, but we had soon plunged into it, hot and strong. It seemed that when Fred was at home at Easter, he chanced to tell his sister, as something laughable, of the queer old lady named Golding, who had interrupted a luncheon party. Mrs. Temple, sitting by, carelessly remarked that she had heard her mother speak of some obscure relative, a cousin, who had married a Mr. Golding. When Fred returned he was out for a walk one day, and in passing a house (her house as it turned out) saw the same old lady at the gate, looking up and down the road as though she expected company. On the spur of the moment Fred stopped; he had plenty of impudence in a gentlemanly way, and inquired into her pedigree, never supposing, he said, that she was the person his mother had alluded to. The old lady, taking all the questions as put *bona fide*, answered them in the same spirit; and Fred found that she really was the cousin. She invited him in, and ordered refreshments. From that day, Fred had been a frequent visitor: and there lay the secret of his diminished intercourse with me.

"I like the old dame," said Fred; "like her uncommonly. She is so genuine and yet so courteous, worth a hundred of the people of the present day."

"Well, I like her too, Fred. But I should never have supposed there was any relationship between her and the Temples. Your mother was the daughter of Lord———"

"You can't judge of people's relatives by themselves," he interrupted before I could finish. "Take two members of the same family; one goes up in life, the other goes down; by the next generation or so, they and theirs will be wide apart in social standing: one in a peer's ermine perhaps, the other selling baked potatoes in the street. That's an extreme illustration, Johnny; but it will serve to show the argument. Female relatives especially get divided; marriage gives all the chances of it."

"Has Slingsby recognized Mrs. Golding?"

"I should think not! When I told him I had been and found the old lady out, he thought I must be getting fit for a lunatic asylum."

"You have been up there a good deal."

"Well, it's just a nice walk, out and in."

"Look here, Fred: it's not the walk that takes you. I can't understand it, though. I never was more astonished in my life than I've been this afternoon. First, at seeing you there, at all; next, at seeing what I thought I did see."

"What was that?"

"You know."

"Well, I have nothing to reply to it," he said, after a pause. "Mind you hold your tongue abroad, Johnny."

"But it wouldn't do, you know, Temple. Between Fred Temple Templemore, grandson to a peer, and Mabel Smith, the wine

462

merchant's daughter, there's a gulf that can't be got over, Fred. You must know that it would never do."

He had a light cane in his hand, and began switching the tufts of grass on that side the path-way; but he did not answer.

"Even if that gulf could be bridged over, Fred, there's another."

"Another?"

"Why yes."

"What is it?" He seemed to be asking the questions mechanically, his mind far away.

"Herself. I don't like to speak of her in this way, Fred, but truth's truth. A poor, afflicted girl, like that, is not—is not suitable for a man to make a wife of."

"I say, how you go dating onwards!" he cried, with a brief laugh that had more of vexation in it than merriment. "It will be year before I shall think of marrying. As to Mabel, *she's* not likely to think of it at all. And she's not much better than a child."

"Do you wish her harm, Fred?"

"Wish her harm! What are you talking of? I would rather shield her from it."

"Yes. But don't you see that the very fact of your going there brings it upon her. She is in love with you already: and what can come of it?"

He was switching the grass perpetually, a frightfully perplexed look on his face. I saw plainly that he had gone over all this in his own mind; but had not the resolution to break through the trammels.

For he, that handsome, courtly fellow, *loved* the deformed girl. Make the best and the worst of the incongruity, *it was so.* Some things in this world are utterly unaccountable, and that was one.

"An end must come to it, Temple. It *must*, you know."

"But it need not come yet. Where's the harm?"

"But look at what it will be for her when it does. The farther it is prolonged, the more cruel it will be."

An expression of pain sat on his, at all times, sensitive lips. He looked straight forward at the sky in the horizon.

"I see your argument, Ludlow. Of course I—I know all this."

"Well, I'll say no more, Fred; I don't want to preach; and you are older than I am. When I saw how it was this afternoon, I could not help pitying Mabel, that's all. She is the last girl a generous man would like to bring pain upon: she is not like other girls."

"I never thought of it quite in this light," he said gently, after a while. "You are right, though, Johnny."

★★★★★★

"Do you mean to pass me, Johnny Ludlow?"

I should have passed her, for I was going along with Budd of Skimmery, and had my head turned to him. Someone had caught hold of my gown. It was Mabel Smith. She was in High Street, walking towards home, an old maidservant with a basket behind her.

This was about a week—ten days perhaps—after the time I had been over there; and the term was now drawing near to its ending. Of Fred Temple I had seen but little since, and we had not exchanged one private word. His mother and sister had come to Oxford, and I concluded he was occupied with them.

"I thought you told me you never walked in the town, Mabel," I said, as Budd strolled onwards. The old servant turned to feast her eyes at a shop-window.

"I scarcely ever do," she answered. "Grandmamma does not let me. But I had to come in today to the dressmaker's to have a cape tried on. You have never been over again!" she added, in a strangely mournful voice, that had a sound of reproach in it.

Again there seemed to me to be a change in Mabel. Her eyes were bright with excitement, her cheeks wore an unnatural flush: and her thin fingers, that looked not unlike birds' claws in their grey gloves, twitched as she held her parasol.

"There's plenty of time yet, Mabel. I have been busy this week."

"Where's Mr. Temple?" she abruptly asked. "Is *he* too busy to come? "

"I daresay he is busy. Have you not seen him lately?"

"Never since the evening you came over and went away with him," she replied, her shining eyes looking straight at me now. "What did you do to him, Johnny Ludlow?"

"Nothing—" I was beginning: and then I felt my own face flush for I remembered what I had said to Fred. Was he staying a in consequence of *that?* It was hardly likely. Mabel fidgeted incessantly with the parasol.

"Mrs. and Miss Temple are at Oxford; Fred is occupied with them I went on. "I have hardly seen him since that morning myself."

"Mrs. and Miss Temple are here!" repeated Mabel. "Do you mean his mother. She is the Honourable Mrs. Temple, is she not?"

"Yes.'

Mabel's face fell. "I see now," she said, speaking more to herself than to me, "they are keeping him away from us. Perhaps they'll never let him come again! We are not good enough for them."

"I don't know anything about it, Mabel. Fred is reading hard, I'm sure."

Mabel stood very still, thinking inwardly, and then, with a catching of the breath, a kind of sobbing sigh, she put out her hand.

"You will come over just once, won't you, Johnny Ludlow, before you go away? It is very dull there, I and grandmamma always alone."

"Yes I will; If I've no time for it, I'll make time. Goodbye then, Mabel."

That same night I met Fred Temple. He was skimming along towards his rooms, with an armful of books, and stopped when he saw me.

"Where have you been burying yourself, lately, Fred? You've been as scarce as sunshine in November."

"Been rejoicing my tutor's heart—going steadily in for lectures all that," he returned. "The mother's here, too."

"Those are just the pleas I setup for you today, Fred."

"Set up pleas for me?"

"I met Mabel Smith in the High. She seemed to think you had finally deserted them, and asked what had become of you."

We were pacing slowly onwards together towards his college. It was one of the loveliest nights ever seen, the moon as bright as day. In changing his position Fred let one of the books fall. I picked it up, and carried it for him.

"I have not been over there, Johnny, since the time you know of," he continued, speaking in a low tone.

"Mabel said so."

"I thought it over that night in bed, Ludlow: what you had said, and what my own common sense showed me. I had driven the thoughts away before—would not think them, if you can understand that. But I took shame to myself that night for a coward; and I strove to put the present and the future before me, undisguised."

"Well?"

"Well, I saw how wrong and heedless I had been; wicked, if you like. I saw that nothing *could* come of it but pain to Mabel. I did care for her, Johnny; I care for her as I believe I shall never care for any other girl in the world; but I knew that the gulfs you spoke of could not be bridged over. The one relating to herself especially could never be spanned; for a man must not, in justice to his possible children, make such as her the mother of them—I daresay," he rather suddenly broke off, "you have heard the reproach of ultra pride cast on my mother."

"Something of that."

"It's a true charge I believe. But with all her pride, Johnny, she has been one of the best of mothers to us: and she has done her utmost to train us to know what's right and to practise it. 'Do your duty as before heaven,' she would say to us when we were little shavers; 'be true to yourselves and to your better con-science, no matter at what cost of pain.' And so—I went over all these things in my mind, and I resolved, be the cost what it might, to break through the—the intimacy."

"It is a cost, I see, to you."

"Yes, it is a cost," he quietly answered, changing his books from one arm to the other. "I deserve it, you know: I should not have been so careless. In future I hope I shall be less selfish."

"Selfish!"

"The word's right, Ludlow. Nobody but myself knows, or ever will know, what my visits there were to me—the intense happiness they brought. I had not the courage to abstain from them, though the still small voice within warned me that I ought to. All I hope is that *she* is not going in for too much pain—for regret."

It struck me she was; but I did not say it. I only said that I thought he had broken it off too abruptly.

"It is hardly good manners, Temple, to have been there so much; and then, without explanation or warning, to drop it altogether. It's not behaving well to the old lady."

"But you don't suppose I'd be guilty of that, do you, Johnny? I intend to call once, perhaps twice, before Term's up, and I shall tell them that, what with reading and what with my mother being here, I have not been able to come before. I might have allowed less time to elapse before making the call, you will say: but the truth is, I have put it off from day to day, hardly feeling sure of myself."

"You mean sure of your resolution when you see Mabel? I cannot *imagine*, Fred, how it was possible for you to get up a liking for her."

"One does not *get up* these things, Johnny; they come of themselves," he quaintly said. "I think the first element in the affair was pity. I looked upon her quite as a child: and the first day I was I here she stood before me, letting me hold her hands, and glanced up in my face with her sad eyes, telling me some of the troubles of her life. Those eyes haunted me till I saw her again.— By the way," he added, again turning abruptly to another topic, "I want you to come with me, the first opportunity we have, and be introduced to my mother."

I said I would go with pleasure whenever he liked: and we walked on in silence, Fred's eyes fixed on the lovely sky.

"A curious fancy comes over me sometimes on such nights at these, Johnny. That the sky there will hereafter be the dome of heaven: one cannot imagine any canopy more beautiful."

He spoke in a dreamy tone. I had never seen Temple in so solemn a mood as he was that night; I had never heard him speak so seriously as he had been just speaking, it was more like a parson than Fred Temple. Close at his quarters we parted, shaking hands and turning our different ways.

I might have been running a minute and a half when I discovered that I had come off with his book. So I went back, and clattered up the stairs to the Temples' rooms, gave a hasty knock and entered.

The lamp was on the table, and Slingsby Temple sat by it, two of his astronomical maps spread out before him on the green baize. He was not looking at them: he was staring angrily at Fred and blowing him up. Fred stood on this side, his face as white as chalk. They had not heard me; they did not see me—at least as it seemed—for Slingsby kept raging on, telling Fred he had been drinking.

"Don't put yourself out, Slingsby," cried Fred—and his voice seemed to have got a change, "it was my father stood there; or his exact image; but there's no need for you to go on like this."

"What's the matter, Fred?" I asked, going forward. "Look here: I forgot to give you the book I was carrying. What's been up?"

They turned to me, Fred with a kind of start; and he told me what it was. Upon entering the college, the lamp fell upon someone standing at the corner of the stairs. Fred looked to see who it might be, and saw his father. But for being agitated, hardly himself, I don't believe he would have repeated it to me: at any rate, before Slingsby.

"It was certainly the face and figure of my father," he said. "He stood in this way"—lifting and curving his right arm inwards. "I thought the arm moved. At first I felt no fear, only very

468

much surprised. It was but for a moment I saw it; the next it was gone."

"If you have been drinking, Fred, it is very disgraceful," struck in Slingsby, in his cold way. "I don't know what else can account for it. No? Nonsense! You must have been, to fancy so absurd a thing as that. It was only one of the gownsmen. Or perhaps a man from the buttery with a tray."

"If it was either, he took the form of our dead father, Slingsby, and vanished afterwards into space. I saw him and looked at him as plainly as I am now looking at you."

"Have you been with MacRae?" demanded Slingsby.

"I have not seen MacRae for days. I had been slowly walking in with these books, talking with Ludlow. Never mind: let it drop."

"Did you see anyone about as you were coming up?" cried Slingsby to me.

"Not a soul. It was all still and quiet. Well, goodnight. I daresay it was somebody or another who had stuck himself there."

"Of course it was," said Slingsby, in his haughtiest manner. "And pray don't talk of this outside, Ludlow," he added. "I should be ashamed to hear of it again; and I think my brother would be."

Fred came out with me: shaking hands in silence, as he looked up and down the stairs.

"It must have been fancy, Fred. That is, some fellow who bore a likeness, you know."

"Perhaps so," said he, in a careless tone as he went in again. "Goodnight, Ludlow."

On the day but one after this, I was leaning over Mrs. Golding's gate with Mabel. It was a Saint's day, and a day I shall never forget; and having leisure I went over early in the afternoon. Mrs. Golding was in her room. Mabel and I, strolling in the garden, came to an anchor at the low front gate.

"I think grandmamma can't be well," said Mabel. "Nearly every day now she has to go and lie down after dinner."

"It is hot, you know, Mabel."

"That's what the servants say—and grandmamma is old. How old should you think her, Johnny Ludlow?"

"Seventy."

"She is seventy-five. Have you seen anything of Mr. Temple?" she went on, with some of her old abruptness.

"I saw him the day I met you in High Street: and yesterday also for a few minutes. He told me he was thinking of coming here; but he has been very busy."

She had her thin fingers up to her face, partially hiding it from me. Presently she put her other hand aside and plucked a small crimson rose from the tree that grew there.

"Which do you like best, Johnny Ludlow: lilies or roses? Here come some horsemen," she continued, giving no time for an answer.

Three or four of them were riding up from the direction of the town. It did not matter much to me who they were, and I'm sure I did not think of Fred Temple: but Mabel's cheeks suddenly took the hue of the crimson rose, and that told me he made one. Yes; there he came, riding on, his bright hair glistening in the sunlight.

Slingsby Temple, Bill Whitney, and a fellow I did not know much of were the others. Whitney nodded to me as they passed. Fred turned aside and rode up to the gate.

"Are you well, Mabel?" he softly asked, bending to shake hands with her. "How is Mrs. Golding?"

"Grandmamma is poorly," said Mabel. "*I* am—very well."

"I feel quite ashamed not to have been up for so long, will you tell her," went on Fred, who had a fine glow on his face as if the wind had caught it. "I will call in a day or two."

"You have been—more busy than usual?" replied Mabel, her voice rather jerky.

"Yes; there's always plenty to do for the reading men as the term draws onwards," he remarked. "I am going for a good long ride to blow off some of the cobwebs that too much work gives the brain. What a nice rose, Mabel?"

Mabel shyly held the crimson rose up to him. "I can pick

another for myself if you would like this," she said; "it is very sweet." And perhaps without downright rudeness Fred could not well refuse the rose: but he hesitated for an instant.

"Thank you: yes, these roses are very sweet," he said, as he took it from her, smelt it, and began placing it in his button-hole.

Nodding to me, and saying *adieu* to Mabel, he backed his horse, and turned him in the direction the rest had gone. At that moment, a low, open cart came tearing round the bend of the road, with a sweep and a bag of soot in it, the horse one of those wretched animals ones hardly likes to look at. Poor and bony though he was, he seemed to have run away, and the man was standing up and lashing him for it.

Whether the animal or the cart touched Temple's horse, or whether, the object they presented and the clatter they made only startled the animal, I know not. I never have known to this day. Fred's horse reared and bounded forward: and Fred, the next moment, was lying on the ground, and the steed flying madly onwards. He had been sitting carelessly: and it might be that one hand was still occupied with the rose and the button-hole. I can't tell; I did not see: I was looking at that wretched cart.

Fred's horse was nowhere: he had dashed round the bend of the road close by, and was lost to sight. The sweep and the cart had dashed', on the other way and must be nearing Oxford. Mabel gave a low, shuddering cry, and I hastened out. It all passed in a moment of time. In another minute, as it seemed, the horsemen were back again: the riderless steed, catching them up, had aroused their fears. Temple was lying perfectly still, face upwards, his golden hair mingling with the dust. "We must get him in somewhere," cried Slingsby, looking at the house. "Who lives there?"

"Mabel," I said, going back to the gate where she stood trembling, "run and tell Mrs. Golding what has happened; ask permission for him to be brought in."

Whitney galloped to the town for medical assistance, and the rest of us carried Fred indoors. The old lady came out in her lace cap, lifting her hands in sad concern. She was most hospitable; the two servants ran about asking what they could do. A mattress was put upon a low table, and he was laid upon it.

The first to enter the house after that was Williams of Trinity, rather a chum of Slingsby Temple's, for he went in also for astronomy. Whitney had met him, and called out what was amiss as he passed at a hard gallop. Fred lay without motion; he just breathed, and by that we knew he was alive. Williams was more affected than you would have thought, as he stood by and looked at him.

"The last time I saw him was last night in chapel," he said, in a low tone, catching up his breath. "We sat together. I was wondering to myself whether there could be another face in the world to match with his. He always looked well in his surplice. It was a surplice night you know."

Someone asked for water, a big bowlful, to sprinkle his face with, and I went to get it. Mabel was sitting on the lower step of the stairs. Her face seemed to have become pinched again just as it used to be; her voice was acute in spite of its low whisper.

"Is he *much* hurt, Johnny Ludlow?"

"I don't know. The doctors have not come. He lies unconscious just as you saw him at first."

"I wish I might go in! *Why* can't I? Grandmamma saw me at the door, and told me to go away."

I had nothing to say to that and went on to the kitchen for the water.

"Perhaps he has only fainted!" cried she, watching me back.

"Perhaps so."

The doctors came, and Mrs. and Miss Temple came. One of the deans came. The house was like a mournful fair. The injury lay in the head, and the surgeons looked grave. Mrs. Temple was very much like Slingsby. Whether she understood who Mrs. Golding was, I don't know: she seemed to pay her great respect on account of her years, and thanked her warmly for what was being done.

"Don't you speak of that ma'am," said the old lady. "I'm sure if he had been the greatest stranger to us, I hope he would have been welcome to a shelter here—happening at my gate, and all. You see, ma'am, we had got to like the young man: he was often here."

"Often here!" repeated Mrs. Temple, her tone as coldly surprised as Slingsby's could have been.

"Yes, ma'am, often. It was a walk for him, you see, out and in, just a nice distance: and he would sit down and drink a dish o' tea with me, or eat away at my beds of strawberries as sociable as you like, just lately I've not seen so much of him; he was engaged, I presume. I trust in heaven the doctors may be able to bring him round."

"You seem to have been very kind and hospitable to him, and I thank you," said Mrs. Temple, seeing nothing but "the walk" in the motive that must have taken Fred thither. She had looked at Mabel in the passage and passed her with a glance of pity: how could any possible ideas associate *her* with her bright and well-born and handsome son?

It is of no use to linger over the day; as good let the end be known sooner as later. Frederick Temple died at dusk, and he never rallied at all. Slingsby was cut up to an emotion man rarely shows; those cold, exclusive natures sometimes are at a blow like this. He hushed it up; but the grief was there.

And Mabel? She did not cry, she did not speak. Her face seemed shrivelled up to its old ugliness; her eyes were dim, and she was just as still as death. Knowing what I knew, and what no one else now knew in the wide world, I read plainly enough that the gleam of sunshine, falling so briefly across her lonely life, had set for ever.

"You remember what happened the night before last," I said to Slingsby Temple below my breath. "That seems very strange *now.*"

Slingsby did not answer.

"Some people would say it was his warning."

"It was nothing but fancy," spoke Slingsby then. "He admitted to me the next morning that it might have been."

"Well, I don't know, he—"

"The less said about it the better," curtly interrupted Slingsby. "Mind that, Ludlow. It would be very painful to me to hear ridicule cast on my brother. A scout was standing there about that time, as I chanced to hear incidentally: it must have been him Fred saw."

★★★★★★

Of course it might have been: or it might not. Who could tell? Some people say the moon's made of green cheese, others say it isn't. Being so far off, down here, we are unable to decide.

One thing only seemed certain. That Frederick Temple, who had seemed to have a bright career before him, who promised to be one of the world's good and great and noble men, had gone to join his father on the everlasting shores.

Seen in the Moonlight
Sequel to Fred Temple's Warning

"I tell you it is," repeated Tod. "One can't mistake Temple, even at a distance."

"But this man looks so much older than he. And he has whiskers! Temple had none."

"And has not Temple got older, do you suppose; and don't whiskers sprout and grow? You were always a muff, Johnny. That is Slingsby Temple."

We had gone by rail to Whitney Hall, and were walking up from the station. The squire sent us to ask after Sir John's gout. It was a broiling hot day in the middle of summer. On the lawn before the house, with some of the Whitneys, stood a stranger—a little man, young, dark, and upright.

Tod was right, and I wrong. It was Slingsby Temple. But I thought him much altered: older-looking than his years, which numbered twenty-five, and more sedate and haughty than ever. We had neither seen nor heard of him since quitting Oxford.

"Oh, he is regularly in for it this time," said Bill Whitney, in answer to inquiries about his father, as they shook hands with us. "He has hardly ever had such a bout: can only lie in bed and groan. Temple, don't you remember Todhetly and Johnny Ludlow?"

"Yes, I do," answered Temple, holding out his hand to me first, and passing Tod to do it. But that was Slingsby Temple's way. I was of no account, and therefore it did not touch his pride to notice me.

"I am glad to see you again," he said, cordially enough, turning to Tod, which was quite a gracious acknowledgment for *him*.

But it surprised us to see him there. The Whitneys had no acquaintance with the Temples; neither had he and Bill been particular friends at college. Whitney explained it after luncheon, when we were sitting outside the windows in the shade, and Temple was pacing the shrubbery with Helen.

"I fancy it's a gone case," said Bill, nodding towards them.

"Oh, William, you should not say it," struck in Anna in a tone of remonstrance. "It is not sure—and not right to Mr. Temple."

"Not say it to Tod and Johnny! Rubbish! Why, they are like ourselves, Anna. I say I think it is going to be a case."

"Helen with another *beau!*" cried free Tod. "How has it all come about?"

"The mother and Helen have been staying at Malvern, you know," said Whitney. "Temple turned up at the same hotel, the Foley Arms, and they struck up an intimacy. I went over for the last week, and I was surprised to see how thick he was with them. The mother, who is more unsuspicious than a goose, told Temple in her hospitable way, when they were saying goodbye, that she should be glad to see him if ever he found himself in these benighted parts: and I'll be shot if at the end of five days he was not here! If Helen's not the magnet, I don't know what else can be."

"He appears to like her; but it may be only a temporary fancy that will pass away; it ought not to be talked of," reiterated Anna. "It may come to nothing."

"It may, or may not," persisted Bill.

"Will she consent to have him? "I asked.

"She'd be simple if she didn't," said Bill. "Temple would be a jolly fine match for any girl. Good in all ways. His property is large, and he is as sober and steady as any parson. Always has been."

I was not thinking of Temple's eligibility; that was undeniable; but of Helen's inclinations. Some time before, she had gone in for a love affair: which would not do at any price, caused some stir at the Hall, and came to signal grief: though I have not time to tell of it here. Whitney caught the drift of my thoughts.

"*That's* over and done with, Johnny. She'd never let its recollection spoil other prospects. You may trust Helen Whitney for that. She is as shallow-hearted as——"

"For shame, William!" remonstrated Anna.

Tod looked at Anna, and laughed gently. "What's this about a boating tour?" he inquired of Whitney. It had been alluded to at lunch-time.

"Temple's going in for one, with some more fellows," was the reply. "He has asked me to be one. We mean to do some of the larger rivers, take our tent, and encamp on the banks at night."

"What a jolly spree!" cried Tod, his face flushing with delight. "How I should like it!"

"I wish, to goodness you were coming! But Temple has made up his party. It is his affair, you know. He talks of being out a month."

"One gets no chance in this slow place," cried Tod fiercely. "I'll emigrate, and go tiger hunting. Is it a secret, this boating affair?"

"A secret! No."

"What made you kick me under the table, then, when I would have asked particulars at luncheon?"

"Because the mother was present. She has got all sorts of queer notions in her head—mothers always have—that the boat will be found bottom upwards some day, and we under it. So we say as little about it as possible before her."

"I see," nodded Tod. "Look here, Bill, I should like to get up a boating party myself: it sounds glorious. How do you set about it?—and where can you get a boat?"

"Temple knows," said Bill, "I don't. Let's go and ask him."

They went across the grass, leaving me alone with Anna. She and I were the best of friends, as the reader may remember, and exchanged many a little confidence with one another that the world knew nothing of.

"Should you like it for Helen, Anna?" I asked, indicating her sister and Slingsby Temple.

"Yes, I think I should," she answered. "But William was not warranted in speaking as he did. Mr. Temple will only be here a few days longer: when he leaves we may never see him again."

"But he is evidently taken with Helen. He shows that he is. And when a man of Slingsby Temple's disposition allows himself to betray anything of the kind, rely upon it he means something."

"Did you like him at Oxford, Johnny?"

"Well I did and did not," was my hesitating answer. "He was reserved, close, proud, and unsociable; and no man displaying those qualities can be much liked. On the other hand, he was of exemplary conduct, deserving respect from all, and receiving it."

"I think he is religious," said Anna, her voice taking a lower tone.

"Yes, I always thought him that. I fancy their mother brought them up so. But Temple is the last man in the world to display it."

"What with papa's taking up two rooms to himself now he has the gout, and all of us being at home, mamma was a little at fault which chamber to give Mr. Temple. There was no time for much arrangement, for he came without notice; so she just turned Harry out of his room, which used to be poor John's, you know, and put Mr. Temple there. That night Harry chanced to go up to bed later than the rest of us. He forgot his room had been changed, and went straight into his own. Mr. Temple was kneeling down in prayer, and a Bible lay open on the table. Mamma says it is not all young men who say their prayers and read the Bible nowadays."

"Not by a good many, Anna. Yes, Temple is good, and I hope Helen will get him. She will have position, too, as his wife, and a large income."

"He came into his estate this year when he was five-and-twenty. But, Johnny, I don't like one thing: William says there was a report at Oxford that the Temples never live to be even middle-aged men."

"Some of them have died young, I believe. But, that's no reason why they all should."

"And—there's a superstition attaching to the family, is there not?" continued Anna. "A ghost that appears; or something of that? What is it?"

I hardly knew what to answer. How vividly the words brought back poor Fred Temple's communication to me on the subject, and his subsequent death!

"You don't speak," said she. "Won't you tell me what it is?"

"It is this, Anna: but I daresay it's all nonsense. When one of the Temples is going to die, the spirit of the head of the family who last died is said to appear and beckon to him; a sign that his own death is near. Down in their neighbourhood people call it the Temple superstition."

"I am glad I am not a Temple; I should be always fearing I might see the sight," observed Anna, a sad, thoughtful look on her gentle face.

"Oh no, you'd not, Anna. The Temples themselves don't think of it, and don't believe in it. Slingsby does not, at any rate. His brother Fred told me at Oxford that nobody must presume to allude to it in Slingsby's presence."

"Fred? He died at Oxford, did he not? "

"Yes, he died there, poor fellow. Thrown from his horse. I saw it happen, Anna."

But I said nothing to her of that curious scene to which I had been a witness a night or two before the accident—when poor Fred, to Slingsby's intense indignation, fancied he saw his father on the college staircase; fancied his father beckoned to him. It was not a thing to talk of.

The afternoon passed. We said goodbye to them all, including Temple, and started for home again. Tod was surly and cross. He had come out in a temper and he was going back in one.

Tod liked his own way. Nobody in the world resented interference more than he: and just now he and the squire were at war. Some twelve months before. Tod had dropped into a five-hundred pound legacy from a distant relative. It was now ready to be paid to him. The squire wished it paid over to himself, that he might take care of it; Tod wanted to be grand, and open a banking account of his own. For the past two days the argument had held out on both sides, and this morning Tod had lost his temper. Lost, it was, again now, but on another score.

"Slingsby Temple might as well have invited me to join the boating lot!" he broke out to me, as we drew near home. "He knows I am an old hand."

"But if his party is made up, Tod? Whitney said it was."

"Rubbish! Made up! They could as well make room for another. And much good some of them are, I daresay! I can't remember that Slingsby ever took an oar in his hand at Oxford. All he went in for was star-gazing—and chapels—and lectures. And look at Bill Whitney! He hates rowing."

That night, after we got in, the subject of the "money grievance" cropped up again. The squire was smoking his pipe at the open window; Mrs. Todhetley sat by the centre table and the lamp, hemming a strip of muslin. Tod, open as the day on all subjects, abused Temple's "churlishness" for not inviting him to make one of the boating party, and declared he'd organise one of his own, which he could readily do, now he was not tied for money. That remark set the squire on.

"Ay, that's just where it would be, Joe," said he. "Let you keep the money in your own fingers, and we should soon see what it would end in."

"What would it end in?" demanded Tod.

"Ducks and drakes."

Tod tossed his head. "You think I am a child still, I believe, father."

"You are no better where the spending of money's concerned," said the squire, taking a long whiff. "Few young men are. Their fathers know that, and keep it from them as long as they can. And that's why so many are not let come into possession of their estates before they are five-and-twenty. This young Temple,

480

it seems, did not come into his; Johnny, here, does not."

"I should like to know what more harm it would do for the money to lie in my name in the Old Bank than if it lay in yours?" argued Tod. "Should I be drawing cheques on purpose to get rid of it? That's what you seem to suppose, father."

"You'd be drawing them to spend," said the Pater.

"No, I shouldn't. It's my own money, after all. Being my own, should take good care of it."

Old Thomas came in with some glasses, and the argument dropped. Tod began again as we were going upstairs together.

"You see, Johnny," he said, stepping inside my room on his way, and holding the door to, for fear of eavesdroppers, "there's that hundred pounds I owe Brandon. The old fellow has been very good, never so much as hinting that he remembers it, and I shall pay him back the first thing. To do this, I must have exclusive possession of the money. A fine bobbery the Pater would make if he got to know of it. Besides, a man, come to my age, likes to have a banking account—if he can. Goodnight, lad."

Tod carried his point. He turned so restive and obstinate over it as to surprise and vex the squire, who of course knew nothing about the long-standing debt to Mr. Brandon. The squire had no legal power to keep the money, if Tod insisted upon having it. And he did insist. The squire put it down to boyish folly, self-assumption; and groaned and grumbled all the way to Worcester, when Tod was taking the five-hundred pound cheque, paid to him free of duty, to the Old Bank.

"We shall have youngsters in their teens wanting to open a banking account next! "said the Pater to Mr. Isaac, as Tod was writing his signature in the book. "The world's coming to something."

"I daresay young Mr. Todhetley will be prudent, and not squander it," observed Mr. Isaac, with one of his pleasant smiles.

"Oh, will he, though! You'll see. Look here," went on the Squire, tapping the banker on the arm, "couldn't you, if he draws too large a cheque at any time, refuse to cash it? "

"I fear we could not do that," laughed Mr. Isaac. "So long as he does not overdraw his account, we are bound to honour his cheques."

"And if you do overdraw it, Joe, I hope the bank will prosecute you!—I would, I know," was the squire's last threat, as we left the bank and turned towards the Cross, Tod with a cheque-book in his breast pocket.

But Mr. Brandon could not be paid then. On going over to his house a day or two afterwards, we found him from home. The housekeeper thought he was on his way to one of the "water-cure establishments," in Yorkshire, she said, but he had not yet written to give his address.

"So it must wait," remarked Tod to me as we went home.'

★★★★★★

"By Jove!" cried Tod, taking a leap in the air.

About a week had elapsed since the journey to the Old Bank, and Tod was opening a letter that had come addressed to him by the morning post.

"Johnny! will you believe it, lad? Temple asks me to be of the boating lot, after all."

It was even so. The letter was from Slingsby Temple, written from Templemore. It stated that he had been disappointed by some of those who were to have made up the number, and if Todhetley and Ludlow would supply their places, he should be glad.

Tod turned wild. You might have thought, as Mrs. Todhetley remarked, that he had been invited to Eden.

"The idea of Temple's asking *you*, Johnny!" he said. "You are of no good in a boat."

"Perhaps I had better decline?"

"No, don't do that, Johnny. It might upset the party altogether," he answered slowly. "You must do your best."

"I have no boating suit."

"I will treat you to one," said Tod munificently. "We'll get it at Evesham. Pity but my things would fit you."

So it was, for he had loads of them.

The squire, for a wonder, did not oppose the scheme. Mrs.

Todhetley (like Lady Whitney) did, in her mild way. As Bill said, all mothers were alike—always foreseeing danger. And though she was not Tod's true mother, or mine, either, she was just as anxious for us, and looked upon it as nearly certain that one of us would come home drowned, and the other with the ague.

"They won't sleep on the bare ground of course," said Duffham; who chanced to call that morning, while Tod was writing his letter of acceptance to Slingsby Temple.

"Of course we shall," fired Tod, resenting the remark. "What harm could it do us? "

"Give some of you rheumatic fever," said Duffham.

"Then why doesn't it give it to the gipsies? "retorted Tod.

"The gipsies are used to it. You young men must have a waterproof sheet to lie upon, or a tarpaulin, or something of the sort."

Tod tossed his head, disdaining an answer, and wrote on.

"You will have rugs and great-coats with you, of course," went on Duffham. "And I'll give you a packet of quinine powders. It is as well to be prepared for contingencies. If you find any symptoms of unusual cold, or shivering, just take one or two of them."

"Look here, Mr. Duffham," said Tod, dashing his pen on the table. "Don't you think that you had better attend us yourself with a medicine chest? Put up a cargo of rhubarb—and magnesia—and family pills. A few quarts of senna tea might not come in amiss. My patience! Are we girls?"

"And I should recommend you to carry a small keg of whiskey amid the boat stores," continued Duffham, not in the least put out. "You'll want it. Take a nip of it neat when you first get up from the ground in the morning. It is necessary you should, and will ward off some evils that might otherwise arise. Johnny Ludlow, I'll put the quinine into your charge: mind you don't forget it."

"Of all old women!" muttered Tod. "Had the Pater been in the room, all this might have set him against our going."

On the following day we went over to Whitney Hall, intending to take Evesham on our way back, and buy what was wanted. Surprise the first. Bill Whitney was not at home, and was not to be of the boating party.

"You never saw anybody in such a way in your life," cried Helen; who could devote some time to us, now Temple was gone. "I must say, it was too bad of papa. He never made any objection while Mr. Temple was here, but let poor William anticipate all the pleasure; and then he went and turned round afterwards."

"Did he get afraid for him? "cried Tod, in wonder. "I'd not have thought it of Sir John."

"Afraid! no," returned Helen, opening her eyes. "What he got was a fit of the gout. A relapse."

"What has the gout to do with Bill?"

"Why, old Featherstone ordered papa to Buxton, and papa said he could not do without William to see to him there: mamma was laid up in bed with one of her bad colds—and she is not out of it yet. So papa went off, taking William—and you should just see how savage he was."

For William Whitney to be "savage" was something new. He had about the easiest temper in the world. I laughed and said so.

"Savage for him, I mean," corrected Helen, who was given to random speech. "Nothing puts him out. But it is a shame."

"I don't suppose Bill cares much: he is no hand at boating," remarked Tod. "Did he write to Temple and decline?"

"Of course he did," was Helen's resentfully-spoken answer: and she seemed, to say the least, quite as much put out as Bill could have been. "What else could he do?"

"Well, I am sorry for this," said Tod. "Temple has asked me now. Johnny also."

"Has he!" exclaimed Helen, her eyes sparkling. "I hope you will go."

"Of course we shall go," said Tod. "Where's Anna?"

"Anna? Oh, sitting up with mamma. She likes a sick-room: I don't."

"You'd like a boat better—if Temple were in it," remarked Tod with a saucy laugh.

"Just you be quiet," retorted Helen.

From Whitney Hall we went to Evesham, and hastily procured what we wanted. The next day but one was that fixed for our departure. And when it at last dawned, bright and hot, we started amidst the good wishes of all the house. Tod with a fishing rod and line, in case the expedition should afford an opportunity for fishing, and I with Duffham's quinine powders in my pocket.

Templemore, the seat of the Temples, was very nearly on the borders of Wales. We were not going there, but to a place called Sanbury, which lay within a few miles of the mansion. Slingsby Temple and his brother Rupert were already there, with the boat and the tent, and all the rest of the apparatus, making ready for our start on the morrow. Our headquarters, until then, was at the Ship, a good old-fashioned inn, and we found that we were expected to be Temple's guests.

"I would have asked you to Templemore to dine and sleep," he observed in a cordial tone, "and my mother said she should have been pleased to see you; but to get down here in the morning would have been inconvenient. At least, it would take up the time that ought to be devoted to getting away. Will you come and see the boat?"

It was lying in a locked-up shed near the river. A tub-pair, large of its kind. Three of them were enough for it: and I saw that, in point of fact, I was not wanted for the working; but Temple either did not like to ask Tod without me, or else would not leave me out. The Temples might have more than their share of pride, but it was accompanied by an equal share of refined and considerate feeling.

"We shall make you useful, never fear," said he to me with a smile. "And it will be capital boating experience for you."

"I am sure I shall like it," I answered. And I liked him better than I ever had in my life.

Numerous articles were lying ready with the boat. Temple

seemed to have thought of every needful thing. A pot to boil water in, a pan for frying, a saucepan for potatoes, a mop and towing rope, stone jugs for beer, milk, and fresh water, tins to hold our grog, and the like. Amid the stores were tea, sugar, candles, cheese, butter, a cooked ham, some tinned provisions, a big jar of beer, and (Duffham should have seen it) a two-gallon keg of whiskey.

"A doctor up with us said we ought to have whiskey," remarked Tod. "He is nothing but an old woman. He put some quinine powders in Johnny's pocket, and talked of a waterproof sheet to lie upon."

"Quite right," said Temple. "There it lies."

And there it did lie, wrapped round the folded tent. A large waterproof tarpaulin to cover the ground, at night, and keep the damp from our limbs,

"Did you ever make a boating tour before, Temple?" asked Tod.

"Oh yes. I like it. I don't know any pleasure equal to that of encamping out at night on a huge plain, where you may study all the stars in the heavens."

As Temple spoke, he glanced towards a small parcel in a corner. I guessed it was one of his night telescopes.

"Yes, it is," he assented, "but only a small one. The boat won't stretch, and we can only load it according to its limits."

Rupert Temple came up as we were leaving the shed. I had never seen him before. He was the only brother left, and Slingsby's presumptive heir. Why, I know not, but I had pictured Rupert as being like poor Fred—tall, fair, blooming as a man can be. But there existed not a grain of resemblance. Rupert was just a second edition of Slingsby: little, dark, plain, and proud. It was not an offensive pride, quite the contrary: and with those they knew well they were cordial and free.

Those originally invited by Temple were his cousin Arthur Slingsby, Lord Cracroft's son; Whitney; and a young Welchman named Pryce-Hughes. All had accepted, and intended to keep the engagement, knowing then of nothing to prevent it. But, curious to say, each one in succession subsequently wrote to decline it. Whitney had to go elsewhere with his father; Pryce-Hughes hurt his arm, which disabled him from rowing; and Arthur Slingsby went off without ceremony in somebody's yacht to Malta. As the last of the letters came, which was Whitney's, Mrs. Temple seemed struck with the coincidence of all refusing, or compelled to refuse. "Slingsby, my dear," she said to her son, "it looks just as though you were not to go." "But I will go," answered Temple, who did not like to be baulked in a project, more than anybody else likes it: "if these can't come, I'll get others who can."

And he forthwith told his brother Rupert that there'd be room for him in the boat—he had refused him before; and wrote to Tod. After that, came another letter from Pryce-Hughes, saying his arm was better, and he could join the party at Bridgenorth or Bewdley. But it was too late: the boat was filled. Temple meant to do the Severn, the Wye, and the Avon, with a forced interlude of canals, and to be out a month, taking it easily, and resting on Sundays.

"Catch Slingsby missing Sunday service if he can help it!" said Rupert, aside to me.

We started in our flannel suits and red caps, and started well, but not until the afternoon; Temple steering, his brother and Tod taking the oars. The water was very shallow; and by-and-by we ran aground. The stern of the boat swung round, and away went our tarpaulin, and was carried off by the current before we could save it.

Well, that first afternoon there were difficulties to contend with, and one or other of the three was often in the water; but we made altogether some five or six miles. It was the hottest day I ever felt; and about seven o'clock, on coming to a convenient meadow nearly level with the river, none of us were sorry to step ashore. Making fast the boat for the night, we landed the tent and other things, and looked about us. A coppice bounded the field on the left; right across, in a second field, stood a substantial farm-house, surrounded by its barns and ricks. Temple produced one of his cards, which was to be taken to the house, and the farmer's leave asked to encamp on the meadow. Rupert Temple and Tod made themselves decent to go on the errand.

"We shall want a bundle or two of straw," said Temple; "it won't do to lie on the bare ground. And some milk. You must ask if they will accommodate us, and pay what they charge."

They went off, carrying also the jar to beg for fresh water. Temple and I began to unfurl the tent, and to busy ourselves amid the things generally.

"Halloa! What's to do here?"

We turned, and saw a stout, comely man, in white shirt-sleeves, an open waistcoat, knee-breeches, and top-boots; no doubt the farmer himself. Temple explained. He and some friends were on a boating tour, and had landed there to encamp for the night.

"But who gave you leave to do it?" asked the farmer. "You are trespassing. This is my ground."

"I supposed it might be necessary to ask leave," said Temple, haughtily courteous; "and I have sent to yonder house—which I presume is yours—to solicit it. If you will kindly accord the permission, I shall feel obliged."

That Temple looked disreputable enough, there could be no denying No shoes on, no stockings, trousers tucked up above the knee: for he had been several times in the water, and, as yet, had done nothing to himself. But two of our college caps chanced to be lying exposed on the boat: and perhaps Temple's tone and address had made their due impression. The farmer looked hard at him, as if trying to remember his face.

"It's not one of the Mr. Temples, is it?" said he. "Of Templemore."

"I am Mr. Temple, of Templemore. I have sent my card to your house."

"Dash me!" cried the farmer, heartily. "Shake hands, sir. I fancied I knew the face. I've seen you out shooting, sir—and at Sanbury. I knew your father. I'm sure you are mainly welcome to camp alongside here, and to any other accommodation I can give you. Will you shake hands, young gentleman?" giving his hand to me as he released Temple's.

"My brother and another of our party are gone to your house to beg some fresh water, and buy some milk," said Temple; who did not seem at all to resent the farmer's familiarity, but rather to like it. "And we shall be glad of a truss or two of fresh straw if you can either sell it to us, or give it. We have had the misfortune to lose our waterproof sheet."

"Sell be hanged!" cried the farmer, with a jovial laugh. "Sell ye a truss or two o' straw! Sell ye milk! Not if I know it, Mr. Temple. Ye be welcome, sir, to as much as ever ye want of both. One of my men shall bring the straw down."

"You are very good."

"And anything else you please to think of. Don't scruple to ask, sir. Will you all come and sup at my house? We've got a rare round o' beef in cut, and I saw the missis making pigeon-pies this morning."

But Temple declined the invitation most decisively; and the farmer, perhaps noting that, did not press it. "It was rare weather for the water," he observed.

"We could do with less heat," replied Temple.

"Ay," said the farmer, "I never felt it worse. But it's good for the corn."

And with that he left us. The other two came back with water and oceans of milk. Sticks were soon gathered from the coppice, the fire made, the round pot, filled with water, was put on to boil for tea, and the tent was set up.

Often and often in my later life have I looked back to that evening. The meal over—and a jolly good one we made—we sat round the camp fire, then smouldering down to red embers, and watched the setting sun, Rupert Temple and Tod smoking. It was a glorious sunset, the west lighted up with gold and purple and crimson; the sky above us clear and dark blue.

But oh, how hot it was! The moon came up as the sun went down, and the one, to our fancy, seemed to give out as much heat as the other. There we sat on, sipping our grog, and talking in the bright moonlight. Temple with his elbow on the grass, his face turned up towards the sky and the few stars that came out. The colours in the west gave place to a beautiful opal, stretching northwards.

"I should like to see the strange stars, opposite to us!" said Temple presently. "What a glorious sight it must be! Sometimes I feel inclined to take a voyage on purpose."

It was singular—I shall always think so—that the conversation should turn on MacRae, the Scotchman who used to make our skin creep at Oxford with his tales of second sight. We were *not* talking of Oxford, and I don't know how MacRae came up. Unless it was that from astronomy we got to astrology, and thence to witchcraft. Up he came, however, he and his weird believings; and Rupert Temple, who had not enjoyed the honour of Mac's acquaintance, and had probably never heard his name before, got me to relate one or two of Mac's choice experiences.

"Was the man a fool?" asked Rupert.

"Not a bit of it."

"I'm sure I should say so. Making out that he could foresee people's funerals before they were dead, or likely to die!"

"Poor Fred was three parts of a believer in them," put in Temple, in a dreamy voice, as though his thoughts were buried in that past time.

"Fred was!" exclaimed Rupert, taking his brother sharply up. "Believer in what?"

"MacRae's superstitions."

"Nonsense, Slingsby."

Temple made no rejoinder. In his eye, which chanced to catch mine at the moment, there was a singular expression. I wondered whether he was recalling that other superstition of Fred's: that little episode a night or two before he died.

"We had better be turning in," said Temple, getting up. "It won't do to sit here too long; we must be up betimes in the morning."

So we got to bed at last: if you can call it bed. The farmer's good straw was strewed thickly underneath us; we had our rugs;

and the tent was fastened back at the entrance to admit air. But there was no air to admit, not a whiff of it; nothing came in but the moonlight. None of us remembered a lighter night, or a hotter one. I and Tod lay in the middle, the Temples on either side.

"I wonder who's got our sheet?" began Tod; breaking a silence that ensued when we had wished each other goodnight.

Nobody answered.

"I say," struck in Rupert, by-and-by, "I've heard one ought not to go to sleep in the moonlight: it turns people loony. Do any of your faces catch it, outside there?"

"Go to sleep and don't talk," said Temple.

It might have been through the novelty of the situation; but the night was well on before any of us slept. Tod and Rupert Temple went off first, and next (I thought) Temple did, *I* did not.

I daresay you've never slept four in a bed. And, that, one of littered straw. It's all very well to lie awake when you've a good wide mattress to yourself, and can toss and turn at will; but in the close quarters of a tent you can't do it for fear of disturbing the others. However, the longest watch has its ending; and I was just dropping off, when Temple, next to whom I lay, started hurriedly and aroused me.

"What's that?" he cried, in a half whisper.

I lifted my head, startled. He was sitting up, his eyes fixed on the opening we had left in the tent.

"Who's there?—who is it?" he said again: and his low voice had a slow, queer sound, as though he spoke in fear.

"What is it. Temple?" I asked.

"There, standing just outside the tent, right in the moonlight," whispered he. "Don't you see?"

I could see nothing. The stir awoke Rupert. He called out to know what ailed us; and that aroused Tod.

"Some man looking in at us," explained Temple in the same queer tone, half of abstraction, half of fear, his gaze still strained on the aperture. "He is gone now."

Up jumped Tod, and dashed outside the tent. Rupert struck a match and lighted the lantern. Nobody was to be seen but ourselves; and the only odd thing to be remarked was the white hue Temple's face had taken. Tod was marching round the tent, looking about him far and near, and calling out to all intruders to show themselves. But nothing met his eye save the level plain we were encamped upon, lying pale and white under the moonlight, and the only sound he heard was the croaking of the frogs.

"What could have made you fancy it?" he asked of Temple.

"Don't think it was fancy," responded Temple. "Never saw any man plainer in my life. The tent had better be closed."

"You were dreaming, Slingsby," said Rupert, as he put down the canvas and blew out the lantern. "Let's get to sleep again."

Which we did. At least, I can answer for myself

The first beams of the glorious sun awoke us, and we rose to the beginning of another day, and to the cold, shivery feeling that, in spite of the heat of the past night and of the coming day, attends the situation. I could understand now why the nip of whiskey, as Duffham called it, was necessary. Tod served it out. Lighting the fire of sticks to boil our tea-kettle—or the round pot that served for a kettle—we began to get things in order to embark again, when breakfast should be over.

"I say, Slingsby," cried Rupert to his brother, who seemed very silent, "what on earth took you, that you should disturb us in the night for nothing?"

"It was not for nothing. Someone was there."

"It must have been a stray sheep."

"Nonsense, Rupert. Could one mistake a sheep for a man?"

"Some benighted ploughman, then, '*plodding his weary way.*'"

"If you could bring forward any ploughman to testify that it was he beyond possibility of doubt, I'd give him a ten-pound note."

"Look here," said Tod, after staring a minute at this odd remark of Temple's, "you may put all idea of ploughmen and everybody else away. No one was there. If there had been, I must

492

have seen him: it was not possible he could betake himself out of sight in a moment."

"Have it as you like," said Temple. "I am going to take a bath. I've got a headache."

Stripping, he plunged into the Severn, which was very wide just there, and swam towards the middle of it.

"It seems to have put Slingsby out," observed Rupert, alluding to the night alarm. "Do you notice how thoughtful he is? Just look at that fire!"

The sticks had turned black, and now began to smoke and hiss, giving out never a bit of blaze. Down knelt Rupert on one side and I on the other.

"Damp old obstinate things! "he ejaculated. And we set on to blow at them with all our might.

"Where's Temple?" I exclaimed presently, looking off, and not seeing him. Rupert glanced over the river.

"He must be diving, Johnny. Slingsby's fond of diving. Keep on blowing, lad, or we shall get no tea today."

So we kept on. But, I don't know why, a sort of doubtful feeling came over me, and while I blew I watched the water, for Temple to come up. All in a moment he rose to the surface, gave one low, painful cry of distress, and disappeared again.

"Good heavens!" cried Rupert, leaping up and overturning the kettle into the fire.

But Tod was the quickest; and jumped in to the rescue. A first-rate swimmer and diver was he, almost as much at home in the water as out of it. In no time, as it seemed, he was striking back, bearing Temple. It was fortunate, for a crisis like that, that Temple was so small and slight—of no weight to speak of.

By dint of gently rubbing and rolling, we got some life into him and some whiskey down his throat. But he refrained in the queerest, faintest state possible; no exertion in him, no movement hardly, no strength; alive, and that was about all; and just able to tell us that he had turned faint in the water.

"What is to be done?" cried Rupert. "We must get a doctor to him: and he ought not to lie on the grass here. I wonder if that farmer would let him be taken to his house for an hour or two?"

I got into my boots, and ran off to ask; and met the farmer at the stile of the second field. He was coming towards us, curious perhaps to see whether we had started. Telling him what had happened, he showed himself all alive with sympathy, called some of his men to carry Temple to the farm, and sent back to prepare his wife. Their name, we found, was Best: and most hospitable, good-hearted people they turned out to be.

Well, Temple was taken there and a doctor was called in. The doctor shook his head, looked grave, and asked to have another. Then, for the first time, doubts stole over us that it might be more serious than we had thought for. A dreadful feeling of fear took possession of me, and in spite of all I could do, that scene at Oxford, when poor Fred Temple had been carried into old Mrs. Golding's to die, would not go out of my mind.

We got into our reserve clothes, as if conscious that the boating flannels were done with for the present, left one of the farmer's men to watch our boat and its contents, and stayed with Temple. He continued very faint, and lay nearly quite still. The doctors tried some remedies, but they did no good. One of them called it "syncope of the heart;" but the other said, hastily, "No, no; that was not the right term." They said Mrs. Temple had better be sent for.

"I was just thinking so," assented Rupert. "My mother ought to be with him. Who will go for her?"

"Johnny can," said Tod. "He is of no good here."

For that matter, none of us were of any good, for we could do nothing for Temple.

I did not relish the task: I did not care to tell a mother that her son, whom she believes to be well and hearty, is lying in danger. But I had to go: Rupert seemed to take it as a matter of course.

"Don't alarm her more than you can help, Ludlow," he said. "Say that Slingsby turned faint in the water this morning, and the medical men seem a little anxious. But ask her not to lose time."

Mr. Best started me on his own horse—a fine hunter, iron grey. The weather was broiling. Templemore lay right across country, about six miles off by road. It was a beautiful place; I could see that much, though I had but little time to look at it; and it stood upon an eminence, the last mile of the road winding gradually up to its gates.

Mrs. Temple was at one of the windows, and saw me ride hastily in. Seized with a prevision that something was amiss, she came out before I was well off the horse.

"It is Mr. Ludlow, I think," she said, her plain dark face (so much like Slingsby's) very pale. "What ill news have you brought?"

I told her in the best manner I was able, just in the words Rupert had suggested, speaking quietly, and not showing any alarm.

"Is there danger?" she at once asked.

"I am not sure that there is," I said, hardly knowing how to frame my answer. "The doctors thought you had better come, in case—in case of any danger arising; and Rupert sent me to ask you to do so."

She rang the bell, and ordered her carriage to be round instantly. "The bay horses," she added: "they are the fleetest. What will you take, Mr. Ludlow?"

I would not take anything. But a venerable old gentleman in black, with a powdered bald head—the butler, I concluded—suggested some lemonade, after my hot ride: and that I was glad of

I rode on before, piloting the way to the farm. Slingsby lay in the same state, neither better nor worse: perhaps the breathing was somewhat more difficult. He smiled when he saw his mother, and put out his hand.

★★★★★★

The day dragged itself slowly on. We did not know what to do with ourselves. Temple was to be kept quiet, and we might not intrude into his room—one on the ground-floor that faced the east. Mr. and Mrs. Best entertained us well, as far as meals went; but one can't be eating forever. Now down in the meadow by the boat—which seemed to have assumed a most forlorn aspect—and now waiting for the last report of Temple.

"Is it here that Mr. Temple is lying?"

I was standing under the jessamine-covered porch, in the rays of the setting sun, when a stranger came up and put the question. An extraordinarily tall and thin clergyman, with grey hair.

It was Mr. Webster, perpetual curate of the parish around Templemore. And knew him before I heard his name, for he was the image of his son. Long Webster, who used to be at Oxford.

"I was unable to get here before," he said. "Is he any better?"

"I am afraid not," I answered. "We don't know what to make of it; it all seems so sudden and strange."

"But what is it?" he asked in a whisper.

"I don't know, sir. The doctors say something about the heart."

One of the doctors appeared just then; and they talked together in a low tone in the shaded porch. Not a ray of hope sat on the medical man's face: he intimated that Temple was dying.

"Dear me!" cried the dismayed Mr. Webster.

"He seems to know it himself," continued the doctor. "Though we have been most cautious not to alarm him by any hint of the kind."

Mr. Webster went in, and was shut up for some time alone with Temple. Yes, he said, when he came out again, Temple knew all about it, and was perfectly resigned and prepared.

There was no bed for any of us that night. Temple's breathing grew worse; and at last we went in by turns, to prop up his pillows behind. Towards morning I was called in to replace Rupert.

"Who is this now?" panted Slingsby, as I took my place.

"It is I. Johnny Ludlow. Do you feel any better?"

"I think he is a little easier," Mrs. Temple put in.

"No, no," he said, just opening his eyes. "Do not grieve, mother. I shall be better off. I shall be with my father and Fred."

"Oh, my son, my son, don't lose heart!" she cried with a sob. "That will never do."

"I saw my father last night," said Temple.

The words seemed to strike her with a sort of shock. "No!" she exclaimed, perhaps thinking of the Temple superstition, and drawing back a step. "Pray, pray don't fancy that!"

"The tent was open to give us air," he said, speaking with difficulty. "I suddenly saw someone standing in the moonlight. I was next it; and I had not been able to get to sleep. For a moment I thought it was some intruder, passing by; but he took a strange likeness to my father, and I thought he beckoned—"

"We are not alone, Slingsby," interrupted Mrs. Temple, remembering me, her voice very cold.

"Ludlow knows. He knew the last time. Fred said he saw him, and I—I ridiculed it. Ludlow heard me. He came for Fred, mother; he must have come for me."

"Oh, I can't—I can't believe this, Slingsby," she cried in excitement. "It was fancy; nothing else. My darling, I cannot lose you! You have ever been dearer to me than my other children."

"Only for a little while, mother. It is God's will. That is our true home, you know; and then there will be no more parting. I am quite happy. I seem to be half there now.—What's that light?"

Mrs. Temple looked round, and saw a faint streak coming in over the tops of the shutters. "It must be the glimmering of dawn in the east," she said. "The day is breaking."

"Ay," he answered: "my day. I shall soon come for you. Where's Rupert? I should like to say goodbye to him. Yes, mother, that's the dawn of Heaven."

And, just as the sun rose, he went there.

That was the end of our boating tour. Ridicule has been cast on the facts, and will be again. It is a painful subject; and I don't know that I should have related it, but for its having led to another (and more lively) adventure, which will be told next month.

497

LEONAUR

ALSO FROM LEONAUR
AVAILABLE IN SOFTCOVER OR HARDCOVER WITH DUST JACKET

MR MUKERJI'S GHOSTS *by S. Mukerji*—Supernatural tales from the British Raj period by India's Ghost story collector.

KIPLINGS GHOSTS *by Rudyard Kipling*—Twelve stories of Ghosts, Hauntings, Curses, Werewolves & Magic.

THE COLLECTED SUPERNATURAL AND WEIRD FICTION OF WASHINGTON IRVING: VOLUME 1 *by Washington Irving*—Including one novel 'A History of New York', and nine short stories of the Strange and Unusual.

THE COLLECTED SUPERNATURAL AND WEIRD FICTION OF WASHINGTON IRVING: VOLUME 2 *by Washington Irving*—Including three novelettes 'The Legend of the Sleepy Hollow', 'Dolph Heyliger', 'The Adventure of the Black Fisherman' and thirty-two short stories of the Strange and Unusual.

THE COLLECTED SUPERNATURAL AND WEIRD FICTION OF JOHN KENDRICK BANGS: VOLUME 1 *by John Kendrick Bangs*—Including one novel 'Toppleton's Client or A Spirit in Exile', and ten short stories of the Strange and Unusual.

THE COLLECTED SUPERNATURAL AND WEIRD FICTION OF JOHN KENDRICK BANGS: VOLUME 2 *by John Kendrick Bangs*—Including four novellas 'A House-Boat on the Styx', 'The Pursuit of the House-Boat', 'The Enchanted Typewriter' and 'Mr. Munchausen' of the Strange and Unusual.

THE COLLECTED SUPERNATURAL AND WEIRD FICTION OF JOHN KENDRICK BANGS: VOLUME 3 *by John Kendrick Bangs*—Including twor novellas 'Olympian Nights', 'Roger Camerden: A Strange Story', and ten short stories of the Strange and Unusual.

THE COLLECTED SUPERNATURAL AND WEIRD FICTION OF MARY SHELLEY: VOLUME 1 *by Mary Shelley*—Including one novel 'Frankenstein or the Modern Prometheus', and fourteen short stories of the Strange and Unusual.

THE COLLECTED SUPERNATURAL AND WEIRD FICTION OF MARY SHELLEY: VOLUME 2 *by Mary Shelley*—Including one novel 'The Last Man', and three short stories of the Strange and Unusual.

THE COLLECTED SUPERNATURAL AND WEIRD FICTION OF AMELIA B. EDWARDS *by Amelia B. Edwards*—Contains two novelettes 'Monsieur Maurice', and 'The Discovery of the Treasure Isles', one ballad 'A Legend of Boisguilbert' and seventeen short stories to cill the blood.

www.ingramcontent.com/pod-product-compliance
Lightning Source LLC
Chambersburg PA
CBHW030746030726
47497CB00001B/154